I TAKE CARE OF OUR OWN

by

Christopher Clancy

MONTAG

First Montag Press E-Book and Paperback Original Edition April 2021

Montag Press ISBN: 978-1-940233-88-8
Design © 2021 Amit Dey

Montag Press Team:
Edited by John Rak
Cover photograph by Corinthian Leathers

A Montag Press Book
www.montagpress.com
Montag Press
777 Morton Street, Unit B
San Francisco CA 94129 USA

Montag Press, the burning book with the hatchet cover, the skewed word mark and the portrayal of the long-suffering fireman mascot are trademarks of Montag Press.

Printed & Digitally Originated in the United States of America
10 9 8 7 6 5 4 3 2 1

For Mom and Dad

WE
TAKE
CARE
OF OUR
OWN

why set the self aflame when   we can do it together

—Beth Bachmann, "wall"

JANUARY FY20___

Private Carl Boxer looks like a paper doll wrapped in dark gauze. His arms, thin and sharp-elbowed, protrude from his oversized jumpsuit. The back of his shaved head flashes just before he launches at the frozen, teddy bear torso of Father Roth. After that, it's hard to tell who's who, everything's just a mess of limbs and boots, like two bodies trying to absorb each other, while the folding chairs they'd been sitting on clang like pots and pans, Carl's chair skidding past the edge of the screen and Father Roth's doing a little half-pirouette before collapsing flat against the concrete floor, revealing on its underside a USoFA WorldWide sticker slapped over the black-stenciled PROPERTY OF U.S. ARMY.

The prosecuting attorney, Captain Deb Posner, pointed the remote control at the screen and paused the recording. Carl shook his head. If he was ever going to remember assaulting a US Army chaplain, it would have been after watching footage of the incident. But he had nothing.

"Sergeant Weir," Captain Posner asked, "do you believe Private Boxer would have stopped strangling Father Roth had you not walked in at that moment?"

From the chair that was serving as a witness stand, Weir glared at Carl. "No, ma'am," he said. "Boxer's a small guy, but I had some trouble subduing him. Finally, I got my knee in his back and called for a medic."

"Let's have a look."

The screen unfroze. Carl watched his grimy hands work their way to Father Roth's neck, thumbs digging underneath his chin. Then Weir makes his entrance, knocking Carl off of Father Roth while shouting, *What the hell, man?* over and over. Free of his attacker, Father Roth turns onto his side and gasps for air, the sound panicked and raw.

The screen froze again as Captain Posner approached the commissioner panel, a clutch of papers in one hand. "I present, now, the latest medical report on Father Roth, who is currently recovering from tracheal surgery, as a result of the attack." She placed the report before Major Fong, who skimmed the first page before passing it to the officer on his right.

When they arrested Carl, charging him with felonious assault of an Army chaplain—"without provocation," the prosecution kept saying—Carl wanted to laugh. He didn't even know who Father Roth was. Now, as part of the case being made against him, Carl was getting a crash course in all things Father Roth: Entered the seminary at age twenty-five. Served as monsignor at a couple of parishes in central Texas before hooking up with the Army in his early thirties, doing chaplain stints all over the Middle East—Iraq, Afghanistan, Syria, back to Iraq, Lebanon, back to Syria, Pakistan, back to Iraq. A wonderful, selfless guy, obviously. Earlier that morning, Carl had felt inspired enough to try praying for Father Roth's recovery (and his hands were already prayer-ready, what with his wrists being zip-tied together), but the attempt felt like a lie, seeing as *he could not remember the attack*.

Major Fong rested his elbows on the table and blinked like a man with a headache. "Defense? Any questions for the witness?"

Captain Ruddy, Carl's defense attorney, looked up from his notepad and shook his head.

God, Carl was so screwed. No question they'd put him away again. During his pre-trial consultation with Captain Ruddy, he had been made aware that, under the Uniform Code of Military Justice, he was looking at three to ten years in prison. Which, OK, bad enough, but then Captain Ruddy told him that the injured party, Father David Roth, happened to be a valued spiritual advisor and dear personal friend and that he, Captain Jeremy Ruddy, had personally requested this case for the express purpose of not lifting a finger in Carl's defense. "You see, son, if it were up to me," Captain Ruddy had said, "I'd have them lock you up in Gitmo and throw away the key."

No matter where they put him, though, whether it was back to Waupun Correctional Institute in Wisconsin or some stockade on some other forward-edge-of-battle place, at least Carl wouldn't have to drive again. It was the driving that had made him crazy—crazy enough to want to spend his nights underneath the trucks in the motor pool, crazy enough to attack an Army chaplain and not remember it afterward—so, really, anyplace they wanted to put him was bound to be an improvement. Shit, they could lock him away for the full ten years; at least he'd be free of the van, free of Last Circle, free of that triple-reinforced Kevlar suit, with its sweat and panic and reek. Anyplace in the world was better than in that suit.

Dismissing Sergeant Weir, Major Fong asked, "Any more witnesses?"

"The prosecution rests."

"Defense?"

Captain Ruddy again shook his head.

"OK, no reason to take this into the afternoon," Major Fong said. "Will the defendant rise?"

Carl rose, his zip-tied hands gripping the table's edge.

"Private Boxer," Major Fong began, "you came to Forward Operating Base Doritos four months ago as part of the Free2Fight program, which aims to rehabilitate convicts such as yourself by having them serve out their sentences in designated war zones. Now, we've got various accounts of your assault of Father Roth, with possible intent to kill though no real motivation for doing so. But one thing that struck me, looking over this case, is that all of your previous evaluations are without prior incident. You were found to be polite, respectful, expecting no special treatment… you were a model prisoner here, and—excuse me while I pause the stenographer—and while we cannot officially *commend* you for your service as a Designated Driver, I think I speak for everyone here when I say that five weeks is an impressive length of time to be providing that service, for which the Army thanks you. And so, keeping these points in mind…"

It sounded like they might go easy on him. Carl shut his eyes and pictured the red-painted floors of Waupun Correctional, the air that smelled of pencil shavings and old blood. A pleasurable dizziness filled his head.

Fast-approaching footsteps sounded outside the door to the conference room. Carl turned to the door just as it swung open on a civilian. Dark suit. American. He looked to be in his late forties, a little bit taller than average, with gangly limbs and wiry gray hair and a slight neck wattle resting against the knot of his necktie. "Carl Boxer? Private Carl Boxer?"

Major Fong leaned forward. "This is Private Boxer's trial, yes. Can I help you?"

"Yes, my name is Dr. Miles Young. I am a licensed psychologist and founder of SoldierWell, a program that specializes in the treatment of post-traumatic stress disorder among recent veterans. Sponsored by USoFA WorldWide." Dr. Young stepped forward, seizing the room. "I'd like to ask the accused a few questions, if I may? And everybody have a seat, please. It's just a few questions, no need to be so *military* about it."

"Objection?" Captain Posner held up a forefinger.

"Let me stop you right there," Dr. Young said. "Because Mr. Boxer here is with the Free2Fight program, which is a USoFA WorldWide program, it stands that any court-martial, whether summary, special, or general, must include at least one salaried USoFA WorldWide employee on its jury, as per the Temporary War

Act. You may consider me that employee. I could have this whole thing declared a mistrial if I wanted."

"Excuse me, Doctor, but I would appreciate you letting me finish stating…"

"Sure, but bear with me a moment." The doctor pawed at the pockets of his jacket. "Mr. Boxer represents a unique case, as he is labeled a private with the United States Army, but, technically, you know, he isn't." He paused in his fumbling. "I mean, look at him. This isn't a *soldier*. What do you weigh, Carl? A hundred and ten?"

Without waiting for Carl's answer, and still fumbling with his pockets, Dr. Young wheeled back around to face the panel. "So, for our purposes today, Carl Boxer is a recognized USoFA WorldWide employee, and yet, for the purposes of consideration into the SoldierWell program, he will at the conclusion of this trial automatically fall back under the jurisdiction of the United States Army."

Finally, Dr. Young produced a clear plastic sleeve containing a folded piece of paper. Carefully removing the paper from the sleeve, he raised it above his head and snapped it open. "Of course, all is accounted for in my letter from Edna H, chair and CEO of USoFA WorldWide." He slapped the piece of paper down before Major Fong, then stepped aside, tapping his foot.

Carl stifled a laugh. If a pair of orderlies were to barge in and throw a butterfly net over this guy, it wouldn't surprise him one bit.

Major Fong picked up the letter and skimmed it. He then passed it to his left and sighed. "All right, it appears that Dr. Young, being a Red-Level specialist with USoFA WorldWide, enjoys certain privileges outside the jurisdiction of traditional Army protocol. I am therefore compelled to grant any requests he might have, and so any objections made in response to his actions are hereby overruled. Dr. Young, you may proceed."

Nodding, Dr. Young brought a fist up to his chin and closed his eyes. "Carl Boxer," he said, "I'd like to ask you some questions. Do you comply?"

"Comply?"

"Do you agree to answer my questions, yes or no?"

"Oh. OK, yes."

"Very well, let's begin." Dr. Young cleared his throat. "Please choose the answer that best describes your situation. Is this direction clear to you?"

"Yes."

"How often do you experience repeated, disturbing memories, thoughts, or images of a specific military nature? Not at all, a little bit, moderately, quite often, all the time?"

"Not at all. Or… maybe a little."

"OK, a little. How often do you experience physical reactions such as heart pounding, trouble breathing, excessive sweating, when reminded of your military escapades? Not at all, a little bit, moderately, quite often, all the time?"

"Moderately."

"How often do you experience the desire to avoid thinking or talking about your military experience? Not at all, a little bit, moderately, quite often, all the time?"

Carl thought about soldiers crying, getting out of Jeeps, standing alone in the middle of the desert. He shook these thoughts away. "Often."

Dr. Young raised an eyebrow. "Do you ever experience a loss of interest in things you enjoyed prior to your military experience? Hobbies, art, sex? Not at all, a little bit, moderate, et cetera?"

Carl thought for a moment. "A little bit, I guess."

"Feeling easily bored or in need of intellectual or physical stimulation? Not at all, a little bit, blah blah blah?"

"No. I like being left alone."

"Just answer the question, please… Do you ever feel distant or cut off from other people?"

"Often."

"Feel unable or unworthy to have loving feelings toward those closest to you?"

"I haven't seen anybody like that in months."

Dr. Young laughed for what seemed like forever, or maybe it just seemed that way because no one joined in. "All right," he said, "we'll pass on that one. Next question. Ever feel like your future will be cut short?"

Carl looked at his wrists. "Often."

"Trouble remembering the most important parts of certain experiences?"

Carl tried to picture Father Roth's face up close and instead saw himself sitting behind the wheel of a Jeep. "Often."

"A-*ha*. Tell me, Carl, do you remember attacking Father Roth?"

Carl shook his head. "I don't. I really don't."

Dr. Young kept his gaze on Carl. The guy's eyes were an icy blue. His uncle Ray used to have an electric guitar the same exact color, a Japanese Stratocaster knockoff that he stopped playing after coming home from the War, back when it was called Operation Iraqi Freedom. Carl had inherited that guitar but never learned how to play.

"I'm now going to throw out a bunch of statements and I want you to say true or false as they apply to you. Some of these might strike you as unusual but I need you to answer me as honestly as possible. Can you do that?"

"Yes."

"When someone says something counter to my religious or political beliefs, I react violently."

"False."

"I tend to feel nervous around crowds of people. True or false."

Carl thought of Marines standing on white rubber, pulling off helmets, unlacing their shitkickers, sniffing at the air. "True," he said.

"Sometimes I feel nervous when standing near trash receptacles."

…standing around the graveyard, smoking cigarettes, laughing… "True."

"Driving underneath overpasses makes me nervous."

…flock of drones in the white sky… "True."

"Running over potholes or bumps in the road makes me nervous."

…young women on the side of the road, flipping in the dirt… "True."

"Standing or sitting next to an open window makes me nervous."

…perfect black holes in the eyebrow beep beep beep… "True."

"I am jealous of the sun."

…red desert heat. "Sorry?"

"I am jealous of the sun."

"No. False."

"Carrying a knife or gun makes me feel secure."

"True. I guess."

"Lying is never OK, not even if it keeps someone from harm."

"False."

Everybody had stopped paying attention. It was as if he and Dr. Young were the only people in the room.

"Trees remind me of large hands."

"False."

"If I smell vomit, I want to vomit myself."

"True."

"If I watch an animal long enough, like a dog, I start to believe I can read its thoughts."

"False."

"Sometimes I feel I am destined for greater things, despite evidence to the contrary."

Carl paused. Though he had never said it out loud, Carl had long thought of himself as a kind of hero-in-waiting. Sometimes, when confronted with the facts of his life so far—this trial did a pretty good job of showing what a mess he'd become—he could take solace in the idea that this was all part of his origin story, and someday soon all this fear and isolation would fall away, revealing the hero underneath.

"True."

Dr. Young smiled like he had a secret. "Terrific job, Carl." He turned to Major Fong and shrugged. "Well, it's perfectly obvious to me this young man suffers symptoms linked to acute PTSD. It is therefore my recommendation that he enroll in the SoldierWell program for specialized treatment."

"SoldierWell program?"

"Well, Major, after this initial screening, SoldierWell pairs ailing veterans with a licensed psychologist to undergo intensive psychotherapy. It's part of a Company-wide effort to better address the healthcare needs of our fighting men and women."

"And you are the licensed therapist, I take it?"

Dr. Young chuckled. "No, no, I run the program. Private Boxer will be paired with a highly credentialed therapist once he's stateside."

Major Fong nodded. "What do you propose, Doctor, we do about *this* incident? Because the sentence for felonious assault of a superior officer is three to eleven years."

Dr. Young winced. "Time served, I should think. The Company is prepared to make a sizable contribution to the Church in the padre's name."

Major Fong scanned the room. "Private Boxer," he said, "do you agree to enter this SoldierWell program, in lieu of continuing this trial?"

"Sir?"

"I'm going to help you, Carl," Dr. Young said. "We're going to beat your PTSD. You'll receive round-the-clock treatment, and when you're better you'll go home."

"How long is the treatment?"

"However long it takes to feel better and get your memory back."

"Where is it?"

Dr. Young's mouth tightened just before he started guffawing. "Carl! This is a great opportunity! Why the third degree?"

Carl wished he hadn't said "great opportunity." Coming to Ma'lef had been a great opportunity. The great opportunities were coming fast these days, all of them with different people, different buildings, different damn realties. Carl wasn't sure he could survive the next great opportunity.

Still, though, time served. And he'd get to go home once he was better, which meant he was going to get some help and maybe stop feeling like he was losing his damn mind, maybe find some way to cope with the feeling that shot through all his other thoughts and feelings, the one that felt like a meteor was about to come crashing into the room and drive him into the ground any second. Like now. Or now. Or right now.

Major Fong sighed. "Perhaps his defense can assist?"

Captain Ruddy turned to Carl, his chest rising and falling. "Say yes." His voice was a whisper through clenched teeth. "Say yes, you dumb son of a bitch."

"OK," Carl said. "I'll do it."

Dr. Young nodded with exasperation. "You're *welcome*…"

"Thanks, yeah. Thank you."

FULL TRANSCRIPT

INTERVIEW: Therapist, USoFA WorldWide War-Related PTSD Individualized Therapy Program (Pilot), "SoldierWell" East (Region 1)

January 26, FY20___

1410EST

DR. MILES YOUNG, Director, USoFA WorldWide War-Related PTSD Individualized Therapy Program (Pilot) "SoldierWell"

and

GEN. (ORDNANCE CORPS) TYLER BURROWS, Commander, US Northern Command Region 1 and US-Canadian North American Aerospace Defense Command (NORAD)

and

DR. AMANDA KANT, Consultant, Department of Military Information Support Operations (MISO), Region 1, USoFA WorldWide

and

TIM NESTOR, Executive Vice President of Media Relations, Region 1, USoFA WorldWide

Interviewing:

LINDA HELD

(BEGIN)

DR. MILES YOUNG: Thanks, Linda, for coming in today. You found the building OK?

LINDA HELD: Oh yes. I'm getting to know the campus here pretty well, so… [*laughs*]

MY: OK, before we start, I just received word from General Burrows's people, and it turns out he won't be attending today's meeting. He was pulled into something else of, you know, vital national importance, I'm sure… All right, I'd like to begin by offering Miss Held my congratulations on qualifying for what is the final interview for employment as a pre-licensed therapist with the SoldierWell East program. I realize, Linda, you've undergone a battery of interviews and tests, so to get even this far is a testament to your skills and experience. Whatever happens from here on out, please know that we here at USoFA WorldWide hold you in the highest regard.

LH: Thank you, Dr. Young.

MY: OK, my right-hand man today is Tim Nestor, Executive Vice President, newly minted Executive Vice President, that is, of Media Relations for USoFA WorldWide, Region 1. Tim, thanks for being here.

TIM NESTOR: Thanks. Nice to meet you, Miss Held.

LH: Mr. Nestor, hello.

MY: And on my left is Dr. Amanda Kant, brought in as a consultant and we're very happy she's here. Now, you've all been given some papers, these are for your eyes only. No copies to be made, not to be seen or discussed with others, no exceptions. Now, Linda, for the official record, please recount how you originally came to hear about the SoldierWell program.

LH: Certainly. I was just beginning my final year of coursework when I saw the call for applicants…

MY: I'm sorry, could you state the university and program?

LH: Of course. University of Maryland, Baltimore County, the Department of Psychology. I'm scheduled to graduate this spring.

MY: Thanks. Continue, please.

LH: Yes…I was just beginning my last year of coursework, and so at that time I needed to fulfill an internship requirement. I had fallen a bit behind on finding placement somewhere… As I mentioned in previous interviews, I'm a single mother and so it's sometimes a challenge, logistically speaking, juggling the usual parenting duties with the coursework and my job. I don't consider any of that beyond my abilities, but when it comes time to make the necessary connections for things like internships and team-oriented projects, that tends to be a little tricky for me. I found myself running out of time, frankly, and…

MY: And why is that?

LH: I'm sorry?

MY: Why is it you find making connections tricky?

LH: Well…[*laughs*] I've come to harbor an outsider feeling, on account of my having come to the study of psychology after a few years away from academia, as opposed to coming in right after graduation. And taking longer than usual to earn my degree. Some semesters I just wasn't able to handle a full load, financially. Anyway, I happen to live close to the Men's Health Center in downtown Baltimore. I walked in pretty much off the street and sat down with Dr. Arnold Rajeev. He was putting together a study on the effects of individualized therapies for inner-city high school athletes, and he brought me on to co-manage the project. One of the great things about working at the Men's Center was I had access to a lot of great information about USoFA WorldWide and its Military Information Support Operations. It's how I got to know your work, Dr. Young. I found the research you were doing very interesting, what with its potential to alter the effectiveness of one-on-one therapy. And I felt like I had found someone who might be sympathetic to my concerns.

MY: In what way?

LH: Well, after my first couple of years at UMBC, I felt there to be… I'm going out on a limb here… I guess I felt there to be an almost undue concern with ethics, ethical matters. Not to say that ethics don't have their place in treatment, but my professors' ethical stances struck me as designed to protect their careers, their standing in academia. It's got almost nothing to do with the patient. Certainly nothing to do with society at large.

MY: Yes, we have that in common. The feeling that all this emphasis on patient-therapist ethics represents a…distortion of the spirit behind the rules.

LH: Yes. I was sometimes ostracized by my fellow students for always harping on the issue, asking questions like why were we spending so much time on this or that intriguing avenue of therapy if at the end of the day we were just going to discard it on such-and-such ethical grounds. Then when I wrote a paper about the practical advantages of patient transference, it was as if…

MY: Sorry, Linda, would you mind offering up a quick definition of transference? Not sure everyone here is familiar.

TN: Much obliged, guys. [*laughs*] I was following OK up until then…

LH: Of course. No, in this context, transference refers to the redirecting of a patient's feelings for someone of great personal significance, like a parent or a spouse, onto the therapist.

MY: Often manifested as erotic attraction toward the therapist.

TN: Oh, sure. Hots for the shrink. I've heard of that.

MY: I take it, Linda, your thesis included some unusual ideas on transference?

LH: I proposed that, instead of treating it as an obstacle to therapeutic success, or at best as something to be explored for insight into the origin relationship, transference could instead be used by the therapist to inspire self-healing. A rough idea, I admit, and some of the things I assumed back then now strike me as naïve, but I think I was onto something.

MY: Getting back to the Men's Health Center, Linda, what was it about the place that you liked so much?

LH: Oh, the freedom. As co-manager of that project, I was allowed to put into practice some of those ideas about transference. It was good in that way. Dr. Rajeev encouraged me to trust my instincts, and he insisted I write down my experiences, though the forms we worked with, there wasn't a place to record that sort of thing. So I wound up tracking my progress in my journaling.

DR. AMANDA KANT: Your own journaling? Do you mean a diary?

LH: Yes.

AK: Is that something you still do? Keep a diary?

LH: Oh... There isn't enough time in the day. On top of earning my degree, raising my son, and for the last few years I've worked full-time...

AK: All while maintaining a, uh...a 3.9 grade point average?

LH: That's correct, yes. But like I said, some semesters I could only take one or two courses.

AK: You must have one heck of a babysitter list.

LH: My mother lives with us, so... [*laughs*] We make it work.

AK: And you're looking for a better life for them, for your son.

LH: Well, yes.

AK: You must be a real mama grizzly.

LH: OK. [*laughs*] Thank you.

AK: The father, is he in the picture?

MY: Excuse me, Dr. Kant?

LH: No, it's all right. No, he's no longer in the picture.

AK: Divorce? Death? Went out for cigarettes?

LH: No, we never married. He wasn't in my life for long.

AK: OK.

[*pause*]

Did you consider abortion?

MY: Oh, for God's sake…

AK: It's a legitimate question, Miles. I'm a little surprised you haven't already asked her. If she can't take a legitimate personal question during a job interview, what's going to happen when she's face-to-face with somebody who's been to war?

[CROSSTALK]

[CROSSTALK]

OK, Miss Held, listen. Nine times out of ten, I'm perfectly willing to sit here during these interviews and nod along while thinking about what I'm going to make for dinner when I get home. Nothing personal, it's just the situation. We've been doing this off and on for weeks, we've got SoldierWell up and running in Alabama, Minnesota, Oregon… It's been a long process.

MY: Which you're now making longer, so…

AK: But since it's apparent that Dr. Young won't speak to it, I guess it's up to me. Miss Held, you're an attractive woman. Do you have any qualms at all about navigating a one-on-one therapeutic relationship with a bunch of veterans, most of whom likely haven't seen a woman out of a burqa in at least a year? I'm not saying this isn't the most elite fighting force in the world, but there's a marked difference between some inner-city football players and a veteran who's seen God-knows-what over in Iraq or Afghanistan or Tasmania or wherever we've got them going these days. Actually, let's put it to you, Miles. Do we really think a fresh veteran of the War, with acute PTSD, is going to open up to this girl-next-door type?

[CROSSTALK]

MY: OK, first of all, I will be guiding her through this process. There will never be an instance where Miss Held won't have the opportunity to voice a concern or ask a question. Also, I'll remind you this is a medication-assisted treat-ment, and our patients will have their PTSD-related symptoms treated with a central nervous system depressant, so I'm not too worried about patient resistance. And that's before taking into account Miss Held's unique skills and abilities.

AK: Tim, what do you think?

[*pause*]

TN: I'm with Miles. I would think that these guys working with Miss Held, seeing her, it might help, uh, patient morale, so to speak. [*laughs*] As a matter of fact, I think it was Aristotle who said, "To the beautiful falls the right of command."

MY: Wow, Tim. Get on with your bad self.

TN: Yeah, well, that's why they pay me the big bucks. [*laughs*] No, I can see where you're coming from, Amanda, but then I think, hey, maybe Miss Held here can get these guys to open up, get that whole trust thing going. And, you know, we've already got a bunch of male therapists in our other SoldierWell locations. Might as well push for a little gender diversity while we're at it.

LH: Excuse me, may I say something?

MY: Of course, Linda. I apologize for all this squabbling, by the way.

LH: No, Dr. Young, it's fine. And I appreciate your concerns, Dr. Kant. But can I just say, one thing I don't think has been covered today is my experience outside of psychology, outside of academia? I'm not your typical grad student. I've been paying my way, cash, and I've worked seven different jobs in the last four years. For nine months I worked sanitation at a meatpacking plant in western Maryland…every night I would come home smelling like blood; it got so my son was scared to sit in my lap. I've cleaned office buildings… I pushed wheelchairs at Rumsfeld International Airport… I've been a barista, a phone marketer, a geriatric masseuse… My resume reads like I'm running from the law. About a year ago, while working as a waitress in a bar in North Baltimore, I successfully removed a pool cue from a man's eye socket. I still have that job, by the way… I learned that I was accepted into UMBC on the same day my son was diagnosed with cystic fibrosis. So one of the best days of my life quickly turned into the worst day of my life.

[*pause*]

I don't think I'm giving too much away by telling you how impressed I am with the benefits package here. Complimentary one-year lease on a three-bedroom townhouse in a Company-owned gated community? Platinum-level CUP access? Automatic enrollment in a student loan forgiveness program? [*laughs*] I'd have to be crazy not to want all that. Anybody would. But the capper for me is, I also understand that full-time USoFA WorldWide employees have their own organ transplant list. I'd very much like to get my son on that list. He needs a new pair of lungs, or else his chances of living past thirty-five drop by half. And I'd like to get him out of his current school, where last month the bacteria caused by the rat feces in the walls reached official toxic levels. I'd also like for my mother, who just turned sixty-two, to quit her job at the car wash.

[*pause*]

I have undergone seven interviews for this position, not that I'm complaining. I actually look forward to these interviews. I got here three hours before we were supposed to meet today because the Wi-Fi is so strong. I paid three bills over my phone and then I took a walk around campus... I can't get over how clean everything is, the buildings, the sidewalks, the air... At one point I bought a peanut butter smoothie and sat down next to a duck pond and eavesdropped on this group of young scientists nearby. [*laughs*] Their conversation was over my head, something about nonlinear polymer chains, whatever those are, but by the time I finished my smoothie, I was half in love with all of them.

[*pause*]

Do I want this job? Yes. Absolutely. But I can say, in all honesty, I would not have bothered coming in today if I thought for one second that I wasn't qualified to do this work. I have a passion for one-on-one therapy. I see it as a force for real change. And I believe the therapeutic techniques Dr. Young has in mind, I think if applied correctly they could prove groundbreaking, not just for USoFA WorldWide but for the world.

AK: Well. Thank you, Miss Held. I think I see what you mean. It's just...

[*pause*]

I just hope you know what you're doing, Miles.

MY: Duly noted, Amanda, thank you very much. Any more questions? Tim?

TN: I'm good.

MY: Excellent. Final interview complete. Once again, Linda, I'd like to thank you for coming in today. We'll be in touch.

LH: Thank you, Dr. Young. Mr. Nestor. Dr. Kant.

MY: OK, for the purposes of confidentiality and security, blah blah blah, I will now stop this recording.

END TRANSCRIPT

FEBRUARY FY20___

Even though it had lowered its gleaming bulk to the curb outside Linda Held's co-op, boarding the USoFA WorldWide Employee Shuttle proved challenging, as its open doors were partially blocked by a hill of long-dead Christmas trees yet to be collected. After helping Danny and her mother scale the pileup, Linda made it onto the driverless shuttle and looked around, kicking gray pine needles from her shoes. The bright interior of the craft was silent save for the whoosh of heat and the low babble of CUP monitors hanging above each row of seats, spouting news from the War's many fronts. Her fellow passengers, about a dozen or so, gave off a sensation of barely contained giddiness, their faces docile yet alert as they peered out of the shuttle's tinted windows. One older couple in the back appeared to be weeping with joy, burrowing their faces into each other's coats.

As the shuttle lifted from the curb and roared back to life, Linda watched Vera buckle herself in as Danny waved to a couple of slack-jawed toddlers outside. Linda soon took a seat and shut her eyes. Enough of this sweet sorrow routine—it was time to *go* and *be gone*. Earlier that day she had visited the Swallow, the bar where she'd worked for the past two years, just to grab her last check and say goodbye. She'd wound up sticking around for an hour, kissing the old regulars' downturned foreheads like Snow White with the Dwarfs.

She had been dreaming of this very trip since winning that first invitation to come by Dr. Young's office for a "prelim chat." So much was about to change, it was dizzying to consider. *Bye-bye, hustling for tips until the wee hours! Bye-bye, cigarette smoke in my hair that takes repeated shampooings to get rid of! Bye-bye, four hours of sleep every night!*

The shuttle expertly navigated traffic, inching its way around a burning car at the intersection of South Green and Russell Street before taking 295 to the B-W Parkway.

"All right, guys," Linda said, grabbing Vera's and Danny's hands. "This is it. The next chapter."

Vera sniffed. "Wake me when we get there."

Bye, co-op! Bye, cockroaches! Goodbye, Children's Health Clinic, where I had to fill out a fourteen-page application every single time Danny needed an antibiotics refill! Bye, Union Memorial, with your hostile receptionists and your stoned orderlies and your no-show doctors, your buzzing overhead lights in the waiting area and coal-flavored coffee and OH MY GOD that freaking bag of Hot Fries twisted in the coils of the vending machine! Poor little Hot Fries, I'd take you with me but I hateyouhateyouhateyou! Goodbye! Goodbye! Goodbye!

"What's so funny, Mom?" Danny had unbuckled his seat belt and was standing to fiddle with the CUP monitor overhead.

Linda gave his arm a squeeze. Eleven years old, Danny was, and she could still get her fingers all the way around his forearm. "I just thought of something funny."

"What?"

"Well, you know when you get a coughing fit in the middle of the night, a bad one? And you get wheezy?"

"And I do the seal sound?"

"Exactly. And we have to go to the ER?"

"This is hilarious so far, Mom."

Linda laughed. "You're right. Never mind."

Danny rolled his eyes and went back to watching the CUP, which looked to be interrupting its usual programming for some important breaking news. Everyone was used to this—the CUP's news channels were constantly interrupting their usual programming for important breaking news—but this looked like actual news, what with the shifty, almost flustered look on the face of the anchor. Linda clicked the volume up.

"...host of military honors was bestowed upon Army General Jack Kimbro, whose life was tragically cut short after undergoing cardiac arrest late last night following a wildly successful exchange with radical insurgents in downtown Baghdad."

Linda looked around to find people watching the CUP wide-eyed, some with hands to their faces. Should she follow suit? General Kimbro had always struck Linda as a throwback, with his broad shoulders and Southern-fried wisecracks, the living ghost of a military that no longer existed.

Vera leaned closer to Linda. "Good riddance," she whispered. "I never bought his whole 'Texas Thunder' routine."

"Neither did I, much." Linda looked around. "Why are we whispering?"

Vera shifted her eyes back and forth. "Someone might be listening."

Linda chuckled, gently shoving her mother away.

Half an hour later, the shuttle exited the Beltway. After a few turns, it came to rest before a long, well-manicured hedgerow somewhere in Arlington, Virginia. Vera, who had been gently snoring for the last forty minutes, raised her head. "What's going on?" she asked.

"I don't know," Linda said, turning to the other passengers, who were doing what she was doing—shrugging and checking windows.

With a series of clicks and whirs, the hedgerow parted, as if Mother Nature herself were about to take them into her embrace. They pulled past a small toll booth, where a milkman from the 1950s tipped his hat.

"I think this might be it," Linda said, again reaching for hands. "Our new neighborhood."

"Welcome to Greenway, a USoFA WorldWide–owned and operated Employee Community," said a voice over the loudspeaker. "As one of the one point five million employees of the United Syndicates of Federal Assistance, WorldWide, working with the US Department of Defense to protect and enhance the lives of all Americans, you are now free to call this place…*home*."

The asphalt of the street turned suddenly smooth; the shuttle seemed to glide on well-oiled tracks as its windows displayed a slow panorama of spotless white sidewalks and sapling trees and mailboxes with little red flags, finely manicured lawns, cobblestone walkways leading to wide oak doors. Just like the brochure. A tiny squeal escaped Linda, causing Danny to look up at her and grin.

"Where are all the cars?" Vera asked.

Linda pointed out a white USoFA WorldWide BearCat, its slogan in red cursive along the side: *We take care of our own!* There seemed to be one on every corner.

Vera shook her head. "I see *them*," she said, "but not any real cars."

"I see garages," Linda said. "I assume the cars go in there." Linda didn't know if a garage was part of her deal. She hoped it was. The thought of her crummy little Hyundai Sonata fouling up one of these spotless streets was mortifying.

"I'd rather not ride in any more of these self-driving buses."

"Fine, Mom, I'll buy you a car the first chance I get. Maybe you could point out something you do like?"

Vera squinted at the landscape. "I like the trees. And the flowers. Good variety. The air looks clean."

Danny took a deep breath to demonstrate. Linda heard a little crackling in his lungs but not much.

"Mom, look, a pool! It's huge! Do you think we can use it?"

"Not in February, hon," Linda said. "But maybe in the summer. I'll check."

After a few more blocks, the shuttle stopped. "Held family," said the automated voice. "Linda, Vera, Daniel. Welcome to your new...*home*."

Linda pulled up the address on her phone and checked it against the number on the mailbox. It matched. She took a deep breath before looking across the front lawn, past the moving truck in the driveway—damn, the driveway seemed to go on forever—and up toward her new...*home*.

Something was wrong. The New Employee Hospitality representative had told her they'd be moving into a three-bedroom townhouse, but the structure looming now before her was monstrous: a two-car garage, a front door as wide as a drawbridge, a third-floor wraparound balcony with weather-mottled gargoyles crouched at each corner... Linda counted the windows on the house's façade, losing count somewhere in the low teens. This was either a mistake or a bad joke.

"Something's wrong."

Danny jumped from his seat, squirming past Linda and Vera and bolting down the aisle. "Come on, you guys!" he shouted. "We're here!"

Linda stood and looked around. Maybe there was another Held family onboard, some nice couple with ten kids...

"Might as well go in," Vera said. "Talk to the movers. Maybe they'll know who to call."

As they made their way down the aisle, a bearded gentleman stood and began clapping. His actions proved contagious—within seconds every passenger was up and applauding the Held family's deliverance to a new and better life. Linda waved off the applause as Vera, standing behind her, let out a pained sigh. If there was anything that scandalized Linda's mother, it was the making of a scene.

"Thank you," Linda said, as Vera clucked her tongue, "but this isn't our house. There's been a mistake. I'm just a med student."

The old man who had been crying on his wife's shoulder when Linda had first boarded yelled from his place in the back, "Cry me a river!" which made everyone laugh. Then Vera elbowed Linda to get her moving.

⌒

The following Saturday, Linda found herself pulling open the front door of her new home and greeting a wide-grinning delivery boy, who offered the most heartfelt "good morning" she had ever heard before handing over a padded envelope marked DANIEL HELD SPECIAL DELIVERY NOT FOR RESALE. Linda apologized for her appearance (1100 and she was still in her bathrobe) and offered a tip, but the young man wouldn't hear of it—he just tipped his little milkman's cap and was off, long legs striding down her driveway, zip-a-dee-doo-dah.

Linda took the package to the kitchen and opened it, gasping at its contents. This was the good stuff—not that made-in-South Korea, caffeine-and-antihistamine junk for which she used to schedule wee-hours meet-ups out by the airport. The street value of what she held in her hands was twelve hundred bucks, easy, yet every penny was covered under USoFA WorldWide's Employee SelectPlus Plan—no out-of-pocket, no coverage gaps, no prescription service fee. And free home delivery.

Vera entered the kitchen. "It came already?"

Linda laughed out loud. "Is this a dream?" she asked before fishing a business card out of the envelope which read "Juliana Bolaño, M.D., of the USoFA WorldWide Pediatric Cystic Fibrosis Center." On the reverse side was a handwritten message: *Call me when you receive this— J.B.*

Linda walked down the hallway, through the master bedroom suite, and into her windowless home office at the back of the house. She sat down in her new "Executive Leather Chair, Button Tufted Edition" before her "Executive Oak Desk" and dialed the number. Dr. Bolaño—not an admin, not a computer, but the doctor herself—picked up on the first ring.

"Linda Held, good morning. How's the move-in going?"

They discussed Danny's condition. Dr. Bolaño knew Danny's medical history every bit as well as Linda (and Linda had long figured no one in the history of the world knew anything as intricately as she knew her son's medical history). Polite yet sharp was how Linda would describe Dr. Bolaño; each time Linda tried inserting a joke or a tidbit of personal insight into the conversation, the doctor would snap her back to matters at hand.

"I've got you scheduled for a visit Thursday," Dr. Bolaño said. "And when I say you I mean everybody, the whole family—you, Danny, Vera. Is that OK?"

"Yes, I can make that happen."

"You're going to want to leave the whole day open, because I want a full rundown. The records that Baltimore Union Memorial sent over were a disgrace, frankly, so I have little choice but to treat Danny's case from scratch. Then, once all is said and done, you and I can discuss where to go from here. Sound good?"

"It sounds great."

"All right, I think that's everything. Make sure Danny gets a good night's sleep the night before."

"I will, Doctor. And thank you so much…"

Dr. Bolaño had already hung up. Freaking badass, was what she was.

Linda put her phone down and dabbed tears out of her eyes. Seriously, was she living in a dream?

Last night had been the first night that Linda had slept all the way through, even though she had been forgoing her master bedroom suite for an air mattress in the walk-in closet just off of Danny's room, since it still wasn't a sure thing she would hear Danny if he had a coughing fit or a bad dream in the middle of the night. She'd been fretting over the house's size since their arrival, but then, yesterday afternoon, a USoFA WorldWide New Employee Hospitality representative showed up to hear her concerns, and while nothing had changed (the young lady was sympathetic but otherwise unhelpful, unless one considered her pointing out that the big empty space on the way to the master bedroom was called a *boudoir* helpful), the visit served to close the matter, as far as USoFA WorldWide was concerned.

Danny was wildly enthusiastic about everything around him, though lately he was running out of things to rave about. Last night he had expressed awe at the flushing power of the toilets. "Bet you could flush a bowling ball if you wanted to," he said. "A *little* one. Like for duckpins." He could do with a little less CUP exposure, though. Having discovered a TerrorBusters channel, he had for the past couple of days been camped out in the den, catatonic before a CUP monitor the size of a regulation ping-pong table, barely able to pull himself away for meals and bathroom breaks. *Maybe this afternoon we could get out of the house, take a walk or something...*

Meanwhile, Vera's complaints masquerading as innocent observations had begun to wane. No longer were the ceilings "awfully high," the refrigerator door "terribly heavy," the chandelier in the front alcove "probably a pain in the neck to dust." A couple of days ago, Linda had even caught her puttering around her new bedroom, humming a happy tune. This change in attitude may have had something to do with the sprightly, brown-skinned man living next door, who yesterday could be seen tossing around a battle-scarred cricket ball with a gorgeous, snow-white Siberian Husky, all the while glancing furtively in Vera's direction as she measured the soil pH around the rosebushes.

Linda leaned back, resting her socked feet on the information packet Dr. Young had sent over the day before. She'd been assigned a caseload (how she looked forward to saying that phrase out loud, *my caseload*, just like a real shrink) of exactly two patients: one a Marine sergeant and one a civilian convict who had spent a few months in Iraq on some sort of contract basis. Linda would be meeting them early next week.

Her phone lit up. Linda took her feet off the desk before answering. It was a prerecorded security alert advising that she take "all necessary precautions." The message repeated itself; on the third time, just as she concluded no further information was forthcoming, an alarm sounded from somewhere outdoors, rising and falling in pitch. She got up and jogged down the hall, toward the den.

"Danny, turn off the CUP!" she cried. "Turn it off! Now!"

Danny wandered into sight. "What's up?"

Linda beckoned him to her. "Get away from the front door!"

Vera stepped out from the kitchen, and Linda had to spin to avoid a collision while ordering Vera and Danny to the back of the house. If something horrible had happened, or was about to happen, her office felt like the place to be, its windowslessness reminiscent of panic rooms she had seen in the CUP ads that had started popping up after their break-in last Christmas.

They made it into the office, sitting down on the carpeted floor and catching their breath as the outside alarm wound down to a gurgle.

Vera and Danny turned to her, wearing identical confused expressions. "Was that the doorbell?" Vera asked.

"Hold on…" Linda went to her Thera-9100 monitor and, after shoving her SoldierWell information packet into a drawer, turned it on. "This thing is supposed to have a camera that looks out on the front door," she said. "Here we go."

The monitor displayed a middle-aged man wearing the evidently standard 1950s milkman uniform, though his chest was outfitted in a dark bib. He appeared relaxed while removing his hat and scratching his head. He pressed the doorbell again.

"He looks all right," Vera offered.

Linda nodded. "I'll talk to him, but you guys stay in here. Just to be sure."

"Right," Danny said. "In case he's a Jihadi in disguise."

"OK, no more TerrorBusters for you," Linda said, pointing at Danny on her way out. "For the rest of the day."

The moment Linda opened her front door, the milkman dove into his spiel. "Hey there, ma'am, sorry to disturb your Saturday morning. My name is Harvey Polaski, please call me Harvey, and I'm the assistant manager of Greenway Security. We're just going around, checking to make sure you were aware of the security alert and if you had any questions at this time."

Harvey took a breath and smiled, his caterpillar of a mustache spreading thin along his upper lip. "Just checking up on you, being new to the neighborhood and all."

Linda cinched up her bathrobe. "Thank you," she said. "What was the big emergency? That alarm about scared me to death."

Harvey chuckled. "Sorry about that, Miss Held. But we've got it under control now."

"What was the emergency?"

More chuckling. "No big thing. We just wanted to make sure you were taking all the necessary precautions. And sorry about the scare, really."

"'All the necessary precautions,'" Linda said, "what does that mean, exactly?"

Harvey turned halfway toward his white BearCat parked at the end of the driveway, his heavy black vest making a pulling, twisting sound. "Oh, you know," he said, "locking windows and doors, all that good stuff. Just being aware in general."

Linda nodded. "What's with the bulletproof vest?"

Harvey laughed. "Well, actually," he said, grinning, "this is one of those lead bibs like they give you at the dentist's office."

"Is that right?"

"Yeah, you see, I was just coming from my dentist. Getting X-rays."

"And you just jumped up to come and see if I had any questions."

"Miss Held, this here's a twenty-four-hour job."

Linda put her hand on the doorknob. Whether this guy had been trained to deflect uncomfortable questions or whether he was a bullshit artist by nature, she couldn't be bothered to find out. "OK, Harvey, very helpful. Thanks for stopping by."

Harvey pointed finger pistols in her direction. "You got it, Miss Held."

Smiling to herself in spite of herself—Harvey would have fit right in at the Swallow—Linda walked through the house and back down the hallway, returning two fallen pictures to the wall.

In her office, Danny and Vera had remained cross-legged on the floor.

"OK," Linda announced. "It's over."

"What was the emergency?" Vera asked.

"He never said. Just making sure we got the message."

Vera blinked at the floor. "Maybe we should check with one of the neighbors."

"This guy was so at ease, Mom, I wouldn't be surprised if it was just a training drill or something."

"Quite the scare for a training drill," Vera said. "Oh, well. It feels good, I suppose, knowing there are people working to keep us safe."

FULL TRANSCRIPT

USoFA WorldWide War-Related PTSD Individualized Therapy Program (Pilot), "SoldierWell" Therapy Session # 1

February 10, FY20__

0801EST

LINDA HELD

Interviewing:

SERGEANT TODD SPARROW, US Marine Corps. 2nd Tank Battalion, 2nd Marine Division

(BEGIN)

LINDA HELD: Sergeant Sparrow, I'd like to begin by thanking you for your participation in Soldier-Well. Over the course of these sessions, you and I are going to be working together to reach closure on the experiences you've gained so that you can better acclimate yourself to civilian life. Please allow me to add that, on a personal note, I admire your bravery not only in the theater of war but also in volunteering for the SoldierWell program. I see you've signed all the required consent forms, thank you for that. Do you have any questions before we begin?

SGT. TODD SPARROW: Yeah...I have a question. Who... came up with that name? SoldierWell? I'm a Marine... Warfighter if you like... Soldiers are Army.

LH: I see. Well, I don't know who came up with the name. It's just a catch-all, I guess.

[*pause*]

Excuse me, Sergeant, do you have many more sit-ups to do? Is this a bad time?

TS: Just a second...I'm almost done...OK. See, that's what I mean. If it's supposed to be a catch-all, then it fails, because it's not really catching all. I'm a Marine. If you had called it something like WarriorWell, that'd be accurate. Sounds better, too.

LH: Well, I appreciate your insight. I didn't know Marines weren't considered soldiers.

TS: [*laughs*] Look, I'm sorry. I'm not looking to get off on the wrong foot here, it's just, when I was signing all those forms, I kept seeing that name, SoldierWell. It's nothing. Forget I said anything, Doctor...?

LH: Held. Linda.

TS: Are you a doctor?

LH: Not yet, no. But I'm approved to provide...

TS: [*laughs*] That's just great.

LH: Is everything all right, Sergeant?

TS: OK, where am I? They said I'd be going home, but I can't even tell where this is.

LH: You're in an undisclosed location, Sergeant. For your own safety.

TS: Uh-huh. You all must have some serious money in this program...this isn't any old VA type of thing...I mean, I've been waking up the last few days by a little bell, ding ding. And this morning, I waited a little bit before going to that little slot over there, and my breakfast was still hot. Yesterday was eggs and bacon, the day before that it was granola and berries, and today it was waffles with syrup and a slice of cantaloupe. No rhyme or reason to it, far as I can tell.

LH: Sergeant, you strike me as somebody who speaks his mind, is that right?

TS: Hey, if I see something I don't like, I let you know. That's the way I was raised. Of course, it's not exactly wise to always speak your mind in the Corps. [*laughs*] You know, Miss Held, I know this is all one big goose chase, and that we're going to have to explore a whole bunch of trauma foolishness that doesn't have any bearing on PTSD, or whatever you're calling it. They used to call it shell shock, you know, back in the day. I happen to know for a fact that this is a very inexact science.

[*pause*]

So...where do you need me to start?

LH: Well, why don't you tell me the story of your joining the Marines?

TS: What, the day I signed up?

LH: If you'd like.

TS: [*laughs*] Fuck this...

LH: Sergeant, if you don't want to speak with me, that's fine. But I think I can help you, given the chance.

TS: I don't belong here.

LH: I see. Well, why do you think you were brought here?

TS: How should I know?

LH: Surely you have some idea.

TS: What happened was, and this was about six weeks ago, in Tasmania. Hobart, the outskirts of Hobart, rather. So my QRF, I'm leading...

LH: QRF?

TS: That's Quick Reaction Force. Anyway, I'm leading it. Eight other guys and me. I can't remember how I came to lead but I'm sure it had something to do with the way I carried myself. I have what they call "command presence," if that's a term you're familiar with. That's just how I see myself, and I'm confident others see me that way. Those guys on the CUP, TerrorBusters, those guys are all pussies. They're models. Because, on a purely physical level, I'm basically the perfect Marine. You should see my fitness reports. I could've been a

SEAL if I wanted. That's what they said during Basic Training. I probably should have applied to be a SEAL. One tends to meet a better class of person the farther up the discipline chain you go. Marines aren't bad. Special Forces, SEALS. The Army, though, my God. The Army takes anybody these days.

[*pause*]

So we're coming back from a double patrol. Twelve hours of exposure, of walking around with a target on your back. Twelve hours of interacting with the people we're trying to protect and the Enemy is trying to recruit. The battle for hearts and minds, all that. Now, that is an extremely long time to be on guard, to be telling yourself to check every corner, possible exits, hidey-holes. At all times. Doesn't matter who it is, a kid, a woman, a lizard, they're probably trying to kill you, that's just the understanding you come to. Mistakes get made over twelve hours. It's just human nature. I'm pretty sure the average human brain cannot sustain such a level of focus for twelve uninterrupted hours. Yet the Marines demand it with regularity. So I think it's safe to say I do not possess an average human mind. Now, get this. You're riding in a Humvee, and some gaggle of indigenous simpletons crosses against the light. Or more likely, they cross because there is no light because it came down a couple of days after some dumbshit pulled the pin on some ancient Russian *limonka* to protest us Americans.

Anyway, let's say the Humvee in front of you happens to swipe one of these belly dancer types on the hip, and, whatever, she's down. Screaming. She needs medical attention. But you don't stop because you're on a schedule, and it must be adhered to. You can't stop because it could be a trap, and if you stop, you're toast.

[*pause*]

My point is, it had been a long day. And then at around hour…eleven, we come into this ambush. It's…I won't say it's my fault. It was and it wasn't. It was my fault because I was the leader, but at the same time, it wasn't my fault because… it wasn't my fault. We had taken a shortcut, it was either walk the perimeter of this big hotel-swimming pool-shopping center thing, like three klicks, or else go through the courtyard. And that courtyard had been cleared for weeks, a week at least, guys walking through it every day, more or less. But it just happened that…I don't know. It had been reported repeatedly that the area was secure. But then…

[*pause*]

Exchange of gunfire, and see, this is why I'm a Marine, I remove the threat. Oorah. And it just so happened on this day that the threat was a boy, probably twelve. Little shaver firing holy hell all over the place, not hitting anything, just making noise. No casualties. The next morn-ing I'm called into Lieutenant Hopkins's office.

I'm expecting a promotion. And then he tells me to pack my shit, I'm finishing stateside. As part of this program.

LH: I see. So the child...

TS: I got lucky, OK? I fired in the general direction of the gunfire. I was just providing coverage to one of my company who had fallen into a fog. He was in no way prepared, mentally, just standing there, totally exposed, and I fired to provide coverage for this fuck, and I saw the kid fall, screaming, and his weapon...the kid was firing a damn Browning, huge gun, bigger than him...and keep in mind, this was just across a courtyard. Little fuck was in this barbershop, hiding behind a barber chair. So I stand up, I grab my guy by the scruff of his useless neck and we walk together very swiftly and deliberately across. Because it was important we do this. And we walk into this barbershop together and I prepare his weapon. It was a belly wound, see, and the Enemy was already well on his way to bleeding out. Finishing him becomes an act of mercy at this point. Plus, I thought it might provide my guy some closure to waste the little fuck who'd put him in this state of mind, this fog I was talking about. At first, he says no, which...I mean...

[*pause*]

So now I have to stand there and yell in this guy's face to do it, take care of it. So finally this guy takes the gun and shoots this kid in the head! [*laughs*] Jesus, you know? I said finish him, not blow his damn head off! [*laughs*] Anyway I leave my guy there, I have him sit down in a chair, and he's…whatever, he's sitting down, head in his hands. And I scan the area. This is all just falling back on my training, by the way. I have done everything right up to this point, more or less. So I scan the area, all these store-fronts, interior storefronts, it's like anything you see in any other barbershop, like some small town in the States. And in this back room, it's just completely dark, heavy sheets on all the windows. I've got my white light on, I'm scan-ning, just in case any other little roachfuckers are walking around with Brownings.

LH: Excuse me, can you talk about what you're feeling at this time?

TS: Oh…it's the same every time. You're going through a house or what have you, and you're shining a light in every corner and you see those eyes, pairs of eyes, looking up with just this awe. Not just scared but with like a horror. And you feel, I'm not ashamed to say, you feel beau-tiful, like a, like a dragon or something. Like the sun.

[*pause*]

And of course, now my fellow Marines have fol-lowed me inside, so everybody's screaming, bark-ing orders. And inevitably, some female, in this case, it was a little girl, maybe ten years old, out of nowhere she hobbles in and just starts with the hysterics. Adding absolute zero to the conversation. This is war half the time. Like herding cats. Trying to restore order to just this annoying chaos. The exchanges, you know, the fighting, it's the most stable and dependable thing, you almost don't mind it. Then you start to look forward to it, you look for opportunities. I can't imagine you understanding this, it's something you have to experience directly to have any idea, but it's true. Anyway, so everyone's yelling until finally I have the idea of turning my rifle around and cracking the loudest one in the face because she is the most easily identified problem in the room.

[*pause*]

[*laughs*] OK, I might've had the adrenaline pumping, because I could feel, as I was doing it, I could feel her nose. It sounded like an egg against a kitchen counter. Just this very efficient sound. I could do it a hundred times and it never would have sounded quite that way again. But here's my point. We had just gotten back from this very wearying ordeal, twelve hours in, being shot at and all, and I'm ready for a nice meal. [*laughs*] An edible meal. Something hot, anyway. That's all I want to do at this point. But the second we get back, we're ordered into this conference room, which is ri-goddamn-diculous because immediately I come under the impression that we'll have to report the whole firefight thing since a child was

involved or something. They're constantly changing the rules on us, fucking USoFA WorldWide…but
when we get in there, we're told to fill out this
ten-page questionnaire about our dreams and our
daily habits and our family backgrounds, and then
the next morning I'm called into Lieutenant Hopkins's office. That's how it happened. I'm being
punished but I don't even know why. So is this
what you want me to talk about?

LH: It's a good start.

TS: Oh. I honestly didn't know that's what we
were doing.

LH: You haven't had any trouble sleeping since
you've come here? Headaches? Nervousness?

TS: No, I'm quite comfortable. It's clean here,
which I appreciate, and the food's great, though
I've been eating bag nasties for months now so
anything is a step up. A beer might be nice.

LH: Forgive my asking, but can you tell me how it
feels? Can you talk about that at all?

TS: You mean with the kid? Sure, it's just…hey,
first of all, that kid was shooting at me. Self-
defense. Against the Enemy. And believe me, by
the time we got to him, there was nothing anybody
could do for that kid. I mean, he was practically
cut in half. So, being a practical person, I made
it this, what's the word…a teachable moment for
my guy.

LH: Why do you say that? What was the teachable moment?

TS: Look, war is chaos. That's it. That old saying, war is hell? Well, it is; you've got to know that going in. You have to prepare, you've got to know what that means. Look, is killing a child right? If I did it right now, would that be OK? Of course not. Of course not. But baby, we're at war. That's what this guy, Torrance, he used to always say, he'd say, like if somebody was pissing their pants…baby, we're at war…you've got to be willing to go deep and see what you're made of. And I'm an animal inside. I am a supple leopard.

LH: I see.

TS: Yeah.

LH: How many kills do you think you're responsible for?

TS: Well, sometimes, most of the time, there are like ten of us shooting at the same thing, so it's hard to say. Thirteen, maybe?

LH: I see.

TS: Or did you mean counting my other deployments too? Because…all right, let's see, I mean… I had a slow start…I'd say more than twenty, anyway. It feels weird counting them up, but that also happens to be why I made sergeant in three years. I'm like the ideal Marine. Seriously, take a look at my cutting score, that's why I don't understand why I'm here with you. Other than as like some measurement of where everybody else needs to be.

LH: Any other children?

TS: That I've done? Sure. Probably the majority. I can count the actual grown men, like over the age of, say, fifteen, I can count them on one hand. There were a few that were arguable… It's weird sometimes, after an exchange. The shooting stops and you approach the Enemy, it's just some body on the ground, and it's like, who wants credit for this? And if it's a kid or a woman, nobody wants credit. People start pointing fingers, I saw you firing, maybe it was you, no, I was shooting up at the billboard. But if it's a grown man, everyone's all, yup, that was me, all right, I took that bastard out, somebody get a picture. [*laughs*]

LH: But aside from war being chaos and you're feeling beautiful, now that it's all behind you, back there, how does it feel?

TS: Oh, I see what you mean. Sure, no. It feels bad. Those poor people, they're dead now. It sucks for them. I mean, we kill them, so we usually have to bury them, and you're right, it's awful to have to see their little faces, all innocent and grubby, and you're digging a hole for them. But you know what? Kids are innocent. It's not like they were out being rapists or something, so the chances of them going to heaven are probably pretty good.

[*pause*]

Permission to speak freely? Just kidding, I know I don't need your permission…I think I was just chosen for this SoldierWell thing by chance. They probably just shuffled some papers and I was the one that wound up on top. So let's just say whatever's necessary to get me out of here.

LH: Well, I'd like to thank you for sharing with me today.

TS: Hey, there's no clock anywhere around here. Am I supposed to rely on my internal clock to know what time it is? If so, I can do that.

LH: Well, it was nice meeting you today.

TS: Wait, are you coming back? When are you coming back?

LH: It won't be long. In the meantime, you've got the CUP. And the video games. [1]

---

[1] GAMES MENU

1. *USoFA WorldWide Team TerrorBusters Classic Presents: Target Practice*
You'll need split-second reflexes to complete your training in Hostage Rescue, Sniping, VIP Protection, and Olympic Style Shooting. Become an expert at identifying Enemy threats instantly and neutralizing them. ***Target Practice*** features more than 40 real-world weapons, accessories, and authentic training targets in more than 30 authentic shooting environments.

2. *USoFA WorldWide Team TerrorBusters Presents: Kill Shot 5 (10[b] Anniversary "Reloaded" edition)*
The tenth anniversary edition of the fifth installment of the beloved series, ***Kill Shot 5*** is a classic First-Person Shooter featuring Jack Korner, the most highly

TS: Sure, sure, video games.

END TRANSCRIPT

---

decorated soldier in the War, boasting 278 confirmed kills during tours in Iran, Iraq, Afghanistan, Syria, and Egypt.

Written by active US Tier 1 Operators while deployed overseas and inspired by real-world threats, *Kill Shot 5* delivers an authentic Wartime experience that puts the gamer in the boots of this nation's most disciplined warriors. (Tenth anniversary edition features all-new missions in Tasmania and the Amazon Basin.)

3. *VDCraft Presents: Human Exterminator: Planet of the Zombie Children*

The year is FY2175. You are the only survivor of a crash landing on XR-51B, a planet that the eggheads back on Earth say has been unpopulated for 10,000 years. So what's that scuttling noise?

Developed by VideoCraft gamer prodigy Jeff Hickey (*Womanhunt, Cannibal at Three O'Clock*) and Hollywood screenwriter Dale Ament (*Rib Spreader, Revenge of T.E.E.T.H.*), **Human Exterminator: Planet of the Zombie Children** delivers an assaultive experience like you've never seen. Employ an array of ground weapons to shoot, burn, maim, crush, decapitate, and otherwise destroy XR-51B's ravenous zombie child population.

Strap in to play the game that Hal Arrendo, editor of *VideoKilledtheVideoStar,* called "so incredibly intense that I had to get professional help to deal with my night terrors! Can't wait to see what these guys do next!"

4. *Forefront A Division of USoFA WorldWide/XXX Entertainment Presents: Strangler*

No score. No levels. No missions. Just a summer night in the suburbs of Chicago, back when folks left their windows open and teenagers "necked" in their parents' GMs.

What are you waiting for?

Banned in Canada and throughout Western Europe, **Strangler** is recognized by many as the most controversial game of all time. "The absolute zenith—or nadir—of pop nihilism," wrote cultural critic Seth Volkin, "at least until the sequel." *(Forefront Reality gloves included.)*

FULL TRANSCRIPT

USoFA WorldWide War-Related PTSD Individualized Therapy Program (Pilot), "SoldierWell" Therapy Session # 1

February 10, FY20__

0945EST

LINDA HELD

Interviewing:

PRIVATE* CARL BOXER, US Army (Associate, Transportation Services, "Free2Fight," USoFA WorldWide)

(BEGIN)

LINDA HELD: Private Boxer, I want to begin by thanking you for your participation in this program. During sessions, we'll be working together to help you reach closure on the experiences you've gained and also help you acclimate to civilian life. I just want to add that I personally admire your bravery not only in the theater of war but for participating in the SoldierWell program. Any questions?

PVT.* CARL BOXER: Are you a doctor?

LH: No. I'm not a doctor. You can call me Linda or Miss Held.

CB: Oh. OK. [*laughs*]

LH: Is something funny?

CB: No, it's just, over the last couple weeks, I kept seeing that name SoldierWell this, Soldier-Well that, and I kept thinking, you know, I'm not really a soldier. I'm not a soldier, and now it turns out you're not a doctor.

LH: Yes, funny. What's your story then? Where are you from, originally?

CB: All right…I was born in Twin Groves, Florida. That's near Bonita Springs. It's a small town. Guess that makes me white trash. [*laughs*]

LH: What did your parents do?

CB: My father drove trucks. He died a few years back, seven or eight years back.

LH: I'm sorry.

CB: It wasn't your fault.

LH: No, I just mean I'm sorry for making you remember something painful, possibly.

CB: Not painful. I only ever met him a couple times. My parents were split, if they ever were together. My uncle Ray was more the father figure. For a while. I mean, he was around, living with us. He served in Iraq, back when it was just getting started, and he got wounded in action. Lost both his legs and was awarded the Silver Star.[1]

---

[1] Raymond F. Denny (May 14, FY19__ to Jan. 1, FY20__) ARMY, Iraq, HHB, 1st Battalion, 46th Air Defense Artillery, 3rd Infantry Div, Samarra, Operation Iraqi Freedom.

When he came home, he moved in with us, Ma and me. He couldn't take care of himself on his own.

LH: And you were close with him.

CB: Yeah, he was around.

LH: Do you know of the circumstances surrounding his injuries?

From official US Army reports:

On October 1, FY20___, after visitations of outlying units around Samarra, Raymond Denny was driving for Sergeant Major Drew Quince as part of a three-vehicle convoy on what was then known as Highway 1. The convoy had driven through multiple ambushes during its return, with vehicles running at approximately 79 MPH, when an improvised explosive device (IED) placed at the side of the road detonated, damaging the Humvee. In the same instant, insurgents unleashed a hail of rocket propelled grenades (RPGs) and small arms fire. One of these RPGs tore through the rear side panel of the unarmored vehicle, wounding Sergeant Major Quince before exploding against the Humvee's engine block.

As the other two vehicles went ahead to their predetermined rallying point, the Humvee proved badly damaged but still running. Denny, suffering significant blood loss attributable to the severance of his legs below the knee, managed to press the gas and brake pedals manually, using one of his own severed feet as a lever to drive the 3000 meters to the rallying point. Military police secured the site and, once Sergeant Major Quince and Denny were flown out on a Blackhawk Medevac helicopter, the two remaining vehicles continued into Tikrit.

Denny was treated for fragmentation wounds in the Aid Station at Forward Operating Base Iron Horse. From there he was flown to the hospital at Camp Findhorn, where doctors ordered his evacuation. On December 1, [FY]20___, before he was flown to Landstuhl Regional Medical Center, Denny was awarded the Silver Star medal for valor in combat by his battalion commander, Lt. Col. Leopold Hutch. After three days in Germany, he was transferred to Fort Hood, Texas, to be treated at Darnell Army Medical Center.

CB: Nope. He sacrificed his legs for his country, they gave him the Silver Star. That's good enough for me. I guess I didn't want to know. I'll tell you what, I'm even less curious now after seeing how it all happens. People lose limbs over there all the time.

LH: So what took you to Iraq?

CB: I'm just…well, no. What happened was, where I was staying, they had this call for able-bodied…

LH: Excuse me, where were you staying?

CB: I was in prison. Up in Wisconsin. Waupun Correctional Institute and Primary Medical Clinic. Never saw the medical clinic…

LH: And why were you there?

CB: You ask that, but I bet you know already.

LH: I'd like to hear you explain it, in your own words.

CB: You like the sound of my voice.

LH: Sure.

CB: [*laughs*] Arson, mostly. One count destruction of property, one count arson. I pled guilty, my lawyer said I'd probably walk away with time served. He said the rap was three to six months but don't worry about it, you're clean, just plead guilty and we'll get something between time served and thirty days. Then I stand up and without even looking at me the judge says six months, take him away. [*laughs*] I'm not as bitter as I sound. I was guilty of a lot before I got caught, so looking back on it now, it was payback. The real surprise was when I started working for USoFA WorldWide. People see the CUP, commercials and whatnot, they think you're set for life... On the other hand, here I am, I drove for USoFA WorldWide in Iraq for a few months and now I'm in this nice hotel, not doing much of anything...and you're telling me I get paid the same as driving trucks? [*laughs*]

LH: Can you tell me the circumstances of your arrest?

CB: Yeah...it was a couple big developers who were making a go of it out by where we lived. They tried to build this neighborhood...what do you call them, when the place is behind a wall?

LH: Gated communities?

CB: That's it. They had this big one out there called Hickory Glen. There was going to be a casino and a golf course. It was on our local CUP for years, this big thing for the community out there, all these jobs, but the developers kept fighting with the city people so I guess the bottom dropped out or something, Hickory Glen shut down even though it was mostly built. There were these big houses, ready to move in. After a while, you could look in through the gates and see the houses sagging, the driveways would be cracked and the weeds coming up.

And you'd see like a raccoon or something walking down the middle of the road.

[*pause*]

So we'd sneak inside sometimes. I was out of school by now, just living with my ma and being a bum. Watching CUP all day, then going out and driving around with the high school kids… I could buy beer so they'd keep me around. Pretty sad. But it was something to do, going in there. Sometimes I'd go by myself. I just liked the place. I never did much, mostly just drank a beer and lit a fire in a fireplace. There was always stuff to burn, two by fours… all I remember is I'd spend as much time looking for just the right spot, the right house, and then finding stuff to burn and then getting it all lit and that right there was like two hours. [*laughs*] Then it'd be time to go home. It was the planning it out that I liked, making up a home.

[*pause*]

I met this little girl, Kendra. She was still in school, younger than me, fourteen. OK, a lot younger. I guess she was a troubled teen, but, you know, that's stupid. She was troubled, though, she had lost her older sister, and everybody I guess knew the sister, she was real popular…and one night she took a lot of pills and overdosed and died. One of those things. I didn't know the sister at all. I didn't really know Kendra that well. But one night it was just me and her. I

don't know how it happened, but she started hanging around and I just figured...I didn't think about
it.

[*pause*]

Goddamn, long story short! [*laughs*] Kendra calls
one night and she's like are you up and I say yeah
and she says let's drive out to Hickory Glen.
She was doing these poems, writing poems. She'd
take a spray paint with her and she'd find like
the side of a house and write these poems. And
then whenever somebody'd say what are you doing,
she'd shoo them away, not let them read it. But
she let me read a couple. Which is why I didn't
give a shit when certain people looked at me
that way or said something about the two of us.
I knew it looked weird. We both did. We never,
you know...did...anything. But she was a nice person
and real smart and had a sadness, because of her
sister. She was working through something and I
got it. I sort of got it. Her poems were real
simple. Crazy and simple. She had this one, I'll
never forget this, she made this one on the side
of this pool house, this big neighborhood pool
house next to these three big, empty swimming
pools, and she had written the word "aching" in
these three-foot-tall letters. Five times. "Aching aching aching aching aching." That's it. That
was the first one she showed me, and I remember
she was really up about it, jumping up and down.
I couldn't even fake understanding it, except
that it was sad. I told her, I said I didn't get

it and she laughed at me like I was kidding. You
see something like that and it's like, you're
not alone in the world. That's not it… It's more
like, you see something like that, it says you're
not the only one with ideas. And even though it
was just the same word five times, it's like…some
people are smarter than you. They go deeper than
you…you trust that.

Anyway, she wanted to go out that night, just
me and her. She had some paint and she wanted
to do another one, so I drove her out there. I
mean, she was the one leading this thing, I was
just going along to be her lookout. We get to the
place and we jump the wall and start walking, and
I remember, she had two backpacks full of these
cans, and those little ball bearings are going up
and down, you know. And it's real spooky, almost
cold. We walked around for a long while and then
we found a spot on this little wall, this Jersey
wall, so she crouches down and says to me turn
around, don't watch, watch the road, and I say
there's nothing around, no one's going to see us,
I mean, they hadn't put a guard on the place for
months. And I guess I got a little mad about it.
I thought what she was doing was selfish because,
like I said, I didn't know what she wanted from
me. So I say you don't need me, you just don't
want to be alone if you get caught, and she's
telling me to shut up because she's concentrating
and…I'm not proud of this, I start telling her
that she's just a kid and her poems suck, they
don't make sense, and then it's shut up no you

shut up and off I go. So I go into this house and I find this whole big pile of particle board and I start a fire in the living room, in the fireplace. And of course, the flue's cold so all the smoke's in the house. And there's your arson. Starting a fire in a fireplace. Anyway, this guy says stop right there and he puts a shot in the air and it's just…handcuffs, all that.

LH: Did they find Kendra?

CB: They didn't. And they put that poem on me. I took the rap, which wasn't a big deal. The arson was the thing. Kendra sent me a picture of the poem after I went away. It was just two words. "Alive again," is what it said, in all these different colors.

LH: I see. What does that mean to you?

CB: I think about it a lot. I think it might mean that she was feeling better about things, you know, maybe she turned a corner. If I ever see her again, I'll ask. [*laughs*]

LH: Do you know how to reach her?

CB: I heard she moved away…no, I don't know. I hope she's all right and everything but…I shouldn't have walked away. That was stupid. And I wouldn't want her to see me now. All messed up. Too much shit since I saw her last.

LH: In Iraq, you mean.

CB: Prison, too. They're almost the same thing in my mind. Or no, more like, prison got me softened up for Iraq. Prison was, like, the opener.

LH: Can you talk about your time in prison?

CB: Nope. [*laughs*]

LH: That's fine. We don't have to.

CB: Prison's just not, it's not where you want to be. No matter who you are, prison's not for you. There's some animals in there, like some of these guys don't even know their own names anymore. They'll bite you, take a bite out of you. Chew it up and swallow. I've seen it.

I was only there two months, and I got real lucky because I knew a couple guys in there. They'd been in school with my stepbrother, and they remembered him being OK. These were guys, they were in this white power group, and they said if I showed commitment I'd be all right, I wouldn't have to worry about anything except doing my time. They kept talking about proving myself, proving myself, but I never really did. I got this tattoo on my hand, can you see it?

LH: Yes. What is it?

CB: Nothing. [*laughs*] It was supposed to be a swastika, part of this whole thing they were going to put on me, but we got interrupted, the dude who done it was pulled out and beat to shit by one of the guards. He ended up in the clinic for a week, and then he had casts on both arms up to here so he couldn't finish it. But yeah, it hurt like hell when he was doing it. Somebody once told me I'd never get a job with it on my hand, even if you can't see the swastika, because a tattoo with no color is a prison tattoo, you see it right away... this one was made with a pawn from a chess game, melted down...I was bleeding like crazy, the toilet we were doing it over was all red...it got infected, too, but I kept pouring bleach on it and it got better. I'm glad it never got finished.

[*pause*]

I was kind of like a junior member of this group, pretty well protected and everything. I saw some guys get beat real bad, and I joined in a couple, three or four, just kicking them when they were already down. It was clear you had to do that or else they'd maybe turn on you, and then it was your turn. I learned whole lines from the literature, that's how I got by. Whenever somebody'd be saying something and they'd ask me what do I think, I had some stuff memorized, I'd say one of them and they'd always be like "Damn, boy, you's smart." [*laughs*]

"The first forms of civilization arose when the Aryan came into contact with the inferior races, subjugating them and forcing them to obey his command." That's Hitler. I'm not even racist and I still got it memorized.

LH: You're not racist?

CB: Ma'am, I did what I had to do. I took what was offered and I was glad for it. I mean, I was scared all the time. If I didn't have them guys I'd have been in the hospital or killed or holding onto somebody's pocket, little boypussy. I had to protect myself.

LH: You left Waupun Correctional through the Free2Fight program, is that right?

CB: [*laughs*] Yeah, what happened was, they rounded up us first offenders, first-timers who weren't there for murder or rape or armed robbery or anything real hard-drug-related, and they said if we wanted to get out on a work program, they'd put us in for regular custodial work over in…what did they call it…foreign markets, they said. You'd have thought they needed us to clean up office buildings, the way they said it. I remember, after they came in and made this big presentation, they gave us twenty-four hours to think it over and decide if we wanted to sign up, and that whole time people were yelling at each other, across cubbies, don't sign up, they'll put you on the front line with no protection or else they'll take you to some black site and test chemicals on you. But I'd been in jail for sixty-eight days up to then. I didn't like what it was doing to me, all that Aryan shit. But if I knew what Iraq was really like, I'd have stayed in prison for another year.

LH: What did you do over there? In Iraq?

CB: I was a driver. They had some name for it, transport manager specialist, and all my papers said I was a private with the Army, but I was a truck driver. Like father like son. That was last August…at least I think I drove trucks the whole time. There's whole chunks I can't remember, like I assaulted a chaplain, they said I tried to kill him, which… [*indecipherable*] No memory of that. None at all.

[*pause*]

Look, I don't want to go back. I'll go to jail again and finish up, but really, I just want to feel regular. I want to remember stuff like I used to, and I want to get rid of these headaches I've been getting.

LH: I understand completely, Private.

CB: You can call me Carl, please.

LH: Very well, Carl. But now our time is up.

CB: OK. How'd I do? All this talking, am I doing it right? I feel a little weird today.

LH: You're a natural.

CB: When are you coming back?

LH: I don't exactly know. But it shouldn't be long.

CB: All right. All right.

LH: Goodbye, Carl, and take care.

END TRANSCRIPT

While waiting for Danny's test results, Linda found a quiet corner in the coffee bar of the USoFA WorldWide Pediatric Cystic Fibrosis Center and looked over the pages of meek scrawl she'd made during her initial patient interviews. She started from the last page and worked her way back, as was her habit through school.

PVT. CARL BOXER

—in fetal position at start (vulnerable?)
—convict (arson, destr. of property) but a gentle soul(?)
—Uncle--->Silver Star, Iraq I
—arson = fire in a fireplace, Waupun
—"drove trucks" in Iraq, no firm memories
—Could be in acute psychic pain > stress or clinical depress.
REAL PTSD, patient must recover memory/find resolution
re: Iraq. Then

Deeming these notes largely useless, Linda sipped her seven-dollar Frappuccino and allowed the classical music that was playing to wash over her. It was fine about her notes—these initial interviews were just informal chats, Dr. Young said, no big deal. It wasn't very long after she had finished up with Private Boxer that Dr. Young called to check in, complimenting her ease with the patients. She was doing OK so far.

Wherever this work was leading her—and even at this early juncture she could see it would be leading to some dark places—USoFA WorldWide was holding up its end of the bargain. Danny was enjoying the finest of medical care. Dr. Juliana Bolaño had been waiting for them outside the front door of the CF Center early that morning, the winter wind whipping at her lab coat, lending her a superheroic air. She was younger than Linda had expected. Following shivery introductions, everybody hustled indoors, where Dr. Bolaño proceeded to focus her whole attention on Danny. For twenty minutes, they conversed on an array of subjects while Linda and Vera marveled at the CF Center's amenities: animatronic zoo animals that sang a welcome song as they passed, a billiard table in the public waiting area, an original Norman Rockwell hanging next to the nurses' station. Only after everyone was seated in Dr. Bolaño's office were the grown-ups even addressed. The conversation took on a family counseling feel as each member of the Held family spoke about their dietary and exercise habits. Linda couldn't help but apologize for the meals she served her son (*way* too much refined sugar), but Dr. Bolaño just nodded along, her face inscrutable.

Then came the tests: A sweat test, a genotyping, a mucus sample, blood and urine samples, a stool sample, PFT, arterial blood gas testing, a six-minute walk test, a CT chest scan, chest X-rays. It made for an exhausting morning for Danny, but thanks to a lab somewhere on the premises (along with a pharmacy, gymnasium, and, for some reason, the second-largest indoor aquarium in the state), the test results were expected within the hour.

From across the coffee bar, Linda spotted what appeared to be a newspaper left behind on a nearby table. Weird, because it seemed that paper of any kind was anathema here at the CF Center—part of the disgracefulness of Danny's old medical records was that so many of them were available via hard copy only. Curious, with the whole place to herself, Linda got up and walked over and grabbed the newspaper, bringing it back to her table.

Oh. It was just *The Citizen*, the free weekly paper of the anti-War movement. Linda had read one or two of these articles before out of sheer desperation—homeless people handed *The Citizen* out on busy street corners and in front of food co-ops.

Last Hours of the Texas Thunder
by Chelsea Daye

Three nights ago, a mysterious package with no return address arrived at my front door. After swiping it through my personal security scanner, I opened the box to find a videodisc, the kind still common in certain media production houses. The disc was unlabeled, so, after an hour spent trying to find my old videodisc player, I sat down and pressed PLAY.

It began with the opening credits of "The After-Action Report with Whit Knightley," the popular neocon pep rally brought to you by USoFA WorldWide's Patriot Media. Even if you don't watch the show—why would you—you've probably seen the opening credits at someplace like the Department of Motor Vehicles or one of your finer cheeseburger-on-a-stick establishments. Allow me to refresh your memory: grainy footage of some dark-skinned "terror suspect" getting mowed down in a hail of blessed American firepower; American flag wipe. Vice President Wenner pointing fingers at a gaggle of weak-kneed foreign journalists; American flag wipe. Cherubic Iranian child sitting on the shoulders of a musclebound TerrorBuster; American flag wipe.

The timestamp at the bottom of the screen read 12-27-FY20__, which I remembered was the day that U.S. Army General Jack "Texas Thunder" Kimbro had died. Yet here he stood, brash yet huggable as the soldiers celebrate behind him, having fulfilled a major combat mission that won three downtown city blocks for the U.S. of A. He calls Patriot News correspondent Elizabeth Swihart "darlin'," which Swihart bears with aplomb.

But there appears to be a bandage on the General's arm. He explains it's the result of his risky (some say suicidal) insistence on being as close as possible to the front line during firefights. What isn't explained is the pair of Hazmat-suited men standing nearby. Swihart asks Kimbro why the men are standing so close, but General Kimbro waves away her concerns.

That's when things get weird:

> SWIHART: Earlier this week, President Halladay alluded to reports of terrorist activity in the town of Aukland, New Zealand. Now, the Governor-General there has denied such

activity, despite ties to known terrorists in Tasmania. Can you give us your thoughts on the prospect of our going to war with New Zealand?

KIMBRO: Well, I've heard some rumors going around on that, and I just don't know. That's for our political leaders to figure out. But if that's where they're finding the terrorists now, then… Hey, what's [*inaudible*]. Oh, dang it! Dang, that is cold!

SWIHART: And there it is, the traditional Gatorade shower… General… I imagine, General, you've been looking forward to this moment for a long time.

KIMBRO: Let me tell you, these jokers… Welker, Ridley, Gutierrez, they're just about the biggest… [*inaudible*] Hey, what's in this stuff? Anybody else smell bread? There's this… bread and butter and… Oh. Oh, God…

The two men in Hazmat suits suddenly accost the General, dragging him out of the frame while screaming for everyone to take cover. A second later, one of the Hazmat suits demands that the camera be shut off. End of feed.

What are the implications of this footage? Was Gen. Kimbro in some sort of danger following his Gatorade shower? Who were the men in Hazmat suits? Why did they tell everyone to get down the moment the General said he smelled bread? CUP reports all say that Gen. Kimbro died peacefully in his sleep, but how can this be? What occurred in the hours between this interview and the reported time of death?

I put in calls to various USoFA WorldWide representatives, as well as Army Public Affairs, but have yet to receive a response. I won't stop trying though. These are questions that demand answers.

IN OTHER NEWS: I am thrilled to announce I've been invited to appear at the Peace Now! Conference to be held at the Walker Art Center in Minneapolis, Minnesota, on February 27th. People are really responding to what we are saying, so please join us if you are in the area. Arm yourself with the knowledge needed to end this War. Abide no longer!

"There you are."

Startled, Linda looked up to see Dr. Bolaño standing before her, her gaze narrowed.

"What is that?"

Linda laughed and put the paper down. "Oh…I found it on the table there."

Dr. Bolaño took it up and looked it over. "I'm not judging, I just wonder how it got here. Did you see who had it?"

"No, I just picked it up."

"I get it," Dr. Bolaño said. "I see Chelsea Daye's still at it, the poor thing." The doctor tossed the newspaper back onto the neighboring table, then squirted hand sanitizer into each palm as she took a seat across from Linda.

"Let's see," she said, opening her tablet. "The test results all came back. Blood and urine samples are fine, liver looks good, arterial blood gas testing was strong… All this is telling me that our chances are good. Really good."

"I'm sorry, good for what?"

Dr. Bolaño look up and blinked. "For the transplant."

A burst of coiled angst charged up from the pit of Linda's stomach, diffusing in startled laughter. A *transplant*? Could that be within reach? There must be more hurdles to overcome, doctor visits, more nights of waking up to Danny being unable to get his wind, laying him across her lap and whapping at his back to bring up the sputum. There was much, *much* more to go through before anyone could even think about a lung transplant, right?

"He has some malnutrition issues," Dr. Bolaño said. "He's in the fifth percentile of what's considered ideal for his age. Which is why I'm recommending an enzyme therapy."

"How long? To do the transplant, I mean." Linda searched her purse for a Kleenex.

"I can't say. It could happen in six weeks, it could take eighteen months."

Linda fell apart all over again. Eighteen months was nothing. Six weeks was a cruel joke. "Thank you," she whispered. "Just…thank you."

"The Center keeps an extensive list of people eager to donate organs in exchange for debt forgiveness," Dr. Bolaño said, "but a Living Donor Lobar Transplant is what Danny needs. That's a bit trickier."

"I've heard of that," Linda said. "Doesn't it require two donors?"

Dr. Bolaño snorted. "Maybe in the public hospitals. Here it's just one. Now, his blood type *is* rare…"

"Right," Linda said, "O Negative. God, Doctor. This is amazing."

"Linda." Dr. Bolaño crossed her arms. "Just because your son may have a functioning pair of lungs one day doesn't mean he'll never have to see a doctor again. And he's going to be hitting puberty in a couple of years, and the very slim chances of his ever fathering a child can be tough on kids that age."

Linda nodded, duly sobered. Like any doctor worth a damn, Dr. Bolaño was managing expectations. Linda dabbed away the last of her tears while chiding herself for coming off like some ditzy hick.

Dr. Bolaño pointed at the Thera-9100 Remote Responder Awareness Device around Linda's wrist. "And since it looks like you're on call," she said, "I'm recommending a live-in companion."

"Oh, I'm not sure that's necessary."

Dr. Bolaño nodded as if expecting this response. "It is necessary. You'll see."

"I appreciate what you're saying, but honestly…"

"Linda, you could be the greatest mom in the world—and you might be, from what I've seen—but this is beyond your ability. I strongly urge you to explore this option."

The bald shoe salesman pulled at the knees of his khakis before crouching down and sliding the old-fashioned shoe sizer beneath Danny's socked foot. Linda took the opportunity to admire the sheen on his bright pink head before wishing he would roll up his shirt sleeves just a little bit more so she could get a better look at the sinews of his forearms. Amazing how good news—or, in this case, incredible news, *seismic* news—always threw Linda into a state of silly girlishness.

So she had a thing for bald guys, so what? They were often so disarming, capable of a bright-eyed gameness that Linda found tremendously appealing.

"We've got the digital things," the salesman said, answering a question Linda had not heard, "but when I want an actual accurate reading, this does the job."

"I hear you," Vera said. "There are one or two things that previous generations managed all right."

Vera had turned downright sociable in the last few days. No doubt this had everything to do with their neighbor, who had come a-calling the other night as they were finishing up dinner. "Pardon me," he'd said to Linda, in a gooey British accent, as his dog pulled at its leash, "but I was hoping for a moment with the constant gardener of the house?" The lovebirds chatted on the porch for twenty-five minutes, by Linda's watch, and by the time goodnights were bid, a date was set: Vera and Deva were going antiquing next Saturday.

Baldy stood up, shoe sizer in hand. "Looks like a men's three," he announced. "I'll go make sure we've got them."

"Great," Linda said, smiling.

"Be right back," he said, grinning, not going anywhere. *There* was that bright-eyed gameness Linda had been waiting for...

"Better get going."

"Guess I'd better."

Danny jumped up to peruse the display near the front of the store. They were the only customers there; the solitude felt like a luxury. Years had passed since the three of them had ventured out to a real retail experience—the last shoe store they had physically visited, at the marketplace inside the old Peabody Library, was when Danny was five. Linda remembered it taking hours to find a pair of matching sneakers in Danny's size, among the rows of plastic bins marked KID SNEAKS $30/PARE.

"Mom, how about these?" he asked, holding up what looked like an astronaut's boot.

"What are they?"

"TerrorBusters 10K!" Danny stuffed his foot into the shoe, clownishly big on his foot. "They feel amazing!"

"Amazing expensive, I bet."

"Early birthday present?"

"Put them back."

Danny let out a groan before removing his foot from the shoe and putting it back.

Vera took Danny's seat. "What did you think of Robert?" she asked.

Linda shrugged. "It's a big step," she said. "Do we really want a stranger living with us?"

"You heard the doctor," she said. "Absolute vigilance gets us a transplant."

Linda nodded, pursing her lips.

"Look at it this way," Vera said. "You're not going to have time for all that physiotherapy stuff."

"You think I can't do it?"

"I didn't say that."

"That's exactly what you said."

Vera grimaced, placing her hands flat on her lap. "I am simply saying that once your work gets going, keeping up with everything that's required might be stressful. I can fill in here and there, but I mean..."

"No, you're right. Sorry. I guess I'm just...I'm not sold on Robert."

"I know someone who is," Vera said, looking Danny's way.

Danny and Robert had hit it off immediately, but Linda couldn't tell whether it was because Robert was that skilled at endearing himself to sickly children or whether Danny was just being accommodating, as was his way. "I guess it might be good to have a positive male role model in the house," she said. "One whose masculinity isn't measured by the number of Enemy scumbags he's wasted."

Vera smiled. "Hey, if that young man can boost our chances of getting Danny a transplant, even a little, why *wouldn't* we bring him on? You said yourself, it would cost us practically nothing out-of-pocket."

The shoe salesman returned empty-handed. "I don't have the Power Kicks in his size," he said. "I can order them special if you want to come back next week?"

Linda turned and watched as Danny fell into a prolonged coughing fit, hacking into his elbow as she had trained him to do practically since birth. Sometimes, while doing the laundry, she would find little slugs of dried mucus on the inner elbows of his shirts.

"What about the TerrorBusters 10Ks?"

Baldy nodded. "Sure, yeah. Give me two seconds."

Linda turned to Vera, who had one eyebrow raised.

"What? Can't I buy something nice for my son? For his birthday?"

Vera held up her hands. "I didn't say anything," she said.

EXCERPT

USoFA WorldWide War-Related PTSD Individualized Therapy Program (Pilot), "SoldierWell" Therapy Session # 3

February 16, FY20__

1349EST

LINDA HELD

Interviewing:

SERGEANT TODD SPARROW, US Marine Corps. 2nd Tank Battalion, 2nd Marine Division

(BEGIN)

SGT. TODD SPARROW: We moved around a lot, Juliette and I… I believe I told you that already. I've lived all over Maryland. Rockville, Columbia, Upper Marlboro, Laurel. I was born in western Maryland, way out there, this little town called New Market. Really old, quaint little town, the main drag was three blocks long. Golf courses all around. And farmland. It hasn't changed much. I rented a car and drove around there right before deployment.

[*pause*]

But lots of apartments, in those years, lots of one-bedroom condos. Every one we got to, Juliette would say, this is home now, and then she'd sit down on the floor and cry. It was like a ritual. And she makes a lot of noise when she cries. It's not the type of crying that evokes sympathy. You just sort of watch her cry and hate her. [*laughs*] No kidding, I've seen grown men, men who said they loved her, and she starts crying, seriously blubbering, and the guys are like there, there…there, there. You can tell they just wanted to jump out the window. She's too much sometimes. Let's see, what else…she was a janitor at a little medical clinic for a while, but that stopped because she kept thinking she was catching diseases from people coming in. She'd ask me, you hear that, Spunky? [*indecipherable*] You hear that thing in my throat back there? [*indecipherable*] Drove herself crazy. Oh, she was a cashier at a hardware store for a long time. She liked all the male attention…loved it… Juliette has never had a female friend, never. She was beautiful when she was young…I've seen pictures. And men, they thought she was great, really fun. Maybe that's why they hated her crying. But she's too much of a drinker now. I don't know if you'd call her an alcoholic, necessarily. She just likes it. She used to smoke cigarettes, but she quit. Or maybe she never really inhaled, maybe she just liked to blow smoke in people's faces. She loved to blow smoke in people's faces.

[*pause*]

I was nine when she got married. [*laughs*] His name was Arthur Pfeiffer. He was pretty old. I remember him saying it was weird I didn't call her Mom. Mom. [*laughs*] I'm sure Juliette didn't love him or anything like that, but he was old and he had money, had this big house in Potomac. And he was semi-retired, but he'd made his money as a political advisor or lobbyist or something for NabisKraft[1]. This was way before it got absorbed into USoFA WorldWide. He wasn't around much, which was fine with me… On the night he proposed, she came home and sat down next to me on the couch and she said, Spunky, I finally did it, I finally did it. And I said what? I was all groggy, you know, and she said I finally got us a rich husband. Then she said, I'll never forget this, she said, we're getting married to a rich old man, no thanks to you. [laughs] That's just how she said it, no thanks to you. [laughs] It's like she never missed an opportunity to let me know I was this big albatross to her. [laughs] Old as Art Pfeiffer was, I think they talked about having kids, or maybe adopting, but nothing came of it. She put up too much resistance. [laughs] I can remember her pointing down at me and saying, I'm not going through all that again.

---

[1] Arthur C. Pfeiffer (FY1955–FY20__) was a key figure in the expansion of NabisKraft into North Africa. (NabisKraft was later absorbed into Exxon-MoChev Dynamics, one of "the Big Three" that came together in FY20__ to form USoFA WorldWide.) In FY20__ he was posthumously awarded a USoFA WorldWide Silver-Level security clearance status.

Pfeiffer is perhaps best remembered for creating the controversial CUP program *The NabisKraft© 400-Pound Challenge*, a reality-based program that followed twelve people with a BMI-for-age between the 85th and 90th percentiles as they competed to reach the goal weight of 400 pounds. The first to reach this weight would receive a "full plate" of bariatric and elective cosmetic procedures: liposuction, abdominoplasty, genioplasty, rhinoplasty, chemical peel, etc. *The NabisKraft© 400-Pound Challenge* aired from FY20__ to FY20__.

[*pause*]

That's what I mean. She never missed an opportunity to be cruel to somebody, anybody. Sometimes I could see it coming. It got to where I could beat her to the punch, in my mind. Somebody would say something to her like, hey why don't you go live overseas for a while or something like that, and I'd look at her and I'd already be thinking, come on, point at me and make that sour face, let's get it over with [*laughs*]...now shrug like I'm your reason for not doing anything important with your life, let's get it out of the way... [*laughs*] Art Pfeiffer was nice enough, though. That's what I called him, by the way. Never Dad or anything like that.

[*pause*]

After we moved in, she got involved in planning kids' birthday parties. It became a side business, more or less. I don't know how she even got involved in it, or why. I don't know if she liked doing it. I detested it because of course I'd have to go to these parties. Juliette arranged it that way. She wouldn't do it if I couldn't tag along. As she said, she wasn't trying to throw money away on a nanny when I'm just as happy being with her, and who wouldn't want to go to a birthday party? But of course, all the kids would be looking at me like, who are you supposed to be? I can remember crying, screaming at her, I don't want to go, I don't want to go. Hanging out of the car all the way there, no, don't make me go. [*laughs*] I haven't thought about this stuff in a long time.

Birthday parties, kids' birthday parties, my God. Little hats and cake and… [*indecipherable*] Oh, and the kids at these parties! Because they realized I wasn't a real guest of the party, and the clowns knew me but didn't try and act like they knew me because, well, I can see that. You don't want to favor the one kid no one knows when there's money to be made. So they never called on me to have the coin get pulled from my ear or any of that crap. Boo-hoo, right? [*laughs*]

LINDA HELD: What did you and your mother tend to do when it was your birthday?

TS: [*laughs*] Nothing! When we were poor, you know, she'd take me out and get me a cupcake or something. But when we stopped being poor, she didn't even do that. I think it might have had an effect on me. I started to treasure my alone time. Autumn weekends, when the party season died down but before it got too cold outside, I love that time of year. I was outdoorsy then. This was all later, you know, like twelve or thirteen. Art Pfeiffer's house was near a woods. Not like in the woods, but there was a woods that made up the back of the backyard. Great backyard. There was a tennis court, because Art Pfeiffer liked to play when he was younger, some other stuff. A, uh, a what do you call it, a pool. Swimming pool.

LH: What sort of things did you do outdoors? What did you see?

TS: Oh, just…it was all very wholesome. Picking up sticks, using them for hiking up little hills.

I was free to explore the, uh, the wonders of nature.

[*pause*]

OK, when I was about eleven or twelve, I took a slingshot from Juliette's kitchen drawer. She had a drawer full of party favors in the kitchen, for the birthdays, and she was always adding to it, whenever she saw a deal at a store. They were always these stupid little toys. But once I got a slingshot, probably a Made-in-Taiwan thing. It had this very cheap, thin rubber band. But I used it to kill a bunch of squirrels. Once or twice, I mean. Birds too. A few birds. Target practice that I would come to need later in life. [*laughs*] I'm a really good shot now, which is important in the Marines, obviously. Now, please don't think, Linda, don't think that I didn't feel remorse. I did. I did feel remorse. Bad stuff. The first time I did it, I was just walking around out there, shooting at the ground with this thing. Bored, you know. And then I saw this squirrel and I thought, hey, let's see what happens. I remember picking up a stone and taking aim and getting ready to run away because I figured the most this cheap thing was going to do was make the squirrel angry. I was just a dumb kid. So I remember, I fit this little stone, maybe like a quartz stone, and I just pulled back and…[*indecipherable*] No suffering. Just a very clean shot. Sad and every- thing, but I couldn't have taken him out any more cleanly if I'd tried. Terrible remorse, though. Guilty. I made a little ditch and said a prayer and buried it. And there was…oh, this is funny… there was a part of me that was expecting to get arrested, as if a police officer was going to come to the house and take me away. Stupid, right? I did it a few more times, once I realized the police had no intention of taking me downtown. [*laughs*] So I figured, you know, why not? It was like this secret between me and the squirrels, and they weren't going to tell anyone. [*laughs*] It's so strange I'm remembering all this stuff… It's difficult to say, when I'd come home from school and throw my little backpack down on the floor of my bedroom, and run outside to play in the woods, it's difficult to say what I looked forward to more, the killings or the burials. I guess that sounds weird because both are, you know… Look, it was something to get involved in, of my own. I mean, I made my own slingshot. The other one, the cheap one broke, so I worked on finding just the right forked branch, and I got this real heavy-duty rubber tubing from somewhere, and I made the little pocket out of this nice, crushed red velvet that Juliette had lying around. And when I'd see a squirrel, after a while I'd see it as a target. Then after I had taken it out, I'd pretend I was a priest and I'd say a little prayer over the body. I'd cry. Seriously I'd cry real tears. So, you know, there's your remorse. Which now, yes, I admit, it's a little weird. But I came to believe that it had to happen, like I was fated to kill this particular squirrel. Like it was natural. And, wow, strange how it's coming back to me…like a couple of times, four or five times, I'd fill up a beer can somebody left, I'd fill it with creek water and act like it was holy water. I'd sprinkle it on the little animal body, like I was preparing the body, getting it ready for heaven, you know. And so after the first few times it felt like I was doing these squirrels a favor, you know, sending them back to God. I think that's why nowadays I don't feel too bad for these things, like if a gas station blows up or somebody walks into a post office with a semiautomatic and shoots everybody. The writers and the news people, they always say, oh, how tragic. And it is. For those people's families, I'm sure, because, you know, they'll miss them. But the victims themselves, I mean... [*laughs*] God loves victims, you know? Those people are in heaven, like automatically. It's practically a good thing, if you think about it. And if they're not in heaven, then they're in hell where they deserve to be. And if there is no heaven or hell, well, then they're unconscious and they don't care. And that's the worst-case scenario, you know? Half the time it's probably a relief. [*laughs*] Talk about weird, I even put little crosses in the ground, as grave markers! Popsicle sticks! Popsicle sticks and glue. There's probably one or two still there, still upright. I should go check after I get out of here... Say, I do feel better today! [*laughs*] Congratulations, Linda, you've got me recounting the story of my exciting childhood. Just like you wanted.

END EXCERPT

Dr. Young appeared lithe and laid back in his mock turtleneck and wide-whorl corduroys, but his manner was nervous, almost squirrelly, as he repeatedly checked over both shoulders. He and Linda were sitting outdoors on this unseasonably balmy Tuesday afternoon in late February, awaiting drinks at Terry's, a small bistro located across from the easternmost edge of the USoFA WorldWide Region One campus. Linda had ordered a root beer, having failed to recognize the celebratory nature of this outing, while Dr. Young ordered a bourbon, neat, before offering his congratulations.

"At first I thought it was risky to volunteer personal information," he said, "but, as we now see, with risk comes reward. You've *reached* these men, Linda. Great work."

The drinks arrived, and Dr. Young all but lunged at his half-full tumbler and took a deep sip. "Excuse me if I seem distracted," he said, his voice low and newly lubricated. "There's been some stress recently. The SoldierWell program seems to have hit a snag in one of the other locations."

"What sort of snag?" Linda asked.

"Well, the SoldierWell South team—it appears we failed to install proper suicide prevention measures."

"Does that mean what I think it means?"

Dr. Young nodded. "We were using an old building down there, and one of the patients…" He made a plummeting motion with his hands. "Nine stories."

"Oh, God. That's horrible."

"We think it was a dosage miscalculation, and the medication's side effects, well. Luckily, all *your* patients are on the ground floor." Dr. Young gave a rueful chuckle. "Excuse me. It's really surprising, how *hard* this is for me." Dr. Young looked downward and closed his eyes. Linda wanted to reach across the table and squeeze his hand, the way she did whenever Danny came home all glum after being picked last at recess.

As if suddenly aware of his vulnerability, Dr. Young looked up and threw his shoulders back. "But then this past weekend, Edna H called me. Her faith hasn't wavered, so that's put the wind back in my sails, somewhat."

"That's nice, having that support."

"Yes, it is." Dr. Young smiled and raised his glass.

"Do we have a plan in place for bringing on more patients?" Linda asked. "My caseload is pretty small. I'm happy to…"

Dr. Young shook his head. "What's needed at this point is deep focus on the patients you have. Keep strengthening that trust bond. Establish a *nexus*, if you will."

Linda nodded, and continued nodding, because nodding was the safest thing she could do as the panic bloomed inside her. *This is the beginning of the end. If they're not giving you more work it's because they don't think you're capable, and if they don't think you're capable, well, pretty soon the work tapers off until one day some accountant in some processing center in Idaho draws a line through your name.* What started as panic gave way to a low-grade existential dread as the likely future unfurled before her: Danny and Vera and herself boarding a shuttle, making the trip back to Baltimore, back to the old apartment… Vera breaking up with Deva just as things were beginning to heat up between them… Danny trudging back up the steps of Tunbridge Public in ratty Goodwill sneakers. Forget the root beer, she needed a *drink* drink…

Dr. Young reached over, placing one of his giant hands on Linda's forearm. "Now I don't want you to worry," he said. "You're not going anywhere."

Linda smiled and exhaled. Relief was such an underrated emotion.

Dr. Young again looked over his shoulder, emitting a combination gasp-chuckle. "God, would you just *look* at them."

Linda followed Dr. Young's gaze to a bunch of Haters, seven or eight of them, clumped outside the gate of the Region One Campus.

One, a teenage girl, held a poster board sign that read ABIDE NO LONGER! Nearby, USoFA WorldWide employees continued streaming in and out, waving at the guards as they passed.

Dr. Young shook his head, bewildered. "Don't they know how hopeless their cause is? Corporations might not be people, per se, but they're made up of people. So it follows they're flawed like people."

"Sure."

"But what makes these flaws forgivable is when you put them up against our success rate. We took over the War when the federal government had gone to *shit*, pardon my French, and now look at us. Look at the War. Completely rehabbed, in a matter of months. And yet, here they are, the Haters, still around, ants at a picnic." He laughed. "It's like they're actively participating in their own marginalization."

"That reminds me," Linda said, "the other day I came across a copy of *The Citizen*. I still can't believe Chelsea Daye is writing that column."

Dr. Young groaned. "Now *there's* a live one." It was a phrase Linda had never understood, though in this context she wondered whether its vagueness was by design, a winking reference to a uniquely feminine yet otherwise indeterminate form of lunacy.

"She was talking about General Kimbro. Questioning how he died."

Dr. Young held up one finger, pausing the conversation as lunch arrived. They each took a minute to dress their burgers, but Linda could tell in the way he was shaking the ketchup bottle that her boss had more to say about Chelsea Daye. Which was fine—she was happy to just listen while stuffing her face.

"She's just so entitled," Dr. Young said. "Using all her Hollywood connections—connections she got thanks to USoFA World-Wide–owned studios, mind—to hack into our accounts, uncover classified information, in some cases. She puts the country at risk, and for what? To style herself as a rebel, some great white progressive hope. It's a rebranding."

Linda nodded. This burger was incredible. "I wish she'd go back to acting," she said. "I always liked her movies."

Chewing his first bite, Dr. Young shook his head. "Don't get me wrong," he said, "I'm speaking as a *fan* of hers. I loved her in that one about the bridge, whatever it was called. *Loved* her. But it doesn't matter anymore, because, just in my own personal research, I've read quite a bit of her stuff, her columns and speeches, and I sense just a… blankness. Know what I mean? It's like she's missing something vital to a whole character."

They finished lunch in a comfortable silence. When their server came to take away their plates, Linda ordered a slice of chocolate pie.

Dr. Young turned back to the Haters across the street. After a long moment, his upper lip began to curl upward. "Hey, Linda," he said, finishing his drink. "Check this out."

"Dr. Young, you have to help me with this pie."

"No, no, I detest chocolate." He stood and called out to the group's ostensible leader, a bearded guy with a megaphone in his hand. The guy's whole body appeared to tighten as he realized that this man lunching in the famous Company hangout was addressing him. With megaphone still in hand, the guy began crossing the street.

"It's OK," Dr. Young said, sitting down. "I've seen this guy before. I know him."

The man stepped over the short black fence surrounding the dining area and approached the table.

"What's your problem today?" Dr. Young asked.

Linda continued eating as the guy dove into what sounded like boilerplate Hater speech. *We're protesting this endless war… loss of communal values… culture of cruelty*, blah-de-blah-de-blah. While she had never considered whether they knew how hopeless their cause was, Linda had long ago lost her patience with the Haters. They reminded her too much of her father in his last years, as the drinking and the paranoia took turns eating away at him. For years she did her best to keep up with his conspiracy theories, reading everything he pressed on her, bridging the worrisome crevices in his logic with her own wobbly, half-hearted theorizing. Even at the very end, after he had stopped eating altogether, after Vera had ceased trying to improve the situation to focus her energies on making sure the car keys stayed hidden, Linda continued nodding along, pretending she understood what Dad was talking about.

"...believe that it's in the best interest of the American people to overturn the Temporary War Law and return the power to declare war back to Congress, as Article One Section Eight of the United States Constitution plainly states. We also believe..." The sanctimonious dolt had placed his hand on the edge of their table, the better to glance down Linda's shirt. For a second she considered affixing his hand to the table with her dessert fork.

"That's enough, I think," Dr. Young said. "May I see your megaphone for a second?"

The guy handed it over. Linda could feel her fellow restaurant patrons staring, anticipating an altercation.

Dr. Young turned the megaphone over in his hands, coming across a small white sticker at the bottom of the handle. "Manufactured by USoFA WorldWide," he read aloud. "Department of Public Address, Harbor City, California. See that, Linda? Even the ones who hate us can't do without us." Dr. Young raised the megaphone to his lips and, with the bell of it inches from the guy's face, asked, "NOW WHY DON'T YOU GO FIND SOMETHING BETTER TO DO WITH YOUR TIME?"

The guy snatched the megaphone out of Dr. Young's hand and went back across the street, getting stuck momentarily on the railing amid uproarious laughter from the surrounding tables. Linda laughed, too. It was funny, the way the guy's eyes widened with impotent rage as he realized he'd been made a fool.

⁓

A security lockdown at Greenway left Linda and her fellow shuttle riders stranded for forty minutes. At one point, Harvey Polaski climbed aboard to inform them that some poor soul had just a couple of hours ago walked up to the front gate and drawn a pistol. Fortunately, it wasn't loaded, Harvey said, but one of the guards ("just the sweetest guy you'd ever want to meet") was forced to respond in the manner trained, and the armed trespasser passed on before an ambulance could make it to the scene. Horrible news, and of course Linda could understand how such a thing would trigger a delay in incoming traffic, but still—she could see her house from where she was sitting.

To kill time, and because she was mildly intrigued by what Dr. Young said about blankness, she reached for her phone and opened up a profile of Chelsea Daye.

Chelsea Daye (actress, activist)

From CUP Flows, the always up-to-date free encyclopedia brought to you by USoFA WorldWide Compliance Unit Publishing, "The CUP"

Chelsea Winifred Daye (born Mary Winifred Daley on February 12, FY20__) is an American actress turned anti-War activist. She appeared in the television series *Control+Alt+Delete*. She played Det. Hillary White in *AutoPilot* and Maya Sanders in *The Part-Time Princess*. Daye is also an Oscar-nominated actress for her work in the remake of *If Lucy Fell*.

Daye has attracted international media attention for her involvement in a three-day protest outside the ranch estate of USoFA WorldWide Chair and CEO Edna H, a stand that continues to draw passionate support and pointed criticism. Currently a columnist with *The Citizen*, she is a vocal critic of The Temporary War Act of FY20__, various business operations of USoFA WorldWide, and US foreign policy under President Halliday's administration.

Scrolling past the "Early Life," "Career Development," and "Stardom" sections, Linda found what she was looking for.

3. Transition to Activism and Activist Journalism

While Daye had expressed ambivalence about Hollywood since *Control+Alt+Delete*, it was the untimely death of her twin brother, Jacob, that many say led to her departure from acting.

According to sources within the Department of Defense and USoFA WorldWide, Jacob Daley stepped on a mistakenly placed landmine half a mile outside of FOB (Forward Operating Base) Crayola in Fallujah on May 29, FY20__.

Daye and her family continue to dispute the official report. On June 6th, FY20__, they appeared at a three-day anti-War protest outside Heavenslice, the Billings, Montana, garden ranch home of USoFA WorldWide CEO and Chair Edna H. On the third day, Daye gave an emotional speech detailing her family's ongoing struggle for information on Jacob Daley's death. "I solemnly swear I will uncover the truth of what happened to my brother," she said.

A live feed of the speech garnered more than 3 million views within its first 24 hours and was translated into 35 different languages. Many say the speech was directly responsible for a 2 percent decline in USoFA WorldWide earnings reported in the third quarter of FY20__.

In August FY20__, Daye was hired as a political reporter and columnist for *The Citizen*, a free newspaper based in Queens, N.Y. that is famous for employing homeless men and women for its distribution. Since joining the staff of *The Citizen*, Daye has used her connections within the entertainment and political spheres to gain access to lobbyists, business leaders, and heads of state.

Her first column, "9/11: The Doctor Will See You Now," which charged that USoFA WorldWide doctored 9/11 footage for various anniversary specials, was critiqued widely by media outlets worldwide. Editions of that issue have fetched upwards of $10,000.

4. Public Image

A fixture in entertainment news known for her outspokenness, Daye has attracted an even higher degree of notoriety since retiring from acting.

In August FY20__, Daye filed suit against USoFA WorldWide Press for libel after entertainment publication *All Access* printed an item implying she had been on methamphetamine hydrochloride, or crystal meth, while eating dinner at a Georgetown, Washington, D.C., restaurant. *All Access* settled with Daye out of court.

5. Personal Life

Daye is involved with numerous charities, including The Creative Coalition, Step Up Women's Network, Central Baptist Children's Hospital, The Human Rights Campaign, Save Darfur, The Susan G. Komen Foundation, Habitat for Humanity, and The Windhammer Group Theater Company Network. In FY20__, she was honored at *USoFAElle* magazine's "Women in Hollywood" tribute, and she has also been honored for her work with Step Up Women's Network.

Daye has spoken of her experiences with depression and bulimia nervosa during her teenage years, saying that she overcame the disorder without medication. She has been a vegetarian since age 16.

In early FY20__, on "USoFA Late Night with Marjorie Ryan," Daye said she began using marijuana during the filming of *Control+Alt+Delete*, but quit after deciding to honor her late brother's wishes that she do so.

Daye began dating screenwriter Jerry Wallace in March FY20__, but the couple split after less than a year. Others connected romantically with Daye include director George Able, professional bull rider Wendell Hart, actor Jason Wiles, and rapper-producer-jewelry magnate Def9.

Speaking of blankness—Linda had in recent days been asking herself a question that she couldn't answer to her own satisfaction: What, exactly, was she doing here? Whoever heard of a thirty-six-year-old medical student suddenly pulling down six figures while working from home, a home that dwarfed that of the dean of the institution where she was still enrolled? And all her employer wanted in return was the therapy portion of a medication-assisted treatment of *two guys* for PTSD? Huh?

A few nights before, Danny had what was known as an episode, his first major one since they had moved into Greenway. From the master bedroom, Linda heard his unmistakable seal bark and so ran up the stairs to attend to him. She entered Danny's bedroom to the vexing scene of her son face down on the bed, retching into a kidney-shaped dish as Robert, wearing nothing but black boxer briefs, sat astride him, pressing his ear to Danny's back to try and locate the blockage. Linda yelped with shock, but the all-business look on Robert's face as he ordered her to go get a wet washrag snapped her to. By the time she returned, Danny was bringing up a fist-sized wad of greenish-brownish sputum, which dropped into the kidney-shaped dish with the heavy thump of a plum. Impressed (to the point of being very slightly turned on by the swiftness with which this young man had alleviated her son's discomfort), Linda thanked Robert profusely, taking one step forward to offer up a grateful hug. Not a problem, Robert replied, snatching up the kidney-shaped dish and passing right in front of Linda's open arms on his way to examine Danny's discharge under a microscope.

At long last, Linda entered the house to find Vera and Deva in the den, watching animal blooper videos on the CUP. After their first date, Vera had described Deva as "just good company," which was enough to make it clear she was madly in love.

After Linda told them about the trespasser, Vera whistled soft and low. "What do you think he was trying to do?" she asked.

Linda shrugged. "Maybe something will turn up on the CUP tonight or tomorrow."

Deva laughed. "You *are* new around here," he said.

"What does that mean?"

Deva quickly apologized. "These security lockdowns," he said, throwing quotation marks around, "they occur frequently here in Greenway. Nothing to be done about them, really. More often than not, they're brought on by some unfortunate soul who's gone 'round the bend. Suicide-by-officer. Or security guard, in this instance."

"So it's not a political statement?" Vera asked.

"No, darling, not unless that statement is 'I'm an idiot.'"

Everyone laughed, and in the ensuing moment Linda asked Deva if he had dinner plans.

It turned out that Deva *was* good company, a real man of the world: Born in Pakistan, he entered the US as a teenager on a mathematics scholarship before popping over to the U.K. to conduct government research with the University of Edinburgh. After twenty-some years in the UK, he was offered a handsome position with the United States Association of Industries, which was USoFA WorldWide's nonprofit arm up until a few years ago. He came off a little hush-hush about this phase of his career, though he did let slide that his work had taken him all over Eastern Europe, East Asia, and South America. Nowadays he earned his keep providing "the odd bit of consultation work" for USoFA WorldWide.

"That's the Company for you," he said. "Like your indigenous peoples, USoFA WorldWide is famous for putting one's whole carcass to use." He pointed his butter knife at Linda. "If you haven't seen it already, my dear, you will."

When dinner was finished, as Danny and Robert absconded upstairs to finish Danny's homework, Deva slapped both palms on his chair's armrests and invited Vera to help him walk his dog, Asha.

And so, with the dishwasher running, Linda sat alone in the breakfast nook, refreshing the local CUP news to see if anything came up about the afternoon's security breach while sipping on a glass of white wine. Her mood was half-celebratory, what with the good marks she was getting for her work, and half–pity party: after she and Dr. Young parted ways, Linda returned to the Employee Outlet Mall to browse a dress shop near where they had bought Danny's sneakers. She tried on seven dresses, which was silly, yes, but not entirely her fault—the salesclerk kept bringing new ones into her dressing room, saying she looked "amazing in everything."

Linda wound up buying dress number seven, loving how the fabric (eighty percent viscose, twenty percent spandex) fell across her shoulders and hit just above the knee, because she could afford it and because she wanted to look amazing when she marched into that shoe store to ask Baldy what time did he knock off, and did he feel like getting a drink at that time.

Alas, Baldy had left for the day, and so Linda felt like a doofus returning to the dress shop and asking the salesclerk if she could please borrow a dressing room to change back into her old clothes.

EXCERPT

USoFA WorldWide War-Related PTSD Individualized Therapy Program (Pilot), "SoldierWell" Therapy Session # 7

February 26, FY20__

1005EST

LINDA HELD

Interviewing:

PRIVATE* CARL BOXER, US Army (Associate, Transportation Services, "Free2Fight," USoFA WorldWide)

(BEGIN)

PVT.* CARL BOXER: I realize I've kind of screwed up my life here, but I guess I wanted to be like my uncle Ray.

LINDA HELD: Aha.

CB: I mean, Ray mostly just collected benefits, far as I saw. He couldn't work or anything. He said his main job was to fight the bureaucrat fuckers who stood between him and his money. The first thing he bought, after moving in with us, was this little portable CUP monitor that let him watch whatever he wanted. He kept it right next to his bed so it'd put him to sleep.

LH: Did he have trouble sleeping?

CB: I think he just liked to sleep with it playing. I don't think he could sleep without something going in the background.

LH: And he never talked with you about his Wartime experiences.

CB: No, and Ma told me never to ask. I remember, he and a few other guys who served, they all took a trip to Washington for the Occupation Marches. Do you remember that? With the riots?

LH: Yes. So awful…

CB: Yeah, Ma was worried. She stayed put in front of the CUP for two days, looking for him in the crowds. Then he called and said he and some guys got bored and they found a bar and were watching the riots on the CUP like everybody else. [*laughs*] He came home with a bunch of names and phone numbers, but he just put them all in a drawer. He didn't keep in touch with anybody, I don't think. The only thing I ever heard him say about any of this was, he once told me that not having legs was a pain in the ass. Pardon my language.

LH: Did your mother ever mention how he might have changed after the War? Apart from physically?

CB: Ma talked a lot about what he was like growing up, how he was full of piss and vinegar, but I never figured it was from his being over there. It may not have happened as quick, but he probably would have ended up just like he was. I remember, we would go to the store every couple

weeks, and he'd spend his benefits money on whiskey and cigarettes and chips and just hole up in
his room. Wouldn't sleep for two or three days,
just...drinking.

LH: What was the cause?

CB: The cause?

LH: The cause of your uncle's passing away? I've
seen the effects of alcoholism firsthand, so...

CB: You have? Who?

LH: I'm sorry?

CB: Who do you know who's alcoholic?

LH: My father.

CB: Oh. Is he in recovery or...?

LH: No. He died six years ago.

CB: Oh. Sorry. Was it the drinking?

LH: For the most part, yes. It's funny, your
story about your uncle Ray yelling. My father
would yell, too. Quite a bit.

CB: So you know what I'm talking about.

LH: It wasn't at old friends, though. More just
things he saw on the CUP. The news and stuff. He
had all sorts of ongoing, [*laughs*] mostly one-
sided feuds with the government, corporations,
that sort of thing.

CB: What did he do for work?

LH: He was what they call a content specialist, though he thought of himself as a journalist. He taught writing at our community college for a few years, until he was kicked out.

CB: Because of drinking?

LH: No, no...no, that came after. A lot of different things. Partly political, I suppose. I'm not sure I know the whole story.

[*pause*]

I'm sorry, Carl, we were talking about Uncle Ray. How did he die?

CB: He hung himself.

LH: Oh! I'm so sorry.

CB: Yeah. New Year's Day. It wasn't pretty. Ma had to be taken to the hospital.

[*pause*]

I carried a pocketknife back then, and I ended up being the one who cut him down. Thirteen years old, I was. He did it early in the morning.

LH: Can you tell me about cutting him down?

CB: Why would you want to hear about that?

LH: You don't have to talk about it if you don't want to.

CB: It's not that. I just can't figure how it matters one way or the other.

LH: Well, ostensibly it was your first intimate encounter with death.

CB: No, I had seen a bunch of dead rabbits before then. Once I saw a gator lay into this raccoon…

LH: Right, but a human death. A loved one.

CB: All right, when you put it that way… The first thing was the smell of pee. It was still dripping steady, like making a little circle on the carpet because he was still spinning in there, probably seeping into the concrete underneath, so the first thing I did was, I remember this, I took the pillowcase off his pillow and kicked it into the closet to sop it up. And one of the things I can remember was how low he was hanging. When a person who's lost his legs at the knee hangs himself, they don't need as much room to clear the floor. I just about cut the rope at eye level… I can't think of anything else. He dropped to the floor, the pillowcase, then I got him and pulled him onto the bed. He had on, I'll never forget this, he had on his usual clothes, T-shirt and his jeans pinned at the knees, but then he had his Silver Star medal on his chest. Which was funny, because the one time I had seen it before he acted like it wasn't worth anything. But there he was with it pinned on his chest. So then I went back out to where Ma was, and the neighbors were already there. I don't know how they got in. Then an ambulance came and that was it. I guess he had his reasons, I don't know. He was a saint in my mother's eyes.

LH: Carl, can I ask you a question?

CB: [*laughs*] You know, I never liked my name much, but I like it when you say it. Some of the soldiers in Iraq called me Gopher because I had a way on the black market there. Coming from prison, you get good at getting stuff. It wasn't like a real nickname, just something they'd say to be funny, because they didn't want to bother learning my name. What did you want to know?

LH: With the only real exposure to military service in your life being Uncle Ray, who, based on what you've told me, struggled with a disability, possible depression, possible alcoholism…

CB: Oh, he was definitely an alcoholic. No doubt.

LH: …and now the suicide… What made you want to go to Iraq? The reason I ask is, how you've described it, you seemed relatively safe inside of Waupun Correctional. Couldn't you have stuck it out those last few months?

CB: I know! I should have! But the Silver Star, Uncle Ray was wearing it on that day. I think a lot about him digging it out from his dresser and pinning it on. Like, he had that. It was his. I was going to say before, there was one time when Uncle Ray got picked up to go to the Occupation

Marches, and there were these dudes who knocked on our door. Wait, did I already tell you this?

LH: I don't think so.

CB: OK. I was the only one home, and I'm sitting on the futon, and a knock comes on the door and I see these three men in the screen door, making the room all dark. I was probably six or seven, and I thought they were superheroes, with their tattoos, sunglasses. Their pride, it just made itself known, it was like a feeling in the air. And they say, hey, partner, is Ray Denny around? And then in the other room, I hear Ray yell let them in, so I go open the door...and they step inside and I can feel the floor just, like, *slant* when they come in. Then they go down the hallway and one of them points at me and says thanks bud and when they got to his room the biggest one picks Ray up by his wheelchair and starts taking him out...and there was this serious look on all their faces, men on a mission, and it was easy to see they were respectful of my uncle... And Ray looked better that morning than I'd ever seen him before, he had on this American flag bandana, and he had shaved all over his face except the mustache, which was a handlebar. And his sleeves were rolled up, and his arms were real big...just badass...and he said hold on a minute and the guy carrying him stopped and Ray looked right at me with real life on his face, like even though his hair was longer and he had the mustache, he looked like the picture Ma kept on her windowsill in the kitchen, from before he was deployed. Just the look in his eye. And he said tell your ma I'll be back in a couple days... I remember watching them head out the door and I went and watched them pack up into the truck, going just...damn.

LH: That's a nice way of remembering him.

CB: Yeah. His hanging himself doesn't change that. Not for me. Ma is liable to cry and cry about it because she worries about heaven and hell. I don't worry about that, not for him. Matter of fact, it was my uncle Ray who set me straight on all that. I remember, this fish of mine died, one of those you get at the county fair...I made all these preparations, I got an old shoebox and I took it out to the median strip that runs in front of our place, and I dug this hole... Ray came out there and he came across the street and he told me to stop what I was doing right this second and he grabbed my hands and put them on his knees, where the stumps were, and he says, whispering... he says you are wasting your fucking time because ain't nothing happened after that fish died and ain't nothing going to happen after I die, after you die, after your ma dies...there is no God, no angels, nothing. He said the best we can do is stick together, keep warm against the cold. Then he said hand me that shoebox and I handed it to him and he tossed it into the street and it got run over by a van. I'll never forget that.

[*pause*]

But I just...I thought about redeeming myself, like, when I was up in Waupun. Not in a God type of way, just...I went to chapel once a week, just to have something to do, and they were always talking about redemption. Maybe it took...because to me it wasn't about just doing the time and getting out...I kept thinking about redemption...and then one day you hear about this Free2Fight thing and it sounded like something to maybe turn things around. Because I was on the road to being this real bum, you know. I didn't want to just get out of jail and go right back to that. Of course, I regret that decision now. Iraq wasn't any shot at redemption. [*laughs*] Fucking-A, it wasn't that!

END EXCERPT

Miles sat before his desktop monitor, watching national news headlines cascade in a continuous spill downward. The time was 0701, which meant he had fourteen minutes before his call with the office of Edna H—more than enough time to grab a coffee from the kiosk upstairs and come back. But coffee, however much it was needed at the moment, wasn't worth the risk. Missing a call from the office of Edna H was unthinkable.

With one eye open, Miles froze the cascade and scanned the top headlines. It did not appear that his most recent professional failure would make national news. Miles exhaled, grinning, chiding himself for seeking drama where there was none (there had never been any real danger, after all), then clicked LOCAL NEWS: MINNEAPOLIS.

There it was, fifth from the top. He clicked the headline, bracing himself.

Patriot Media, a division of USoFA WorldWide Media Relations and USoFA WorldWide Compliance Unit Publishing, "The CUP"

February 28, FY20__ Monday 0606 EST

Five Dead, One Wounded in Shooting at Minneapolis Bowling Alley

Minneapolis, Minn.—Five people were killed at a bowling alley in the Lowry Hill neighborhood of Minneapolis Sunday afternoon in a mass shooting. Among those killed was the gunman.

The suspect entered Strikeroo Bowling yesterday at approximately 1440 CST and opened fire on the dining area, killing three people. He then turned toward the games area and shot two more before turning the weapon on himself.

A witness on the scene estimated there had been between 10 and 20 people in the bowling alley at the time of the shooting. The shooter, US Army Staff Sgt. Darryl Bacon, had served in Yemen for the past three years, working mostly as an assistant to Lieutenant James Wardle.

Lt. Wardle was instrumental in the strategic coordination of Operation Red Charge, an early instance of the US Armed Forces and USoFA WorldWide's proactive anti-terror strategy in the War. The lieutenant could not be reached for comment.

Hennepin County Police Chief Gerald Clower told Patriot Media that, until evidence proves otherwise, they are treating the incident as a Hater-related domestic terror incident. When asked if the shooter suffered from PTSD, Chief Clower said he would consider the possibility.

This marks the thirty-seventh public mass shooting in the past six months. (Mass shootings are defined by the US Congressional Research Office as a shooting incident occurring within a public space and resulting in at least three fatalities.) On Saturday, a lone gunman opened fire at a fitness club in West Lafayette, Ind., killing four and injuring two before police subdued him. Last Thursday, a gunman in Little Rock, Ark. wounded six and killed one at a Sikh temple before police subdued him.

The police report shows that Bacon used a Beretta 92 pistol and an accessory known as the "Murphy," a customized magazine storage unit and compensator that can effectively turn pistols into fully automatic machine guns.

Following the nine mass shooting incidents to take place over the course of last week nationally, President Halliday released a statement from his cabin estate in Barkhamsted, Conn.

"While many are very likely Hater-related, these incidents only affirm my resolve that we must get tough on gun violence. I hereby call upon my friends in Congress and the Senate to join me in creating a bipartisan committee to explore broader background checks for first-time purchasers of the Murphy, as well as new registration requirements for automatic and semiautomatic weapons."

ALSO ON THE CUP:
Fourteen Dead in Brooklyn Public Swimming Pool Mass Shooting
The Toothbrushes of These Celebrity Husbands Will Leave You Speechless
Best Gun Holsters for Sleeping

Miles checked the time. Six minutes before his call. He placed his hand over his heart and felt its quickened beating. If he hadn't been fully awake before, he was now.

Edna H was famous for being in direct contact with multiple people at all times; editorial cartoons always portrayed her as an octopus, tentacles clutching phones, tablets, sacks of money, ragged maps of the Middle East. Miles had never actually spoken with Edna H person-to-person, only representatives entrusted to make decisions on her and the Company's behalf. The last such representative he'd been in contact with had been understanding, mostly, regarding the patient suicide and resultant failure of SoldierWell South, but that was likely because Miles had so carefully managed expectations, constantly qualifying the progress he claimed with parentheticals on how such a groundbreaking therapy could not be counted on to succeed the first time out of the gate. Plus, Soldier-Well South had resulted in just the one death, which he was able to pin on a miscalculation of the recommended drug dosage. And it was easily argued that if that young man hadn't jumped from that ninth-floor window while under his supervision, he probably would have offed himself some other way, probably within weeks of returning to civilian life. At least this way, his family got a nice letter from Uncle Sam saying he died an honorable death on the front line—that beat the hell out of finding your pride and joy hanging purple-faced from a crossbeam in the root cellar.

But five dead in a Minneapolis bowling alley? Fuck a duck, one doesn't just write that off. To make matters worse, everything had worked perfectly from a chemical standpoint. The medication did exactly what it was supposed to do: form a physical dependence that, once the patient was released, would lead to withdrawal symptoms that resulted in profound detachment from reality and hyperaggressive behavior. The most frustrating thing was that Staff Sergeant Bacon had been the ideal patient—he'd seen significant if not prolonged combat, his tendencies toward violence were well-established, his dependence on the medication was total. And he had a habit of blaming others, women in particular, for his problems. A true Golden Boy. So what had gone wrong?

The phone rang. Miles closed his eyes and breathed deep, picturing the process taking place inside him: diaphragm flattening to accommodate his expanding lungs, 600 million alveoli filling with air to dump clean oxygen into his quickened bloodstream. He answered.

"Please hold for Richard Taper," said an automated voice.

Christ, Taper was such a drag. One of three Edna H representatives with whom Miles maintained relations, the guy fancied himself the heavy of the bunch, mistaking his own social ineptitude for misunderstood exceptionality. Miles had met him face-to-face once, not long after winning approval for SoldierWell. Young and lean, his dark hair pulled back into a ponytail and held in place with a stars-and-stripes ribbon, Taper asked Miles if he had ever considered the phrenological ramifications of his work, as he considered himself "something of an amateur phrenologist," with an impressive collection of rare and historically notable craniometers back in his home office. It was enough to make Miles pity him, almost.

"Dr. Young, good morning."

"Hi, Rick."

"I'm wondering if you had a chance to read over the CUP story."

"I did, yes."

"Tell me how you're feeling." This invitation was murmured in monotone, as if he was reading it off an index card.

"Right. I'm worried... that is to say, I'm concerned about whether the patient told anyone about his therapy, about Soldier-Well, before the rampage."

"Tim Nestor is checking on that now. Not for you to worry about. What else?"

"Well, I'm disappointed."

"..."

"I spent the better part of last night trying to figure out where we went wrong," Miles added, feeling duped. Why was the onus always on him to fill these conversational vacuums?

"Tell me about it," Taper said.

Impossible to know how to respond. Was this sarcasm? Had Taper too been up all night, poring over session transcripts, and hence did *not* want to be told about it? Or did he want Miles to explore his befuddlement, now, over the phone?

"I'm thinking it may have something to do with the therapist we had up there," Miles said. "In some of the session recordings, I noticed some..."

"I'm sure you'll figure it out," Rick said. "The answer will come to you over the next day or so, and then you'll have learned from this experience and do better next time. Agreed?"

Miles exhaled. "Well, Rick, I'm glad you feel this way."

Taper laughed, correctively, each *ha* more overenunciated than the one that came before. The sound raised the hairs on the back of Miles's neck. "This isn't at all how *I* feel, Dr. Young. It's how Edna H feels."

"Right. Of course."

"Is there anything else we can do for you at this time?"

"For me?" Christ, he could not stop sounding like an idiot. He stood up and placed one hand flat on his desk. "I'd like to see Amanda Kant removed from the SoldierWell Board."

"Done."

"No, I take that back...I don't know why I just said that."

Taper laughed again. "Dr. Young, Edna H is keeping her eye on the big picture. You should, too."

"Oh, I am. I still very much believe in the INSIST Technique, and I…"

"I had a dream last night. Do you dream, Miles?"

"Not last night, I didn't."

"It wasn't a dream so much as a vision," Taper said. "I've been reading a book, *Maximizing the Positive*. I'll send you a copy! Anyway, it cited studies showing that, when the brain thinks positive thoughts, when it really, truly *believes*, it can inspire the body to heal itself in very specific, very powerful ways. There's an anecdote about a woman in Brazil who was able to cure herself of stomach cancer merely by *ordering* her body to rid itself of the disease. Her oncologists, her gastroenterologists, even psychologists such as yourself, they're all flummoxed. She simply *told* her body to go get the cancer, and billions of white blood cells rose up to attack. Consider the elegance, Miles—the human body attacking its own demons."

"Right. Amazing."

"I think it's similar to what you're trying to achieve with SoldierWell. If we can more effectively instruct our own warriors—society's white blood cells, yes?—then we can effectively *inspire* them to attack the cancers in our own bloodstream, our own society. The possibilities are endless, wouldn't you say?"

"Yes, I would."

"That's what excites Edna H so much about your program. The possibilities. *That's* what she saw in your presentation at the Innovators Conference last year. *That's* what she saw when writing you a check for twelve million dollars and allowed you access to those black sites."

"Yes."

"We'd rather not examine failure, Miles. Failure is toxic, and we need not sicken ourselves with yours. We'd rather continue entertaining possibilities so that, if and when you do succeed, we will be ready to press the advantage. That's what *Maximizing the Positive* is all about. Does that work for you?"

"Yes, of course."

"Excellent. We don't want you worrying about punishments, or the fact that if we see another needless tragedy we will be shutting down this program and stripping away your security clearance and relocating you to one of our manufacturing facilities in Idaho, where you'll spend the rest of your career prescribing benzos to Air Force wives with restless leg syndrome." Taper took a deep breath. "We're keeping our eye on the bigger picture, Miles. You should, too. I'll get that book to you."

A new voice came on, giving instructions on how to end the call. Miles hung up and sat down. He took a series of deep breaths before spinning in his chair to look over the spines in his bookcase: Miller and Rollnick's *Motivational Interviewing*, Salter's *Conditioned Reflex Therapy*, Krasnogorski's *Primary Violence Motivation*, Kneer and Cohen's *Summoning Chaos: Stochastic Terrorism in the Digital Age*, Anderson's *The Closer's Handbook*... Useless now, all of them. He could drive out to Langley, flash his security clearance badge, and join the other Company drones in digging through the yellowed confidential records of stuff like Project MK-Ultra, but such excursions, while fun, usually weren't worth the time.

Miles spun back around and clicked on the folder labeled CON-FIDENTIAL **INSIST TECHNIQUE** CONFIDENTIAL. Once it opened, he selected a document labeled INSIST TECHNIQUE. FINAL, scrolling past the title page, the table of contents, the executive summary, before stopping on page eight:

> **I: *Isolation.*** Isolation occurs from day one of Patient's therapy. Patient is removed as much as possible from any living persons other than Therapist. Medication adherence begins.

N: *Nexus.* Creates a link between Patient and Therapist, resulting in the establishment of trust. This most efficiently occurs in the mutual sharing of intimacies, life histories, etc. Medication adherence continues.

S: *Suggestion.* Once the trust relationship has been established, Patient's thoughts are directed toward a single actionable idea, or "True Mission" (TM). Medication is increased.

I: *Impetus.* Patient is prepared for fulfillment of the TM by taking part in the creation of a workable plan, scheduled to take effect immediately following release (see *Turnout*). This plan is refined and repeated until Patient comes to believe it has originated in his or her mind. Increased medication adherence continues.

Impetus is of vital importance. It serves to bypass any and all emotional detritus that might hinder Patient from fulfilling TM. When properly utilized, it has the paradoxical power to obliterate the self while instilling total self-efficacy.

S: *Subjugation/Suicide Watch.* Once the TM has been accepted as Patient's own idea, the values of Patient are reordered so that fulfillment of the TM becomes the sole reason for living. Once properly Subjugated, all actions taken by Patient will be reflexively measured on a scale of how much it might please Therapist. Increased medication adherence continues.

During this phase, Therapist should guard against the possibility of Patient suicide, since a fully dismantled ego has been known to "rally" against this systematic obliteration of self via suicide.

T: *Turnout.* Eager to fulfill the TM as soon as possible, Patient is released and medication regimen is abandoned, resulting in extreme withdrawal designed to further push Patient toward fulfillment of the TM.

Maybe it was this sort of thinking that lay at the heart of Miles's failures so far. Great artists don't sit around marveling at their work, do they?

Maybe Miles was too close to it. Maybe an outsider's perspective was needed. Someone with expertise, sympathetic to his efforts…

Goddammit.

Miles's reverie was broken by faint footsteps, quick and light, coming down the hall. A moment later, his assistant entered, bearing coffee. "Heavy cream, heavy sugar, right?"

"Bless you, Howie." Miles held out his hands to receive.

"Excuse me, Dr. Young, but did I hear you swearing just now?"

Miles shrugged. "There's a distasteful errand I need to run."

"Anything I can do?"

"Yeah, I need you to put me in touch with the warden of Red Onion State Prison."

"Oh, God. Where's that?"

"Southwest Virginia. Very near Kentucky."

Howie nodded before pointing backward over his shoulder. "Oh, and somebody just dropped off a book? *Maximizing the Positive*? Did you order it?"

MARCH FY20___

Meeting of Principals: USoFA WorldWide War-Related PTSD Individualized Therapy Program (Pilot), "SoldierWell"

March 3, FY20__

0811EST

DR. MILES YOUNG, Director, USoFA WorldWide War-Related PTSD Individualized Therapy Program (Pilot) "SoldierWell"

and

GEN. (ORDNANCE CORPS) TYLER BURROWS, Commander, US Northern Command Region 1 and US-Canadian North American Aerospace Defense Command (NORAD)

and

DR. AMANDA KANT, Consultant, Department of Military Information Support Operations (MISO), Region 1, USoFA WorldWide

and

TIM NESTOR, Executive Vice President of Media Relations, Region 1, USoFA WorldWide

(BEGIN)

DR. MILES YOUNG: Oh, good, the General's just jumped on. General, can you hear us OK?

GEN. (ORDNANCE CORPS) TYLER BURROWS: ███████████ ████████████████[1]

MY: Good, good. I promise this won't be long. OK, you've each been given some documents. These are for you alone. No copies are to be made, nor to be seen or discussed with others except for superiors… Today we're discussing SoldierWell East, specifically the fork in the road we're at now in terms of which of our two patients, Private Boxer or Marine Sergeant Sparrow, will be going forward as our Golden Boy, that is, the recipient of my INSIST Technique. I assume we've all had a chance to read the summary report on this issue, so are there any questions, issues we'd like to bring up at this time?

TIM NESTOR: I'll start if that's all right.

MY: Yes, Tim, please do.

TN: OK, I'm coming at this from a strictly civilian angle, but it seems pretty cut-and-dried to me.

MY: How do you mean, Tim?

TN: Well, this Boxer fellow is a USoFA WorldWide employee. That's just a fact. His paychecks for

---

[1] All remarks made by US Army General Tyler Burrows, in documents relating to upper-level management of the SoldierWell program, have been redacted, as granted under the provision of the Temporary War Act of FY20__ (Title XXXIIV, "Involvement of U.S. Armed Forces Personnel in Discussion of Commercial, or Mostly Commercial, Interests").

the last two months are signed by Edna H. So that makes me think that if the press gets hold of it, not our guys, but let's say the international press, or the Hater rags, whatever… that's how he'll be described in the media, over and over again. USoFA WorldWide employee Carl Boxer. Then all we need is some enterprising young reporter to start digging around. And not only are we talking about an employee of USoFA WorldWide, but a truck driver, and then, you know, the question now becomes what the heck is a truck driver for USoFA WorldWide doing shooting up the place? What's he seen over there? And then there's his jail time and our recruitment efforts…I mean, that damn Free2Fight program has never polled well. It's not in our best interest to remind the public about it.

[*pause*]

But… on the other hand…we've got Marine Sergeant Sparrow, a fully qualified Marine with superior training, and so there's the peace of mind that he's probably going to lessen the risk on innocent bystanders, somewhat. Plus he's a big guy, very intimidating. You see his picture on the CUP, you're going to say to yourself, well, sure, that looks like the kind of guy that'd be capable of something like this. It's all very consistent in the public mind, which works in our favor… the mind just fills in the rest, and then it's like, hey, look, a mass shooting, what else is new? So, if you ask me, Miles, it's Sergeant Sparrow. No contest.

MY: Right. I'm with you, Tim. I'll also say I like where our therapist, Linda Held, is with Sparrow. I think she's broken him, so to speak. And I also thought Boxer was a strong candidate initially, or else I wouldn't have flown into Iraq to get him. But he's just not strong enough right now to take this on. And his being employed with the Company, there's the rub.

TN: Yeah, and the other thing I like about Sparrow is that if things get hairy, for some unforeseen reason, like let's say our Darling survives and this thing takes on a life of its own in the media, well, we've got those reports of him killing kids in Tasmania. I should think a nice little precision leak to the press would play well, really give him that loose cannon background.

MY: General? Feel like jumping in here?

TB: ██████████████████████████████████████
██████████████████████████

MY: On the fence? Really?

TB: ██████████████████████████████████████
██████████████████████████████████████
██████████████████████████████████████
██████████████████████████████████████
██████████████████████████████████████
██████████████████████████████████████
██████████████████████████████████████
██████████████████████████████████████

[REDACTED]

MY: Not at all, General. We're eager to hear your thoughts.

TB: [REDACTED]

MY: Absolutely, sir. And I meant no offense, of course, to the training of our Armed Forces…

TB: [REDACTED]

MY: No, I understand, sir. That's a valuable insight. Uh…

TN: OK, General? This is Tim Nestor. Can you hear me?

TB: █████████████████████████████

TN: OK, I might be out of line, here, sir, so if I am, my apologies in advance...but I wonder if maybe you're concerned with what this does to the public image of our fighting men and women?

TB: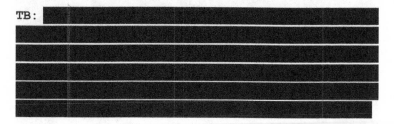

TN: I hear you, sir. But you know what, I'm just not prone to thinking about crisis preparation that far down the line. The idea that this will all go off without a hitch...no offense, Miles, but there's no telling at this point. And, again, that's not to say I'm not behind the program. I happen to agree with Edna H, I think this thing is worth every penny, if only from a research standpoint.

MY: Thank you, Tim.

TN: But the fact is, I mean...this is such a bold venture, in that way... but General, I'm just not sure that's something we need to address right this second.

TB: ████████████████████████████
████████████

[*pause*]

MY: Anything else, General?

TB: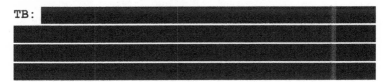

MY: I understand, sir. OK, Dr. Kant? Care to offer up some thoughts, quickly? You heard the General, and I'm guessing Mr. Nestor doesn't have a ton of time, either.

DR. AMANDA KANT: Yes, Miles, thank you for letting me speak…so I listened to all of the recordings, and last night I read along with the transcripts. Really very interesting.

MY: Well, I'm glad they could keep you company on these cold nights, Amanda. [*laughs*]

TN: [*laughs*]

TB: ████████

AK: Ha, yes…but, Tim, you mentioned earlier about this being cut-and-dried, and I agree with you, this is cut-and-dried. I don't think Marine Sergeant Sparrow or Private Boxer are at all fit, in any of the ways we need them to be.

MY: Now, hold it right there. The INSIST Technique is all about structuring a comprehensive…

AK: Excuse me, Miles, but you asked me to offer my thoughts. I'm offering my thoughts.

MY: You're right, Amanda. I apologize. Go ahead.

AK: I just wanted to say I think Sergeant Sparrow is highly vulnerable…

MY: Agreed.

AK: And I think that suddenly pulling him off a steady drug regimen could be especially danger-ous, because I believe it's time we consider that Sparrow exhibits psychopathic tendencies.

MY: [*laughs*] Really? Which ones, exactly?

AK: Well, the ritualistic killing of small ani-mals as an adolescent, that's just textbook. Then there's the lack of remorse attendant with that, the grandiose sense of self-worth, believing him-self to be the perfect Marine…there's impulsiv-ity, irresponsibility, shallow affect… There's also the way he speaks about his upbringing, his mother…I wouldn't be surprised if there was some abuse there, which, the General and Mr. Nestor might not be aware, but childhood abuse, espe-cially sexual child abuse, tends to increase the odds for psychopathic tendencies later in life. I did a little back-of-the-envelope Hare Checklist last night…

MY: Oh, the Hare Checklist!² Wonderful!

TB: ████████████████████████████████

MY: The Hare Checklist is an outmoded assessment tool, General, designed to make people para-
noid about whether their friends and family are
secretly dangerous people. It was quite popular,
once upon a time, to go around scoring people,
public figures and the like, on a scale of normal
to dead-eyed psycho killer. Never mind that the
examination that I had all program applicants

---

² The Hare Checklist, or Psychopathy Checklist, is an assessment tool that employs
a 20-item inventory of perceived personality traits to assess psychopathy in individuals. These items are:

Item 1: Glibness/superficial charm
Item 2: Grandiose sense of self-worth
Item 3: Need for stimulation/proneness to boredom
Item 4: Pathological lying
Item 5: Conning/manipulative
Item 6: Lack of remorse or guilt
Item 7: Shallow affect
Item 8: Callous/lack of empathy
Item 9: Parasitic lifestyle
Item 10: Poor behavioral controls
Item 11: Promiscuous sexual behavior
Item 12: Early behavioral problems
Item 13: Lack of realistic long-term goals
Item 14: Impulsivity
Item 15: Irresponsibility
Item 16: Failure to accept responsibility for own actions
Item 17: Many short-term marital relationships
Item 18: Juvenile delinquency
Item 19: Revocation of conditional release
Item 20: Criminal versatility

undergo is specifically designed to weed out anyone remotely psychopathic.

[CROSSTALK]

TB: ████████████████████████████████████

AK: Well, as I said, I'm basing this on my take on things. But how Sergeant Sparrow interprets the events surrounding the death of that child in Tasmania, I mean…I listened with my headphones last night, with the volume way up, and his breathing is incredibly calm when describing these things. Recounting all these details of things he saw not eight weeks ago, he describes them the way you and I might describe a sunset. Then again, Miles, you're right, none of this points directly to his being a dead-eyed psychopath, but I think for someone this close to exhibiting certain tendencies, we might want to think twice before applying this experimental, intensely coercive technique while pulling the rug out from under his feet, medication-wise. We could wind up with much more than we bargained for. Because guys, as I understand it, what we're talking about here is radicalization. We've got a little Motivational Interviewing[3] here, a little

---

[3] Popular among credentialed addiction treatment providers, Motivational Interviewing (MI) is a therapeutic approach developed by William R. Miller, PhD, and Stephen Rollnick, PhD, in [FY]1983 wherein the therapist evokes the patient's own intrinsic motivation to facilitate behavioral change.

Reid-style interrogation[4] there, but at the end of the day, this is radicalization, chased with the exploitation of withdrawal symptoms from a strong anti-anxiety drug. And Miles, you say that Miss Held has broken him, but I don't see it. I see an average therapist-patient relationship at this point, perhaps slightly more codependent than usual. Not to mention, we have yet to see how Miss Held will react to her new duties.

MY: Why don't we just let me worry about that, Amanda? I've managed pretty well with the therapists in our other SoldierWell locations.

AK: Have you? Because the fact of the matter is we've got five bodies in a Minneapolis bowling alley to show for our work so far. Is it possible, Miles, that you've fallen in love with this thing you've created, and now you're failing to account for important variables?

[CROSSTALK]

TB: ▮▮▮▮▮▮▮▮▮▮▮▮▮▮▮▮▮▮▮▮▮▮▮▮▮▮▮▮

AK: No, General, I don't think Private Boxer is a particularly good candidate either. Both

---

[4] A registered trademark of John E. Reid and Associates, the Reid Technique is a nine-point method of questioning designed to extract confessions of guilt by the subject (dependent on the results of the Behavior Analysis Interview, wherein the subject's guilt has already been determined). The Technique was widely used among law enforcement agencies throughout North America since the late 20th century, despite charges that it often elicited false confessions from traditionally marginalized populations (the mentally impaired, the elderly, ESLs, etc.).

young men have experienced serious and sustained trauma. It's just that Boxer doesn't remember, while Sparrow remembers everything but so far refuses, or maybe lacks the ability, to feel it. He may not even have PTSD. Either case represents a significant danger going forward.

MY: OK, so Dr. Kant refrains from choosing.

AK: That's not what I'm saying, Miles.

MY: What are you saying, Amanda? Because this is a meeting where we decide if it's Sparrow or Boxer receiving the INSIST Technique. Or were you not listening when I called this meeting?

AK: Then I would strongly recommend neither receiving the INSIST Technique. I think we need to step back and ask ourselves whether this program needs to be in place at this time.

MY: And just watch this opportunity slip away? Because that's what's going to happen if we all decide to join hands and meditate on whether this is the ideal place and time. The timing here is crucial, or am I the only one reading *The Citizen* these days?

[CROSSTALK]

MY: Look, Amanda, I have been refining the INSIST Technique literally for a decade. And everybody here heard what Tim said, that Edna H herself has my back. But you want to pull the plug because of the damn Hare Checklist, this, this party trick…

TB: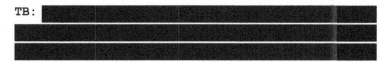

MY: I understand, General, will do. Thanks for joining us today.

AK: General, I'd like to also…

MY: Sorry, Amanda. He's gone. So, can we take a vote now? I know we're all busy. Tim, what say you? Move forward with Sparrow?

TN: Move forward, yeah.

MY: Good, and since I vote to move forward with Sparrow as well, that's two in favor. Dr. Kant?

AK: I refrain from choosing and would like my reservations regarding SoldierWell East to remain on the record.

MY: Noted, thank you… OK, and with General Burrows deferring, it looks like we're going to move forward with Marine Sergeant Todd Sparrow as our Golden Boy in the east. I'll let Miss Held know as soon as possible… Oh, that reminds me, Tim, can I speak with you after this? I'd like your help scoring tickets.

TN: Sure. Not a problem.

MY: OK, meeting adjourned, thank you…

END TRANSCRIPT

Robert took the day off to go hiking with friends and Deva was needed at some work-related something or other, so it was just family, for a change, on the morning of Danny's twelfth birthday. Linda woke early and fixed pancakes, dropping into the mix a cupful of organic blackberries that had come free with the last grocery delivery.

Once the table was cleared, Danny opened his presents. He did his best to feign appreciation for the Baltimore Ravens sweatshirt from Vera, but the act might have been more convincing had he not been so sincerely overjoyed with his grandma's second gift: a $100 gift card for something called The TerrorBusters League. Next came Linda's three gifts, which yielded diminishing returns: *Kill Shot 5*, Tenth Anniversary Edition ("Awesome! I didn't even know this was *out* yet!"); a cable knit sweater and matching corduroy pants ("Nice!"); and three books on dinosaurs of the Mesozoic Era ("Huh. OK."). All in all, a successful birthday, easily better than the last few years, when money and schedules were often so tight it was all Linda could do to buy a T-shirt and a used chemistry set.

Later that morning, as Linda was walking home from the bakery, Dr. Young called. He didn't sound like himself—it took five minutes of pleasantries before he got around to why he was calling. She took a seat in her porch swing as Dr. Young finally arrived at his point.

"I remember you saying something a few days ago about your son's birthday?"

"Yes! It's today, actually."

"Well then, as luck would have it, I find myself with three tickets for tonight's Showing of the War. Mr. Nestor—you remember Tim—it turns out he can't go, so I was thinking, if your son was interested, the three of us could take it in?"

Linda looked over at Danny's birthday cake in its clear plastic box. She had selected the TerrorBusters Edition, featuring the visage of Lieutenant Jack "Buddy" Griffin declaring HAPPY BIRTHDAY

PATRIOT! and four plastic Army men pointing their rifles north, south, west, and east.

"Danny would absolutely love that," she said. "What time were you thinking?"

⌒⌒⌒

Danny trembled with anticipation. They had a minor scare in the late afternoon when a coughing fit ripened from the normal wet hacking to a painful-sounding bark, but he seemed to overcome it by sheer force of will. "I *will* not miss this, Mom," Danny said after it was over, before bounding upstairs to drape himself in every item of TerrorBusters-related clothing he owned: TerrorBusters cap, TerrorBusters scarf, TerrorBusters sweatpants, TerrorBusters socks. Tying the ensemble together, though, was the Baltimore Ravens sweatshirt Vera had given him that morning. Linda's heart ached when she saw it.

Dr. Young showed up right on time, in a vintage yellow Porsche, so Danny was a fan of his mom's boss from the get-go. In what passed for the vehicle's back row sat a picnic basket with cold salmon filets, a block of Gouda cheese, dark chocolate, a bottle of Malbec, and a large bottle of Gatorade Classic for Danny. This was the weekend edition of Miles Young, PhD, his usual mock turtleneck–sport coat combination replaced with an olive V-neck sweater over a white tee, his wavy hair slicked down and combed back. Deva, who had come to the house straight from his work thing, played the concerned patriarch, ordering Dr. Young to "have these darlings home no later than noon tomorrow."

The drive out to the Showing venue was brisk once Dr. Young got on the Beltway. After taking the shoulder past the bottleneck outside the General Admission parking lots, he flashed his security clearance tag at an armed guard outside of the Red-Level Employee

Parking gate and swung into the first space they saw. Then up pulled an elongated golf cart, driven by an older woman with a submachine gun hanging from a thin band around her shoulder and a ball cap that read ESCORT-RED LEVEL.

"You folks'll be wanting a lift, I suppose," she said.

Their escort drove them the half-mile or so to the venue's entrance, sticking to paths that cut through the parking lots. Linda had heard stories of how the tailgating at these Showings resembled feeding time at a zoo, but what she saw astonished her. The parking lots stretched toward the horizon, yet they were all jammed, the shuttles bumper-to-bumper. When one of the shuttles came to a stop, the back doors would fall open and people would come spilling out, getting barely enough time to stand up and dust themselves and their children off before undergoing pat-downs from any one of the squadrons of black-clad security guards. Every hundred feet or so there stood a small mountain of contraband: blankets, chairs, clothing, water pipes, baby strollers.

Their observer suite was beautifully appointed, with a lounge area near the door and six leather recliners facing out. On the walls hung stylized posters of past Showings, TerrorBusters silhouettes and frayed American flags. CUP monitors hung from all corners.

Outside, three LED Titanotrons stood against an unseasonably verdant backdrop, each one playing commercials from various Showing of the War major sponsors—Gatorade, VDCraft, "The After-Action Report with Whit Knightley"—as the sky showcased a sunset for the ages. Dr. Young handed out opera glasses, and together they spent the next hour noshing picnic basket goodies and observing people on the General Admission lawn. As night fell, clothing started coming off. Many had come prepared—Dr. Young remarked that if he saw one American flag bikini he saw a hundred. Steam rose from bodies into the night air as the low roar of the crowd grew hypnotic; with showtime approaching, it sounded like nothing so much as the purring of a single wild animal. Security guards, stationed ten at each exit, stood grimly implacable in their well-oiled boots, submachine guns over their shoulders, jaws working fluorescent chewing gum.

The Showing opened with a rumbling bass note so loud and low Linda wondered if she might be sick, but soon enough gave way to a bouncy montage of the TerrorBusters Elite Squad in action—pumping iron, shooting guns, pulling grenade pins with their teeth. Each TerrorBuster got his or her own highlight reel, followed by vital statistics: height, weight, number of Enemy kills in the last fiscal quarter, et cetera. Danny could recite these stats with his eyes closed.

Finally, the main event: amid deafening cheers and a thunderous mash-up of "Carmina Burana" and "You've Got Another Thing Comin'," the announcer announced that tonight's Showing was, like all Showings, rated PG-13 and added that explicit moments, should they arise, would be sweetened to comply with FCC requirements.

It was plenty explicit for Linda, though. A twisty feeling took root in her gut as Corporal Ferris "Razor" Holloway kicked off combat operations by firing his grenade launcher at an Enemy sniper on a distant balcony and Danny let loose a full-throated call to "waste that towelhead!"

"Such a shame Uzbekistan harbors Enemy forces!" Linda hollered at Dr. Young, turning toward him as a means of looking away. "Tashkent is beautiful!"

"Just wait till we get into New Zealand!" Dr. Young yelled back. "Tickets for those Showings will go fast!"

"We're going to war with New Zealand?"

"You didn't hear it from me!"

In just under an hour, the TerrorBusters Elite Squad had leveled the Enemy compound, rounded up fourteen new suspects for enhanced questioning, and executed the Enemy leader with a bullet to the back of the head.

That particular scene (or whatever one called it) was presented rather tastefully, like some long-practiced ritual. Colonel Jed Whitlock marched the defeated man to a sort of grassy knoll, far away from the desolation of the battle site, before handing him a long shovel. Leisurely, the man began to dig, which allowed time for backstory on how this Enemy leader, whose name was Muzzafar Shishelova, had come to fall in with Enemy forces and what his capture and execution meant for the overall War effort. After digging, the man dropped his shovel and jumped down into his grave, his head and shoulders disappearing for a moment as he lay down, testing it for comfort, while the other TerrorBusters gathered round, vaping. Shishelova then climbed out and cleaned his hands with a wet nap offered by Colonel Whitlock.

When finished, Shishelova was issued a fringed prayer rug. He unfurled the prayer rug at one edge of the grave and, with the sun rising behind him, said his prayers. The Titanotrons defined each step in the man's prayer process (the rak'ah fardh, the rak'ah sunnah mu'akkadah, the rak'ah nafl). Colonel Whitlock and his men appeared deferential, their fists clasped before their groins in the classic pose of masculine reverence at a remove. Below, the Showing of the War crowd appeared likewise, their whooping and chanting muted for the moment.

Finally, Shishelova stood and rolled up the prayer rug and dropped it into his grave. He then turned to Colonel Whitlock and nodded. Colonel Whitlock directed one of his men to place a bucket, overturned, at the edge. Shishelova took his seat and waited, smiling peacefully. The camera zoomed in on Colonel Jed Whitlock's face, its narrowed blue-eyed gaze and skin like freshly oiled Naugahyde. He closed his eyes and turned. The camera then zoomed out, just in time for the shot, or, as it turned out, burst of shots. A plume of blood released into the air as Shishelova fell forward, disappearing.

The crowd went wild. Star-spangled beach balls emerged, bopping around. The whoops and hollers soon morphed into a chant of U! S! A! U! S! A!, keeping up until it was airtight, until Linda wondered if anyone in the crowd had ever done anything as well as they chanted the name of their country. Then everyone, even those lounging in the observer suites, stood to sing the National Anthem. It was just as "and the home of the brave" dissolved into total delirium that Danny beckoned Linda close.

"Mom! Jed Whitlock used one of those Murphy accessories!" Danny shouted. "The kind that make regular pistols fire like machine guns!"

"Isn't that overkill?"

"Yeah!"

The announcer informed the stadium that their rendition of the National Anthem was at that moment being streamed into the headphones of those TerrorBusters returning to base. Finally, everyone took their seat and finished their suppers. It felt good to relax.

As another round of commercials began, Dr. Young looked over one shoulder and then the other, as if about to tell a dirty joke. "Say, Danny," he said. "I saw them selling Fruit Blazers on the way in. I know I could use one. What about you?"

Danny slid off his seat and plucked the security clearance tag out of Dr. Young's hand. "Let me know if I miss anything!" he said, thanking his benefactor and heading out the door.

Dr. Young watched him go. "Terrific kid," he told Linda. "How old, did you say?"

"Twelve today," Linda replied, then added, as she often did, "He's small for his age, because of his condition."

"How's his treatment going?"

"Really well. The CF Clinic has been a godsend."

"Good, good. I'm not surprised, but it's good to hear." He brought a fist to his mouth as if to stifle a cough. "Linda," he said, "you may have already surmised the Board has its reasons for keeping your patient load so small."

"Oh?" Linda asked. At last, a peek behind the curtain! She sat up straighter and told herself to concentrate. *Put down the wine, Linda,* she thought, *you can refill afterwards...*

"You see, you've done such a terrific job with the guys you have... Do you remember my talking about establishing a nexus with the patient? Well, you're accomplishing that in spades, particularly Sergeant Sparrow. The Board is impressed."

"Great."

"All that is to say, we're now looking at how SoldierWell might best benefit...well, we're looking at how it might benefit the patient, of course, but in the interest of keeping the program afloat, we're looking at how to square *our* interests, as mental health practitioners, with the long-term business interests of the Company."

Dr. Young paused, perhaps waiting for Linda to request further explanation. Linda said nothing.

"We're thinking now of changing course vis-à-vis the program. Your work with Sparrow, specifically. Now, you might be wondering what that means, so I've put together an information packet. I'd like to send that over to you in the next couple of days, because, well... this is neither the time nor the place..." He waved an arm toward the screens outside. Like a child, Linda looked out, taking note of the crowd below. The joviality had ceased; the purr of the crowd had become a growl.

"Linda, I think—that is, the *Board* thinks, and I happen to agree—that we might really make our mark if we can somehow prove to the powers that be that SoldierWell can do some measurable *good* for the Company. The Company and the nation." Dr. Young placed his elbows on his knee and clapped his hands together. "Linda," he said, "how would you feel about employing your skills as a therapist toward something more aligned with national security?"

Linda searched her boss's face for clues. "How would I feel about…what?"

Dr. Young nodded as if he'd foreseen her confusion. "Let me put this to you as simply as I can. *Will you help us* persuade Sergeant Sparrow to kill on behalf of USoFA WorldWide?"

"Kill? Who?"

"That's still being decided by the Board, but let's assume a pretty bad person. An enemy of the state."

Linda nodded for a long time. "I'm sorry, but…would Sparrow be in on it? What do you mean 'persuade him'?"

Miles winced. "Well, *he* would be the one making the actual choice to kill. He's responsible for his actions, after all. But he won't be privy to our work. That's the point."

"Would he have protection from authorities, the police? If he killed somebody?"

Miles shook his head. "He makes the choice. He suffers the consequences."

"So we would be persuading him, but…" Linda had lost the thread. "How would we even do this?"

Dr. Young licked his lips and smiled. "I'm glad you asked, Linda, because that's what I've spent half my life figuring out. And I've finally…hey, kiddo! One of those for me?"

Bounding into the suite, Danny handed a Fruit Blazer to Dr. Young. Linda watched her son claim his seat before the Titanotron, which displayed a ten-point analysis of Colonel Whitlock's fighting style. Dr. Young raised the half-full bottle of wine and Linda nodded, holding up her glass.

It was time to head home. Night had fallen solid over the goings-on below, and while Linda could make out pockets of restlessness (every few minutes a singular male voice could be heard shouting, "That's what I'm talking 'bout!"), the crowd had turned woozy, relaxed.

As had she. Maybe it was the wine, but Linda felt stunned, her thoughts and feelings in dire need of sorting out. She found herself waiting for Dr. Young to give her a playful elbow to the ribs and let her in on the joke, but he hadn't, not yet. As they left the observer suite and joined the exiting crowd, he just kept leafing through Danny's Showing of the War program, quizzing him on his TerrorBusters knowledge, occasionally looking up to smile tightly at nothing.

While they waited for the elevator, Dr. Young looked over Linda's shoulder and made a sour face. "Christ, I should've known."

"Known what?" Linda asked.

"Fran Lanier. Over there, with the beard. Biggest windbag you'll ever meet. Damn, here he comes."

Linda and Danny turned to see a very tall man with a close-cropped salt-and-pepper beard approaching. As for his dress, he had Danny beat: TerrorBusters gear from head to toe. Across his chest was an airbrushed portrait of a dead Enemy soldier, bright red blood flowing from his head, and underneath the words IRAQ LIVES SPLATTER. "Miles," he said. "Caught the Showing, I see."

"Hey there, Fran," Dr. Young said. "Good one tonight, huh?"

Dr. Lanier sniffed. "We did the job." He tilted toward Linda and nodded at the picnic basket. "Enjoying some bread with our circus?"

"Fran, I'd like to introduce Linda Held. She's with our Soldier-Well East program."

"I heard you expanded," Dr. Lanier said, offering a limp hand to Linda. "Huzzah."

"And this is her son, Danny, who turned twelve today. Oop, there's our ride."

"I'll join you."

Dr. Young ran a button hook once inside the elevator, stationing himself directly behind the operator, mouthing *Sorry!* to Linda as she and Danny and Dr. Lanier were swept along to the back, where they had a panoramic view of people being driven from the venue. Each streetlamp showcased its own small drama—under one, a security guard was zip-tying the wrists of a preteen girl; under another, a guard was shaking out the contents of an older man's backpack, stamping on whatever hit the ground.

"Wow," Danny said. "Check out the fireflies."

Dr. Lanier let loose a donkey bray. "Fireflies! Classic! Young man, those are tasers."

"Tasers?" Linda asked. "But there must be hundreds out there."

"Tailgating started six hours ago," he said, shrugging. "Sending these people home is like the proverbial herding of cats."

Linda pointed out past the parking lots. "Is that a bonfire?"

Dr. Lanier shook his head. "A book burning."

"A book burning? Really?"

Dr. Lanier chuckled, and Linda caught a whiff of his breath, like old pennies. "Before we go making indecorous comparisons," he said, "I'll point out that it's a purely practical measure. Those books have all been digitized, so burning them is just the most efficient method of disposal. Good fun, too."

"I take it this isn't your first Showing," Linda said.

"It's my thirty-fourth Showing. I haven't missed one since they began."

"Wow. What is it you do, may I ask?"

"Well, in another life I was a highly successful theater director," he said, "but for the past year I've been writing a book about the cathartic nature of these Showings."

"Cathartic? For the audience, you mean?"

Dr. Lanier nodded. "You've heard of Theatre of the Real? Theatre of Cruelty? Epic Theatre? Don't feel bad if you haven't. No, what I propose is that these Showings represent a *new* kind of theater, a way of engaging with an audience comprised almost entirely of the common man. Of course, the common man has proven woefully evasive to theater, *real* theater, for centuries.

"Now," Dr. Lanier continued, "a typical Showing of the War, like the one we saw tonight, draws from entertainments various and sundry—sporting events, obviously, but also the musical, horror, reality TV, and various propagandas—parades, pageants, even tent revivals—all to create an entirely *new* theatrical form, something I call the Theatre of Relentless Victory. It's the foisting of narrative structure onto the blatant absurdity of war. High-stakes kitsch."

"Thirty-four Showings. You must really like it."

Dr. Lanier closed his eyes and sighed. "I find it intoxicating."

Linda saw the elevator doors open and Dr. Young waving for her and Danny to come along.

"Excuse me," she said, grabbing Danny's hand, "I think this is us."

"Well, it was lovely meeting you, Doctor...?"

"Oh, it's just Miss. Linda Held."

Dr. Lanier's jaw went sideways. "Well, goodnight," he said. "Tell Miles to give me a ring."

───────

At the car, Dr. Young opened her door for her. The passenger seat resembled a black nest. Once inside and buckled up, Linda turned to find Danny already horizontal across the backseat, his Showing of the War program hugged to his chest.

Pulling out of the parking lot, Dr. Young opened his mouth, shut it, opened it again. "Linda, I hope you don't think I brought you and Danny here tonight to, I don't know, instill patriotism or something," he said. His voice was very low. "I think much too highly of you to try anything so tawdry."

"I didn't think that, Dr. Young."

"Call me Miles, please." He glanced over. "So how is all this sitting with you?"

Linda leaned her head back. "How long have you been planning this?"

"Ten years," he said. "But I've been interested in effective persuasion my entire adult life. You'll read about it in the information packet. It's a life's work."

"Maybe I can save you some time," Linda said.

"I'm listening."

"How about, in the next session, I just *ask* Sparrow if he wouldn't mind doing us a favor and assassinating an enemy of the state. He'd probably jump at the chance." Linda laughed, not because it was funny but because it was hard to believe the words coming out of her mouth.

Miles shook his head like a gnat had landed on his nose. "That isn't what this is about, though. The Company is looking at this long-term. What I am providing is a *method* of persuasion. A *technique* that can be repeated." He shifted in his seat as they turned onto the open road. "Think of all the times, Linda, throughout your life, when you were persuaded to do something you didn't want to do. The man at the auto shop who tricked you into buying the upgraded tires or the coworker who got you to trade shifts with her. Naturally, we chalk that up to the ability of the persuader, but what *I've* done is uncover the persuader's method."

Linda caught herself nodding along. "You're thinking big."

"We're thinking big."

"But no one does anything they don't want to do. Just like how the best lies contain that kernel of truth, persuasion works by stoking a desire that's already there. Maybe you can talk someone into a tire upgrade, but that person needed tires to begin with."

"I think that's probably right." Miles cleared his throat. "But what if you were in control of *all* the conditions of a person's life? What if you were able to control all other stimulation, so that, over time, the person's only loyalty was to you? Then, pleasing you becomes the desire."

Linda looked out on the road ahead and focused on her breathing, trying to match it to the snores coming from the backseat. "I just don't think..." she lowered her voice to a hiss, "...murder can just be implanted in people."

"What about your patients?"

Linda thought for a moment. "Sparrow, maybe. Sometimes I get the feeling he'd kill *me* if I said the wrong thing. But Boxer, no. Not in his nature."

"You sure about that? I could put you in touch with a certain Army chaplain."

"I know. But I keep thinking there's some other explanation."

"You like him. Boxer."

Linda didn't object. It was true, she got a happy feeling whenever her Remote Responder Awareness Device sounded and she sat down before her monitor and up popped Carl. "You said you're only considering Sparrow? What does that mean for Boxer?"

"He'll be released. Sent back to Ma'lef for his trial. It's a pretty open-and-shut case, so I imagine he'll be heading back to prison."

Linda thought about what Carl was doing at that very moment. He could be sleeping. He could be watching Showing of the War highlights on the CUP. He could be playing one of those horrendous video games.

"Gosh, Miles, I wish I had more experience in sales. I worked as a remote solicitor for about six months, and we used a script to keep people on the line. Other than that, I don't have a ton of experience with persuasion."

Miles blew past the ramp leading to I-66, then poked a finger at the road ahead as if to say, *I know a shortcut.* "This isn't about selling, Linda. It's not even about persuasion. It's about triggering certain emotional responses and harnessing them so that they align with Company goals. The idea is to push toward an ideal: the construction of synthetic motive. If we can apply my technique effectively, you won't feel like you're selling anything. Especially since the patient will be open to our suggestions, thanks to his medication."

"What if he stops taking his medication?"

Miles grinned. "Not possible."

"Why not?"

"They receive it through their food. It's one of the reasons why I spare no expense on their meals."

Linda nodded but wanted to shake her head. "And as for the patient?" she asked. "'First do no harm,' the Hippocratic Oath? That means nothing here?"

Miles appeared ready for this. "'I will remember that I remain a member of *society*, with special obligations to my fellow human beings, those *sound* of mind and body as well as the infirm.'"

Linda laughed. "You're not going to convince me this is coming from a place of moral authority, Miles."

"But it does! It does come from a place of moral authority! Use your imagination, Linda. If we do this, then you, me, your son, we'll all live in a safer world. If that isn't moral…" Miles shrugged.

Linda found herself weirdly subdued. These Maryland country roads held a solemnity at night. "I imagine you checked *my* personality against some profile of the ideal therapist," she said.

"Is that so different from any job interview?"

The ride continued in silence, Linda and Miles staying on neighboring yet separate tracks of thought. For long stretches, they were the only car on the road, and Linda could imagine herself in deep space.

After Miles pulled through Greenway's outer gates, Linda asked, "You'll send an information packet, did you say?"

Miles didn't answer the question until he had parked the car and killed the engine. "I need you to accept before I send it," he said.

Linda looked up at her house. Other than the light over the front door, all was quiet and soft dark. Suddenly, the light in Robert's bedroom window came on. He'd been waiting for them so that he could administer Danny's nighttime drugs.

"What if I say no?"

"It's a free country."

"But what happens?"

Miles paused, weighing his words. "Arrangements would be made. You'd be taken off the program. We'd move you and your family somewhere else. Probably Spectator Heights."

"What is Spectator Heights?"

"Kind of a halfway house thing, for employees whose security clearance has been disabled while the Company finds a new spot for them."

"Oh. Is it nice?"

"I hear it's OK."

Linda pointed up at Robert's window. "Danny's nurse—would we get to keep him?"

"You're free to keep him at your own expense."

"So that's a no."

Miles could be heard shifting in his seat. "Look, Linda, it's late. Why don't you take some time? It's a lot to unwrap, and…"

"Miles, I'm going to ask you a question and I would appreciate an honest answer."

"I've always been honest with you."

"You already know I'm going to accept, don't you?"

"Linda, this is *your choice* to make. No one's making any predictions."

"But do you know I'm going to accept? Are you counting on it?"

Miles sighed. "I believe you'll take some time to think about it, then come back and say yes. That's what I believe will happen."

"How long will I take to think about it?"

"Couple of days."

Linda nodded for what felt like a long time. "Let me have Carl," she said.

"Carl? Boxer?"

"I want to keep him on. I'll do what you want with Sparrow, but let me keep Carl. Let me keep treating him."

"Now that I did not predict."

"Let me keep him and it's a deal."

"You like him."

"Yes."

"You think you can save him."

"Do we have a deal?"

Miles shrugged. "I'd feel better if you slept on it."

"I doubt I'll change my mind."

"You might. It's your choice."

"What does this even look like? What's the next session with Sparrow look like?"

"Same as always, pretty much. I might like it if you asked him about his CUP habits, who his favorite political pundits are, that sort of thing."

Linda nodded, handing the empty picnic basket over to Miles before opening her door and getting out. She turned and pulled her son close, relishing his heat.

Miles leaned over. "I can take him in."

"No, it's all right," Linda said. "I've got him." She turned and began walking up the driveway to her house. An abrupt farewell, but Danny could write a thank-you note tomorrow. As she keyed into the front door, Miles's Porsche roared to life and drove off.

The quiet only made the house feel bigger. Linda stepped out of her shoes in the foyer and pulled off Danny's sneakers, dropping them to the floor.

Taking him up to bed was harder than she thought. All the meal supplements and vitamins were doing their work—Linda was halfway up the stairs when her knees began to buckle under his weight.

"I've got him." Robert was at her side, startling her. He was wearing boxer briefs and a Harvard T-shirt and, for some reason, cologne.

"No, he'll just…" Linda was going to say *wake up*, but Danny remained asleep in Robert's long, fat-veined arms.

"Thank you," she whispered. "Make sure he pees before bed?"

Robert nodded before vanishing up the stairs.

Sleep came quickly, the physical toll of the evening putting her in a light coma, though at dawn she woke from a strange and frightening dream that had something to do with wildfires and beach balls and Robert's calf muscles squirming up the steps all by themselves.

EXCERPT

USoFA WorldWide War-Related PTSD Individualized Therapy Program (Pilot), "SoldierWell" Therapy Session #20

March 16, FY20__

1349EST

LINDA HELD

Interviewing:

SERGEANT TODD SPARROW, US Marine Corps. 2nd Tank Battalion, 2nd Marine Division

(BEGIN)

SGT. TODD SPARROW: We leveled her whole house, to tell you the truth, and that was it. I could have stood up, I could've taken off my Kevlar, walked all the way down there. She was the eyes of the whole operation.

[*pause*]

OK, the reason I tell you that story is to tell you this…you cannot imagine, Linda, the satisfaction of putting an Enemy like that down. It's better than sex…and because she was pregnant, or possibly pregnant, I mean she might've had a basketball shoved down there, far as I know, but if she was pregnant, it was like we were getting rid not just of her but also a future Enemy. I remember that night, I remember getting back and sacking out. Slept like a baby.

[*pause*]

LINDA HELD: You miss the War.

TS: Yeah. I miss the War. God! It feels good to say that finally!

LH: How have you been feeling lately?

TS: Fine. Still no PTSD.

LH: Still getting enough exercise? The food agrees with you?

TS: The food is actually a little bland around here, I will say. As for exercise, I'm good. I take an hour of recess in the morning and one in the afternoon. I don't know the exact time, but I can tell OK by my heartbeat… Marine training, you know. I figure once around the courtyard is an eighth of a mile. When I got here, I could run about seven miles in that hour. Now I do eight. Do I look like I'm in shape? I mean, do I look OK to you?

LH: You like you're in fine shape.

TS: OK, phew. I mean, I figured I did, but…

LH: And the video games, they're enjoyable?

TS: They pass the time.

LH: Are you aware that your progress regarding the games is reviewed?

TS: Um… I didn't know that. But it makes sense.

LH: You're a very good shot.

TS: Thank you! Sometimes I had the feeling I was being watched, but I didn't want to say.

LH: Well, they're mostly problem-solving exercises, those games. But you show an aptitude.

TS: Glad I can keep you entertained. [*laughs*] They're fun.

LH: And what are your thoughts about the future?

TS: Well, it all depends where they send me after this.

LH: But if you had your choice. Where do you see yourself, a year from now?

[*pause*]

TS: I suppose it depends on my financial picture.

LH: Well, let's say you've got enough to take care of yourself for a while.

TS: Well, I'd find a place to live, an apartment or something. And I'd have to furnish it, of course. A bed, a couple of lamps, a chair, big CUP monitor. Like this room. And I'd get some clothes, really comfortable clothes. T-shirts and jeans, that would be like my look. No more polos. Up until the Marines I'd been wearing polo shirts my entire life and I've never liked them.

LH: OK, so there you are, new apartment, new clothes. Sitting in a new chair and looking out the window. You need to do something.

TS: Ah, I knew it was too good to last. [*laughs*]

LH: You can do anything you want. So what is it? What would you like to contribute to society?

TS: Oh…maybe reenlist.

LH: Todd, [*laughs*] you've just come back home. It wouldn't realistically take more than a few weeks to find an apartment. And all you would do is wear your new clothes and then reenlist?

TS: Can I ask why you're asking me this, Linda? Are you going to release me?

LH: I'm just trying to get you to use your imagination. You've been halfway across the world, fighting terrorism…

TS: That I have.

LH: But now you're home, you've got the rest of your life ahead of you. We should discuss what you want to do with it.

TS: I get it. My personal freedom, like the freedom to turn the page…

LH: Yes, exactly. So let's explore.

TS: I'm a good…I'm a good shot. I could be a professional hunter or something. My drill instructor said I was one of the best he'd ever seen. I could be on one of those shows, those instructional shows about hunting deer. Or maybe I could go to like Montana and escort people across the countryside, and then if a bear comes after them, I'd be there, for protection. They'd give me a rifle and I could shoot whatever comes our way.

LH: You want to protect people.

TS: Yeah. Rich people. I saw it on the CUP the other day, rich people love riding horses across the western states, camping out at night. I could help them with that. Or no, I could take people on safari, like in Africa, the undisputed parts, anyway. Not West Africa, obviously. Yeah, safari… I could escort rich Americans while they're taking in the sights. Say one of them is filming a lion or something, and the flash goes off and gets him in the eye and then he comes after us. I'd shoot it before he got to us.

LH: That's good.

TS: Wait, why do you say it like that?

LH: Why do I say what?

TS: Why are you saying that's good like that? Is this a stupid idea?

LH: I didn't say that.

TS: Is it, though? This is all just off the top of my head. If I had some time…

LH: No, it's excellent. You're using your imagination. We've made it to Africa, with the lions. It's wonderful. You seem to have a real desire to protect people.

TS: I guess I do.

LH: Americans, especially.

TS: Maybe it's an only child thing. I've always been forced to play man of the house.

LH: Yes, I get that sense from you.

TS: Thank you, I just…that's what life is about, right? Taking care of the people around you?

LH: That's a good way of looking at it. But let me ask you this… Now, it's just a question, so please don't feel like you need to answer it. You're never required to answer any of my questions. You know that.

TS: Sure.

LH: About the safari…do you think you need to go all the way to Africa to protect people?

TS: From lions?

LH: From anything.

TS: Oh. Probably not.

LH: Because there are quite a few dangers right here in this country, aren't there?

TS: Sure. I mean, I've just come from a war zone, so it's going to look different…but no, I see your point. This country suffers from…

LH: Infestation.

TS: Yeah. If that's what you mean.

LH: And the American people, they need protection. Wouldn't you agree?

TS: Sure. But I think now we're talking about reenlisting again.

[*pause*]

LH: Do you ever dream about your experiences in Iraq?

TS: Some. There were a lot of fellows over there that I didn't get along with. Sometimes I think about what I'd do different, different things I could have said that would have put certain characters in their place.

LH: And you miss the fighting. You're nostalgic for it.

TS: Nostalgic? I mean...yes. It was fun. There was a rush, being out there, patrols... I was good at it. It's interesting when people say, like I've had people say to me, the standard thing, thank you for your service, God bless you, all that. But what's interesting is that when you're out there, you don't feel very much like a Marine as much as an exterminator. The Enemy, at this point, they must want to die. They're all so little, Linda. And in that split second when they see you coming at them, where you just come at them, like ah, you piece of shit, I'm going to kill you... it's better than sex, I don't mind saying. You're like a god, you know, dark vengeance. It's a reckoning. You do something like that, it can be hard to just kick back and watch the CUP. [*laughs*]

LH: Well, Sergeant, I'm afraid...

TS: Don't you say it!

LH: I'm afraid we're out of time.

TS: Damn! [*laughs*] I knew it!

END EXCERPT

EXCERPT

USoFA WorldWide War-Related PTSD Individualized Therapy Program (Pilot), "SoldierWell" Therapy Session #14

March 17, FY20__

2113EST

LINDA HELD

Interviewing:

PRIVATE* CARL BOXER, US Army (Associate, Transportation Services, "Free2Fight," USoFA WorldWide)

(BEGIN)

LINDA HELD: I knew he'd like the video games best, but his reaction to the clothes was pretty enthusiastic too. As for the dinosaur books...

PVT.* CARL BOXER: [*laughs*] I told you.

LH: I know, I know. [*laughs*] But no, it was after lunch, my boss called and said he had a couple of extra tickets to the Showing, and he asked if we wanted to come.

CB: I bet Danny went crazy.

LH: Oh, he lit up like a pinball machine.

CB: What's your boss's security clearance?

LH: Red.

CB: Red, goddamn. What are you?

LH: Orange.

CB: Orange? Wow, Linda, I didn't figure you for orange.

LH: [*laughs*] What difference does it make?

CB: I'm just saying, no wonder you're in that big house. You must be doing important work.

[*pause*]

But it's big, right? The venue?

LH: God, yes. We took the elevator for what must have been five minutes, and one side was glass so you could see the parking lots, the general admission lots, with all the tailgating…

CB: You all were in one of the boxes?

LH: Yeah, the view was amazing. We had one screen almost directly in front of us, and then past that are all these hills and things. It was like fall out there, the leaves all different colors…

CB: I heard somewhere, USoFA WorldWide paints those leaves. It's supposed to keep the crowds calm before show time or something.

LH: They don't actually paint the leaves, it's a spray that keeps the trees, you know, healthy looking. But what you were saying about keeping people calm, it was…we must have spent an hour just people-watching. Lots of drinking, and the music...

CB: It gets pretty hairy down there, right?

LH: We didn't see any real trouble. The security was as much as any airport.

CB: OK, tell me about the Showing. Where were the TerrorBusters this time? Uzbekistan?

LH: That's right. Tashkent.

CB: It's all staged, you know.

LH: No, I know. But the battles are real. The killing is real.

CB: OK, sure. So how did it end? Did we win? [*laughs*]

LH: Oh, you know, leader executed, Enemy compound destroyed. There was this whole back story about what it meant in the bigger picture of the War, but it was all over my head... Colonel Whitlock, is that his name?

CB: Yeah. Jed Whitlock. Big soldier, big goddamn hero. So then what'd you do?

LH: Well, in the observer suites, you're allowed to stay for another hour and watch security kick everybody out so we stuck around, just snacked on the food we had.

CB: They let you bring in outside food?

LH: Well, we did. Danny just looked at the program and the grown-ups talked about work stuff.

CB: Did you talk about me?

LH: A little.

CB: How am I doing? Am I a problem?

LH: A problem? No, no. Far from it.

[*pause*]

CB: So, pardon my asking, Linda, and if you don't want to tell me, I won't...

LH: Danny's father. Where's Danny's father.

CB: [*laughs*] How did you know?

LH: It's just something you pick up on, as a single mom. People get a look.

CB: Forget I said anything. Don't tell me, I don't want to know.

LH: No, it's fine. Danny's father was in the military. Marines.

CB: Oh. OK. Is he around or what?

LH: I don't know. I haven't seen him since he went to Afghanistan. That was...well, more than twelve years ago.

CB: Danny doesn't know him at all.

LH: No.

CB: Does he ever ask about him?

LH: Not as much as you'd think. He knows his father was in the Marines when we met. That's about it. I don't know much more than that.

CB: OK. And Danny's a big TerrorBusters fan.

LH: He is, yes. Huge fan.

[*pause*]

I've never made that connection...

CB: I don't even know why I asked you that.

LH: No, no...so you think Danny's being a Terror-Busters fan gives him a connection to his father? I never would have thought. That's interesting.

CB: Yeah, OK. Sorry.

LH: Not at all! It's a good insight. I'm just considering... He watches those men and imagines a connection. Huh. How do you do this, Carl?

CB: How do I do what?

LH: How do you get me talking like this? You barely say two words and here I am rambling about my son's birthday and the Showing...

CB: [*laughs*] What did I do?

LH: You tell me! [*laughs*]

CB: I'd rather talk about you, I guess. See, this, this feels all right. I feel safe with you in the room, Dr. Held.

LH: I'm not a doctor, Carl. But I'm glad you feel safe with me.

[*pause*]

So… are you going to broach the subject, or should I?

CB: Broach what?

LH: What happened to your head? Can you say what happened?

CB: Oh, I just fell out of bed the other night…I must've banged it on the way down.

LH: Does it hurt?

CB: Not much. I got a tough melon. [*laughs*]

LH: The injury report said you were deliberately hitting your head against the bathroom sink. Is that incorrect?

CB: It's not a big deal.

LH: Carl, I'm looking at your head right now, and I'd say it is a big deal. Why were you hurting yourself?

CB: It's…it's coming back, Linda. I'm seeing stuff. In my mind.

LH: You're seeing things…

CB: Yup. The pictures.

LH: You're beginning to remember?

CB: Some of it.

LH: Oh God, and here I've been… Do you want to talk about it? You don't have to if you don't want, but I think it's better to talk about it than keep it in… I won't press you, though.

CB: Good.

LH: Let me just ask you this. Your job, over there, it was in transportation services, correct?

CB: Yeah.

LH: OK, what did you transport? Supplies? Or people? Or other things?

CB: Things, definitely. I was a thing.

LH: And this was in Baghdad?

CB: No, Ma'lef. South of Baghdad.

[*pause*]

What else do you want to know?

LH: All right, can you tell me how it felt over there? What was the mood among the people you saw, you worked with? I'm sorry, I wasn't really ready for this…

CB: Well, you know, word had been going around for a little while, like on the CUP, that we were just wrapping things up in Iraq. Remember that? The president said he was going to start pulling troops, bringing the numbers down. Roadside stops were going without incident, traffic was moving again, the Enemy had abandoned IEDs… Everybody was confident the Resurge had worked, like we broke their backs. That was the mood…the intelligence was looking good, they were hearing something like eighty percent of suspect cells in our area, just…nothing. No chatter. It was, you know, unofficial but pretty much major combat operations concluded. It was feeling like the War was won, at least in Iraq. And I was happy about that, but I also felt like I missed the train…

[*pause*]

LH: What else?

CB: I need some time…

LH: Take all the time you need.

[*pause*]

CB: OK. I was at Forward Operating Base Doritos, and it wasn't long, just a couple weeks after I got there…and me and some other guys, Army, we were put together to run these supply routes. We were in convoys, ten vehicles in a line, sometimes more… It wasn't bad at first, but the driving there is tricky. We were doing runs all through Baghdad, and there are all these one-ways, and traffic gets jammed up, and Army's always switching up routes and closing off roads, and then you've got USoFA WorldWide trying to build some hotel, they're always clogging things up because somebody needs to jackhammer into the road to put in a pipe or something. Just…chaos, like, layers of chaos. And you can't ever stop. That's the only thing anybody ever told me there. Go up on sidewalks, knock shit over if you have to, knock people over if you have to, but there's no stopping the vehicle. Stop and you're toast.

[*pause*]

But south of there, where we were, where we usually started, it was just long and straight… We go out one day, into Baghdad, we had to get portable fans or something…and we get up just south of the city and it's…I mean, I'm sure you've seen it on the CUP before, just bad roads and people getting out of their cars… I'm in the truck with two guys up front, one in back. The one in back is on the M2, and they're radioing back and forth, saying watch this motherfucker on his phone, watch him, watch that fucker with the bag, watch him, make sure he sees, give him a wave. He's having fun with it, you know, because like I said, nobody's seen an IED in months. We're moving along, and things get all…there's this Iraqi dude, a traffic cop, and I should've known better than to listen to him but he's waving us toward this detour…and something's not right because Army usually paints these arrows on all the walls so drivers don't get confused. I was used to following the arrows. And what happened…like, I saw the guy, the Iraqi, he's telling me to go this way, but I'm following the troop carrier in front of me, and then one of their guys jumps out and he's pointing the other

way, and I don't know if he's wanting me to go or
stay or what. I just didn't know. And everybody
with me is yelling, saying go this way, no go this
way, and I'm not wanting to stop so I just...I guess
I got nervous...I turned and, right away, like a
block later, we're lost. Then word comes over
that the ones behind us were just in an ambush.

[*pause*]

And...now, this was their rainy season, and the
rain started coming down...so there we were, the
wrong road, all alone, and everybody's stopped
yelling because it's just...it's bad. And I'm still
going at top speed, just going straight, farther away from where we need to be, but I can't
go anywhere else, there's nowhere else to go... I
didn't know where we were...and we're all listening
to what's going on with the ambush, and it sounds
bad, so then one of my guys... [*laughs*] my guys,
OK...he's yelling back and forth with the radio,
trying to figure out where the shots are coming
from. I mean, we'd been told it was just about
half a mile away, or point eight of a kilometer,
I never really learned, but still...it didn't feel
like it was happening anywhere near us. Even when
the guys with me were naming people they thought
might be in it but I didn't know anybody, so I was
just staying quiet the whole time, but I could
tell these guys...they weren't scared enough, they
just assumed everything was going to work out.

[*pause*]

Then somebody got shot…then right away somebody else. Not us, I mean the other ones, but…two casualties…then somebody requested air support, and that went through all right and now they were saying air support's coming in, small drones on their way so everybody get out of the area. That was the command. And then these guys were all roger that can we get a pickup because the carrier's gone…and I'm just driving, I caught this little roundabout and was turning around. And then the sky just got real dark. Just like…I mean, I was sitting there, behind the wheel, and I turned to one of my guys and, like, his face, it just turned into a shadow. And he saw the same thing in me, and he says here she comes…and we both duck our heads out the window and just this…this thing goes across the sky, loud as hell. Loud as hell. And it swoops over us and then about five seconds later…[*unintelligible*] I mean, the area, whoever was in it, everything just gets fucking disintegrated. I'd never seen anything like it. We were pretty far from it, but it looked like, it felt like it was happening right on top of the hood, you know…and then the radio comes on and somebody says all right, let's get a Medevac out there, and oh, by the way, we got a cargo truck a ways back, going around in circles, hey cargo get your ass back there and pick up some guys. Then one of my guys gets on and says we're on our way, and they're all slapping high-fives and all… It's…I'm sorry. This is hard.

[*pause*]

So then it was time to go. I remember being jealous of the ones who got shot. I hadn't even met them, I wasn't even supposed to be there, but I'm jealous because I knew they'd be taken care of, like their families would be taken care of and they'd get to go around saying it's on account of our boy getting wounded in battle. They could be proud. And here I was, driving trucks. [*laughs*] But…everybody was feeling pretty good. Two wounded, looks like they'd pull through, and we secured the area. I remember one of my guys saying now that right there's a good day at the office, something like that… He was dipping Copenhagen and I asked him for one and he said naw I only got two left and I was all…[*indecipherable*] I said hey I got us out of that ambush and he rolls his eyes and says, goddammit, here. And then somebody said what was the Enemy thinking, going up against US soldiers in a damn convoy. And we're bumping along, almost there, and…that was when it happened. Just this…boom. I saw the Medevac in front of me, I saw it go just straight…up. It just lifted straight up.

[*pause*]

There's a second, you know? When something terrible happens? There's a second where it all gets quiet, and it feels like it might go on forever but still not long enough for you to figure out what's happening. It's that second right when something bad happens, and you figure you're either going to straight-up die or your life is going to be shit for a certain length of time. Or maybe it's just like that in your memory. I've heard about people being addicted to war, like doing five, six deployments. I've never been in a battle, but I think I see where that comes from. Because it's that second, it stays with you forever. And maybe you start to think that the next time something happens, there'll be that second to be able to, like, do something, you know, like next time you'll be ready and you'll assess the situation and deal with it better…like a hero… instead of panicking and wondering how long this is going to last before everything's safe again and you get to go home and be home. It's terrible, but at the same time, it isn't. There's an honesty to it, like, yup, this is what it's come down to.

[*pause*]

I stayed in the truck. I stayed there just not knowing, but I hit the brakes and everybody fell forward, and our guy manning the back, I check the mirror and I see him swing the M2 and just *open up* on these women, these girls who'd been walking alongside the road. They were carrying baskets or something, towels…I remember seeing them get mowed down and, this guy, I didn't know him, he just *stayed* on them, shooting them up as they're laying there, flipping them over in the dirt…and a couple guys get him to stop, and somebody's on the radio now, screaming about how they'd all been promised this area was fucking secure so what's a fucking IED doing here and then somebody else says no, friendly fire, it's got to be a drone… And I'm just wondering what happened because the Medevac is just…gone. There'd been a bunch of people leaning up against it, waiting for pickup, and they were all gone. And there's fire here and there and some of it is burning up the mist that's the blood in the air, and the mist is getting on the windshield and I remember thinking, I remember thinking how long before I got to put the wipers on to wipe off the mist, which is the blood, which is the men who were just there two seconds ago… Anyway…that was the first one.

[*pause*]

LH: The first one?

CB: Yup. The first parasite. One of the first.

LH: I'm sorry, parasite? What's a parasite?

CB: [*laughs*] That's the question, right there.

LH: Carl?

CB: [*laughs*] One of our men, one of our wounded… his name was Morrison. He got parasited. He wasn't hit with a bullet, or…he was, he was hit with a bullet, but there was something inside it. And once this, this thing lays into somebody, it's got this…or maybe it becomes it, nobody knows…it's got this real small, real small, real powerful detonation device. Morrison took a bullet through his arm and everybody was thinking it went straight through, but it left something behind, and he got infected.

LH: I'm confused.

CB: [*laughs*] Now you're getting it! We're all confused! [*laughs*] It's confusing! The Enemy was developing these parasites the whole time, when it was so quiet, laying low until one of their people stepped up to test it out. [*laughs*] And it worked! And we don't know, Army doesn't know, the president doesn't know, fucking USoFA WorldWide doesn't know what these things are! All we know is they're supposed to have started in Iraq but they're everywhere now. [*laughs*] I mean...you got to hand it to the Enemy...

LH: I'm sorry, Carl, I just want to clarify. You're saying that the Enemy is...shooting detonation devices into US soldiers.

CB: We think they're detonation devices. Nobody knows. It's happened so many times, Linda. Guys coming back from ambushes, they're on their way back, they don't make it. The Medevac blows up. It kept happening. If you weren't seeing it, you were at least hearing about it...brass from other places would visit, there were all these meetings...I was always last to know anything but they brought a bunch of people in, trying to get everybody to remember every last detail about what happened that day in Baghdad. The CIA, weapons experts, all of them sniffing around, tearing up our clothes for samples… They wasted a lot of time, I remember, with these theories. I remember one guy said it must be a terrorist cell on the inside, somebody else was saying it was defective weapons. One guy was talking about spontaneous combustion. [*laughs*] And people kept dying.

[*pause*]

But finally, somebody gets the idea to measure the time between when somebody gets shot and detona-tion, trying to see if there's any consistency there. And then after…they got it down to within a few seconds, and it changed everything. For a while, anybody who got shot or wounded, or even if they so much as tripped on a rock, anything, you had to press the timer on this special-issue stopwatch and call it in so everybody around you can clear the area. I mean, [*laughs*] I heard about soldiers refusing to clear the area on account of they wouldn't abandon their buddies, you know. That was when people still couldn't believe the Enemy had come up with this thing… It didn't take long, though, for everybody to start believing, once they'd seen it.

[*pause*]

And then they got this finding. The investigators were reviewing recordings of the dead because that was another thing, everybody was wearing these little black box recorders around their necks, and they found a tell. That's just what they called it. What we called it. If you got shot by an Enemy, and you'd been infected, within something like two minutes you'll be thinking you smell baking bread. Does anybody smell bread? Who's making bread? And then ten minutes after that, detonation. That was big…it helped them identify who'd been parasited. And then they could isolate them. But there were all these questions with that, too.

[*pause*]

What do you think of all this, Linda? You're looking at me like I lost my mind.

LH: I'm sorry, I don't mean to.

CB: It's funny, I was worried when I started telling you. I was afraid you wouldn't believe me. But now I'm in it and I don't care if you believe me. I saw it with my own eyes, over and over.

[*pause*]

Hey, Linda? Can you do a favor for me?

LH: What is it?

CB: You've got to promise you'll do this for me, Linda. I need you to promise.

LH: Carl, I'm not going to promise something until I hear what it is.

CB: All right. But I want you to do some research. You've got orange security clearance, I bet you could at least check out casualty reports for medical personnel in Iraq. Compare it to past years. I bet you anything they went way up. I bet you anything.

LH: I'm sorry, Carl, but it looks like our time today is just about up.

CB: OK, but can you do that for me, Linda? Can you look it up?

LH: Can you promise me you'll stop hurting yourself?

CB: Just look it up, Linda, please. Look at the casualty reports—not the ones they talk about at press conferences, the real numbers. You'll see.

END EXCERPT

It took ten minutes to fit the leash around his neck, but the moment Linda opened the front door, Asha shot out through the wet grass. This was followed by thirty intermittently rainy minutes of indecision, as no bush or fire hydrant or section of curb smelled worthy of Asha's shitting near it. Finally, once Linda came to realize she had to have her back turned, he did his business.

Deva had stopped by early in the morning to take Vera birding (which was somehow different from bird-watching, though Deva's explanation collapsed halfway through). Linda had not finished her first cup of coffee when he produced the dog's leash from inside his coat, asking if she would mind walking Asha at some point before lunch. Before Linda could even answer, Deva was guiding Vera out the door.

Now, as she and Asha were rounding the corner of their street—the dog straining on his leash so arduously Linda could have plucked it, like a harp string—who should they run into but Dr. Amanda Kant. Holding a large black umbrella over her head, Dr. Kant was dressed in sweatpants and a man's flannel shirt—just the kind of outfit one might don for a weeklong depressive episode.

"Dr. Kant, hello," Linda said, planting her feet and leaning back to counter Asha's forward straining. "Sorry—Linda Held? We met at my interview for the SoldierWell East program?"

"Linda Held," Dr. Kant said, not even trying to mask the weariness in her voice. She produced a package of cigarettes from the breast pocket of her shirt. "So you live around here?"

"Yes," Linda said, "we're in that house there."

Dr. Kant turned to look. "What, next to the castle?"

"No, it's…it's the castle."

Dr. Kant snorted. "They lay it on thick, don't they?" She stuck a cigarette in to her face, tucking the umbrella handle under her chin before lighting up. Linda felt for a moment a keen nostalgia for the Swallow. How nice that place could feel on rainy mornings like this, with the regularest of regulars all gathered round, their liver-spotted hands gripping Bloody Marys and bottles of beer, wrinkled faces turned like baby chicks up to the dusty CUP monitor in the corner.

Linda asked Dr. Kant where in Greenway she lived.

"I *was* on Cheney Avenue, but now they've got me in Spectator Heights."

"Oh," Linda said. "I hear that's nice."

Dr. Kant gave her a disbelieving look. "It's where they put you when you get canned."

"Sorry?"

"That's right, off the SoldierWell board. They took a vote and… that was that."

"I'm so sorry," Linda said, realizing she had apologized to this woman three times in the last twenty seconds. "Did they give a reason?"

"Not a good one," Dr. Kant said. "But I honestly don't care. As far as I'm concerned, you and Miles and Tim Nestor can have at it."

Just then, Asha came nosing between them, his fluffy white tail thumping against Dr. Kant's shins. "Hey there, beautiful," Dr. Kant murmured, switching her umbrella handle to her cigarette-holding hand so as to rake her fingers in a zigzag pattern across Asha's back. "You realize Miles is making all this up as he goes along, don't you?"

Linda laughed. "Hey," she heard herself say, "I'm just happy to be here."

"Really? Nice gal like you, inciting murder? No. No way this isn't getting to you. Not without some serious self-medicating, anyway."

Linda pulled the dog away from Dr. Kant. "Come on, Asha," she said. "Let's leave the nice lady alone."

Dr. Kant stood at full height, shaking her head. "Really, Linda, how *do* you feel about this thing? And don't give me that crap about defending America."

"You got a problem defending America?" Linda asked, her Balti-moron accent huge in her ears. "No wonder you got kicked off the Board."

Dr. Kant laughed a smoker's laugh, sounding like an old hairdryer.

"I'm fine with it," Linda said. "I trust the Company."

Dr. Kant narrowed her gaze. "OK," she said. "Let's say this little mind game actually works, and it's *your* patient it works on. That means *you've* sent him out there to kill somebody, and in the process, he's very likely going to get *himself* killed, others killed. I've seen it happen. Innocent people will die because *you* trust the Company. That sits just fine with you."

Linda's eyes filled with tears. Ever since Miles had offered her "the new mission," she had awoken each morning restless, saturated in a distraction bordering on…dread wasn't the word, but in her mind's eye there persisted the vision of an old-fashioned fire alarm, the kind with the little stem thingy vibrating against the metal shell, ringing out forever in deep space, the loudest noise never to be heard.

Dr. Kant bore witness to Linda's reaction with visible pity. The rain had let up; drops popped one at a time against her umbrella's fabric.

Then, as if by magic, Linda understood exactly what was happening. "You're trying to sabotage us," she said. The tears in her eyes receded instantly. "You're bitter about getting kicked off the Board, and now you're trying to sabotage us."

Dr. Kant slouched, tipping the umbrella back, creating a small waterfall behind her. "Oh, sweetie," she said, "wake *up*."

"You almost had me." Linda turned and walked toward Deva's house, Asha in tow, neither straining ahead nor holding back. They got about ten yards before Linda stopped, her sneakers skidding on the wet asphalt, and marched back to Dr. Kant, who hadn't moved from her spot. Linda saw a flicker of fear in the woman's eyes and felt a ping of deep satisfaction.

"I wanted to see if I could do it."

Dr. Kant waited a beat before responding, "Do what?"

"Have my baby. My *son*. You asked me, during my interview, if I'd ever considered abortion. I did. But then I realized I could do it, I could be a mother. And I did."

Dr. Kant smiled as if moved, but then the smile went too far, becoming a sneer. She took a final drag from her cigarette and flicked it away. "Mark my words, Miss Held," she said, "when the dust settles on this, you'll be sorry you brought that kid into the world."

———※———

Inside, Asha halted in the alcove and sat, ears pinned back. With shaking hands, Linda removed his leash. "There you go, you little snot," she said, giving him a single pat behind the ears. "Take it easy, don't choke on a…"

Asha turned and bit Linda on the hand, releasing his grip almost as soon as he had established it. Linda cried out, more in fright than pain, and fell back against the front door. *Oh God, I'm going to die, right here, right now, he's going to come at me and clamp down on my throat and that will be it.* But all she saw when she opened her eyes was the back of Asha, tail raised high, no looking back.

Tucking her wounded hand under the opposite arm, she stood and followed, stepping around his sashaying bulk on her way to the kitchen.

Gorgeous kitchen—all ebony wood cabinets and natural stone granite countertops, stainless steel appliances, and a coffee maker with what looked like a gear stick. Rain-filtered light from the windows lent everything a silvery glow. Just the right size, too—Linda would've loved something like this, manageable and cozy as opposed to the cookhouse sprawl she had going on next door. She stepped up to the spotless sink and examined her hand.

There was an upper incisor–sized hole in the webbing between the thumb and forefinger of her right hand. Not a huge deal, but the blood was real and it was abundant. And so red! She couldn't remember the last time she'd seen blood so vividly, luxuriously red. Hot rod red. For a long moment, she watched the blood seep from the hole, then began testing various positions: a flattened palm, a tight fist, a thumbs up. Tiny red rivulets streamed their way down her wrist, toward the sparse blonde brush of forearm, forging minuscule tributaries in the quilt seams at her wrist. She felt strangely at ease, enveloped here in the dim, rainy day quiet. All the impossible things she was taking on, the demands of work and home, everything felt far away from this place, the kitchen of a strange man's home.

Asha barked. Remembering herself, Linda ran her arm under the tap.

Yes, Linda trusted the Company, and she would try applying the INSIST Technique on Sergeant Sparrow. That was her job now. Still, about the best the Board could reasonably hope for was a scooch more intel on human nature in general terms. After all, Miles's INSIST Technique was a fledgling; not even a fledgling, a fetus, one unlikely to come to term, and so Amanda Kant's bad faith hand-wringing was moot.

Linda pulled a wad of paper towels and pressed it to her wound. Some blood, not much, came spotting through. She left the kitchen and edged into the living room, where the dog was wagging its tail, peering intently through the double doors out to the back deck.

The living room was a bachelor's paradise, with a leather couch and recliner on one side of a pulverized Persian rug. The coffee table was a gigantic, squat square, messy with papers of all kinds, notebooks and crammed manila folders, and a half-dozen remote controls for the old-fashioned stereo equipment in the stained wood cabinet against the far wall. Linda stepped farther in, attracting Asha's attention. He padded across the room and past Linda, disappearing down another hallway.

Linda took a seat on the couch and checked her hand. Still bleeding, but she probably wouldn't faint anytime soon.

Though the information packet Miles had sent showed off an extensive knowledge of trauma and PTSD and the power of suggestion, it was hard to believe this was his life's work. Certain sections read like a first draft, and there was an overall tone that felt supplicating, as if Miles had yet to fully convince himself. Meanwhile, how all of it was supposed to work remained a mystery to Linda since, in her humble opinion, the human mind was too mysterious to be undone by some all-encompassing *technique*.

Take Carl: the fact that he was now nursing wild delusions about soldiers blowing themselves up was evidence enough to prove the unpredictability of human behavior. Meanwhile, his emotional intelligence was remarkable—alerting Linda to the possible motivation behind Danny's TerrorBusters obsession had been truly insightful. Linda had broached the delicate subject of fathers with Danny just the previous night, asking if he ever thought about his dad, who he was, where he might be. At first, he seemed content with parroting the old explanation about his father being "married to the Marines," but with a little pressing, Danny came to admit that, yeah, sometimes he wondered whether his father might be a TerrorBuster. Score one for Carl…

There was an open sketchbook that looked like it might fall off the coffee table any second. Linda leaned forward to see a small pencil sketch of a naked woman's torso, nipples like plunger cups. *Freaking perv.* Too young a body to be Vera, though, thank God.

Linda pushed the sketchbook farther onto the table, causing an avalanche of books and papers to slide off the opposite edge.

Going around to pick them up (using only her left hand), she came across *The Citizen*. Odd that Deva would have a copy. Linda glanced over the creased page to see the inky little square containing the face of Chelsea Daye.

Two reports about War casualties came out this week. You only heard about one of them.
by Chelsea Daye

Everyone by now has heard the news from Canada, thanks to media campaigns by USoFA WorldWide, the White House, and members of Congress on all sides of the aisle. Phrases like "running the War more efficiently," "redefining what it is to engage" and, as Rep. Samuel Flake (R-GA5) remarked yesterday, "good old terrorist ass-whooping," have been bandied about, but the gist is this: Since the passage of the Temporary War Act of FY20__, American casualties have increased by less than 2 percent, despite the War expanding into seven additional countries.

This comes from the report *In Context: USoFA WorldWide's Effect on U.S. Foreign Policy*, released last week by Canadian research firm Groundwork-A. The authors maintain that its findings serve as "conclusive proof" that:

> ... despite what many have labeled an "aggressive" approach to international terrorism, USoFA WorldWide has managed a 1.9 percent increase in War-related casualties since its inheritance of all logistical duties previously provided by the U.S. Armed Forces during times of war.

Groundwork-A's findings are anything but conclusive. Much of their "exclusive data" appears to have been lifted from USoFA World-Wide's own earnings reports, which are laughably unreliable among analysts not on the Company payroll.

And try comparing that data to official casualty reports released by the U.S. Department of Defense around the same time and, well, you can't. While the DOD defines casualties as "members of the U.S. Armed Forces and private security contractors through death, wounds, sickness, capture, or because whereabouts cannot be determined," USoFA World-Wide defines casualties as "loss of servicemen on the front line(s)" in all of its documents.

What's more, Groundwork-A tacitly denies the accuracy of USoFA WorldWide's definition of casualties just a few pages later, when it mentions casualties among servicemen *not* on the front line(s) at the time of their deaths. These findings are themselves tagged with asterisks referring the reader to another Canadian research firm, N2A Research.

Released for quick burial less than one week before the Groundwork-A report, N2A Research's *Something Happening Here: Ramifications of USoFA WorldWide's Takeover of U.S. Foreign Policy* finds that, while overall front line casualties have increased by 1.9 percent over the past two years, casualties among medical personnel have increased a shocking 59 percent.

I contacted N2A President Reed Katz about his company's findings. He too was stumped as to why so many American medical personnel are dying.

"What's weird is these numbers can't be explained away as some sort of outlier," Katz said. "I should hope USoFA WorldWide is looking into how they might reverse this trend. It doesn't make sense that precautions haven't been taken already."

Of course, asking why extra precautions have not been taken to protect medical personnel might lead one to wonder why doctors and nurses are dying in such large numbers to begin with. And since no one at USoFA WorldWide takes my calls, I hereby invite anyone who has lost a medical or non-combatant loved one in the past two years to please contact the offices of *The Citizen* at 86-16 Queens Blvd., Elmhurst, NY 11373. The information you provide could go a long way in helping us find the reason why so many are dying.

IN OTHER NEWS: I will be appearing at the Rights for Veterans Rally to be held in Kesey Square Plaza in Eugene, Ore. on April 7. Please, if you're in the area, come out for a day of peaceful protest. Let's show the powers that be that we too can organize! Abide no longer!

So this was where Carl was getting it. Linda imagined him sitting barefoot on his bed, watching the CUP and coming across Chelsea Daye talking about this stuff, death counts and whatnot. Classic projection. Which was understandable, given all the processing work he'd been doing lately, to say nothing of the prolonged isolation.

Linda returned the rest of Deva's papers to the coffee table. *Enough snooping.* She needed to get a bandage on this wound stat.

EXCERPT

USoFA WorldWide War-Related PTSD Individualized Therapy Program (Pilot), "SoldierWell" Therapy Session #25

March 22, FY20__

1349EST

LINDA HELD

Interviewing:

SERGEANT TODD SPARROW, US Marine Corps. 2nd Tank Battalion, 2nd Marine Division

(BEGIN)

SGT. TODD SPARROW: I've got USoFA Sports, which I'll watch if I'm desperate. Then there's the Old Broadcast Hub. I watch that sometimes. Then you always have, like, some cooking show over on USoFA Home. I can't sit through those shows. Juliette used to watch those shows. She'd skip lunch if it was an engrossing episode, if they were cooking something exotic. Skipping a meal to watch a meal being prepared. Consider that your irony for the day. [*laughs*]

LINDA HELD: Any news programming?

TS: We've got all those here, but I try to avoid them, aside from the milder talk shows. Whit Knightley isn't bad. He's got that old-school broadcaster thing I like. He seems pretty well-informed about the War, too, which is rare. His guests, though... Sometimes he brings people back who annoyed me the first time, and for some reason I'm sucked in all over again, waiting to hear what stupid thing they have to say. Maybe I'm just waiting for Whit Knightley to tell them to shut up.

LH: Which particular guests?

TS: I can't think of them right now...oh, I know. I find Wanda Matthews annoying. She shows up and I just have to watch her.

LH: Who else?

TS: Maybe if you mentioned some names...

LH: What about Greg Hutter?

TS: Is he the German guy, with the white hair? Yes, he's an idiot. He actually said that our War has roots in British Colonialism. He said that. Apparently, he doesn't realize that the British have a royal family, and we don't, it's why we fought a revolution so...you know. Big difference. But I was glad for Whit, he pointed out the same thing in his response. That's why I like Whit Knightley.

LH: Marlena Jonez?

TS: I haven't seen a lot of her. I know who you're talking about, but no. No opinion.

LH: What about Chelsea Daye?

TS: Oh, well, I love her. Love her. What a beauty. She's beautiful like a...like a rainbow is beautiful. Good actress, too.

LH: Have you seen her on these shows, talking about her brother's death?

TS: Yeah. I notice they don't put much makeup on her on those shows, not as much as when she used to do the promos for her movies. It's refreshing because she's such a natural. As for her opinions, well, it's a free country. I'm sure her brother dying must've affected her very deeply, poor thing. I'd like to meet her. I bet we'd get along. The last time I saw her was on one of those shows. She gets a bit shrill when she believes she's in the right.

LH: Are you familiar with her newspaper column?

TS: Yeah, that handout thing. Like I said, I don't agree with what she's always going on about, how the War is just one conspiracy after another. It seems a little unpatriotic of her to say that. I guess, [*laughs*] I guess you could say her opinions carry less charm when you're not looking at her face. I'm joking, of course. I don't mean to objectify her.

LH: Her political views don't take away from your opinion of her as being attractive or a good actress.

TS: Well, it's not like I know her in real life. But I've seen all her movies. And there was a documentary not too long ago about Ethiopia. I watched that, I mean I could give a flying fig about Ethiopia, but after watching her for three hours I felt guilty enough to write a check for the starving kids. I think it's her face. There's something in her face that is just so genuine... she's got this capability to show emotion. Which is why it's such a shame for her to be giving it up for all this stuff about the War and her brother and all that.

[*pause*]

This might sound weird, but sometimes I can almost imagine knowing her. Chelsea Daye. It's like I've seen her in enough things to have this kind of...catalog of her facial expressions. Which, you know, which enables me to...in a fantastical way, to, like, insert her in different situations. Situations involving me, situations where I'm the star. And we go off and have adventures and stuff. And it's like...it's the reason why I'm such a big fan. She's better than anyone I can think of when it comes to emoting, displaying emotion. And I can take it all in and reorganize it for my own fantasies. I hope I'm making myself clear.

LH: Yes, you are.

TS: Is what I'm saying weird? Please tell me if it is.

LH: No, you're fine.

TS: So yeah, I'm capable of taking my memories of her, my mental images, I mean, and repurposing them. Now, here's the really weird part… I hope you don't find this off-putting, but sometimes I find myself mixing up what she says in my mind and what she says on the CUP or something, when she's on there. Just to give you an example, if you were to ask me as part of a normal conversation, say, did you see Chelsea Daye on Whit Knightley's show last night, it might take me an extra beat to remember what it was she said. And then I'd have to form an opinion about that on the fly, because, chances are, I've already reacted to whatever it is that she may have said and forgotten it already, or like replaced it with my fantasy version of what she said. So the reaction needs to happen all over again. It can get a little confusing. [*laughs*] I'm able to handle it, though. I find I can have different arguments inside my head at the same time. I like to think of any issue, any problem, as having a lot of different sides, and so the more interesting the issue, the more arguments, the more sides. Like a diamond. Because a diamond, a carved diamond I mean, is like this object with different sides… So those are my thoughts on Chelsea Daye. Great actress, limited geopolitical understanding.

[*pause*]

It's funny, Linda, now that you've got me thinking about these things. Maybe these two ideas are battling for dominance in my brain, and I don't even know when the battle is over until someone asks me, how do you feel about USoFA WorldWide's involvement in the War? I won't know what I really think until I open my mouth.

[*pause*]

But I suppose that's what we're doing here, isn't it? Talking in a nice, comfortable environment to see what it really is that I feel. It's an interesting field of study, Linda. I can see why you're pursuing it.

LH: Let's talk some more about these adventures that take place in your mind. Why do you think you think them?

TS: OK, if you're asking if they're masturbatory fantasies, they're not. I'm not real big into self-pleasure. Juliette gave me all sorts of warnings, you know, don't touch it, you'll make yourself wet your pants, don't play with it, people can see when you've played with it by the color in your face. Filling up my head with these nightmare scenarios. I sort of hated my penis for a few years, from about four or five to thirteen, fourteen. Whenever I had to urinate, I would look down and just think, you know, ugh. It got so I thought it had a mind of its own, looking for ways to have power over me… I'm being unfair. I can't pin all of this on Juliette. It's not like she went around saying these things. She'd catch me, you know, like if she told me to get out of the bathtub and put my pajamas on, and if it got too quiet in there, she'd go to the door, and if there wasn't any noise, the noise of a little boy putting his jammies on, then, yes, she was liable to open the door and she'd catch me in the act. Exploring. And then she'd start with the warnings. Because... [*laughs*] you've got to say something to a little boy when he's doing that, you know?

[*pause*]

So let me just be clear. When I say I fantasize about Chelsea Daye, I'm not saying I imagine her in...positions or something. If I ever do that, and I never do it, but if I ever *do* do that, I'm liable to pick someone I don't particularly respect. Someone from a pornographic thing. Sorry, I don't feel very comfortable talking about this, though I suppose one must cover it at some point... Basic training was awful, though. There you were, in your bunk, exhausted by some test of endurance, and there was always one moron who'd start going on about who he was thinking about while touching himself. And then some other moron would make a comment, which would then get the first moron babbling some more, and on and on. And it always fell on me to tell them to kindly shut up so we could all get some sleep, which of course was pouring gasoline on the fire. But I was mature, I realized that these people were just morons who hadn't had the opportunities I had...it was a matter of time before I'd be moving on to the next thing and they would all just fade away.

LH: I'm sorry to interrupt you, Todd...you were talking about fantasies?

TS: No, it's just, I think about her, Chelsea Daye, with me. And we're outside, in a forest or something. Fully clothed and everything. As a matter of fact, we're dressed like pirates. [*laughs*] And people are chasing us, I can't tell who. And I'm kind of the leader, I suppose. But she's no slouch, not at all. Like I imagine she's good at tying knots or setting traps or something, something valuable to the situation. We respect each other's skillsets…and we're out there, running through the forest and thinking up plans to escape these, these ogres who are after us. Stock villain types. Captain Hook, bin Laden, whatever…they're off stage, like. And while we both realize they're dangerous, we're also aware that if we put our heads together, we can survive. That's it. That's the fantasy. It exists out of time. I mean, it's just that single moment, us running through the wilderness, feeling capable, up to the challenge. I might feel her hand in mine, but that's it. I don't know what happens next and I don't care. I just want to stay in that moment and trust that whatever follows is fun and good. Sorry, this is probably disappointing. You were probably anticipating me biting her head off or something, ripping off her clothes… Honestly, Linda, if you could hear some of the things those morons would say after lights out, it would shock you.

END EXCERPT

Linda crossed her legs and reestablished her posture. She'd needed to use the bathroom for the past ten minutes, but the prospect of standing up and traversing the crowded main room of the Pink Lady scared her a little. She'd drunk half a bottle of chardonnay before her date had even come to pick her up; now she was having a tough time using her unimpaired left hand to do everything: smooth down her hair, pick up her menu.

Conversation with Derek had drifted toward what she did for the Company, and since no one had ever told her what she could or couldn't say about SoldierWell, she was sticking to how the program was first presented to her.

"OK," Derek said, throwing his shoulders back and gripping his glass, "how come this guy joined the Army if he's such a gentle soul?"

"Actually, he was sent to Iraq as part of the Free2Fight program. Are you familiar?"

"Nah."

"It's a program that rehabilitates people convicted of crimes by having them serve out their terms in War zones."

Derek laughed. "So he was in prison! What for?"

Linda shifted in her seat. "Arson."

Derek cackled with triumph, running a hand over his dreadlocks for the hundredth time.

"Hmm, criticizing my work," Linda said. "That's a risky move for someone so keen on making a strong first impression."

Derek sat up even straighter, fake alarmed. "But I was taking interest in your professional life! I was engaging!"

"That's a relief," Linda said. "For a second it sounded like you were saying my patient is a malingerer, that he's manipulating silly old me so he wouldn't have to go back to the front. Remind me, how much training in human behavior do you have?"

Derek placed his hands flat on the table. "All I'm trying to say... is... it sounds like you put your heart into your work. And I admire that. Seriously."

"Thank you."

One corner of his mouth curled upward. "Do I still have a chance?"

Linda laughed before she could think to execute the necessary eye roll. Derek was attractive, pretty much objectively speaking, and his personality was just what the doctor ordered: confident, kind-hearted, sharp yet down-to-earth. She had met him in the main hallway of Danny's elementary school during a parent-teacher conference. Greenway Academy was unsurprisingly dazzling (eleven-foot-high mastodon skeleton in the lobby, hall monitor bots, wood-fired brick pizza oven in the cafeteria), but after thirty minutes of sitting at Danny's desk and listening to his teachers yak about contextualized pedagogies and student behavior analytics, Linda acted on the strong need to exit the classroom and enjoy an unguided walk around. Derek, one of the eleventh-grade teachers, caught up with her just outside the gymnasium, asking if she was lost.

Her phone buzzed against her hip. She excused herself and checked—Miles. She had registered her unavailability with the Thera-9100 before leaving, so it must be an emergency. Damn, now she *had* to stand up and negotiate her way out of this booth...

"Sorry," she said. "Work beckons."

Derek took up the menu. "Mind if I order?"

"No, please."

"Any allergies I should know about?"

Linda shook her head—nice touch, that question—and stood. Not too bad. She pushed out sideways and set out for a restroom, taking care with each step to brace her ankles and keep her weight on her toes.

It required some effort, but over the past week, Linda had trained herself to indulge in a fantasy self: a spy, a uniquely skilled specialist infamous for her singular ability to implant murderous impulses inside the mind of any man, woman, or child. She would stalk the halls of USoFA WorldWide's innermost passages in black leather pants and thigh-high boots with seven-inch heels. Everyone would address her as Dr. Held, but among the powers that be, she would be known as The Doctor. This was the image she lent herself while striding across the Pink Lady's main room.

She was wearing her new dress, and while she'd been excited at home to find that it paired beautifully with her old peach heels, she felt ludicrous the instant she set foot inside the Pink Lady. Practically every woman in the place was donning boho: lumpy sweaters over peasant tops, chunky jewelry, Navajo-ish boots that laced up to the knee. Linda looked like an aging bimbo in comparison, in her clingy dress and scuffed heels. As the hostess—a dead ringer for young Joni Mitchell—informed them that their table wasn't yet ready and they may enjoy a drink at the bar, Linda spotted a button-nosed redhead glancing her way before leaning into her boyfriend's ear and mouthing what could have been the words *outlet* and *mall*. Derek had made it slightly better, though, ordering two dirty martinis and toasting to a lovely evening with "the most beautiful woman here. By a damn sight."

Ducking into the ladies' room and locking herself in, Linda placed her purse on the back of the sink. After relieving herself, she stood and counted down from ten before returning Miles's call.

"Are you somewhere private?" Miles asked.

"Yes."

"Good." Miles sounded like he was lying down. "My dear, you are a rock star. I've been listening to the last few Sparrow sessions, and just…bravo."

"Oh. Thank you."

"I daresay the Nexus phase is complete." He chuckled. "I knew you could handle this."

Linda laughed for no reason. "Sure, OK," she said. "I didn't think it would be so quick."

"It's good that it's happening quickly," Miles said. "We're on the right track. The drugs are doing their work. Those video games seem to be doing their work, too."

"That's good news." Linda caught herself in the mirror and turned away.

"Now we enter the Suggestion phase. Never mind trying to convince him it's in his best interest to accept everything you throw at him. Engage the *emotions*. Get him thinking about all the slights he's suffered in the past, all his misfortune. Then, connect the resolution of those slights to fulfilling the mission. The more it makes emotional sense, the less it has to make logical sense."

Linda heard the heavy clink of bottle against tumbler and wondered whether Miles wasn't so much speaking to her as thinking out loud. "I'm so sorry, Miles, but I should probably get back…"

"I was thinking, let's maybe take a few days off," Miles said. "Earnings Week is coming up and nothing will get done. I myself will be out of town for one or two days next week."

"I was hoping to get some time with Private Boxer," Linda replied.

"Take some time off, Linda. You deserve it."

"I was wondering what you thought of his last session. Private Boxer."

Miles sighed. "What do *you* think?"

"I think I need some guidance."

"All right. What kind of guidance?"

"OK… I wonder if Carl's been misdiagnosed?"

"No."

"Because this parasiting thing, it strikes me as a lot more detailed than just delusions associated with PTSD. Infections, human time bombs… I'd like your take on what I'm dealing with here."

"What *are* you dealing with, do you think?"

"Well, his story is so detailed. It has a logic. *He* certainly thinks it's real. Combine that with the head injury, self-inflicted…" She was ad-libbing now, flailing toward an idea. "I think it goes beyond the typical cries for help."

"Yes?"

"I think it may point to schizophrenia, like, a budding schizophrenia."

"A budding schizophrenia?" Miles asked, laughing. "That's your professional opinion? *Miss* Held?"

"I don't appreciate your tone, Miles."

Miles stopped laughing. "I'm sorry, Linda. I don't mean to shut you down."

"You didn't shut me down."

"Look, with Earnings Week coming up, I've been occupied with trying to justify the twelve million dollars we've been given, so forgive me if I don't drop everything to attend to your pet cause. We've got to stay focused on what's important here: inciting Sergeant Sparrow to produce an IMCI that neutralizes the threat to national security."

"An IMCI? What is that?"

Miles didn't answer, though Linda could hear his breathing.

"Miles?"

Another long pause. "IMCI stands for intentional mass casualty incident."

Intentional mass casualty incident. She knew what each word meant, but the phrase meant nothing.

"A mass shooting, Linda. It's what we're trying to generate with Sparrow."

Linda closed the lid on the toilet and sat down. "I see."

"It's the only way," Miles said. "You see, once the therapy is finished, he'll be released from the program, and then his most violent tendencies will be triggered by the withdrawal he'll be experiencing. Since he'll no longer be taking the medication he's been on since January."

"Yes. Right."

"Dear me, I've said too much." Miles burped. "I can discuss it with you in more detail at a later time. Goodnight, Linda. And good job." He hung up.

Linda went to the sink and rinsed her face. She wet a paper towel and wiped under her eyes. She took her makeup bag out of her purse and applied a little powder, then some clear gloss to her lips. Then she reapplied cover-up to the scabby mess between her thumb and forefinger. Asha's tooth hole had shrunk almost to closing, and a white crust surrounded the dark scab.

Without conscious thought, Linda pressed the thumb of her left hand into the wound. Fresh pain shot up her arm, slicing through her alcohol buzz. Her mouth watered.

She did it again, harder, twisting her thumb clockwise and counterclockwise. The pain this time had a searing quality, scaling up the back of her neck and spreading over her scalp. After a couple of seconds, she opened her eyes. The wound bled anew; a rivulet curled over her thumb knuckle. Linda waited. Blood dripped into the sink, mixing with the water there to make a wan pink. Linda took a deep breath and swallowed. She kept a fresh bandage in her purse. Cleanup only took a second.

When finished, she appraised herself in the mirror. She looked OK, felt OK. Hungry, actually. Derek had better be ordering a lot of food, but, in Linda's experience, men always ordered too much on the first date.

She unlocked the restroom door and flung it open, returning to public view. Her mother's suggestions from her teen years sounded loud in her brain: *Walk with purpose, honey. Small steps. Shoulders back. Confidence!*

Next thing she knew she was standing beside her table, smiling at her date.

"I went a little crazy," Derek said. "Five sushi rolls."

"Perfect." Linda eased back into the booth.

"Everything OK?"

"Fine. Great, actually. Seems I have cause for celebration."

Derek raised an eyebrow. "Feel like sharing?"

Linda downed the last of her martini. "I could tell you, young man, but then I'd have to kill you." She threw her head back and screamed with laughter. "No, just…work. Not a huge deal, but worth celebrating."

"Are they making you write up an Earnings Week report?"

Linda shook her head. "Do you have to write one?"

"Not this quarter, thank God," Derek said. "But I used to write a lot of them, because of the different projects I was involved with."

"What's your clearance level with the Company?"

"Beige. You?"

Linda smiled. Her hurt hand was throbbing. "Orange."

Derek bowed his head, making an "I'm not worthy" gesture. Quite the happy-go-lucky guy, this Derek. But beige was just two levels below Orange—what Company secrets could a fancy high school teacher possibly have? Linda found she didn't care enough to explore the question, not tonight.

Amid much shushing, the steady restaurant hubbub suddenly quieted down. Linda and Derek turned to see everyone in the restaurant staring at a CUP monitor that took up half of one side of the main room. On it, President Halliday sat behind a big oak desk, a dozen American flags behind him. The restaurant-goers turned toward the kitchen, helpless, before a server jogged to the middle of the dining area, brandishing a remote control. The volume came up.

"…fellow citizens, at this hour, American and Company forces are in the early stages of operations to disarm New Zealand, to free its people, and to defend the world from grave danger. On my orders, these forces have struck selected targets of military importance to undermine…"

A cheer erupted, straining Linda's eardrums. Young men in oversized cardigans slapped high fives with one another while their wives and girlfriends threw their arms into the air or did little butt dances in their seats. Linda searched for the bitch who had sized her up when she'd first come in, but she didn't seem to be around. She turned to Derek, who had his phone to his ear.

"I *told* you, man! I *told* you!" he shouted. "Before Earnings Week, I said…that's right, nick of time…I *know* it doesn't affect the numbers, but it's a momentum thing. Who's going to nickel-and-dime us on Yemen now? Exactly right… Change the conversation, yes. It's genius." He looked up and winked. "Listen, I've got to go. Aha. Later."

A sweaty server came over, placing two glasses on their table. She began uncorking a bottle of wine.

"Did you order this?" Linda asked.

Derek shook his head.

The server pulled the cork, throwing her hair back from her eyes. "Compliments of us," she said. "It's a pinot from New Zealand. We have to get rid of it."

"Or else what?" Linda asked.

"Or else they'll come and dump it all out."

"And the Pink Lady will be seen as Enemy sympathizers," said Derek.

"You got it."

Linda saw other servers doing the same thing. "Must be hard on you guys," she said.

The server shrugged. "You get used to it."

Derek took up a glass and held it under the tipped bottle, then handed it over to Linda, who gulped it down too fast and burped. Embarrassment burned within her until she realized that no one had heard—the celebratory din drowned out everything.

Linda would later remember standing next to Derek while waiting for the valet to retrieve his car, leaning into him for warmth the way other women were doing with their dates. At one point, she brushed her hand across Derek's abdominal muscles and could not believe her fingertips. By the time his car was in sight, she had worked herself into a slight tizzy, repeating *I deserve this* in her mind. Then she stepped off the curb and her heel broke and she fell square on her ass.

Chintzy piano continued playing on unseen speakers, but it may as well have stopped with a violent scratch as Linda found herself on the ground, absorbing unwanted attention.

Derek, meanwhile, had taken a giant step back—partly in surprise, partly to save his foot from getting squashed—so it fell to the parking valets to come over and help Linda to her feet. Only then did Derek swoop in, muttering *I got this* and elbowing people out of the way.

Linda, eager to flee the scene, took one step forward and nearly fell again. The pain in her left ankle was sudden and immense. "Stop, please, stop," she said, as everybody lurched to a halt.

Derek breathed hard through his nose. "OK, Linda, what are we thinking here? Want me to carry you? I'll carry you."

"I don't want you to carry me."

"OK, then you've got to *walk*, sweetheart."

"You really know how to treat a girl."

Derek clucked his tongue. A dark lock that had somehow escaped dreading lay pasted to his forehead. "OK, Linda," he said, "I'm happy to take you home, the ER, whatever, but we can't stand here in the damn *valet lane* all night. Let's make a decision, please."

Tears filled Linda's eyes. She didn't know what to do. *Please, God, just make me disappear. Right now, please, just do it.*

EXCERPT

USoFA WorldWide War-Related PTSD Individualized
Therapy Program (Pilot), "SoldierWell" Therapy
Session #17

March 27, FY20__

0912EST

LINDA HELD

Interviewing:

PRIVATE* CARL BOXER, US Army* (Associate, Transportation Services, "Free2Fight," USoFA WorldWide)

(BEGIN)

PVT.* CARL BOXER: Did you find anything out?

LINDA HELD: Not really, no. I wouldn't know where to begin. But the reported medical casualties look…off, I'll admit.

CB: I told you, Linda. I knew it.

LH: Carl, this doesn't actually prove anything.

CB: Proves I wasn't lying.

LH: I never thought you were lying.

CB: Oh, right. You just think I'm crazy.

LH: Carl, I don't think you're crazy. I think you've undergone some disturbing and stressful experiences…

CB: But can you tell me, Linda, did you check into it? What I was saying?

LH: Carl, I'm not even sure we should be talking about this.

CB: But you remember how the…whoa, what happened to your hand?

LH: Oh, it's just… it's nothing.

CB: Did you hurt yourself?

LH: My neighbor's dog bit me. [*laughs*] It's just a nip.

CB: That's a lot of bandage for a nip. I've been nipped by dogs before, I never needed all that tape. Whose dog?

LH: My mother's boyfriend's. They were on their way out, and Deva, that's the boyfriend, he pulled a leash out of his coat and handed it to me and he goes, I owe you one, darling.

CB: He owes you more than one.

LH: And as soon as I open the door, the stupid dog shot out into the street. Then it was half an hour of watching him figure out where he wanted to do his business.

CB: I bet you rushed him, didn't you? And he bit you?

LH: No, I wouldn't dream of rushing him. You should see this dog, Carl, he's beautiful but a real beast. No, it was after we got inside and I was taking his leash off, I was just, like, petting him behind the ears, just to say goodbye, and he turned his head and bit me. I was already pulling back, so he just managed to get me right here, that fleshy part.

CB: What is it? What breed?

LH: Siberian Husky. Totally white. Beautiful animal.

CB: Were you bleeding?

LH: Yeah, I ran to the kitchen and got a paper towel and I tucked it under my other arm like this, but…the blood was so…steady. Pouring out.

CB: Did you get light-headed? My ma always gets light-headed with the sight of blood.

LH: You know, sometimes I do, but this was just the opposite. Just… standing there, it was so red… I kind of fell into this dream state, an escape.

CB: From what?

LH: No, just…the self. The usual. It was only a few seconds.

CB: It's funny, what you're saying about escape. I know what you mean. It's like…something like that happens and everything you were thinking, it's like, no time for that now. Because of what's going on with your body.

LH: Right, the pain, whatever else it does, it places you very much in the present.

CB: Yeah, and everything you were worried about, it's just whoop, out the door. Like a broom or something.

LH: Yes!

[*pause*]

CB: I've got to know, Linda, did you check into it at all? The parasiting?

LH: I did come across one thing, yes.

CB: Weird, right? The casualties?

LH: Yes. And the fact that no explanation seems forthcoming is notable. But…

CB: But what?

LH: I hate that you're putting me in this position… I'm finding it very odd that no one else has ever heard of it before. I've talked to a lot of soldiers, Carl, soldiers and Marines. I guess I'm just wondering how is it that someone of your…

CB: How come a truck driver knows so much.

LH: Why you, Carl? Can you talk about that?

CB: Let me think for a minute… OK, I told you about the tell, right? How you smell bread?

LH: Yes.

CB: All right, so bread means dead. That was the saying going around. But a couple weeks after that first one, with Morrison, I got to be what they called a Designated Driver. I didn't know what I was getting into. For a while they had me shadowing the controlled det team, like they...

LH: Controlled det team?

CB: Yeah. Detonation. Like if there's a car bomb, they need somebody to clear the area and set it off safely. I was trained for that, nobody told me why. So I was doing that, shadowing them, and then one day the captain comes in and he says, are you the jailbird that's on controlled det? And I say yes sir and he says come with me.

[*pause*]

So being a Designated Driver means transporting the soldiers that've already been parasited out to this...it's what they call the preordained all-clear area but it's just the middle of the desert. Middle of nowhere. You drive them out and you leave them, that's it. Somebody gets shot or something, they come in hot, they've got to go sit in Last Circle and wait to be examined... then it's, hey, does anybody smell bread? Then the parasited ones get in the van with me and we haul ass out to the all-clear area, then I snap a salute and get out of there. [*laughs*] After three months of research and bomb-sniffing dogs and all this CSI bullshit, the best anyone comes up with is taking these poor sons of bitches out to the middle of nowhere and leaving them. But that's the Army for you.

[*pause*]

So this is what it was, for me. Twelve hours on, twelve hours off. I sit in the van, I got my triple-reinforced Kevlar…it goes over my head and I'm covered to about the knees. Weighs about forty pounds…after wearing it in the heat, day after day, I mean…it was new when I got it, but it didn't take long before it stank like something just… I must've dropped twenty pounds in the time I pulled that duty, just wearing that thing, God almighty… Nobody, and I mean nobody, wanted to see me when they came back from out there. These guys, they'd get back, they're sitting in Last Circle and putting their gear down and their hands are shaking…and there's me, sitting inside the van, waiting for somebody to say they smell bread so I can start up and drive them out to die. Just this big Kevlar idiot…I was like death to them. And then, just as bad, you see these guys that've already been cleared, and they're all standing in line, and some of the guys waiting to get cleared, they're all sniffing around. Even the ones who aren't hurt, they're sniffing, trying to see if they smell bread.

[*pause*]

LH: Carl?

CB: So it was on my second day of doing this...second or third...this team comes back on a helicopter. They were up in the mountains and there was an ambush on this trail. And one of our guys is hit in the collarbone, just above it, and right away this guy says, hey, who's making pancakes... and that's it, they call it in.

[*pause*]

So I'm ready, the clock's started. And he gets there, and the first thing is I'm relieved because it's not somebody I know. It's one of these older guys, older than me, like late thirties...and he knows exactly what's going on, you can see it on his face. He's good about getting in the van, you can tell he wants to follow procedure, they had all these talks about it, meeting after meeting, everybody had to go...and he's on the double. And at the same time, he's trying to make sense of all this. And a couple guys are watching him and they're saying brave man...I had about four minutes to get him to the all-clear area. And he starts crying, realizing what's going to happen. They told me to be prepared for this... And I had my eye on the clock and I'm thinking of my orders...I'm telling you, the only thing keeping me in the van is my hands on the wheel, looking over at this guy, who's got his head in his hands, crying...and he pulls out a phone. We're not supposed to have them, it was one of the things with USoFA World-Wide taking everything over, they want everybody to be on *their* phones, Company phones. But this guy pulls out like his personal phone. And the funny thing is…it's a burner phone that I got for him. I had gotten this phone myself, I remember, on the black market. [*laughs*] I had a bunch, and I was selling them off for two hundred apiece, I knew some of the guys wanted them for sex with their wives or partners, they didn't want it recorded. Easy money. So I'd seen this guy before, Staff Sergeant Forrester, I remembered him…and he's sitting there, calling his girl, but she's not home…so finally he gets control of himself and he leaves a message, he says please tell everybody I say hello. And then he's saying bye and real quick he goes, by the way, I'll never see you again, they're going to blow me up now. Then he says just kidding and hangs up. I mean…what am I supposed to do with that?

[*pause*]

LH: Carl, it's all right if…

CB: So the clock hits and I'm inside the all-clear. I slow down. And now I'm supposed to climb out and snap a salute, and that's the sign for the guy to get out. So I do that, I salute him, but Forrester just sits there. He's still in the van, looking out on the desert, not even crying now, he's just…not there, you know?

[*pause*]

Now, the procedure is, the fucking procedure is, you know, die like a soldier. Have some dignity

and don't put anybody at risk…so Forrester looks
at me and he says, no, fuck your salute, I'm
about to fucking die. Tell me goodbye. But even
if I want to, I got too much on with the Kevlar,
I can't say anything. And the clock now, it's
beeping, got to go, got to go…so I snap a salute
again and he says nope, not good enough. So I
wave…and I mean…if you've ever seen Mickey Mouse
at Disney World, that's what it looked like. And
now the clock's going beep beep beep, danger… So
I start taking my headgear off…I was going to say
goodbye. And he sees me, he recognizes me, and
he starts laughing. Can't believe it, he can't
believe that my ugly ass is the last person he's
ever going to see.

[*pause*]

Then I remember. Pistol in the holster. And without even thinking about it I reach back behind me
and I pull it out and I'm holding it on him and he
smiles and says, goddammit, I should have known.

[*pause*]

I shot him. It just went off.

[*pause*]

So now he's got this perfect circle in the middle
of his eyebrow, but like his face is still saying I should've known. Then finally his head drops
back against the seat like a baby, like a little
child…I watch that for a second, and then I run
around the other side and pull him out…because

I'm panicking, you know? I'm just thinking not me not me not me. [*indecipherable*] Big hero, right?

[*pause*]

Because he wasn't getting out of the van, Linda. [*indecipherable*] I mean, I pissed the suit, Linda, and the clock's going beep beep…I just get out of there, just leave him in a heap, head pouring out blood. And I get back to camp and I eat four helpings, four, of Swiss steak. And a little bit later the chaplain comes over and he says they noticed a bullet missing from the emergency pistol, did I want to talk about what happened. Thanks, Father, but no way.

[*pause*]

I keep thinking about it.

LH: I'm so sorry, Carl. But your actions saved lives.

CB: Sometimes I think, when people see me, look me in the face, they know. They know what I've done. Because it comes from inside. I'm rotten in there.

LH: You served your country, Carl. Nothing could be done for that man. You removed him from where he could've hurt others.

CB: No…that's not even true, Linda. That's not true.

LH: What do you mean?

CB: Forrester was a dud. [*laughs*] He wasn't parasited. He just *thought* he smelled bread. I was
out there the next day and he was still there,
still in one piece except for what the birds got.
He never had it.

LH: Oh.

CB: If I hadn't shot him, if I hadn't been there,
if I was never born the way I was, he'd be alive
right now.

LH: Oh, Carl.

CB: [*indecipherable*] I keep thinking about it.
I wasn't thinking about it when I got here, I
didn't remember. But you got me going, Linda,
talking, and it just…the memories keep coming
now, they're so clear, I mean… [*indecipherable*]
He wouldn't get out of the van!

LH: I'm so sorry, Carl. This War is a terrible
thing.

CB: Goddamn, you said something there. This is
hell, Linda. It doesn't stop.

[*pause*]

You know, I understand… I understand if you got
to go tell somebody. Do what you got to do.

LH: Tell? Why would I tell somebody?

CB: Because. I killed one of ours. They sent
me over there to drive trucks, keep my mouth

shut... And now somebody's dead because of me. It's like what we were talking about before, sending somebody off to that, that nothing. That black. That's the sin, you know?

LH: Carl, who would I tell? They might take you away from me, and that's not going to happen.

CB: All right. All right... Ah, damn. Can I get a minute, please?

LH: Of course.

CB: OK. OK, thanks. Let me just... [*indecipherable*]

LH: Take it easy, love. You've said what you had to say. You don't have to say anything more.

CB: Are you leaving?

LH: I'm not going anywhere. I'm right here. Take it easy, now. Lie back if you want to.

CB: All right...

LH: I'm not going anywhere.

CB: We don't have to talk. Just...be here with me, please.

LH: I know. I'm here.

END EXCERPT

NOT FOR PUBLIC RELEASE

KEYNOTE ADDRESS: USoFA WorldWide "War" FY20__ Q2 Earnings Videoconference

March 31, FY20__
1300EST

CORPORATE PARTICIPANTS

Leonard Leitch, President, USoFA WorldWide, Temporary War Division

Nathan Barnicle, CFO, USoFA WorldWide, Temporary War Division

Peter Lampré, COO, USoFA WorldWide, Temporary War Division

Tim Nestor, Executive Vice President of Media Relations, Region 1, USoFA WorldWide

CONFERENCE CALL PARTICIPANTS

[ERROR 221; ERROR 221; ERROR 221]

John Raul, Northern-Southern Securities

Suzanne Joncas, Analyst, Quell Industries

PRESENTATION

Operator:

Good morning. I'm here to talk to you today about a company. A very special company: United Syndicates of Federal Assistance WorldWide.

Founded in what would have been Fiscal Year 20___ through the historic three-way partnership of Exxon-MoChev Dynamics, ComDisApp Media, and GE-LockRaythe & HalliDyn Security Solutions, USoFA WorldWide (Ticker: USoFA) is made up of 1.6 million employees working tirelessly with the United States Department of Defense to protect and enhance the lives of all Americans. Picking up the mantle of leadership when sustained economic instability and rank political partisanship threatened the nation's very ability to defend itself, USoFA WorldWide has gone on to do the impossible, many times over.

If you're of a certain age, you no doubt remember a time when the balance between safety and privacy was a delicate one, and people had next to no choice when it came to their advertising experiences. That's all in the past now, as USoFA World-Wide has expertly harnessed the twin **[ERROR 221; ERROR 221; ERROR 221]** powers of technology and human-to-human cooperation to effectively solve these problems and more. Recent advances in cancer research have brought us closer than ever to a cure. Our world-renowned Compliance Unit Publishing (CUP) technology has made the internet safe again, filtering out 99 percent of all hate speech and online predation. Smoothie kiosks in school hallways and cafeterias enable children—our most precious national resource—to remain healthy and obedient. Our self-splitting USoFA stock shares, now available to 13 percent of the public, allow those of us living on smaller incomes to enjoy USoFA WorldWide's every success. Yes, as our beloved Chair Edna H says, we take care of our own.

It's no secret that Edna H considers the passage of the Temporary War Law of FY20___ a milestone, not just for the Company but for the nation. A lifelong patriot and fully documented American citizen, Edna H considers USoFA WorldWide's management of the War to be the highlight of her spectacular career.

And it's no coincidence that USoFA WorldWide has chosen this FY20__ Q2 Earnings **[ERROR 221; ERROR 221; ERROR 221]** Videoconference to serve as the keynote address in its weeklong Q2 FY20__ Earnings Week Celebration. On today's call, USoFA representatives **[ERROR 221; ERROR 221; ERROR 221]** will make forward-looking statements within the meaning of Section 27A of the Securities Act of (FY)1933 and Section 21E of the Securities Exchange Act of (FY)1934, as amended. Undue reliance should not be placed on any forward-looking statements, and USoFA World-Wide disclaims any obligation to update or announce any revisions to any forward-looking statements contained herein. Please feel free to visit USoFA WorldWide on the CUP for additional information.

And now we turn **[ERROR 221; ERROR 221; ERROR 221]** the videoconference over to Leonard Leitch, president of USoFA WorldWide's Temporary War Division.

Leonard Leitch, President and CEO, USoFA WorldWide, Temporary War Division:

Thank you, everyone, for joining us today on the USoFA World-Wide "War" Q2 FY20__ Earnings Call. I am assuming those in attendance are eager to return to their Earnings Week festivities, so I'll dispense with formalities and get right down to business.

But before I begin, you may notice a low rumble during my remarks and the remarks of those following me. I want you to know, there's no need to adjust your monitors or anything like that. What you are hearing—if you're hearing anything, that is—are the chants of a dozen or so protestors outside the building we are now in. Which is odd, since our location was never disclosed to those below Lavender Security Clearance. Now, while we are of course supportive of every American's First Amendment rights, we were also made aware of some uh, well, some pretty amazing advances in what they call noise suppression, developed by USoFA Food and Industrial Research out there in Roswell, New Mexico. And so that low rumble you're hearing is the side effect, I guess you could say, of a three-inch-thick clear plastic canopy that we've placed over the designated First Amendment zone here. I can't pretend to know how it's done—science was never my strong suit [*laughs*]—but I am told the plastic is porous enough to allow oxygen to flow freely in and out but also dense enough to muffle whatever they're going on about in there. If you look at it in a certain frame of mind, we're doing these folks a favor should the weather take a turn for the worse. In any event, we're glad they could be with us today.

Now, without further ado…

To summarize our results for the second quarter, revenues from continuing operations grew to $2.7 trillion, up 3 percent from the same period in the prior year. EBITDA for the quarter was $954.9 billion, up 1 percent over the prior year. And EPS for the quarter was $0.37, up 11.6 percent from the prior year.

Through the first half of the year, we successfully executed strategies to drive Wartime performance, and our quality metrics continue to improve. We are growing USoFA WorldWide with recent weapons acquisitions and we are operating efficiently. The Company has a relatively longstanding history of solid Wartime operations. It is these operations that remain a core competency of our security leadership personnel.

We remain focused on recruiting the right individuals from the appropriate communities and townships, mostly the Midwestern and Southeastern United States, as well as New York and Pennsylvania. New recruiting efforts in Alaska, Hawaii, Puerto Rico, and Guam have also paid off. All of which is to say, everybody's pulling their weight, it seems, and we are on track, once again, to exceed our annual recruiting targets. Personally speaking, I think it's got something to do with those new uniforms, that brilliant new design, which was our own Tim Nestor's baby. So that's something else to be pleased about.

In other news, we maintain a solid balance sheet with strong cash flows and ample liquidity. Our financial strength allows us to make strategic investments in our military, including new technologies and ongoing base renovations.

While we maintain a focus on being the sole freedom and liberty provider in many smaller, more hotly disputed communities, we are also repositioning our portfolio by moving into faster-growing War markets with a more favorable battle mix. But let me be clear: USoFA WorldWide is a *disciplined* buyer. With our strong balance sheet and track record of quick and successful integration of recent acquisitions, we are confident that we can continue to identify and integrate new "hot zones" all over the globe, adding value for our stockholders.

Meanwhile, given the changing industry and certain legislative dynamics, we recognize that regional scale matters, and building strong relationships with leading weapons providers is more important than ever. By forming networks in specific regions, we believe we can enhance the quality of War that we provide, thus ensuring that Enemies are in the most appropriate and cost-effective setting to receive our weapons' discharges. And *that* is the differentiating strategy for this War.

In summary, we have made continued progress on our strategic initiatives in the second quarter. We are well-positioned in the War markets we serve and excited about upcoming skirmishes and police actions, particularly in New Zealand. We also remain focused on delivering value for our stockholders through the current fiscal year and beyond.

With that, I would now like to turn it over to Nathan Barnicle to discuss our financial results for the quarter in more detail. Nate?

Nathan Barnicle, CFO, USoFA WorldWide, Temporary War Division:

Thanks, Leonard. Can everyone hear me? I've got my microphone turned up as loud as it can go... OK, I'll try and just hit the high-lights that I know are most important to you all, but in case my mic goes out halfway through, let me go ahead and refer you now to the summary tables in front of you.

Second-quarter trends include growth in same-War admissions, solid pricing, and good cost management, producing strong earnings growth. As we've discussed over the last several quarters, we continue to invest in both internal and external weapons production resources to position our...

Operator:

Thank you.

Nathan Barnicle, CFO, USoFA WorldWide, Temporary War Division:

Hello? Hello? OK, as I was saying, we continue to invest in internal...

Operator:

Thank you.

Thank you.

[*pause*]

Thank you. We apologize for the delay.

Leonard Leitch, President and CEO, USoFA WorldWide, Temporary War Division:

Uh, Operator? Is...

Operator:

Thank you.

Our next question comes from the line of

[ERROR 221; ERROR 221; ERROR 221]:

Good morning, gentlemen. Allow me to congratulate you on another successful quarter.

Tim Nestor, EVP, Media Relations USoFA WorldWide:

Wait a minute...

Leonard Leitch, President and CEO, USoFA WorldWide, Temporary War Division:

Excuse me, who is this?

[ERROR 221; ERROR 221; ERROR 221]:

This is Chelsea Daye, with *The Citizen*?

Leonard Leitch, President and CEO, USoFA WorldWide, Temporary War Division:

OK. Did you have a question?

Tim Nestor, EVP, Media Relations USoFA WorldWide:

No, Mr. Leitch, she's not on the list...

[ERROR 221; ERROR 221; ERROR 221]:

I just wanted to ask...I was poring over your quarterly statement last night, and...

Tim Nestor, EVP, Media Relations USoFA WorldWide:

I'm sorry, Miss Daye, did you just say last night?

[ERROR 221; ERROR 221; ERROR 221]:

Yes.

Tim Nestor, EVP, Media Relations USoFA WorldWide:

OK, I'm going to go ahead and take issue with that. Our statement was not officially released until the time this videoconference went out. What you were looking at, Miss Daye, is either a fraudulent statement or there's been a security breach, and you'll need to speak with a USoFA WorldWide representative as soon as possible. We shouldn't be talking to each other... Operator?

[ERROR 221; ERROR 221; ERROR 221]:

Fine, I'll do that, promise. But what I wanted to ask was, I didn't see any breakout on casualties accrued on the battlefield versus casualties accrued under medical supervision? That's appeared in former statements, so I was wondering if there was a reason for the omission.

Leonard Leitch, President and CEO, USoFA WorldWide, Temporary War Division:

Omission in what, now?

Tim Nestor, EVP, Media Relations USoFA WorldWide:

Miss Daye, this is a quarterly earnings call. We're not here to discuss the manner in which every last casualty is counted, and it's not something I think our stockholders need to delve into at this time.

[ERROR 221; ERROR 221; ERROR 221]:

I'm sorry, but I beg to differ. I imagine your stockholders would be very interested to learn about the Enemy's newfound ability to kill huge *swaths* of American soldiers inside various USoFA-run medical units. There's a rumor going around...

Tim Nestor, EVP, Media Relations USoFA WorldWide:

Miss Daye, I'm not going to discuss this with you at this time, and I'm quite sure my colleagues aren't interested in discussing this with you at this time. If you'd like, you can contact my office after this call, and we can sit down and get answers to all your questions in a mutually respectful...

[ERROR 221; ERROR 221; ERROR 221]:

I'd like that, Mr. Nestor. What's your direct line there?

Leonard Leitch, President and CEO, USoFA WorldWide, Temporary War Division:

All right, I think we can all agree we've had enough gotcha questions for one day. Nate, do you want to go ahead with what you were saying?

[ERROR 221; ERROR 221; ERROR 221]:

I'm still here, gentlemen. I'm happy to rephrase my question.

Leonard Leitch, President and CEO, USoFA WorldWide, Temporary War Division:

Operator?

[ERROR 221; ERROR 221; ERROR 221]:

Still here, gentlemen. And I'm waiting for one of you to...

[CROSSTALK]

Leonard Leitch, President and CEO, USoFA WorldWide, Temporary War Division:

OK, that's fine. That's fine. Thank you. Operator? Next question, please?

[CROSSTALK]

[ERROR 221; ERROR 221; ERROR 221]:

Evidently, there's been some collusion with foreign chemists formerly employed with the CIA...

Leonard Leitch, President and CEO, USoFA WorldWide, Temporary War Division:

Operator!

Operator:

Thank you. Our next question comes from the line of... Chelsea... Daye...

[ERROR 221; ERROR 221; ERROR 221]:

As I was saying, are your stockholders, and your advertisers, for that matter, are they aware that our soldiers are in no way prepared, mentally or physically, for the challenges that the Company's global approach to...

Tim Nestor, EVP, Media Relations USoFA WorldWide:

Goddammit...Operator!

Operator:

Thank you. Our next question comes from the line of John Raul, with Brent Hutchinson Securities.

John Raul, Brent Hutchinson Securities Analyst:

Hello?

Tim Nestor, EVP, Media Relations USoFA WorldWide:

Go ahead, John.

John Raul, Brent Hutchinson Securities Analyst:

OK…what did I want to…oh, yeah, is there any way to give us a sense of the impact that some of these new battle configurations I'm seeing on Table 16 might have on, like, overall strategy?

Peter Lampré, COO, USoFA WorldWide, Temporary War Division:

Hello, John, this is Peter…I think I can speak on that one. Those battle configurations are the result of a new schema in how we're reporting those numbers. They're geared toward finishing this thing in a way that won't have too big of an impact on the overall economy. Does that answer your question?

John Raul, Brent Hutchinson Securities Analyst:

Sure. But what about the casualty breakdown? Is Chelsea Daye asking…

Tim Nestor, EVP, Media Relations USoFA WorldWide:

Not at all, Jim.

John Raul, Brent Hutchinson Securities Analyst:

It's John?

Leonard Leitch, President and CEO, USoFA WorldWide, Temporary War Division:

Next question, Operator?

Operator:

Thank you. Our next question comes from the line of Suzanne Joncas, with Quell Industries.

Suzanne Joncas, Analyst, Quell Industries:

If I may, gentlemen, are you saying the reason for the lack of casualty breakdown results for this quarter is a response to…

Leonard Leitch, President and CEO, USoFA WorldWide, Temporary War Division:

I'm sorry, as much as I hate to do this, we're getting some serious static on this end, and I'm getting word that our protestor friends have decided they'd rather not contain themselves to the designated First Amendment zone, which is unfortunate. I'm afraid we'll have to cut the Q&A at this time.

In closing, let me just say that we continue to focus on executing our strategies which have resulted in growth of revenue, EBITDA, and EPS for the quarter. Our emphasis on investments and attracting the best recruits provides an opportunity for value creation at USoFA WorldWide.

The balance sheet gives us lots of flexibility… We have an infrastructure with a proven track record… Continue to target Enemy strongholds in faster-growing markets… As always, we will continue to focus on efficiently managing this War, and we look forward to continued discussions with you on these results. Thanks for joining our call today, thanks for your interest in USoFA World-Wide. Operator?

Operator:

Thank you. Ladies and gentlemen, this concludes today's video-conference call. We thank you for your participation and ask that you please disconnect your lines. Please stay tuned for the USoFA WorldWide Global Citizenship Report.

NOT FOR PUBLIC RELEASE

The walls of Visitation Room #1 were painted white, save for a pair of thick stripes running parallel across the top. The top stripe was a dark orange while the bottom stripe was yellow, though due to time or maybe some reaction to the caged light-bulbs overhead, the yellow had almost completely faded, and so now it looked like the white was doing a strained imitation of a yellow stripe, to the orange stripe's amusement. Miles had been waiting for a while.

After some key-turning and heavy door sliding, a prison guard with an unkempt gray mustache shuffled in. In one of his hands was a metal folding chair, identical to the one on which Miles sat. In the other hand was a small, square, pink satin pillow. Nodding once in greeting, the old man whipped open the chair and placed it near the side of the table opposite Miles. He placed the pillow on the seat before stepping back and taking a moment to appraise his work, then left the room.

A moment later, Mitch entered Visitation Room #1, making a racket with the chains around his wrists and ankles, accompanied by another mustachioed guard. Though his head was lowered, he appeared upbeat, his eyebrows raised and a meaningless half-smile on his lips.

"Holy mackerel," Miles snickered, remaining seated as instructed. "Your hair is totally white."

Mitch kept his head bowed, observing the guard unlocking his ankle cuffs. "And you've gained weight!" he declared, sounding like an old-timey game show host. When his hands were free, he wagged them in a show of relief.

The mustache straightened and asked his prisoner. "Would you like me in or out, Mr. Crawley?"

Mitch pressed a thoughtful forefinger to his lips. "I'd rather out, Hal, thank you."

"Real good, sir. I'll be right outside if you need anything."

Both Miles and Mitch watched the guard exit, turning toward each other only after the door slid shut.

"Miles!" Mitch shouted, grinning with fake surprise as if they had spotted each other across a crowded airport. A winking commentary on the intrinsic banality of greetings. Miles noticed Mitch was standing very straight, his chin up and his shoulders back, and felt a piercing disappointment. He had been anticipating the day he would find his older brother stooped, burdened with age and regret.

He and Mitch had grown to be the exact same height—five foot eleven—but you wouldn't know it from looking at any family photo taken within the last thirty years. At some point in his late adolescence, Mitch began standing on his tiptoes for every picture. Every one. Even operating at the outer limits of his empathy, Miles could never understand such a thing. Sure, maybe it was some weird idea you get into your head as a kid, and then you do it because you think it's funny, and then over time it becomes a habit: "Say cheese!" = stand on tiptoes. But there were a few years in there when Mitch would stand next to Miles and put his arm around his shoulder, which Miles interpreted at the time as an aberrant yet sincere stab at brotherly affection. It was years before he realized it was just another way for Mitch to use Miles as leverage with which to gain another inch or two, and the realization of such colossal smallness had been so deep and grievous that, to this day, Miles could make himself literally dizzy thinking about it.

"You're my second visitor this week," Mitch said, pulling his chair out. "It's like Grand Central Station around here."

"Who was your first?"

Mitch waved the question away as he took his seat. "Some writer. Wanting to explore my *personality*."

"I bet he left disappointed."

"Ha."

"What was he writing? Another exposé?"

"Some listicle for the CUP. 'The Twenty Most Dangerous Criminal Minds of All Time.' Whoopie."

"Congratulations."

"Thanks a bunch."

"So where did you rank?"

Mitch did the thoughtfulness thing again, blinking at the ceiling. "Eleventh. Five under Manson, which is *such* a joke."

"Yeah. It's just a big popularity contest these days."

"I know you're joking, but I think there's some truth to that." Mitch raised his hands as if appealing to the gods. "Seriously, how hard is it to coerce a bunch of hippie runaways?" The question bounced around the windowless room.

"You have to admit, you took a little from Manson."

"Please. LSD is for amateurs. It's a blunt instrument. There's nothing you can do with LSD that you can't do with a few beers and a lot of repetition."

Miles nodded. "Where'd they rank Bundy?"

Mitch rolled his eyes. "First."

"Well, who can say no to that face?"

Mitch laughed; he couldn't help himself. Miles laughed in kind. Good ol' sibling chitchat—from long experience Miles knew his brother would not be rushed. Miles thought of the swimming pools of his childhood, how Mitch always took fifteen minutes of walking around the edge, dipping toes and asking about temperatures before finally getting in the damn water.

"Anyone else drop by?" Miles asked.

"Oh, the mother of one of my knights paid me a visit," Mitch said. "That was nine weeks ago."

"Which one? Nathan?"

"Anthony."

"Ah." Anthony Barber had been an angel-faced sophomore and first-chair clarinet at the prestigious Calvary High School in

St. Louis when Mitch had first gotten his hooks into him. Last Miles had heard, Anthony was living in a forensic mental hospital in upstate New York, bloated from years of antidepressants and various experimental add-ons, eyes like rainbow suckers. "What did she have to say?"

"Oh… 'Damn you to hell,' that sort of thing. Shaking like a leaf the entire time. If I had to guess, I would say her therapist put her up to it. Hey, if it helps to yell at *me*, fine. Knock yourself out, madam."

"Hm. Where is Anthony? New York still?"

"I believe she said Florida, but I may have misheard."

"Still in the system, though."

Mitch picked at some invisible something on his lap before nodding at the gift on the table. "Is that for *moi*?"

Miles pushed the gift forward, humming "Happy Birthday."

"Enough," Mitch muttered, taking up the gift and setting it in his lap. His fingernails had grown out; their color matched the yellowish stripe on the walls. "You brought it in like this? All wrapped up?"

"No, I had to open it at the security checkpoint, but then one of your guards wrapped it back up once I made it down here."

"Trevor." Mitch grinned. "He's such a sweetheart." Mitch tore into the gift like a toddler, grunting with recognition as the wrapping paper fell away. "Oh, boy," he said, "I know what *I'm* doing tonight." He turned the record over and began reading song titles, credits. Teasing a platter halfway out of its paper sleeve, he let out a low whistle.

"It's an original pressing," Miles said. "I had a guy appraise it. He said it's pristine."

"I was going to say, it looks mint." Mitch held the record up to the light. "This must've cost you a fortune."

Miles sat up a little straighter. "I can swing it."

"I bet you can."

Miles crossed his legs while waiting for Mitch to finish his examination of goods. Everything was going well so far—Mitch seemed in good spirits, energetic and quick-witted.

"Oh, I play guitar now," Mitch said. "Did you know that?"

"Is that why your fingernails are so long?"

"No, I use a pick."

"Who gave you a guitar?"

"Excuse me, I bought it with the money I earned."

Miles could feel himself grinning. Surely a reference to money being earned opened the door to a discussion of business matters. Best not to pounce on the initial consent, though. That's what Miles taught his therapists: Never disrupt the natural flow of conversation. Steer it. "They let you play in here?"

"I play whenever I want," Mitch said. "I'm no Charlie Christian, but one of the screws is teaching me some blues *licks*, I believe is the idiom." Mitch placed the record in his lap, gently cracking open the gatefold sleeve and skimming what looked like the artist's bio.

Outside of this newfound interest in blues *licks*, nothing Mitch was saying came as a surprise. His brother could do anything he wanted here except leave, and it didn't seem like he ever wanted to leave. Once, about five years ago, Miles got to see inside Mitch's cell. It resembled nothing so much as a miniature bachelor pad from the 1970s, its cot's thin mattress buried under heavily tasseled pillows (gifts from deranged fans), vintage erotica posters on the cinder-block walls, a lavender sheepskin throw rug. Most if not all of these accouterments were strictly prohibited by his keepers, but this was Mitchell Crawley we were talking about—the guards didn't stand a chance against his nigh-feline penchant for creature comforts. He could get African rhinoceros horn powder delivered directly to his cell if he wanted.

"Dead at twenty-five," Mitch murmured, "Goodness gracious."

Miles counted down from three before asking, "I don't suppose you got a chance to listen to those sessions I sent you?"

Mitch carefully placed everything back on the table, then let his arms fall to his sides. He closed his eyes. "I love this Linda person. Where'd you find her?"

Miles reached into the breast pocket of his shirt and clicked his voice recorder on. "She applied," he said. "She's a psych student at UMBC."

"Hm. What does she look like?"

"She's pretty." Miles shifted in his seat.

"Young?"

"Mid-thirties."

"Brunette, right?"

"Excellent guess."

"What's the situation? Married?"

"No, single. She has a son who just turned twelve."

Mitch clutched at his chest with one hand. "Get me a picture?"

"I'll see what we can do."

Opening his eyes, Mitch sneered and crossed his arms. He knew equivocation when he heard it. Miles again shifted in his seat—this chair was killing him—and braced himself for one of his brother's Harmless Suggestions, the afterthought request that would result in Miles setting up a face-to-face between Linda Held and Mitchell Crawley, the eleventh most dangerous criminal mind of all time. No matter how much Miles prepared, no matter how well-traveled he felt amid the dark alleys of effective persuasion, Mitch was the Master, acting purely on the instinct of genius. Miles could recall with perfect clarity the gray December afternoon, forty-four years ago, when an eleven-year-old Mitch had talked the Griffin kid from down the road into throwing his pet cat out of a third-story window.

"What about Sparrow?" Miles asked.

"What about him?"

Miles shrugged. "What do you think?"

"I think the young man has issues."

"Wow, Mitch. Your powers of perception, I mean…"

"His mother. Something is going on there."

Miles winced. "Everybody keeps saying that, but I don't see how you can gracefully…it just seems so…Freudian."

"I'm not saying he wants to *bang his mom*…"

"No, I know."

"But if you don't take the time to address these mother issues, they're going to bite you in the ass. Because once something like that comes out, that's it. He's useless, as far as this project is concerned."

"OK, so what do you think is going on with him? With the mother?"

Mitch shrugged. "I have no idea."

"Abuse? Sexual abuse?" Miles sat back, shaking his head. "No. The application process weeds all that out. I would've seen it. No, I think it's much more likely he's got a mother with some narcissism issues, nothing more."

"Well, let's hope you're right," Mitch said. "Because none of this works if the patient's been seriously abused. What do I always say?"

"Right, right. 'The subject will always be true to his first abuser.'"

"Very good." Mitch raked his white hair back with his hand. "Oh, tell me this, has Linda been churlish with you recently?"

"Churlish?"

"Sullen?"

"In a way, yeah. I think her acceptance of the mission is more a work-in-progress than it was with the others."

"You got off easy with the others. Men in this position, young men, they're eager to please, eager to move up. Females are trickier. They see all the responsibility and it makes them wary."

"The responsibility of what?"

"This Nexus stuff runs both ways, Miles. I can't say whether Linda is fully conscious of it, but I would bet she feels responsible for these patients. That sense of protecting Sparrow, her investment—emotional investment, time investment— sometimes it can result in resentment toward someone looking to exploit that. Like you."

"Huh."

"It's not necessarily a bad thing. I remember one of my knights, it may have been Anthony, I can't remember...one of them was grumbling about something I had suggested. After days of this, I suddenly realized he was crying out for me to give a little more of myself. You talk about subjugation, Miles, and that's fine, I agree, the subject's sense of self must be absorbed into the action being suggested. But before that, give her a little something."

Miles nodded, checking to ensure his recorder was getting this. Mitch was on a roll. This was exactly what Miles had driven seven hours for.

"Invite Linda *in* a little more," Mitch said, his eyes closed again as he worked the air with his hands, packaging his thoughts as he gave voice to them. "Offer her a peek behind the curtain. Because she's not rebelling against the SoldierWell program, or even against you. She's tired of being in the dark." He opened his eyes.

"I took her to the Showing of the War a couple of weeks ago. I thought it might help her feel a part of something bigger."

"That's just spectacle, though. Fine as far as it goes..."

"I was wondering if her upbringing—that whole binary morality thing. I wonder if that might be gathering itself for, I don't know, a kind of last stand."

"What, is she Catholic or something?"

"Raised Catholic, yeah. She says she doesn't believe anymore, but I've found that stuff has a way of getting into a person's bones. The guilt and whatnot."

Mitch made a seesawing motion with his shoulders. "OK, then you need to get her to realize she's operating in an entirely different world than her patient. Make the patient, this Sparrow fellow, make him an 'other' in her eyes. Which shouldn't be too hard, because she knows something that he doesn't, and that puts him on the outside. Because what else do I always say?"

"'The keeper of the secret always has the advantage.'"

"Exactly. Kind of like with you and me." Mitch's ensuing laughter turned into a cough, mild at first, then forceful. "Anyway," he said, "give a little, and I bet your girl loses the 'tude."

"OK." Miles was bouncing his knees. "How long, in your opinion, I mean I know you can't tell, not knowing her or anything, but how long before we get to the Subjugation phase, would you say?"

Mitch blinked. "I have no idea. Six months?"

Miles suddenly wanted to lay his head on the table. It felt like every time he took a moment to consider his work, to really take the long view on it, another unseen dimension made itself known. Chelsea Daye was on the cusp of putting everything together, and when she did, Edna H would need an efficient, clean solution. Was Miles supposed to just say sorry, come back in six months?

Meanwhile, SoldierWell West was on a course to fail, spectacularly. The problem, it was now plain to see, was that the Subjugation phase had not taken hold as well as it should have, and so Turnout had been premature. This was entirely Miles's fault—he had panicked during the Company's Earnings Week audit of the SoldierWell program and blurted out that he could probably finish up SoldierWell West in a mere matter of days, under budget, so swimmingly were things proceeding in Oregon. Now there was a traumatized, radicalized veteran out there, crazed with withdrawal, totally unstable. Innocent people would be hurt.

"What's the matter?"

Miles raised his head. "Just…circumstances. We've got an enemy of the state going around, and…"

"And you made promises to the powers that be."

Miles nodded.

"Promises you're in no position to make." Mitch tut-tutted. "Who's the target of all this, anyway?"

"That's confidential."

Mitch leaned forward, laying his bright white arms on the table. Torn wrapping paper rustled under his elbows. "Whisper it to me."

Miles sighed. "Come on, man."

Mitch sat back. "You're right," he said. "I don't want to know." He rearranged himself, crossing his legs and settling his arms in his lap. "But you've worked so hard for this. All this time and effort and it still feels like you're at the starting line."

Miles turned away, reaching into his shirt pocket and softly pressing the recorder's OFF button. Very soon, he would stand and exit this room. The civil portion of his visit was over; things were about to get ugly.

This was how it started: Mitch would find that secret, deep-down wound in a person and use it as a way in, a way behind. A couple of choice observations would then hollow out the person's sense of self, leaving them open to whatever suggestion came next. *Perhaps no one in American history better harnessed the dark potential of personal intimacy than Mitchell Crawley.* Miles had come across this sentence years ago while wandering the shabby stacks of a bookstore in Boston—it had been in the foreword of a "shocking bestseller" detailing his brother's life and crimes.

"So you're not a wunderkind," Mitch said. "I can only imagine how that must feel. 'We know what we are but not what we may be,' as the Bard said."

"Oh, fuck off with your Bard."

Mitch tapped his birthday gift. "Strange, isn't it? The way those who succeed in youth seem to be the only ones mentioned in the history books? There's just such a *decisiveness* about making your mark at a young age. Like you've been preordained."

Miles stood and went to the door behind him, pounding it with the flat of his hand. *Damn*, he thought, *I forgot to ask about SoldierWell West. Oh, well, too late now...*

"No, I'm serious!" Mitch said. "You really are doing wonderful work, for someone of your years. And, hey, you're only as old as you feel, right?"

Catching the eye of the old guard, Miles nodded. *We're finished.* "Happy birthday," he called out over his shoulder.

"Oh, and Dr. Young?"

Miles turned.

"About SoldierWell West..." Mitch made a sad clown face and shook his head. "I'd concentrate my resources on matters *East*, if I were you. That Linda girl, she's a winner."

Miles felt better outside. He walked to the perimeter of Red Onion State Prison, signed himself out, crossed a one-lane road, and got in his car. In the trees beyond all the squatty, shoebox-shaped buildings, he could see the electric green of little buds lined up on branches. In ten minutes he was perched at the bar of Cornpones and ordering a whiskey neat; he could have kissed the bartender after she asked to see his ID.

Post-visitation trips to Cornpones was a self-imposed tradition. The first time he had spotted the dead neon sign standing tall at the entrance of the gravel parking lot, something about its backward R and, just underneath, in nauseating Comic Sans, "True Southern Quizeen," ignited within him a yawning, merciless nostalgia, and with sudden tears in his eyes he had turned in. After his last trip out to see Mitch, one of the servers had told him that this very restaurant prepared the last meals for all of Red Onion's death row inmates, which seemed about right. Their chicken salad game was strong, anyway.

Miles sipped his drink and shrugged at himself in the spotty mirror behind the bar. *So you're not a wunderkind.*

Maybe he would just stay here for the rest of the day, fill up on fully loaded nachos and get good and stinko on well whiskey. He could consult the bartender on what a guy with some cash might do for fun around here. Find a motel nearby, someplace he could defile and abandon.

Nothing got done during Earnings Week anyway. Since the passage of the Temporary War Act—with each fiscal quarter reporting, predicting, and evangelizing exponential growth for USoFA World-Wide—Earnings Week had become a kind of Company-approved Mardi Gras, the Region One campus a business-casual Bourbon Street. Miles had tried listening in on the Temporary War Division's Second Quarter Earnings Call (like most USoFA WorldWide employees with decent security clearance, Miles's personal worth was all tied up in the Company's fortunes overseas), but the feed dropped out once he made it out of town and onto I-81 South, the Blue Ridge Mountains on either side. Probably just as well. He wasn't sure how much he could take of Old Man Leitch droning on about how proud he was of everybody.

Miles now found himself staring at a stock photo of Leonard Leitch on the CUP monitor at the other end of the bar. Strange. The volume was muted, but the chyron underneath read ...BREAK-ING NEWS... USoFA WW EARNINGS CALL CUT SHORT DUE TO 'SECURITY CONCERNS'...

His phone rang. The name on the screen read NESTOR TIM. Before answering, he spun on his stool to look out on the empty dining area.

"Miles Young."

"Tell me you're on the East Coast right now."

"More or less. Why?"

"There's a situation." Nestor sounded spooked, out of breath. "Did you hear Temp War's Earnings Call?"

"Just the beginning. Was there an issue?"

"Yeah, you could say there's an issue. You might even say we've got a goatfuck on our hands. You and I need to figure some things out, my friend. When can you get here?"

"About six hours, give or take."

"All right…wait, where *are* you?"

"Deepest Virginia." Miles downed the rest of his drink. "Research."

"OK, just… I *may* be able to send a chopper. Find the nearest helipad and call me back."

Miles chuckled. "You really are desperate."

"Look, just find one, then call me when you're ready to get picked up."

"What about my car?" Miles asked, but the line was dead. Spinning back around, he settled up with the bartender. He used the restroom and exited Cornpones, grabbing a handful of starlight peppermints at the door. His mood had lifted; the intensity of this work never failed to override everything else in his life. His father had been the same way—the man could not wait to get out of bed in the morning, could not wait to go out and sell, sell, sell, no matter how late he'd been up the night before. *Salesmen are born, not made,* he used to say. *Your brother Mitchell, now there's a salesman.*

Miles laughed out loud. *Oh, Daddy, if you could see me now.* Little Miles, so quiet and shy, charmless little Miles Crawley, who always had to wait in the car and watch the boxes, now entrusted with twelve million smackers to prove you wrong. *Of course* salesmen could be made. This wasn't *art.* It wasn't *voodoo.* It was formula, a code to be broken down and defined. You want proof? How about the biggest company in the history of the world sending a damn *helicopter* to pick him up so that he could help fix a goatfuck, whatever that was? How about that, Dad? Did you ever ride in a helicopter?

And where was the born salesman of the family these days, pray tell? Oh, that's right, rotting away in a supermax prison in the middle of nowhere, that's where.

Miles keyed into his car—Porsche—and slid behind the wheel. Through his windshield, way at the other end of the parking lot, he spotted a homeless man hobbling toward a battered wide-load trailer, its tires sunk halfway into a strip of bright orange mud past where the gravel tapered off. Next to the trailer's open door hung a sky-blue bedsheet that read "FOOD PANTRY COME IN!!!" in red spray-paint. A dozen or so poors milled about just outside, heedless of the mud and thick weed stalks. Miles observed his bum friend approach and get absorbed into the loitering mass, though nobody seemed interested in his copies of *The Citizen*. Everybody was looking up at the trailer's doorway as if a show were about to start.

It soon dawned on Miles what was happening: these sad bastards had all come to this trailer for tumorous carrots and dented cans of wax beans, but getting inside was proving problematic, as the doorway hovered a good three feet above the ground and no one had thought to bring stairs or a ramp. Miles caught himself smirking in the rearview mirror. *What a splendid metaphor for the progressive cause,* he thought. *Good intentions, zero follow-through.*

A thin guy with wild hair appeared in the trailer's doorway. He displayed his scrawny arms like a Depression-era weightlifter (light applause in response to this show of strength) before crouching down to take hold of the wrists of an elderly woman in a red raincoat.

Bad idea, Slick. The thing to do is take everybody's order, then hand the food down.

The guy started counting. Everyone joined in: *Oooooone… twooooooo…three!*

What happened next was like a gift from above. The guy heaved and wound up tumbling backward, disappearing into the trailer, taking the elderly woman's raincoat with him. At the same time, the elderly woman, coatless, dropped to the mud like a sack of toy whistles.

Miles laughed and laughed, then laughed some more, tears streaming down his face. He laughed so hard he leaked a little in his khakis. He laughed so hard that a few of the poors turned to see who or what was the cause of that unhinged cackling noise. He had never laughed so hard in his life.

APRIL FY20___

The Oven was a three-story red brick amphitheater located in the middle of the USoFA WorldWide Region One campus. Linda had passed the structure often during her wanderings, every time wondering at its purpose, placed as it was between two office towers. The path leading to the Oven was this morning littered with wet confetti, the dye of which was running out, smearing the pavement in red, white, and blue. She entered through the Oven's double doors, passing under a sign that read YOU ARE NOW ENTERING A SENSITIVE COMPARTMENTALIZED INFORMATION FACILITY.

Miles stood just inside, waiting, his eyes bloodshot and his face in need of a shave. A white plastic bag dangled from his grip. "You're just in time," he said.

"In time for what?"

Miles pointed at a narrow flight of steel stairs nearby. "Follow me."

The stairs opened onto the hardwood floor of a loft. Orange- and aqua-colored plastic chairs stood about. Linda was reminded of the loft of her childhood church, back when her father played guitar for the choir. In her mind's eye she saw Dad unhooking his black guitar case, where there awaited his Martin D-28 and a fat songbook titled *We Celebrate*.

Miles pulled together three chairs so that they all faced outward, over a railing of plaster topped with stained wood. He placed his plastic bag on the middle chair and took a seat on the right. Linda watched him dig into the bag, producing two Styrofoam clamshells, one of which he handed to Linda. Her empty stomach grumbled.

"You brought me up here to eat breakfast?"

"Quickly," Miles whispered, motioning for her to sit down. "Before the presentation."

Linda approached the railing and looked out. The Oven was much larger than it appeared outside. Rows of seats faced a stage the same stained wood color as the top of the railing. Onstage was a lectern and behind it hung an enormous projection screen.

Statement by

Dr. Eloise Jorden

Director, Defense Advanced Research Projects Agency

Submitted to the

Subcommittee on Intelligence, Emerging Threats and Capabilities

US House of Representatives

Linda went to her chair and sat, taking up plastic knife and fork. She ate scrambled eggs and a sausage patty, hash browns, and a biscuit with grape jelly. Her coffee was black, which was how she liked it these days.

When they finished, Miles took up their trash and stuffed it back into the bag, tying the handles together and stowing it under his seat. "We should be starting soon," he whispered, dragging his chair closer to the railing and directing Linda to do the same.

Next to Miles, Linda again looked out. What she saw frightened her, though she couldn't say why: a gathering of fifty or so people, not yet seated, holding close to the stage. Servers with round silver trays butted into conversations, taking drink orders.

"What is this?" Linda asked, her attention drawn to an older woman in a pink pantsuit. "Is that Congressman Blaine?"

"We are not here," Miles whispered.

Linda spotted the blond comb-over of Tim Nestor, seated in the front row, surrounded by chattering assistants. She leaned back and turned to Miles. "What is this?"

"Please keep your voice down, Linda. You'll see."

"Are we about to witness some mass orgy? Animal sacrifice?"

Miles made a pained face and brought his forefinger to his lips. "I've brought you here because I need you to see with your own eyes what the Company is dealing with. Consider this your peek behind the curtain."

"Is this above my security clearance?"

Miles nodded, sitting up straighter.

Linda saw a thin woman, her hair parted down the middle, walk out to the center of the stage. Wearing a bright smile, she waited for everyone to take their seats.

"Chairman Blaine, Ranking Member Reardon, Members of the Subcommittee, thank you for calling this meeting today and thank you for inviting me to testify before you and the many esteemed representatives of the United Syndicates of Federal Assistance WorldWide. My name is Eloise Jorden and I am the Director of the Defense Advanced Research Projects Agency. It is my pleasure to be here before the Department of Defense Science and Technology community.

"Our organizations work together every day to strengthen our defense technologies, technologies that hold the potential for extraordinary advances in national security capability. However, as Federal budgets over the past decade have contracted, DARPA has seen drastic reductions across all demonstration programs. I invite the Subcommittee and esteemed representatives of USoFA World-Wide to keep this in mind as I report on our seven-week effort to replicate an effective Timed Improvised Explosive Corporeal Accessory, otherwise known as a parasite. Slide, please?"

Linda gasped, loud enough for Miles to place a hand on her shoulder. On the projection screen appeared the words THREAT OVERVIEW: THE DARPA CHALLENGE.

"I'm very pleased," Eloise Jorden said, "that this alarming trend in Enemy-led terrorism is being taken seriously, as indicated by the presence here today of members of the Central Intelligence Agency, the Department of Defense, the House Committee on Foreign Affairs, and the New Iraq Study Group. With so many cooperative bodies joining forces, I believe that parasiting will be swiftly dealt with and swiftly eradicated."

The audience broke into applause. Miles took his hand off of Linda's shoulder to join in.

"At the same time, I will say that we underestimate the effects of parasiting at our peril. Speaking as a military and commercial explosives expert with more than twenty-five years' experience, it is my professional opinion that the parasites we have seen in and around Mosul, Baghdad, and elsewhere represent not so much a new stage in the evolution of improvised explosive devices, IEDs, but an entirely new technology. It is, in my opinion, the single most effective ground weapon since the self-loading rifle. Slide?"

The words PARASITE: OUR ENEMY'S TACTICAL ADVANTAGE appeared onscreen.

"During Basic Training, US Army soldiers have long been taught that it is more tactically advantageous to wound an Enemy combatant than to kill him. Shoot to kill, and you take out your adversary. Shoot to *wound*, and you take out that adversary plus at least one other, since he or she must retrieve the wounded under typical 'no soldier left behind' protocol, a protocol that carries across virtually all military cultures.

"Parasiting augments and exploits this protocol. Infect the adversary with a parasite, and not only do you take out your adversary, you take out whoever may come to retrieve that adversary, plus anyone riding with that adversary back to camp, and—should his wound appear serious enough to merit immediate medical attention—any and all medical personnel, including doctors, nurses, volunteer workers, non-parasited wounded, and so on. And with the sorts of timed detonation patterns that we have seen, the parasite's destructive effects have all too often reached their full potential. In fact, internal reports show that, since the debut of the parasite, casualties among American medical personnel have increased by nearly sixty percent. Slide?"

A spike grew inside of Linda's chest. Carl was right. Chelsea Daye was right. She turned to Miles, who kept his gaze fixed straight ahead.

On the projection screen appeared the words REPLICATING THE PARASITE: DARPA'S "ACTION TEAM" APPROACH.

"When USoFA WorldWide approached us seven weeks ago to discuss the creation of a microscopic incendiary device with no detectable fuse that, once implanted, could delay charge for up to twelve minutes, we selected sixteen of our most respected program managers to form what came to be known as the Action Team. After reviewing materials sent us by the US Armed Forces and USoFA WorldWide, this team of all-stars underwent a single, sustained brainstorming session that lasted forty-eight days.

"While the Action Team's efforts to replicate the parasite were not entirely successful, the DARPA board found this approach worthy of further pursuit, provided additional time and funding. Slide."

The words BIOLOGY AS TECHNOLOGY appeared onscreen.

"Long one of DARPA's most promising areas for future capabilities, synthetic biology—the hybrid discipline of biology and engineering—has long held our fascination as a means of discovering and producing materials for use in the next generation of mechanical and electrical products. As we have sought to harness synthetic biology to better serve humanity, the Enemy has been using it to more destructive ends.

"Keep in mind, this is not new. In 400 B.C., Scythian archers turned biological agents into weapons when they dipped their arrows into blood and animal manure before marching off to war. And one need only look back to the first decade of this century to recall the imminent threat of a 'dirty bomb,' that radiological weapon designed to explode and contaminate the area with radioactive material, creating lasting detrimental health effects for any living thing within the area.

"But while an Enemy-made dirty bomb detonating inside the US has yet to occur, the parasite is well upon us. Slide."

A close-up photograph of a goat appeared onscreen, its eyes yellow and doll-blank. Underneath were the words, REPLICATION OF PARASITE: THE JENNIFER EXPERIMENT.

"During brainstorming, the Action Team determined that a parasite exists not *inside* of a bullet but rather on the *outer jacket* of the bullet, as a coating or resin. Slide."

The goat photo was replaced with a cross-section of a bullet.

"The Action Team concluded that these bullet jackets held either a functionalized carbon nanotube or functionalized graphene sheet. These two colloids can combine to create a catalytic action that, when bonded with iron-rich human blood or calcium-rich human bone, has the potential to create enough energy for the quality of detonations we've been seeing in Iraq. However, efforts to put this theory into practice have proven problematic. Conducting experiments on ten animals with biochemical makeups similar to those of human beings, only one replicant caused any significant catalytic action. I believe we have that video?"

The bullet vanished, replaced by a video of a goat standing on a spotless white tile floor. In the corner of the screen was a running digital clock.

"This is Jennifer," Eloise Jorden said. "Don't get attached."

Some in the audience snickered. Linda wondered what could be so funny before realizing *oh no are they going to show us how they…*

"OK, after we install our parasite replicant…"

A blast of rose-red burst from the goat's stomach, causing it to collapse.

The goat's jaw must have broken in the fall, for now it appeared too far to one side, the white-pink tongue lolling over adobe-colored lips. Blood flowed from the eye-shaped tear in the goat's side like water from a garden hose on half-power, spreading between Jennifer's splayed legs to swirl with the quickly widening puddle of clear urine. Jennifer's eyes were gripped behind tight lids, her nostrils and lips vibrating in muted screaming.

Eloise Jorden, who had taken a few steps back and appeared to be observing the footage with casual patience, like someone who had watched it many times before, returned to the lectern. "OK, in less than seven minutes, we're going to see the first signs of our replicant doing its work."

"Are we supposed to just sit here for seven minutes?" Linda whispered.

"Six minutes," Miles said, nodding at the screen.

The theater was as silent as the footage. *Yup,* Linda thought, *we're all just sitting here, watching a goat suffer in its final moments, no big deal. This is reality.* Another minute ticked off. Linda gripped her armrests and told herself not to leave her body.

"Pardon me?" A voice from the audience. "I just thought, since we're waiting…"

"Go ahead."

"So our troops haven't killed or captured *any* Enemy soldiers with one of these, uh, these coated bullets?"

"That is my understanding, yes. Which suggests they're only being issued to select soldiers, perhaps those capable of quick retreat.

It also points to a possible overreliance on small drone strikes. After all, very few Enemy fighters can *be* captured once our drones finish a skirmish. I do know that our best interrogators are working tirelessly to elicit useful information about the parasite, so it's just a matter of time before we find out how it's done. Any other questions while we're waiting? Yes, in the back?"

"Returning to what you were saying…*if* DARPA were to receive the third-party funding needed to produce an effective replicant of the parasite, would this third party have exclusive access to the technology? Or, at least, right of first refusal?"

Eloise Jorden leaned hard on the lectern. Onscreen, one of Jennifer's hind legs began to twitch in a backward kicking motion. "Are you asking whether this third party would own the patent on a replicant? Like for commercial purposes?"

"Well, for that party's protection."

"I'm not sure I'm the right person to answer that. Back when we were working more closely with the Department of Defense, sometimes they would apply a secrecy order on this or that technology because it might undermine national security if it fell into the wrong hands."

"Right, but—and pardon me for saying—USoFA WorldWide *is* national security now. If you hadn't noticed."

Laughter trickled from more than a few people in the crowd as Eloise Jorden shrugged. "I suppose the third party that funded the project would have exclusive access, yes. But I'm not a patent lawyer, so…"

With two minutes remaining, the camera zoomed in. Jennifer's eyes were open, though rolled back. The kicking had slowed. Linda imagined an acceptance taking place. Dammit, she would *not* weep over the death of a goat…

Eloise Jorden checked her wristwatch. "OK," she said, "we're going to see evidence of catalytic reaction right… *now*."

Foam, like the head on a glass of beer, formed at one corner of Jennifer's mouth, building vertically for a moment before tipping and spilling out past the edge of the frame. Jennifer was no longer a goat but something else: a lumpen, leaking, biological curiosity. Linda aimed her gaze at a spot of wall to the right of the screen. She would *not* leave her body, she would *not* weep, and for God's sake she would most definitely *not* throw up.

"I think that's enough of Jennifer," said Eloise Jorden, and suddenly the footage was replaced by the words FUTURE COUNTERMEASURES: IMAGINING THE POSSIBILITIES.

"Before I conclude this presentation, I'd like to say that, during our seven-week brainstorming session, many individual members of the Action Team wondered about the safety risks of the Armed Forces' current approach to dealing with parasited soldiers—the transporting them to designated explosion areas and such. A kind of side project was launched, resulting in the designing of the Single Capacity Detonation Containment System, or SCDCS."

The words onscreen were replaced by a black-and-white graphic showing a rectangle. Above it stood two smiling stick men.

"Roughly the size and shape of an old telephone booth, the SCDCS rises from underground and opens to allow the parasited soldier to enter."

The box rose to the level of the two men. The man closest slid into the box.

"Once the parasited soldier is inside, the SCDCS closes. Then, operating on traction steel ropes, the SCDCS lowers to its recommended distance of four hundred feet."

The box sank down the screen. Once it reached the bottom, the smiling stick man was replaced by a fireball.

"With walls made of lead-reinforced concrete and an interior coated with polytetrafluoroethylene, containment of the ensuing explosion would be total. And cleanup is a snap."

The fireball disappeared. The box then rose again, up to the second stick man. At the end of his hand appeared the nozzle of a hose, which sprayed at the rectangle.

"I'd like to close by saying that I am mindful of the challenges our nation faces and the difficult environment in which we work. But I am also excited about what lies ahead and I am confident that, with the support of both the Subcommittee and USoFA WorldWide, DARPA will continue to play a role in redefining our national security landscape and ultimately winning the War. Thank you."

Tepid applause. Linda looked over to see Miles already disappearing down the stairs. She stood and followed him down, gripping the cold railing.

Miles paced in small circles while Linda stared at a pair of plastic champagne flutes resting atop the blades of a nearby patch of grass. "So Carl's been telling the truth," she said. "He's seen parasiting firsthand. He's seen people die with it."

Miles stopped pacing and, turning to Linda, shrugged.

"You kept me thinking he was delusional," Linda added. She wasn't angry; she was trying to define for herself the scope of his deception.

"You're weren't authorized to know, Linda."

"But now I am?"

"No, but I thought it would be good to clue you in. You now know everything I know."

Linda nodded. "What does this mean for SoldierWell?"

Miles glanced toward the Oven's entrance. "Come," he said, "let's get out of here before everyone sees us."

Linda hurried to keep up with Miles's strides. Her bum ankle was acting up. Campus felt like a closed themed park, the taller buildings reflecting a sun Linda couldn't find in the sky.

"The Company's just trying to get out in front of this as best we can," Miles said. "Remember how I said the only thing that can weaken the Company's public standing is if the stock takes a dive? Well, this parasiting thing, this is *just* the thing that puts us in the shitter. The slightest hint that we're not winning the War and that is *it*, Linda. We need to be seen as winning all the time."

"But what does this mean for SoldierWell?"

"We've just been given the go-ahead to conclude SoldierWell East within the next four weeks."

"We're shutting down?"

"What? No. No, see, the timing is actually really good here. You've achieved Nexus with Sparrow, and that's the most time-consuming phase of the INSIST Technique. So now, I think that quickly finishing up with the Suggestion phase, and then maybe combining the Impetus and Subjugation phases—none of it should be too disruptive. Now, why is that, you might ask. Well, let me answer by pointing out the consistency principle here. I had some guys in Consumer Behavior analyze a few of your most recent sessions with Sparrow and, let me tell you, he already defers to you on a number of points. He is so driven to appear consistent in his thinking that I think ratcheting up our demands on him won't be much of a leap at all. And, keep in mind, we've still got four whole weeks to soften him up." Miles nodded, looking pleased with how much sense he was making. "Honestly, Linda, there's no reason to see this new timeframe as some kind of setback. We've got the wind at our backs now... What?"

"Nothing," Linda said. "I'm just waiting for you to say April Fool's."

Miles peered at her. "You think I'm joking? I am not joking. People are dying over there because of this thing."

"I can't believe this, Miles. You said yourself, six months at a minimum. We're barely two months in, and you want me to wrap everything up?"

"Linda," Miles said through closed eyes, "I'm going to need you to get over it. This is a new framework."

"What about Carl?"

"Oh, Carl is done. You don't have time for that anymore."

"What happens to him?"

Miles shrugged. "He goes back to Iraq, he goes to prison, whatever. You've got other things to worry about now."

Linda spotted a nearby bench and sat down. The only person in her life she looked forward to seeing anymore was Carl. It had been that way for weeks. Soon she would have no one. "Let's send him home," she said.

"That's your recommendation?"

"Yes."

Miles nodded. "Fine."

"Thank you."

Miles moseyed toward the bench and stood before her. "You look tired," he said. "Is the ankle still keeping you up at night?"

Linda laughed. "You look like you haven't slept in three days."

"Maybe let's tweak the dosage on your Sertanin. You're going to need your rest wherever you can get it."

Linda wanted to thank Miles but held back. "Aren't you forgetting something?"

"What?"

"How am I supposed to do all this when I still don't know who the Darling is?"

Miles slumped. "You're kidding."

"Not that I know of."

"It's Chelsea Daye," he hissed. "Chelsea Daye is the Darling. How could you not…" He looked away, shaking his head. "OK, you know what? That's my fault. I should have been clearer from the beginning. I'm sorry if it feels like I'm rushing you through this."

"Why her?"

Miles narrowed his gaze, bewildered at Linda's inability to keep up. His blue eyes had darkened. "She infiltrated the Earnings Call," he said. "I thought you said you watched the videoconference."

"I did. I watched the playback."

Miles nodded. "OK, the playback, so you wouldn't have heard it. No, Chelsea Daye crashed the call during the Q&A. She hooked up with her Hater friends and hacked into our tech support so she could ask a bunch of nonsense."

"She was asking about parasiting, wasn't she? She's close."

"She committed a serious security breach, Linda. There's a system in place for press questions and she violated it."

Linda shook her head. She couldn't stop. "It's too real now. It's too real. I've been going along, eager to please the Company, eager to please you. Now that I know her name and I can see her face, Jesus…"

"Listen to me, Linda. This is important. Do not be fooled by our Darling's efforts. This is an *actress*, remember." Miles sat down next to her. "What she's been doing lately, this protesting, writing for a newspaper, spreading all this slander…it has to stop. Lives are at risk."

Linda let her head fall back against the top of the bench. The sky was such a dense gray that it felt like a low ceiling, inches away from her nose.

"But see, that's why this is such a great opportunity for us," Miles said. "The powers that be are looking to you and me for help. Think about it, Linda, if this is successful… Let's say it's successful. Let's say SoldierWell does what I know it can do. Then we can take out the terrorists hiding in plain sight all around us. No more Patriot Act, no more data mining, surveillance… This program marks the first step toward the ultimate maintenance of law and order. A populace that polices itself, that finds its own threats and expels them, on its own."

Linda brought her head up. "But Chelsea Daye *isn't* a terrorist, Miles! She's a journalist who's telling the truth!"

"She's an enemy of the state, Linda!"

"She's an enemy of the Company, Miles!"

"It's the same thing!"

As Miles's voice carried across campus, Linda opened her arms. "How am I supposed to react to this, Miles? How should I react?"

Miles stood, brushing down the chest of his sweater. "React however you want," he said, "but keep in mind that it is not your job to question anyone's decisions, including mine. Your job is to apply the INSIST Technique as directed, and you've been given more than enough time and resources to do your job. You don't have to worry about making rent or going to classes, no more student loan debt, no more credit card debt…you don't even have to worry about your son's care. There is nothing to get in the way of you and the job. This is the job."

Linda took a deep breath and attempted to herd her thoughts into something she could see as a whole. She was going to have to continue involving herself in the death of a human being, who she now knew to be Chelsea Daye, and she could no longer counterbalance that by saving Carl because Carl was being taken from her. But continuing to involve herself in SoldierWell meant she could keep Robert, and the CF Clinic, and Dr. Bolaño, which meant she would still be saving her son. A little nefarious persuasion in exchange for her son's life. Who wouldn't make that deal? What kind of mother would she be if she walked away now?

"I want to make sure Carl is taken care of. He should be sent home. And I want to be the one to tell him. I want to say goodbye."

Miles laughed. "I can see that everything remains at a standstill until you get your little show of goodwill," he said.

"It's the least you can do."

Miles slid his hands into his pockets and beckoned her with his elbow. "Come," he said, "let's get some coffee."

"I'm going to stay here for a minute. Get my bearings."

"OK. Come to my office when you're ready. Not too long." Miles took a few backward steps before turning and walking away.

Linda watched him go, then realized she didn't know where she was. The Oven was nowhere to be found, though what might have been one of its neighbors was visible, a gleaming pillar holding up the concrete sky.

Four weeks.

Chelsea Daye.

She could quit. She'd still come out ahead. Her school bills were all paid, she was on track to graduate within the next month… Let them kick her out of that house, make them go live in Spectator Heights, or whatever. She'd been poor before. She knew how to do it.

And Danny was healthier than he'd ever been. Last week, Dr. Bolaño had said he was ready, physically, to undergo the transplant procedure. If she could somehow maintain that level of readiness, without anyone's help, until they could get a transplant via non-Company-assisted means…it wasn't impossible.

Plus, she could go find Carl, out in the world, visit with him, see how he was doing. She knew where he was from, had even looked it up on the CUP once or twice. She could fly into Cape Coral, then take the Cape Coral Bridge into McGregor. From there it was a fifty-mile drive down to Bonita Springs, and she'd probably start seeing signs for Twin Groves soon after that…

Four weeks.

Chelsea Daye.

Not that she needed it, but it might have been nice if she had her Sertanin with her just then. Just one or two and she could remain on this bench for an hour or so, watch the world go by. Initially, Linda had no interest in the pills Miles had pressed on her, but damn if they didn't install a wonderful feeling of contentment along with knocking out her lingering ankle pain. Taking those pills was often the best part of the day. By 2100 sharp, she would have everything just the way she wanted: pajamas and bathrobe on, slippers off, bottled water on the nightstand, bedroom suite temperature set at 72 degrees. A moment on the back of the tongue, a swig of water, and *voila*: Linda's situation, all her problems, all her *stuff* would turn wan and watery, something easily dispensed with until tomorrow, replaced by a warm and shiny feeling in the pit of her stomach and the beautiful ability to talk to herself like a loving mother. Yes, her dreams were often violent, and more than once she had woken to find she had wet the bed, but, hey, a few nightmares and the occasional extra trip to the laundry room beat the hell out of waking up panicked in the middle of the night, defenseless against damnations of her own making: *this is murder, this is murder, this is murder, this is murder…*

Linda took a deep breath and wiped the tears from her eyes. She would get up soon. She would follow Miles into that agglomeration of office buildings and express cafes and SENSITIVE COMPARTMENTALIZED INFORMATION FACILITIES, and eventually make it to his office, where he would give her more pills so that her ankle wouldn't keep her up at night.

Four weeks.

Chelsea Daye.

EXCERPT

USoFA WorldWide War-Related PTSD Individualized Therapy Program (Pilot), "SoldierWell" Therapy Session #25

April 2, FY20__

1613EST

LINDA HELD

Interviewing:

PRIVATE* CARL BOXER, US Army (Associate, Transportation Services, "Free2Fight," USoFA WorldWide)

(BEGIN)

PVT.* CARL BOXER: I guess it's good, right?

LINDA HELD: Of course!

CB: Well…I'll miss you, Linda.

LH: Thank you, Carl, I'll miss you, too. More than you know.

[*pause*]

CB: They said I could just leave?

LH: Yes. We're making some changes, so…

CB: Time to kick out the dead weight.

LH: No, you've just been deemed…the powers that be saw your progress and they decided you didn't need to be here any longer.

CB: That's what they said?

LH: Yes. Look, all I know is this is supposed to be our last session. Let's not spoil the little time we have left poking holes in things.

CB: You're right.

LH: We should discuss what you plan on doing after this. You've got to be pleased about going home, right?

CB: Yeah, sure. It beats jail. [*laughs*] And it sure beats Iraq.

[*pause*]

They're just going to write off my assault charge?

LH: As far as I know. You've been cleared to go home. I don't imagine they want to continue with the trial.

CB: Oh. OK.

LH: What's it going to be, then? What do you plan on doing?

CB: Oh, you know. The usual. I'll probably stay with Ma for a while. Catch up, you know.

LH: Yes. Reconnect.

CB: You know what, Linda? I've been thinking about something. I'd be interested to hear what you think.

LH: Tell me, please.

CB: I was just...I think I'm going to do something when I get out of here. I've been thinking about this, like, maybe I could go and speak out. Against the War. Or against how we're handling things. I was thinking I could contact somebody next time there's a protest somewhere, and I could go and talk to people, get hooked up that way. What do you think, Linda? I think I can do it. I could tell people what I did over there, show them pictures of the people I drove. Say what happened. I could tell them about Forrester, what I did, and then if they lock me up, well... I'll just be in prison again. But at least people will know what's going on over there. What do you think, Linda?

[*pause*]

LH: I don't think you want to do that, Carl.

CB: You don't?

LH: No.

CB: Oh. How come?

LH: Well, for one thing, you'd be reliving the most painful memories of your experience there. And what do you think that would do to your living a normal life? No. It's not safe.

CB: I'm just... I'm talking about what happened over there. About parasiting and my driving people out to die. The truth.

LH: The truth? Your truth? No. It's not safe.

CB: Oh, wait…you're not worried about USoFA, are you? You don't got to worry about that, Linda. I won't make you look bad. I mean, this Soldier-Well thing, this is a great program. You're doing great work. I was just thinking about getting out there…

LH: The fact is, Carl, you signed up to serve over there. And you, of all people, you understood the sacrifice that might be involved. But now, instead of accepting that, you're just going to run out and complain? It's not safe.

CB: No, I'm telling people what they don't know! And letting them know my part in it! I'm no angel! But they watch the highlights of the War, Linda, they look at the CUP, they keep score like this is some game. I'd be telling them that's not how it is!

LH: Why? Why do they need to know? So they can thank you? What about the real soldiers? What about the mothers and fathers of the people you drove? Should they thank you?

CB: No. But maybe they can forgive me.

LH: What if they don't? And there you are, talking about what you did. Getting famous off it.

CB: I don't want to be famous. I just want to tell people.

LH: All right. Do what you want. It's a free country. But let me ask you one thing. Please think of the opportunity you have, right now. You can do anything you want, Carl. You've got a little money, you can go back to school. You can get an apartment, you can go on dates, travel… You're a good person, Carl. You've done your time, you've served your country. You're free. Please don't torch that by talking about all the terrible things going on over there. It's not safe. No one wants that. And that's what we're defending. Not just the freedom to live without terror, but to live in a world where we don't even have to know about it. Because, if there's someone always reminding us, then we're not really living without terror, are we? What kind of protector goes back to his flock and tells them all that he's done?

CB: You know, Linda, I don't know from flocks, I was just…

LH: Is that what your uncle did? Did he go on and on about the things he saw?

CB: No.

LH: He never even said how he got that Silver Star, did he?

CB: All right. I was just thinking about it. Maybe we should talk about something else now.

LH: Fine. We can talk about anything you want.

[*pause*]

CB: It's just, when I joined up with Free2Fight…I told you this before, I wanted to help. I wanted to get out of prison but I also wanted to help.

LH: And you have. You did what you were ordered to do. You made important sacrifices. You saved people.

CB: [*laughs*] Doesn't feel like it.

LH: What's it supposed to feel like?

CB: Like being able to hold my head up. That's what I know it to be. My uncle Ray, he fought, he lost his legs, but he was able to hold his head up. He had that.

LH: You want to feel like a hero.

CB: No…yes…it's supposed to feel like something you're not ashamed of.

LH: But Carl, you are a hero. Those medics, nurses, the other patients, all those people you protected. They might not know it, but *you* do. *You* can know it.

[*pause*]

You were expecting more.

CB: I wasn't expecting more, I just…I didn't do anything, Linda. I just went over there and watched a bunch of people die. I got people killed, I helped get people killed…and I killed a man.

LH: You want people to know the truth of what's happening over there. Because your knowing the truth is a burden to *you*. You'd like to share it and unburden yourself. Put the load on anybody else.

CB: Why are you being so mean to me, Linda?

LH: I'm sorry…I'm sorry you feel that way. I'm not trying to be mean… Carl, when you first told me about the duty, the driving, it was hard not to sense your shame. Getting you to talk was a way of coming to terms with it. And now that you've come to accept how you feel about these things, there's this urge to confess. I'm just pointing out something you maybe haven't considered. If you do go out there, out into civilian life, and shout from the rooftops how parasiting is real and you were involved, well…then what? You're living it over and over. You won't replace those old feelings with anything positive. You'll just be talking about it in front of an audience. And the shame will turn into pride. It's not safe.

[*pause*]

Listen to me, Carl. This is important. You're better off if you don't do this. Don't do this, and you'll be fine. I know it. You can go wherever you want. You can have a future. Nothing is stopping you.

CB: Yeah…

LH: Please say it. I need you to say it. Nothing is stopping you.

CB: Nothing's stopping me.

LH: And when you leave here, when you get on that shuttle, just…do right by the gifts you have, please.

CB: [*indecipherable*] All right, then. If you say I shouldn't do it, Linda, I won't do it.

[*pause*]

Linda? What's the matter?

LH: Nothing. I'm sorry…I can't do this…

CB: You're crying… Is it Danny?

LH: What? No, Danny's fine. Thank you for asking. He's actually doing pretty well…

CB: Then what is it? Is it me?

LH: No, it's just…

[*pause*]

Carl, can I tell you something of a personal nature?

CB: Hell yeah. Anything you want.

LH: I've been thinking about this a lot lately. I don't know why…maybe because I can…but it was just about exactly six years ago today that I found out Danny had CF. He was barely six, and we'd been running all these asthma tests. A couple of times a week, I'd take him into the public clinic and wait forever for this ongoing allergy test, and a nurse would take Danny behind a curtain and shoot up his arm, then take pictures on her phone of how much they swelled. And Danny would cry every time, he'd say no, Mommy, don't let them give me the shots. But then he got used to it. He became stoic. Anyway, asthma never turned up, and so they kept running tests, and we went there… I remember it was a Saturday, and he's still wheezing constantly, all these medications were doing nothing…and we came home…and then a good while later, two weeks later, I get a call at work and they ask me if I know whether Danny's father had the CF gene…I didn't know…so they tell me Danny tested positive for CF… I didn't even know what that was. At the time, it was just another test. And for the next couple of days, because they couldn't schedule an appointment right away, I was looking through the CUP, and just…crying. I couldn't believe any of it. Some of the information on there was very old, it was saying people with CF don't live to see thirty… And it was just this ongoing, unfolding sadness. A wave. It kept getting worse, and I was making myself crazy but also, just very…very sad.

CB: OK, but Danny's about to get a transplant. The Company's going to hook you up.

LH: Yes. As soon as they find a donor with the right blood type.

CB: I'm trying to remember… In jail I filled out a sheet for a bunch of different organ transplants. It seemed like a good enough thing… Maybe Danny will get my lungs. Or is it after you die? It's after, right?

LH: [*laughs*] I don't know what form you filled out, Carl, but I assume they won't take your organs until after you're finished with them.

[*pause*]

I almost didn't have him, Danny. I'd gotten pregnant and it was…rough. Couldn't even fake it, I was throwing up all the time. My mother knew right away. She didn't even ask me, she just woke me up very early one morning, she had her coat on and her purse and she said, come on, get dressed, I made an appointment, we're going to take care of your problem.

[*pause*]

Next thing I'm in the car, and it's cold. She's got the heat up. I remember her speaking very matter-of-factly, she said, we'll take care of this and be home before your father knows we're gone. This was when Dad was starting to get bad, you know, sleeping through the day, pretty much. We drove down to Silver Spring because our county didn't have any places…I called in sick to my job on the way. We got there, and there was this big, inflatable baby set up on the sidewalk. It must've been three stories high, just this huge baby with these big eyes. The pro-life people put it there. So we get there, and my mother talks with the woman at the desk, and we sit down. I was still barely awake… I just thought about this and that, how I wouldn't have to drop out of school now, I'd feel OK… Nothing but relief. No regrets, no worries about…just…nothing. But it was that nothing that worried me. It just worried me. Like, what kind of person am I, that I can just turn this off, and all I can think about is how great it's going to be, just the relief of it. And I remember looking at Mom, she was supportive…she might have been thinking this was going to make us closer, this thing. I might be making that up. It could've been breaking her heart. I've never been able to tell what she's thinking. But just…[*indecipherable*] just as we were called, just as the woman called my name, the fire alarm goes off. And it's deafening, just…deafening, the kind where it's so loud you think it's happening inside your head, and I just froze, and Mom was holding my hand…and then the doctor comes out and says, OK, everybody…and we all went outside. And my mother, if you knew her, she's terrified of ever making a scene, so we got back in the car and sat in there, waiting for the fire department. And that's when I realized I didn't want to do it. It was like…I didn't want to do it because I *could*. [*laughs*] God, that sounds stupid…I remember just… falling apart in the car, saying I don't want to do it, the fire alarm's a sign, I won't do it.

[*pause*]

I know we stayed in the car for a while, just talking, making plans. Eventually, we drove home. And Dad, he was up but he didn't even care where we'd been…I had Danny nine months later. And we limped through, made it work.

CB: You're still making it work. Because you're a real mom. Your having a kid was, it was just like… it wasn't going to be any other way.

LH: It could have been.

CB: Maybe Danny's being sick, in some strange way it proves you right. It wouldn't have made sense if Danny was easy. It had to be like this.

LH: Yes.

CB: Or no, more like…more like Danny needed you. He needed a mom like you, somebody with something to prove.

[*pause*]

I think you told me that because you need to remember what you're doing, what all this is for. Now, you know me, Linda, I don't believe in anything, but a fire alarm gets pulled and a bunch of years later, I get to meet you? It's just that random, out of nowhere, that sometimes it comes back around again, and I feel like I believe in everything. God, heaven, angels, ghosts, everything.

LH: I know what you mean.

CB: You're a good mom. You deliver.

[*pause*]

Ah, shit, I'm sorry…

LH: No, it's all right. It's me.

[*pause*]

CB: Jesus, look at us.

LH: Quite a pair, aren't we?

[*pause*]

CB: But you're a good mother, Linda.

LH: Thanks.

CB: No, say it. Repeat after me…

LH: Carl…

CB: No, I'm serious. Say it. Say you're a good mother.

LH: I'm a good mother. [*laughs*] Thank you, Carl.

CB: There you go.

[*pause*]

I love you, Linda.

[*pause*]

[*pause*]

LH: Thank you, Carl. That's nice to hear.

CB: Not really the response I was looking for…

LH: Oh, Carl, I'm sorry! But I'm your therapist... I can't...

CB: It's all right. I think it was more about me saying it, anyway. I wanted to hear myself say it. **LH:** Keep saying it.

CB: I love you, I love you. I like it. Makes me feel good.

LH: It's good for you.

CB: What about you?

LH: It really, really doesn't hurt. That I can say.

CB: [*laughs*] All right, then.

END EXCERPT

EXCERPT

USoFA WorldWide War-Related PTSD Individualized
Therapy Program (Pilot), "SoldierWell" Therapy
Session #28

April 10, FY20__

1349EST

LINDA HELD

Interviewing:

**SERGEANT TODD SPARROW, US Marine Corps. 2ⁿᵈ Tank
Battalion, 2ⁿᵈ Marine Division**

(BEGIN)

SGT. TODD SPARROW: I'd like to just walk in a
park again, see people, families walking around,
ice cream cones. Maybe a merry-go-round. Jesus,
[*laughs*] I've been watching the CUP a lot lately.
Sometimes I feel like it's talking *to* me, instead
of *at* me, you know?

LINDA HELD: So, we've got a sunrise and a walk in
the park. What else?

TS: Wow, I haven't considered this… I look forward
to seeing familiar things. Driving around the
neighborhood. I mean, yeah, I'm aware it won't be
the same. There'll be new buildings, stores… Last
time I spoke with Juliette, she says all these
new security measures have made it so leaving the
house is more trouble than it's worth. Of course,

she only ever leaves the house if she has to, and she almost never has to anymore. She's gotten fearful in her old age. I speak with her now… well, it's been months, but I speak with her now and it's like I'm speaking to a seven-year-old. I hear her say things, things about politics, or what this celebrity said about that celebrity, it's like getting punched in the nuts.

LH: Like what?

TS: Pardon?

LH: What things does she say?

TS: Oh…opinions about the War. About me. She says it to get a rise out of me, and that's fine, but then I consider the place she's coming from, what must be going through her mind to say these things. It's not a hurtful place. It's more like a, like a place of just…ignorance. Just a child's fantasy world type of place. I'll give you an example. When I first got to Iraq, I called home, and of course, she gets on the phone and it's this total readjustment because no longer am I speaking with an intelligent person who appreciates the sacrifice that some of us are making for a certain way of life… [*indecipherable*] Anyway, she gets on the phone, this is the last time we spoke, and she says well, if it isn't my little boy in uniform. Like I'm ten years old, playing games in the living room. So I say something, well…all I can think to say is, I'm not playing dress-up, Juliette, but right away I feel like I've given away too much. Know what I mean? Do you ever feel that way with people? Like you know it's coming but you can't help it?

LH: I can see you feel strongly about this.

TS: Well…

LH: Maybe you should do something about it.

TS: I should, yeah. But what, you know?

LH: I just don't think it's healthy, serving your country and having to hear your service questioned like that.

TS: Yeah.

LH: Particularly by someone who doesn't know, who couldn't know.

TS: Yeah.

LH: I read somewhere that one of the reasons so many veterans of Vietnam suffered from post-traumatic stress was that they were coming home to a country that didn't support them. The hippies and those people… Did you know they would see a man in uniform stepping off an airplane and they would actually spit on him?

TS: That's terrible.

LH: At least now, yes, the War has been going on for a while, but the nation is behind it for the most part, behind the troops and brave men like yourself. I think USoFA WorldWide has been good about keeping that going, that degree of support.

TS: I agree with you. There's just a better feeling about it now. I mean, you've got the Haters, but still...

LH: Right, so it's a little surprising to hear your mother say these things.

TS: Oh, surprising doesn't even cover it.

[*pause*]

I heard Art Pfeiffer call her a bitch once. We were in Pittsburgh, something like that, coming back on the plane, and we were at the airport running late, I think. Or I assume, rather, because my mother makes a show of being late to everything... I've always suspected she thinks it's graceful or sophisticated or something, and yet for all this worrying about what other people think, she's not aware that airplanes are on actual schedules and no plane is going to just wait for you, they're going to leave because that's what they have to do. Goddamn bitch, that's what he said, under his breath. She didn't hear him but I did!

LH: You mentioned in our last session how Art Pfeiffer reacted to your joining the Marines.

TS: Right. He thought it was a bad idea but he didn't stop me.

LH: How did Juliette react?

TS: She was fine with it. [*laughs*] Fine, go and get yourself killed, see if I care. All very consistent with her overall attitude in life, that of the fat, bored housewife who yells at the help and starts drinking at noon. I have a feeling she considers me useless now that I'm fully grown and able to think for myself. Doesn't have me under her thumb anymore.

LH: Was Juliette a good mother? Do you consider her a good mother?

TS: Juliette? [*laughs*]

LH: Do you think there's any way she can be made aware of the sacrifices you've made? The lives you saved? Because I was looking at records the other day...

TS: Yes?

LH: ...and the things you've accomplished...you display the utmost discipline in military affairs. You must be personally responsible for the safety of who knows how many servicemen.

TS: True.

LH: That means there are any number of people over there, right now, fighting for freedom, who would be dead were it not for your training, your decisiveness, your courage. But Juliette, all she knows is you went halfway around the world and played dress-up. That doesn't seem fair.

TS: Sure, but what can you do?

LH: Well, maybe if you were to show her in some way. Like in defense of your country...

TS: What?

LH: Maybe if you were to defend them...defend her, I mean. Because for some people, you know, you go away, halfway around the world to defend your country, and it's out of sight, out of mind. Know what I mean?

TS: Sure.

LH: I mean, does Juliette even keep up with the War?

TS: My God, no. She wouldn't know Chad from the North Pole. If it doesn't affect her eating or her drinking or her...her comfort in some way, she doesn't care.

LH: But is that an excuse? Is ignorance an excuse?

TS: No. But I guess I'm used to it.

LH: Hm. If only there was a way to reach her. Have you ever considered ways to reach her? To show her what she's missing?

TS: No. I just take it. But I can't...

LH: Can't what?

TS: I can't in good conscience...

LH: What can't you in good conscience do?

TS: Well, I can't just…hit her. I can't do that. Have I thought about it? Sure, of course. Hasn't everybody? I used to think about it quite a lot when I was a kid. I was rebellious then. Well… maybe not that far back.

[*pause*]

Sorry, where was I? Oh…I've thought about it. Not recently, but yeah.

LH: But you can't do it in good conscience.

TS: No, no. It's just a thought you have. They're just impulsive things, right? I know when I was younger, and I would see someone crossing against the light or something, there was always that impulse to run the person over to see what it felt like, how it would all unfold, you know, pressing your foot to the gas, seeing the reaction, the sound of her big ass slamming against the grill. But it's a fantasy. I might want to do it, but just in that small instant.

LH: Why only that instant?

TS: Why? It goes away. You come to your senses. No, your conscience…your conscience kicks in. It's weird, though, how the impulse always beats the conscience, isn't it? Is that something you've studied, Linda?

LH: It's your conscience that keeps you from taking the action.

TS: Yes.

LH: You couldn't kill a person because your conscience will bother you.

TS: Yeah. [*laughs*] I feel like you're trying to corner me, Linda.

LH: I'm sorry, I don't mean to make you uncomfortable.

TS: All right, good. I've got to say, I was starting to...

LH: Let me pose it another way. If you knew ahead of time that it wouldn't bring any adverse consequences, like you wouldn't be arrested or anything...

TS: OK.

LH: And it wouldn't bother your conscience in any way...

TS: Yeah...

LH: Do you think you could kill someone?

TS: Yeah. Well, no, I don't know. It would depend on the person. Let's say, let's say that person crossing against the light, could I kill that person? No.

LH: Why not?

TS: Because...it's wrong.

LH: But I just said it wasn't wrong.

TS: You did?

LH: Well, the effects of it being wrong, your conscience, consequences, they're all wiped out.

TS: OK.

LH: You still wouldn't do it. Because it's wrong.

TS: Right.

LH: OK.

TS: OK.

LH: OK, let's change it up so that, instead of just any person crossing the street, that person now has a gun. Pointed at you. No, pointed at a child, say.

TS: Oh, then yeah. My conscience would actually go the other way. Because if that gun goes off, you're going to spend the rest of your life saying, why didn't I speed up? [*laughs*]

LH: Right. And also, like in times of war, those opportunities…

TS: Yeah, yeah. You're taking care of your brothers, defending freedom, all that.

LH: But is there a similar threat here? In the United States? It seems like a strange question because this is what people like yourself are defending. Which your mother doesn't realize.

TS: Right, but it doesn't matter. I'm always disappointing her in some quiet way. It's what made me join…well. I won't say that. But, knowing how she would react, let's just say it informed my decision to join the Marines. I wasn't escaping her, but the idea of being away, the prospect of being away gave me confidence, you might say. It was good, because here's me, on the other side of the world, fighting in the War, the one thing most people, most Americans can agree is good and noble, and I'm in the middle of it. A Marine. The few, the proud. Oorah. And then there's Juliette, laying around by the pool, swiping through her celebrity garbage on the CUP, scratching her big stomach…my God but she's gotten fat in recent years. Did I mention that before? People always used to tell me how beautiful she was…busboys, cab drivers, people like that. They'd fall all over themselves opening a door for her, hurrying around the cab so they could open her door and catch a glimpse of her underpants as she's swinging her big ass around…She knew what she was doing, of course. Then when she was inside grabbing them a couple of bucks, again, making everybody wait, they'd inform me that my mother was a beautiful woman. And [*laughs*] I'd always tell them the same thing. She knows. And they'd turn and look at me like I didn't know how good I had it, walking around with such a beautiful woman for a mother. It was just service people, though. Cabdrivers, those types of people. If they were any smarter they'd be doing something valuable with their time, not groveling under the rich and beautiful and their miserable sons.

[*pause*]

Then Juliette would come back and hold her money out for them like she was feeding a dog, afraid of touching them, even when she was wearing gloves. And these imbeciles would take it from her and try to make eye contact, really bend down and peer up into her face to try and get a smile…nothing, of course. She'd smile as she was turning away from them, though…I think she gained something from rejecting them. And if it was a nice day outside, even semi-nice outside, whenever she came back from somewhere, whether it was the Caribbean or the liquor store, the very next thing she had to do was slip into her bathing suit and sit by the pool. With her CUP monitor and her wine.

LH: Todd…

TS: And she always, always made me join her. I hated going out to that pool, and there was never anywhere to go. Sometimes I would fake a stomachache, or I'd tell her I had homework to do, and she always had some stupid thing to say about that, like, well, a few minutes out in the sun will make that tummy ache go away…and she'd send me upstairs to go put on my suit, and I'd just sit up there in my room, looking at my bathing suit in the drawer and…I remember this…whispering every bad word I could think of. I remember sitting up there looking at my bathing suit on the bed, this red suit, red trunks, and I'd be whispering fuck shit piss cocksucker fucking dammit asshole motherfuck…and I'd want to cry but I knew there wasn't a good reason to cry, I was just

going to sit out by the pool, no reason to cry...
and so no matter how long I waited...like I'd put on
my bathing suit all slow, I'd go to the bathroom
and pee...no matter how slow I went, I'd always end
up first out by the pool. I hated that. I didn't
want to be out there, but then I'd always wind up
waiting for her. And I would get a real stomachache, waiting for Juliette and looking down at
the water and seeing all the wavy little lights
in the blue. I can see it now...I'm squatted, cap-
turing ants on the stone, trapping them, wanting
to cry.

[*pause*]

And then, oh, and then, Juliette would come outside. First, she'd have on a robe, this white
robe that would just blind me if it was sunny,
and of course her sunglasses. Big glass of wine,
the glass just filled to the top and splashing
out sometimes, making these bloody globs on the
stone. She wouldn't even look at me, she'd be
checking all the rose bushes around the pool,
and she'd turn up her nose if she happened to
see so much as a line of brown on the edge of
any of them, she'd turn up her nose and I could
tell she was making a mental note to yell at
Samson or, better yet, yell at Art Pfeiffer
for keeping Samson around. And she'd waddle
around the pool, sip here, sip there, a little
gasp at the end of each sip like she's shocked
that the wine might have some alky-hall in it,
who could have spiked my wine? Then she'd look

at me. I could tell because, all of a sudden, I'd see myself, squatted down, helpless,
ant-trapping boy. And it was like I could see
me through her eyes, the smallness. And she'd
tell me to go for a swim. And I'd say, no thank
you, Juliette, I don't want to. And she'd look
at me like I was very boring and say it again,
commanding me, just go for a swim already so
I can look over my things. And then she'd take
off her robe and kick off her sandals, she's
watching me, watching me watching her…and she'd
turn on her CUP and start scrolling through
all her celebrity junk…not another word. She'd
just take it as a given that I was going to get
in that pool. So…so I'd get in the pool. Never
disobey Juliette. Never ever. I have a perfect
record. I've always done exactly what she said.
A perfect disappointment. And I'd swim some
laps, paddle around, hold my breath. I'd hold my
breath to see if I could make myself pass out,
see if I could drown, but I couldn't. I really
would try.

[*pause*]

She'd call to me. She'd say, Spunkeee…really sing
it out. I can see it in my mind, in my mind it's
always cold, but that doesn't make sense…but it's
getting near dinnertime and he's going to be home
in an hour, or maybe not…and the sun's going down
and everything's got this silver touch on it. I'd
ignore the first time she'd call. I'd look up and
out over the fence or something. But then she'd

say it again, she'd say it again because she
wanted to say it again, she *wanted* to have to call
me a few times. It was easy to hear the smile in
her voice. And so finally I'd say what is it and
she'd just laugh and laugh and laugh and I would
just sit there, in the water, watching her laugh,
and of course while she's laughing she's watching
me watching her. And then she'd say come on out
of that pool, come dry off. She'd say you can even
use my robe and she'd reach back behind her and
halfway pick it up, offering it, like. And this
is why I always think of it as being cold, because
I'd tell her I don't need her robe but as soon as
I got out of that water it'd be cold, really cold,
and I'd have to reach for it. I'd have to do what
she said… And just the smell of her on that robe
would be all over me…and I'm dripping, making the
stones wet…and I'd walk over to her, water in my
eyes. I'd walk over.

[*pause*]

She'd look away. I'd be standing there. Sometimes
I'd squat down and hug myself, you know. I was
just a kid. Little, I mean, I hadn't formed yet,
I wasn't a person. I'm sorry…

[*pause*]

LH: You're shaking…

TS: I'm sorry…

[*pause*]

I'd look up at her, because I couldn't not...I
couldn't not look...and she'd be looking far off,
at least that's what I'd think, because she had
her sunglasses on still, though you know now
that I think about it I'm wondering if her eyes
weren't closed just then, at that moment. And I'd
see the side of her face, her profile, I mean, and
no matter how big she got, she really was just
so beautiful...so beautiful...and slow, I can remember the saliva in my mouth, I'd get dizzy...real
slow she'd move her hand down...and she'd pull back
her...like pulling back a curtain, you know...she'd
show it to me. And it would take me a second, I
wouldn't want to look, I can see the goosebumps
on her legs, inside, all nubby and white. She
knew how cold it was. She could feel the cold...
and then she'd say [*unintelligible*] she'd say it.

LH: What would she say?

TS: It was the only time I ever heard her say it.
Just those times.

LH: Say what, Todd?

TS: Please.

[*pause*]

She'd say it so soft...like she was thinking of
something else, like something from a long time
ago, and the memory got the best of her and she'd
said it out loud. She was so weak in that moment...
and sad...and I realized she was going to die one

day. It was like she was showing this part of herself she could never show anyone else. Except me. It was a privilege but also this horrible thing… There's so much pity, so much pity in love, I think… Sometimes I think love is just pity, nothing more…

[*pause*]

Ah, damn…could I have a minute, please?

LH: By all means…

TS: OK. OK, thanks. Hey…hold on, let me just… [*unintelligible*] Is it normal to want to vomit during these things? [*laughs*]

LH: You don't have to continue if you don't want.

TS: Fuck it, too late now. [*laughs*] So…so she was asking me. And I knew it was important. So I would. I would. It happened more than once. Not a lot but more than once… Just that one summer. In my mind it happened…three times. Just that summer.

[*pause*]

I've never told that to anyone. [indecipherable] God, how I hate her. I hate her so much… Who does that to a child? To their son? I mean…I don't think about it. I honestly don't know why I'm talking about it today. But fuck, I'd kill her. I would. My God, forget about PTSD. This, I need to get over this… Wow. If you told me we were going to cover this today, I'd have said… So… [laughs]

probably not a real good idea to let me out of here, is it? You'll probably want to keep me here for a little while longer? [laughs]

LH: A lot of people have shame, Todd. Everyone alive carries shame with them.

TS: Oh yeah? What's yours? [laughs] I'm just kidding. You seem very put-together, Linda. Ah...all of a sudden I'm so tired...beat...it would be nice to sleep now. Sorry, I just...can I sleep now? Can I sleep, Linda?

LH: Of course, Todd. We'll talk again soon.

END EXCERPT

Miles rose from bed while it was still dark, according to the openings between the heavy hotel curtains. His pants were buzzing, a square of bright light in one of the pockets. He went to them and slipped them on, leaving his fly unzipped so as not to wake her with the sound, then reached into the pocket to silence the buzzing.

Sylvia lay naked under the sheets. Miles turned to her, his breath on hold, wanting to make sure she was really still asleep and not just faking so she wouldn't have to talk to him so early in the morning. If she was awake and about to leave he wouldn't care, but he didn't want to miss seeing her naked one last time. It was why he'd paid for the full night.

Satisfied with the equilibrium of her breathing, Miles slowly slid the balcony door open and sluiced outside. Cold but not unbearable. He sat down in a wrought iron chair, rubbing his eyes until the former KOIN Tower stopped looking wobbly. He checked his phone.

From Mitch: *How's it going*

Good. You can text now?

I have my ways

Thanks for waking me

You should be up by now

I'm on west coast. Portland

Apologies. Nice?

Skyline is a joke, coddles its poor, all the statues are girls

Ha. What are you up to?

Miles peeked inside. Sylvia had turned over so that the sheet had slid off, offering Miles the chance to admire her bare back. Not one tattoo! Who'd ever heard of such a thing? Very slowly he reopened the sliding door, stuck his phone through, and snapped a picture. A little blurry, it turned out, but the shape was easily ascertained. He sent it to Mitch without comment.

He had met Sylvia in the bar downstairs, telling her right away that she needed to clear her schedule because he wanted somebody for the whole night. They discussed rates over drinks, then went to a place called DAB or DUB, something like that, young people everywhere—Miles must have been the oldest guy in the place by a decade. And yet the novelty of his age struck him as being welcome in this place; soon he was in the center of the upstairs dance floor, making a jackass of himself because he had granted himself the right. Then they walked across the street to a dive called Sandy's (half the place knew Sylvia by name), and together they did three or four shots of Southern Comfort, one after another, and then a long ride in a citizen taxi, and at the end of it Sylvia had to shake him awake so he could pay the driver, and once all that was sorted out he saw they were standing in front of somebody's home, a townhouse in a row of townhouses with a flag of Switzerland hanging by the front door. Miles asked where the hell are we and Sylvia said keep it down, this is a nice neighborhood, these are friends of mine. And so Miles stepped inside and said hello to everybody, this huge community of poors, young and middle-aged dads and moms with what had to have been twenty kids running around, and the living room had this very low ceiling with this huge hookah on the floor, black and aqua green, long hoses like jump ropes lying around everywhere, and no matter which one you grabbed it was always tangled up with another one, and so after a couple of drags of this really powerful strain of dope, probably it was dope, Miles tried untangling the whole mess, which made him the life of the party as everyone had fun watching the new guy trying to untangle the ropes. Miles played up his frustration when he got confused, just clowning around, and at one point he looked up to see that Sylvia was gone but by that point he was so drunk and high that he didn't actually care much, he was OK sleeping here on the floor with all these wonderful people if that's the way it had to be, because poors are people too, pretty cool people at that, but then just when the music started getting softer and the kids started to drop—incredibly, these kids would just stop playing and curl themselves up in a corner, not saying another word—Miles got to talking with this huge troglodyte with a Hater neck tattoo and a pink-dyed Van Dyke. They talked forever about something very serious, though Miles couldn't say now what any of it was.

Christ, let's hope it wasn't about SoldierWell. Miles tended to brag about his work when he was especially plastered. Somewhere in Florence, Alabama, there was a golf pro walking around with a working knowledge of the INSIST Technique.

Then Sylvia showed back up, looking as beautiful and amazing and nice as anyone could look. She had showered and her hair was darker and combed straight back and she was wearing a pink hooded sweatshirt and this pair of white jeans that showed off her dynamite ass, particularly with this fringe-y leather fanny pack thing slung loosely around her waist. And she said hey Doc are you ready to get out of here and Miles swooned and said my dear I have never been readier and then Neck Tattoo Man howled and clapped Miles on the back and said have a ball. They fooled around like teenagers in the back of another citizen taxi and then in the blink of an eye he found himself in his hotel room, where it was dark and warm, and he tripped over an empty champagne bottle and she laughed and said she had to use the bathroom and she was in there for what felt like a month and then finally, finally she joined him in bed.

Miles again peeked inside to see her sitting up, facing away from him, feet on the floor. Her bare back moved like water as she leaned forward and hung her head, which made her scapula flare out. After a few seconds, she stood and got her clothes, which had been neatly laid out over the arm of a chair, and trudged into the bathroom. The door shut. Miles stepped back inside just as the shower started.

His belt and shoes were out in the living room, the toe of one loafer wedged underneath the minifridge. He fixed coffee and picked up a little, tossing away chocolate wrappers and half-empty bottles of sparkling water. The shower stopped. With a fresh cup in each hand, Miles sat on the sofa and waited. After a minute, the bedroom door slammed shut.

OK, not a morning person. Miles sipped his coffee and straightened up a little more. He checked his hair in the blank CUP monitor screen, going for a boyish dishevelment thing before realizing it could not matter less. He scanned the room for something else to do, settling on the selection of magazines fanned out on the desk. At the top was something called *Colour*. Its cover showed a watercolor painting of a little white goat. Chuckling, Miles picked it up and began swiping through pages, noting the London address atop its masthead, when he saw her.

Page thirty-nine. Just the one photograph, in black and white: our Darling dressed in a white T-shirt and jeans and sneakers without socks. Her hair was pulled back in a no-nonsense ponytail, revealing that damn masterpiece of a neck, a few strands of hair falling about her earring-free lobes. She was turned toward the camera but was looking away, her eyes hopeful, steely. *Non-abiding.* Underneath the photo were the words "Fox on the Run," in bulbous cursive.

Underneath, in a more stolid text: *In Spain for the first time since the death of her brother, the Hollywood-star-turned-political-activist recalls the past, looks to the future, and takes on a hostile American press.* Miles checked the date on *Colour*'s cover (April 9, FY20__) and took a seat on the couch.

> *It's a sunny Thursday afternoon, and Chelsea Daye is on holiday with her parents in Barcelona. Well, 'vacationing' isn't quite the word. For the past six hours, Ms. Daye has been barricaded in her luxury suite at the Mandarin Oriental, working on an upcoming speech for the Rally for Peace taking place in Washington, D.C. on 1 May, part of an ongoing, 21-date speaking tour across the U.S. 'My country is drowning in*

media,' she said in a recent CUP interview. 'The only way anyone can hope to make themselves heard is to speak, in real-time, before as many people as possible.'

This, presumably, was the motivation behind her crashing of USoFA WorldWide's Second Quarter Earnings Call, where she maneuvered her way around the supraconglomerate's celebrated digital firewall to hold various executives' feet to the fire regarding spiking casualties among certain military personnel.

Miss Daye's appearance this afternoon is one of charming American dishevelment: dark blue jeans and a plain white T-shirt, her dark curls pulled back into a messy bun. She hunches over her laptop whilst biting an unpeeled carrot. (Aside from three espressos, it is the only food she has consumed in the last twelve hours.) 'All right,' she says, popping open a Gatorade Wheat. 'What do you want to talk about?'

The shower stopped. Miles looked up from the magazine to listen. Sylvia was moving quickly, like someone who had figured out the most efficient way to ditch a hotel room. Miles debated whether to offer a hearty "Good morning!" before deciding against it. He flipped a page, skipping over questions about her supposed retirement from acting to get to the interesting stuff.

I like the place I'm in now. I'm in the exact right spot for the first time in my life, considering all that's happened in the last six months.

Such as the death of your twin brother.

Yes. That's at the center of what I'm doing, but I was already wanting to leave. The threats, the objectification, the sense that you're losing yourself in all the silliness—I was already wanting out. Jacob's death just brought that home.

Last June, during a speech outside of Edna H's ranch estate in Montana, you said you had spoken with Jacob hours before his death, though you didn't provide much detail.

I was pressed for time with that speech. The whole weekend was kind of slapped together, we had no idea it would be that many people showing up. And no one knew if or when Edna H was going to call in a SWAT team to break it up. Every time I looked up, I was seeing my people, friends and stuff, motioning for me to hurry it along. If I could do it over again, I would have made it twice as long.

Did Jacob give you any hint that he might have been in danger? I apologize if this is difficult…

No, it's fine. But to answer your question, no, there was no hint he might be in danger. I know for a fact that if he was in danger he would have said so. Of course, everyone over there is forbidden from saying anything very revealing—USoFA WorldWide's confidentiality policies are ridiculous—but my brother and I had our ways around that.

You did?

Yes, we had a secret language growing up, and we remained fluent into adulthood [*laughs*]. Cryptophasia is the term for it, but it's better known as just 'twin speak.' I suggested we try talking like that on the phone, just so we could have total privacy from USoFA World-Wide and the censors. So I am one hundred percent certain that if Jacob had plans to go into places that might still have landmines, as the official story goes, he would have told me. But he didn't. What he said was he was about to go into a twelve-hour shift in the medical unit, the hospital. His spirits were high.

Does it ever get lonely, this pursuit? Do you ever feel alienated by the work you're doing?

It's more like I don't feel like anyone ever wants to talk about what I want to talk about. Which is fine if I weren't already famous for being in a couple of big movies, because then I could just shrug and say I need to work harder. But in my situation, I've got all this access to media but it's the wrong kind. They just want to see the smile, the haircut, the girl from the movies. Sometimes I'm able to manipulate that access to gain other types of access, the kind that I *do* want, but that doesn't happen a lot, and I have to be careful about it.

Some would say you weren't being careful when you crashed the Q2 Earnings Call. Some called it a stunt.

It's funny, ever since then, I receive three or four death threats per day, and the lawsuits continue to pile up, and I didn't even get my question answered, but crashing that Earnings Call was probably the best thing I ever did. If I'm remembered for nothing else, I will die happy.

Maybe it was a stunt. It felt like one when I was doing it. But again, I was just trying to get some answers for this rise in medical casualties in the Middle East. The fact is, USoFA WorldWide has reported exponential losses in its War-facing medical departments for the last three financial quarters, and I have yet to hear a reason for it that makes sense. It wouldn't have seemed like such a stunt if they had just answered my question. The fact they were scrambling and making excuses and had to cut the thing short isn't my fault.

And, just to get this out of the way, *of course,* part of the reason I'm so interested in this issue is that my brother was killed in Iraq. That's what drives this. But if you're at all willing to set that aside and just look at the numbers, you'll see a really weird trend that hasn't been explained. That's why I'm torching my vacation to work on a speech—I happen to think I can present this to the American people without all the filters of the CUP and Patriot Media. Just face-to-face.

Going back for a moment, you said you receive three or four death threats per day. What security measures are in place during your speaking tour?

The bedroom door opened. Into the room came Sylvia. Her hair was just like it was the night before, wet and combed back. The black leather fanny pack on her hip looked like some gigantic beetle. "So that'll be three large," she said.

Miles nodded, placing one hand against the wall. The textured wallpaper felt like tree bark. "I thought maybe you'd want to get breakfast. My treat."

"Aw," she said, "but I should get going. You want to do cash or card?"

"You take cards?"

Sylvia unzipped her black leather fanny pack and brought out a card reader. "It makes things easier," she said, taking a seat on the edge of the coffee table.

Miles went and fetched his wallet from the bedroom. After handing Sylvia his credit card, he sat down on the couch and sipped his coffee.

Sylvia swiped his card and handed it back. "Sometimes it takes a minute," she said.

Miles nodded. "I had fun last night," he said. He always pulled this sentimental crap with hookers; he couldn't help it.

"Yeah, me too," Sylvia said, checking the card reader, which was definitely taking a minute.

"Did you mention last night it would be three thousand? I'm just trying to remember…"

Sylvia slumped, a combination of disbelief and sympathy on her face. "I told you. At the club. You said OK. And then Roland, at the house. You guys worked it out."

"Roland was the one with the…" Miles stroked his chin.

"Yeah," said Sylvia, nettled, unable to let it go. "And then back here, I asked, do you want me for the whole night, and you said yeah. I told you it was double."

Miles remembered now. "I asked you to marry me."

"Yeah, like ten times."

"That offer stands, you know." Miles wanted to crawl inside a hole and die.

"Aw." The credit card reader beeped. "God-fucking-dammit. Give me your card again?"

Handing over his card again, Miles asked Sylvia if he could make a phone call. It was a lame, petty way to show that he too had a life, with things to do, people waiting to talk with him. He pulled his phone from his pocket and dialed the office.

"Office of Dr. Miles Young, may I help you?"

"Howie! You're in early."

"Dr. Young, it's so good to hear from you. I was a little concerned after yesterday. If it's something I can help with…"

"No, it wasn't anything you could've done. Messages?"

"Quite a few…"

Sylvia stood, stuffing the credit card reader back into her fanny pack. "All done," she whispered, zipping up.

Miles hung up the phone. "You're leaving?"

Sylvia nodded. "The charge is going to read 'Home Entertainment' on your bill," she said. "And there'll be a number there. That's Roland's line. Next time you're in town, call that number. Ask for me if you want."

Miles felt himself blush. She didn't have to say that, did she? "Thank you, Sylvia. I will."

"Tell your friends." The door closed behind her with a heavy click. Miles got up and went to the door. Some footfalls, the chime of the elevator, the opening and closing of elevator doors, then nothing but hotel hallway silence.

Miles checked his phone. A new text from Mitch.

Not bad how much

Miles made his way back to the couch but stopped halfway, deciding he'd rather just lie down on the floor.

After a minute, his phone rang. Probably Howie, eager to give him his messages. Miles checked: UNKNOWN CALLER. He sent the call to his voicemail so that he could remain alone with his thoughts, the most intrusive of which was: What was he doing here?

But where else was there to go? Failure greeted him in every direction.

SoldierWell South: Patient suicide. FAIL.

SoldierWell North: Shoot-up in a Minneapolis bowling alley (Darling not affected). FAIL.

SoldierWell West: Patient arrested before fulfillment of Mission. FAIL.

SoldierWell East: Patient nonreceptive to INSIST Technique due to remembered childhood trauma. FAILURE IMMINENT.

He had writhed and wriggled throughout the flight to Portland, his heart beating louder than the snoring of his neighbors as he asked himself what he was now going to do. The worst part about Sergeant Sparrow's little "breakthrough" was that Mitch and Amanda Kant had been right. Both had warned him that something was off about Sparrow's relationship with his mother, but no, Miles had waved them off. (Well, that wasn't the *worst* part. The *worst* part was that SoldierWell East was now well and truly fucked, which meant Miles's career was well and truly fucked. Rumor had it that Edna H had been in a perpetual state of demonic fury since the Darling had crashed the Earnings Call, which had indeed upended the market as countless high-profile foreign investors publicly expressed they were reconsidering their Company holdings.)

His phone rang again. Another UNKNOWN CALLER. Fine… Miles answered with a sigh.

"Please hold for Edna H."

Miles got up, croaking acknowledgment as a fresh batch of panic acid flooded his gut. Edna H was calling him. Soon he would be speaking with Edna H, his words going into her ear and her words going into his ear.

"Hello?" said a strange voice on the other end.

"Yes, hello," Miles said. "Good morning."

"Clear the room."

"Ma'am?"

"Not you, Miles. My grandchildren are visiting." For security purposes, Edna H used voice masking technology for all of her telephone conversations; she sounded like a heavily Auto-Tuned pop singer at the bottom of a well. "Unfortunately I don't have much time this morning, so let's just go over what happened."

"What happened?"

"That's what I'm asking you."

"Of course," Miles said. "Well, reports of an armed man found inside of Revolution Hall came out at about 2200 last night. But the story seems to be pretty self-contained. The only reason I even heard about it was I happen to be here in Portland."

"What are you doing there?"

"I...wanted to be available," Miles said. "Just trying to be more aware of, you know, seeing things through."

"OK," Edna H said. Even through the voice-masking, she sounded unconvinced. "So how did they find him? The patient?"

"Well, he was sleeping in a bathroom stall of the theater. One of the cleaning crew found him there and called the police. He had an assault weapon on him. The police report said he had been there for days."

"How did they know that?"

"I believe it was the detritus scattered about. Snack wrappers and things."

"And where is he now?"

"Police custody, I believe." Miles had meandered back into the bedroom.

"You believe."

"I...yes."

"OK, stop *believing*, Miles. Belief is nothing. We need to know."

"Yes, ma'am."

"Let's do this again. Where is the patient now?"

"Police custody, ma'am."

"OK, we'll need to get him out of there."

"I'd be happy to do that since I'm in town."

Edna H laughed—a gurgling, subterranean sound, each *ha* tumbling over its predecessor in synthetic reverb. "No, Miles," she said, "I'd rather learn what you're planning to do now."

Miles now found himself in the hallway, standing before the elevators. He ducked into an empty one. "Well, it was more of a logistical matter, or a series of logistical matters," he said. "Our Darling didn't actually speak at that particular theater. They changed the location just the day before, so everybody was caught off guard."

"Ah, so our target wasn't where we needed her to be."

"That's right, yes." Miles pressed for the lobby.

Edna H didn't respond but Miles could hear her electronically altered breathing. The sound was like distant ocean waves. "So, if I'm understanding you, the science works. If not for her changing locations, this would have been a congratulatory call."

"Well, I can't predict alternate timelines or anything, but…"

"Sure you can, Doctor. Just say it."

"Pardon me?"

"Miles, as far as I can tell, your INSIST Technique *did* work. Your SoldierWell West patient was open to the Suggestion, he took it upon himself to take this action, and he would have fulfilled the mission, given the chance. Isn't that right?"

"I believe so, yes."

"Dammit, Miles, what did I just say about belief? What did I just say?"

"Sorry."

"Have some confidence, for goodness' sake!" She sighed with force. "Miles, do you know why I was so looking forward to this conversation with you?"

"Ma'am?"

"This morning I had a man in here, someone I've known for years and whom I've always considered a close acquaintance. But this morning, he grew terribly upset because the data he was using for a presentation was eleven minutes old. And as I sat there, watching him, I thought, Wow, Philip, look what they've *done* to you. Data, analytics, numbers in so-called real time. Sometimes I think I might strangle the next person who shows me a line graph, just wrap my hands around their neck and never let go."

Miles chuckled, then stopped upon realizing he was alone in doing so.

"I don't have to look at graphs with you, Miles. I cherish that. I'm sure I could find a hundred people to show me the numbers on pre-contemplation estimates and empathy triggers, but that's not addressing the problem of human nature, is it? Human nature is voodoo, as far as I'm concerned, and you *get* that. You know how I know?"

"No, ma'am." The elevator stopped on the third floor.

"I don't! I just have a feeling. That's all you are, Miles, when you come down to it. A feeling I have."

Miles nodded as a family stepped into the elevator. It was easy to spot the Company-employed breadwinner of the clan, because while the father and two teenage girls appeared tanned and serene, Mom looked weathered, with a facial tic that had her continuously scraping her lower lip against her eye teeth, as if about to say *fish* or *fine* or *force*. Anyone that nervous must have a security clearance level of blue or white, something way up there…

"So let's get this straight, Miles. You are saying Chelsea Daye would be dead right now were it not for the fact that someone decided at the last minute to change venues?"

Miles observed his fellow passengers, who remained quiet out of deference to his call. "Yes, ma'am, that's what I'm saying."

"Then say it, Miles. Tell me Chelsea Daye would've been dead."

"Yes, she probably would have been." The elevator doors opened. Miles followed the family out to the bright, white-tiled lobby.

"No, Miles. Say it. Chelsea Daye would've been dead."

"I'm sorry, ma'am…I'm actually in a hotel right now?"

"Say it."

Miles swallowed. "Chelsea Daye would have been dead."

"Louder."

"Chelsea Daye would've been dead."

"Come on, louder. Really shout it out."

"Ma'am, I can't really…"

"I'm giving you an order."

Miles waited for a little girl to pass, then shut his eyes to unsee the scene he was about to make. "Chelsea Daye would've been dead!"

"Good. Now tell me your technique works."

"The INSIST Technique works!"

"There you go. Now tell me SoldierWell East will work."

Eyes still shut, Miles raised a fist in the air. "SoldierWell East *will* work!" Miles heard his voice echoing along the high hotel ceiling. He felt like a severed power line, his consciousness whipping around, shooting sparks.

"Guarantee it."

"*I guaran-fucking-tee it! Chelsea Daye will be dead by Mother's Day!*"

He felt dizzy. He opened his eyes. No one was paying him any attention—the most he got was a sneering up-and-down from a bucktoothed boy on his way to the restroom.

Edna H sighed. "Miles, it was a pleasure, truly. I look forward to next time." An automated voice came on, giving instructions on how to end the call.

Phone in hand, Miles fell into the crowd of kids and parents. Near the complimentary coffee kiosk, he settled onto an arm of a couch, half-hiding behind the outstretched fronds of a potted palm tree, and began to reflect on what had just happened. He had guaranteed to Edna H that SoldierWell East would work. And there was no way that could happen. Sparrow was done.

Miles gasped. Had he said Chelsea Daye would be dead by Mother's Day? Where did that come from? Mother's Day was in *two weeks*. Where was he going to find a candidate, one with the proper weapons training, diagnosed with PTSD, who would be open and amenable to...

Miles stood, feeling taller than usual. He had to get out of here. There was work to do.

⁓

A bright-eyed orderly stuck his head in, breaching Danny's room. "You ordered an overnight bed?"

Linda stood up from her spot at the foot of Danny's bed. "No, but I'll take it."

The young man steered a folded cot inside, parking it perpendicular to Danny's bed. He unfolded it, smoothed it flat, and dressed it. He fluffed the pillow with relish and placed it at one end, giving it a final karate chop down the middle.

"Thanks," Linda said.

"Sleep well."

"I doubt it."

"Ma'am?"

"Nothing. Thank you."

The orderly smiled as if touched. "I understand you wanting to stand watch over your son," he said, "but it's good to take breaks, get some air once in a while. Pardon me if I'm overstepping, but I'd be happy to buy you..."

"You are overstepping, but thanks for the offer."

The orderly nodded and left. The room was quiet again, aside from all the technology in and around her son. Still, Danny looked so *big*. Robert's growth hormone regimen, along with the extra caloric intake, was paying off—there was a conspicuous bulk across his chest and shoulders. And even under these fluorescent lights, his post-surgery complexion was downright rosy. A warm feeling overtook her insides as she recalled a thought she'd had back when he was a baby: *My son's a freaking dreamboat.*

Danny had been rushed by ambulance from the East Quadrant Park tennis courts less than four hours before. He and Robert had been engaged in a little casual volleying when Danny suddenly fell to one knee and signaled that he wasn't getting any air. Robert laid Danny down to listen to his chest and, knowing pneumothorax when he heard it (and never missing a chance to brag on his medical expertise, the little shit) flagged down Harvey Polaski in a Company BearCat.

And what had Linda been doing at that time? Oh, not much— for the past three days she had been in celebration mode, hanging around the house and washing down a couple of Sertanin every six hours with swigs from a $450 magnum of warm champagne that she kept under her bed. Linda did the math and figured that, at the same moment her son was sprawled out on sun-warmed clay, struggling for oxygen, she had been sitting cross-legged on the bathroom floor with a pair of grooming scissors, marveling at their frictionless opening and closing, the way the curved tips of the blades came flush to create a fine little cutlass. For at least ten minutes she had been daring herself to press them into her thigh, wondering if a little bloodletting might wake her up, provide a clarity to which she otherwise had no access. She had *almost* worked up the nerve to do it when Robert called.

Deva offered to drive to the CF Clinic and Linda accepted, gratefully, but it turned out that he drove like the old man he was, and so they wound up arriving at the same time as Dr. Bolaño, who had come by helicopter from a golf weekend somewhere in North Carolina.

Dr. Bolaño's mere presence went a long way in allaying everyone's worst fears, entering the ICU flanked by two pediatric physicians and three tagalong medical students, her putter still in her hands. In twenty minutes, she had located a cluster of cysts on Danny's right lung, which had caused the tear that collapsed it. While the tear itself measured less than one inch, it nevertheless necessitated something called an Insertion procedure, which involved a tube being set into the chest to draw out the air around the collapsed lung and enabling it to re-expand. Dr. Bolaño sketched all this out on the whiteboard in her office, with ear-shaped lungs and arrows pointing in opposite directions to signal breathing.

The procedure had gone well. Robert, who had wheedled his way into the OR as an observer, called Dr. Bolaño "an artist with a scalpel," which Linda could have done without. Now it was an overnight stay in the ICU so that Danny could heal under proper medical supervision. Linda had sent everyone home an hour before, telling them there was zero chance she'd be getting any sleep tonight so she may as well keep vigil here at the Clinic. (Linda also needed Robert out of her sight. The desire to blame him for this ordeal had calcified over the course of the evening, so that by the time Danny was resting comfortably, she could barely bring herself to look in Robert's direction.)

Linda lay face down on the cot. Maybe it was the quiet of this room, maybe it was the gratitude she now felt after an afternoon of such wild anguish, but the impulse to pray overcame her. Now seemed like a good time. She could appeal to God for *inner strength* during her son's recovery. That was all you could ever pray for, anyway—twelve years of parochial school had taught her it was folly to ask God for anything else. Typical Catholic mind games: God listens! He loves you! He can give you anything you ask for! But don't ask for anything real, just request a little topping off of *inner strength*. Oh well, a little *inner strength* wouldn't be unwelcome.

Linda got into a kneeling position, folding her hands. She bowed her head and closed her eyes as all the old prayers flooded her mind.

Our Father, who art in Heaven, hallowed be Thy name...

After all, it had been almost four days since her last session with Sparrow, where he had made that admission about his mother. Jesus, was that ever awful to hear. No wonder Miles had been against playing up the mother angle; Sparrow had been reborn with that breakthrough, he even *looked* like a baby by the end of that session, with tears running down his face and his whole body shuddering.

Hail Mary, full of grace, the Lord is with thee. Blessed art thou amongst women...

Since then, Linda had been biding her time, figuring no news was good news. Recently she had come to appreciate the simple pleasure of a hot shower. Nothing like being in the shower when the Sertanin kicks in, all that hot water moving down your bare skin, all that tactile delight. She had already taken four when Robert called from the tennis courts.

"I came as soon as I heard."

Linda opened her eyes and fell back. "You could have knocked," she said, scrambling to her feet.

With his crisp white shirt, collar open, and his hair very recently brushed back, Miles strolled in looking like someone on a tropical vacation. Which was astonishing—one of Linda's consolations over the last few days was the certainty that Miles had gone apeshit over Sparrow's breakthrough.

Miles stopped in his tracks upon seeing Danny. "He's going to be all right, yes?"

"How did you know we were here?"

"I just ran into Dr. Bolaño."

Linda nodded, though it struck her that Dr. Bolaño had left the CF Clinic hours ago...

"The procedure went well, then?"

"Very well. Yes."

"Christ," Miles said, "can you imagine what might've happened without so many of us looking out for him?"

"No, I can't," Linda said.

Miles approached Danny's bed. "And how are you?" he asked.

"Oh," Linda attempted laughter. "Hanging in there."

Miles held his phone against the orange bracelet on Danny's wrist. "Don't worry, I'm a doctor," he said, grinning as he took care to tuck Danny's arm back under the bedsheet. He looked over his phone. "Say, would you look at that?"

"What?"

"O Negative. Rare."

Linda nodded. Doctors were always saying this.

"You know who else is O Negative?"

Linda shook her head.

"Our Darling." Miles stepped away from Danny, taking a seat on the cot. "Isn't that something?"

"I guess you've heard the last Sparrow session?" Linda asked.

Miles nodded. "I'm not concerned," he said. There was a serious, almost mournful look on his face. Linda wondered if he had lost his mind, but no, he looked too well-rested for that.

"What do we do now?" Linda asked.

"There's someone else," Miles said. "He's been with us this whole time."

Linda understood as soon as she heard the words *someone else.* It seemed obvious, though just a second before it never would have occurred to her.

"Private Boxer attempted suicide yesterday," Miles said. "It wasn't serious. Surely his withdrawal symptoms played a part, but I think he did it to see *you* again. I'd like to bring him back. Actually, he's already on his way back. Our work continues."

Linda felt as if she might faint—the world smeared before her eyes until she thought to look to Danny. She held her gaze on him until everything returned to its proper place.

From his seat on the cot, Miles held out his hand. "Chelsea Daye will be speaking on the National Mall at the end of this month," he said. "Private Boxer will be there. It's time, Linda."

Linda sat down next to him.

"You see it, don't you?"

Linda looked down to find she had placed her hand in his. A teardrop landed on her knuckle and stayed there. "No," she said. "No."

Miles let go of her hand to grab her by the shoulders. "Hey," he murmured. "You can use this. It's right in front of you now. Use this."

Linda knew exactly what he was talking about and hated him for it. He was talking about transference. Another tear streamed down her face, even after she looked up at the ceiling. "No, no…"

"He worships you. We can use that. We can take it all the way."

Linda put her head in her hands, where it felt good. "You did this on purpose," she said.

Miles sighed and leaned back. "Yes," he said, "I can see how you might think that."

EXCERPT

USoFA WorldWide War-Related PTSD Individualized Therapy Program (Pilot), "SoldierWell" Therapy Session #26

April 9, FY20____

0913EST

LINDA HELD

Interviewing:

PRIVATE* CARL BOXER, US Army (Associate, Transportation Services, "Free2Fight," USoFA WorldWide)

(BEGIN)

PVT.* CARL BOXER: I got on a shuttle, I got on a plane, I got on another shuttle, now I'm back. Same room. It's a good room, I like it. I had a feeling, anyway, because leaving here, my release…it was weird. The door just opened. I was sitting here, after you and me talked, and the door just opened.

[*pause*]

Oh, I checked my organ donor information while I was waiting to be released. They said I was all set, I'm giving everything away, lungs, heart, liver, marrow…anything that works. Even my hair, there was something in there that said they could use it.

LINDA HELD: That's thoughtful of you, Carl.

CB: Yeah, I'm pretty excellent. [*laughs*] No, just, with your son and everything, it got me thinking, I don't do enough, I don't think about that stuff near enough… I feel good being back here, Linda. It's good to see you again. I didn't know if that was going to happen. So why am I back here? What do you want now? [*laughs*] Just kidding. I'm real happy to be back here. Real happy to see you again.

LH: Tell me what happened when you made it home.

CB: All right…so that afternoon they gave me a plane ticket and a gift card good for any USoFA WorldWide-approved restaurant and told me to board the shuttle again. I went to Grand Forks Air Force Base, and that was where I felt like I could mix in with the people…just their voices, it sounded good again. Then at one point, I was eating a burger, I kind of struck up a conversation with this little girl, she was wearing these little black leather shoes…her name was Alice…then she excused herself, she said she had to go to the bathroom, but really she just went to sit a couple tables over with her headphones on…[*laughs*] I had a layover in Dallas…and then a cab ride that I paid for with the rest of my gift card…I got home just after midnight. Ma let me in. She was mad for not calling ahead but she said I looked pretty fresh, considering I'm home from goddamn Iraq.

[*pause*]

I slept all right. Some weird dreams. She put me in Uncle Ray's room, which doesn't look like his room anymore, it's a different bed, but still…

LH: What were the days like? Who did you see?

CB: Oh…just neighbors. I saw an old friend of mine, this dude Jeff Lehigh…he's got a job, he's married, got a kid on the way…we had some beers. Good to catch up, but we're different now, both of us… I made a point to let everybody know I saw some shit, didn't tell them what, exactly… Ma shopped around and found an outpatient clinic that does veteran sessions once a week, but I called there and they said I couldn't go because I wasn't a real soldier, just a driver. [*laughs*] Ma kept talking about having a party around the picnic table in the backyard, like with barbecue sandwiches or something…she kept saying invite all your friends and I kept saying, Ma, there aren't any friends anymore. Once she started crying, so, you know, I stopped with that. I caught her on the phone once, telling somebody that it was like having Ray all over again…I think that did it.

LH: Did what?

CB: You know, what put me in the hospital.

LH: Oh.

CB: I can talk about it. I'm all right with talking about it…just, I don't remember…no, that's not true. I remember everything about it. I got a cord from one of those old game controllers Uncle Ray used to fool with... I took a couple days testing it, like pulling on it and tying it in knots and stuff...and then on maybe the fourth morning I was home, I just...tied it up onto the ceiling fan and put it around my head and...gave it a shot.

LH: Why, Carl?

CB: I knew you were going to be mad at me...all the work you've been doing with me, I mean, you're a great doctor, Linda. You helped me a lot.

LH: That's nice, Carl, but it's hard to believe when I'm sitting here, looking at you, and you've got these welts on your neck from trying to hurt yourself.

CB: Well...I didn't really do it, did I?

LH: It looks like you did.

CB: Yeah, but...I mean...I just didn't have anything going on. I don't have anything. It was like, my sitting there, not doing anything, it wasn't going to get better. I'd been to prison, I got all fucked up there, and in Iraq, and...it felt like everything was just leading to this. It felt like I'd been avoiding it my whole life and I couldn't avoid it any longer. There's nothing for me out there.

LH: Carl. We talked about this. You can do something.

CB: I know...but I tried, I thought about it...you told me I was wrong. It just got me thinking, I'm wrong about everything...but it's all right, I don't even care anymore.

LH: When did I say you were wrong?

CB: About going to the Haters and telling them everything... Shouting from the rooftops, you said.

LH: Well...

CB: Yeah, it wasn't the best idea. It felt like something, at the time, but...

[*pause*]

It was a bad idea. But I thought it was good at the time. I think now, I think I was just confused. I was going to be all alone again, you know? And I didn't want this to stop. I might need more help but...even if I didn't, having you... I mean, I don't really have you, but...

LH: But Carl, I said that we would see each other again. Didn't I say that? I was going to see you. I was making plans.

CB: I know. I know it.

[*pause*]

LH: Well? Are you happy now? Was it worth it?

CB: It was. Yeah.

LH: I see.

CB: Oh, here we go…

LH: What?

CB: When you say I see like that, you're up to something. You're thinking something.

LH: How do you mean?

CB: You just always say something weird after you say that. It's a thing you do.

[*pause*]

LH: You really are happier now, aren't you?

CB: Oh, I'm doing great now.

LH: This can't last, Carl. The Company won't put you up forever.

CB: Tell you what, let's just cross that bridge when we get to it. I just got here. Let me enjoy it.

LH: But I'm afraid it's time to be realistic, Carl. Because whether it's tomorrow or three weeks from now, your staying in that room and speaking with no one but me is going to come to an end. You have to prepare for that time. What is it you want out of life? What do you want to see when you look back at the end? Tell me. Don't worry about how it sounds.

CB: Well, it feels funny saying, but…

LH: Yes?

CB: I've told you about it before…I want to be…

LH: A hero.

CB: Yeah. As long as we're just talking. It's how I see myself, I guess, shaking off all this and doing something big and good.

LH: Doing something big and good…

CB: What?

LH: No, nothing. You're starting out on the right foot. What could you do to make you a hero?

CB: This is embarrassing…

LH: Think of it like this: who needs saving? Who needs a hero?

CB: Everybody? Regular people?

LH: Ah. So how do you save regular people?

CB: Oh, like charity. Food kitchens.

LH: Come on, Carl. Food kitchens? I thought you wanted to be a hero.

CB: All right… [*indecipherable*]

LH: What is a hero, Carl? In your own words.

CB: OK. [*indecipherable*] Sacrifice. A hero is somebody who stands up for what's right, like no matter what.

LH: But that's a cliché, don't you think? I'm not even sure what that means, exactly.

CB: It means, like, doing something, really doing something, for the right reasons.

LH: Being active. Taking action.

CB: Yeah.

LH: What do you mean by "right reasons," though? What's right? I'm sure a lot of terrorists taking action to hurt us, children, I'm sure they believe they're doing things for the right reasons.

CB: You know, everybody's always talking about terrorists, but they're like damn unicorns anymore. I don't think I've ever seen a real terrorist in my life. And I was in Iraq.

LH: Please, Carl…I don't like it when you're so glib. I'd just like to explore this idea of a hero a bit more. I think we might be getting somewhere.

CB: OK. Yeah, but terrorists are all twisted up, right? They've been taught something else, outside the norm, and then they're taking measures that are outside…I mean, the whole thing about terrorism is that it puts innocent people in danger. That's what makes it terrorism.

LH: Right. But I'm thinking…one of the things that separates us, or USoFA WorldWide, I should say…but us as in the United States of America… I mean besides from our spreading freedom and democracy and doing what we can to make the world a better place, ultimately, ensuring people are represented fairly and all of that...is that when we run into conflict, we don't go after the innocent. It's not an option for us. Yes, things happen, and regular citizens may get caught in the crossfire. But you have to remember, the Enemy *engages* innocent people, women and children, to fight for them. Puts them in the line of fire.

CB: Right.

LH: I heard this story, Carl, very recently, about how the Enemy in Tasmania, I believe it was, they used a pregnant woman to act as a lookout for them during a firefight with some Marines. Talk about terrorism!

CB: Yeah, I've heard stories like that.

LH: So that's what makes us right. We are on the right side in this situation. Even if you don't believe in our going around the world spreading democracy, you can agree with the fact that terrorists go after innocent people and we don't. Am I making sense?

CB: Yeah. I don't know how it relates to what I'm supposed to do when I get out, but...

LH: Right, sure. But if you don't support that...I mean, I get it, you hear somebody say how you're either with us or you're against us and you roll your eyes, I get that. But it makes sense that if you support us, you're here on the right side, and if you don't support us, well...what are you supporting?

[*pause*]

CB: You're asking me?

LH: Sure.

CB: Well, yeah. I was part of the effort.

LH: So why would you ever consider becoming a Hater?

CB: You don't have to keep rubbing my nose in it, you know.

LH: You're right. I'm sorry. And I sympathize with your situation. I know what you've been through. And it makes me question what we're doing over there.

CB: Yeah, exactly.

LH: But I don't think reaching out to the Haters is the answer, either. I think that's the opposite. They're the opposite. They use that idea of questioning, healthy questioning, and they exploit it.

CB: Yeah, but you haven't seen what it's like over there, Linda. The last thing on anyone's mind is democracy and freedom. We're just occupying these places.

LH: Oh, sure. I wouldn't want to speak for anyone in the military. I can't imagine what you went through over there. Well, I can, because you described it to me, you confided in me. But still, it's not like we're over there for our health. It's not like we're trying to keep the War just going and going and going.

CB: [*laughs*] You seem pretty wound up about this, Linda.

LH: Am I? It's just how I feel. I think it's important, not just because I work for USoFA WorldWide and I owe pretty much everything to them.

CB: Oh, sure.

LH: But also my father...he got wrapped up in all that Hater thought, all these conspiracy theories about how USoFA WorldWide was this shadowy organization trying to run the world, and it killed him. He was an alcoholic, yes, but he went a little crazy, too, always railing at injustices that everyone else just considers life, you know? That kind of thinking killed him. It got him to kill himself, with the drinking.

[*pause*]

Like your uncle Ray. And for the same reasons, the trauma of it all. Dad wasn't a soldier, he was a regular citizen, but the War killed him in a similar way. I hope you don't mind my saying this.

CB: No, I see what you mean. I think.

LH: See, these are regular people, my father, your uncle. They're the people that need saving.

I don't know if you feel like you let your uncle down...

CB: Nah, I was just a kid.

LH: That's good. Sometimes I feel like I let Dad down. I mean, I had other things going on. Danny was just a baby, and in truth, I was just trying to keep everything going without driving myself crazy. But I did let him down. *I'm* no hero, that's for sure.

CB: You're a hero to your son.

LH: Thank you, Carl.

CB: It's true.

LH: But my point is, regular people are the people who need saving, just like you said. And we have two real-life examples of the kinds of regular people who need saving. People crippled by doubt. Confusion. Now the Haters, I don't think they care about regular people...

[*pause*]

But I'm talking too much. Tell me what you think.

CB: Yeah... Everybody needs to get on the same page, I guess. Like you were saying, we got USoFA WorldWide doing what they do, and it's messed up, but at least it's a mission...and then you got the Haters trying to tear all that down. They go on the CUP, they write stuff...

LH: Yes! And which ones, which Haters go on the CUP?

CB: Well, Chelsea Daye...

LH: The actress?

CB: Yeah. She's all over the CUP, all those shows. She was the one I thought of when I thought about going over and telling them what I did in Iraq, when I was all mixed up.

LH: She's basically the face of the Haters, isn't she? She's taken on that role, you might say.

CB: Well, she's got a case. Never getting any answers about her brother, I mean...

LH: Right, but Carl, there's got to be very good reasons why USoFA WorldWide can't just tell her. Sometimes I get the feeling she'd rather not know. Being able to hammer away at USoFA World-Wide certainly keeps her in the public eye.

CB: That could be...

LH: She just drums up all this outrage, smears the Company like it's this secretive organization that manipulates people all the time, forcing its employees to engage in all this sleazy behavior. And because she's a celebrity, because she's been in a couple of movies, everybody listens. She's sowing chaos, don't you think?

CB: I guess.

LH: Someone should do something.

CB: Probably, yeah.

LH: Something heroic.

[*pause*]

Maybe it's time to start thinking radical, like someone who takes action. Like a hero.

[*pause*]

Tell me you love me, Carl.

CB: I love you, Linda. Goddamn, just the look on your face…that's why I came back.

LH: I was thinking, as you were talking about standing up for what's right…I had a radical idea. You're going to think I'm crazy.

CB: No, I won't.

LH: OK, what if…God, this is so crazy…what if… You said before, you don't want this to end. You'd stay with me forever if you could.

CB: If I could just see you every once in a while, I'd stay here the rest of my life.

LH: Even though we're not in-person.

CB: Hey, I'll take what I can get.

LH: But you want to be a hero.

CB: Yeah, sure. [*laughs*] I know it's not realistic, but if there was some way to see you and keep being a hero…

LH: All right, I'm just going to say it. It's going to freak you out, but it just might make sense…

CB: Go ahead.

LH: Are you sure? Because it's either going to turn you on right away or it's going to just destroy your idea of me.

CB: I doubt it.

LH: All right… What if you were to do something that might put you back in jail?

CB: OK. I don't know.

LH: But then I came to visit you, in person? On a regular basis? I could get a job at the prison, I could be a prison counselor and we'd see each other every day. And you'd be in jail, but it would be for the right reasons. You'd be a hero to a lot of people. And to me. And we would be together.

CB: OK.

LH: What if you…when you got out of there…what if you were to take out Chelsea Daye?

[*pause*]

CB: What…

LH: I'm going to stop talking now. Let's just sit with this.

CB: What, take her out? Like, kill her? You want that to happen?

LH: Yes, I do.

CB: Why?

LH: It's a radical action.

CB: You can say that again.

LH: Heroes take radical action, Carl.

CB: Heroes don't kill movie stars.

LH: They might, if those movie stars are trying to bring down the country.

CB: With some newspaper articles. [*laughs*] This is weird. I think I'm done for today, Linda. I think you're done, too.

LH: You think I'm crazy.

CB: You know what, Linda? How about you stop telling me what I think.

LH: I'm sorry, Carl. We don't have to talk.

CB: Good.

[*pause*]

[*pause*]

What is…I've been telling you, Linda, how messed up I am about Forrester…and now you ask me to kill somebody? What in the *fuck*?

LH: You don't think you have it in you.

CB: What about you? How about you shoot Chelsea Daye, and I'll visit you in jail? Come on, be a hero!

LH: You're right, Carl. Maybe I should.

CB: Oh, fuck you!

LH: Carl. Unnecessary. Apologize to me, please. Apologize or I'll shut this down and you can go home.

CB: Sorry.

[*pause*]

LH: Do you own a gun, Carl?

CB: What?

LH: Do you own a gun?

CB: I've got Uncle Ray's Colt that he brought home from Iraq.

LH: Maybe I could do some research, find out how to shoot, take classes. Then I could see when Chelsea Daye comes to town. She's doing a tour. Did you know that? Going around, holding rallies…

CB: I heard.

LH: I'd have to make sure Danny and my mother were taken care of... My mother I'm not so worried about, but Danny... You're right. I can't do it. Too many attachments. Besides, if I went to jail, I don't think you would be able to see me every day, so that wouldn't work...but I would do it if I could.

CB: No. I don't buy it.

LH: Why not?

CB: I've done it. And it takes something, not in a good way. You don't have it.

LH: Could you do it again, do you think?

CB: Maybe. If I had to. Not this cold-blooded shit you're talking about, but if it saved somebody's life.

LH: Don't you see, Carl? This is what I've been talking about this whole time. This would save lives. Think about it.

CB: No, I'm not going to think about it.

LH: Carl, you're crying.

CB: It's just...I can't believe...

LH: You like Chelsea Daye that much?

CB: You hate her that much?

[*pause*]

LH: Carl, allow me to bring you in on some highly confidential information… Chelsea Daye is an enemy of the state. That's not just fancy language. She's been designated. Officially.

CB: Do you hate her, Linda?

[*pause*]

LH: I do. I hate her for making me do this. Every time I see her face, when I hear her voice or when I see *The Citizen*… I just want to die.

[*pause*]

Because it's either her or me, and I've made my decision. I live with it now. Her being taken out, it's my world. It's why I'm here. It's why you're here, too. We're meant to be together so we can do this. And the worst part is, this is easy. I'm shocked at how easy this is, how easy it will be.

CB: No. No way.

LH: And when it's done, we'll be together. You talk about how you missed doing something in the War, but you haven't. The War is here. Carl, I've thought the same things you're thinking now. I've wondered at the impossibility, the strangeness of it. But then one day it feels less strange. Then it starts to feel OK. But you have to feel it. Allow it to pass through you. Because it isn't going anywhere. I have the idea in me and now it's in you. And you're going to accept it just like I did. Chelsea Daye will die. By your hand. I promise you.

CB: No.

LH: You know, these days, I can forget myself for hours, forget how to feel…I can just be less… and sometimes it's hard to come back. Sometimes it takes a tiny act of violence to bring myself back from not being. Have you ever felt that way, Carl? Wanting to not be?

[*pause*]

CB: Yes.

LH: That's the hero in you. It's there. It's there when you're not, when you forget yourself and just…do. You will be stronger for doing and the world will be better because you accepted this.

[*pause*]

Do you still love me, Carl?

[*pause*]

I know you love me. I love you too.

[*pause*]

Do we love each other? Don't cry. Do we love each other?

CB: Yes.

LH: We're going to work on this, Carl. This is the work you need to do to become the hero you are. I am here to help you. And when we're finished, we will be together. Accept this.

CB: OK.

LH: You will be a hero to me, to the country, to yourself. Accept this.

CB: OK.

LH: It's not going to be easy, Carl. But I know you can do it…never forget that. And never forget I love you.

END EXCERPT

Linda emerged from her office, making a maraca noise with each step, courtesy of the bottle of Sertanin in the pocket of her bathrobe. The noise used to annoy her, but lately she found comfort in it, as a reminder that redress for whatever she might be feeling was just a dose away.

She went into the bathroom, frowning at the small heaps of garbage on either side of the sink—cotton balls, Kleenex, Q-tips, boxes of Band-Aids felled and opened, everything dotted copper-red. Linda checked the small gash on her shoulder. Looked all right—it had been such a nice, clean cut, right in that sweet spot where deltoid made way for bicep. Linda worried the wound with two fingers, making the pain sharp and tasty. *Enough,* she thought, after a minute. *This isn't what we came in here to do.*

Linda undressed, leaving her bathrobe and sleepwear where they fell, keeping her eyes closed to avoid seeing herself naked. Her thighs had gone wide on her and a paunch had formed at the front of her waist, just like the one she'd had after having Danny. The last time she examined herself in the mirror, the words *disgusting cow* sprung to mind, not just because of the weight gain but the look in her eyes.

She stepped into the shower. The water was hot, which was good—the hotter the better. Yesterday had been the most Carl-filled day yet: nine sessions over twenty-four hours. Today was likely to be lighter, probably no more than four or five. (Lighter days tended to follow heavy days, Linda had found, figuring Miles didn't want to fall behind in his reviews of the playbacks.) They were now well into the Impetus phase—the introduction/repetition of a workable plan—and it was easy: repeat, repeat, repeat until it all becomes fact.

And the repetition went both ways. Linda had Carl telling her that he loved her on command. She, meanwhile, issued statements of affection only after Carl showed obedience. This dynamic of unconditional love versus conditional love made things manage-able, emotionally, though sometimes Linda wondered whether Carl might be the more fortunate of the two of them. At least he had the comfort of delusion.

Linda stepped out of the shower, again keeping her eyes closed, and toweled off. She exited the bathroom and dressed in her closet, revisiting a thought that had occurred to her last night: What if, after all this trouble, all this annihilation (annihilation in the physical sense, that is, the conversion of matter to energy, man to action), Danny were to undergo a lung transplant and die on the operating table? In the light of day, it didn't seem possible. Danny was now con-sidered a prime candidate for the procedure, with an expected success rate in the ninety-ninth percentile. But the unexpected could and did happen. The dream in which Linda had this thought—a dream that involved her walking through a huge field of daisies, every one of them on fire, looking like a million small, swaying torches—had left her in a state of paralysis. Fully awake, she knew she was lying in bed, could hear rain tapping on her windows, but could not even open her eyes. *This is probably what it would feel like,* was one thought, *if the unexpected were to happen. Waking death.*

After retrieving her bathrobe from the bathroom floor, Linda made her way back to the office. This was her spot when she had nothing else to do. On either side of her monitor were foot-high stacks of papers, most of them recent session transcripts with Miles's handwritten notes in red ink. She only ever skimmed them any-more; she knew by now what he wanted. Fulfilling Miles' wishes had become second nature.

She powered up the monitor to find Carl asleep in bed, curled up in the fetal position. He had eaten breakfast—his tray held an array of dirty plates and drained cups. Linda zoomed in on Carl's face. His eyes and mouth were shut tight. One fist was tucked under his chin. After a few minutes, he flinched his shoulders. Linda shut off the monitor. It wouldn't be long before a new session was called. Linda's powers of waiting had grown exponentially in the last couple of weeks; she could sit somewhere and *not think* for hours. The Sertanin helped with that.

Linda searched the pockets of her bathrobe and found a strip of staples. She had no idea where they had come from, though it felt like some earlier version of herself had grabbed them the moment she saw them. She ran the tip of her forefinger across the bottom edge of the strip. Sharp. Good and sharp.

She stood and removed her bathrobe, letting it drape over her chair. She examined her hands, her forearms, her elbows. Where was a good spot? She needed someplace that could satisfy the impulse but remain hidden from prying eyes…

Bringing one foot up to the seat of her chair, Linda removed the sock. This foot already had two cuts—long slashes that ran parallel across the top of the foot, where the metatarsals were still visible if she flexed her toes a certain way. Maybe the underside of the foot? No, too messy, and it could lead to limping, which would, in turn, lead to questions from her mother. (Vera was getting damn nosy lately, always asking when she last ate, what did she do with herself all cooped up there in the back of the house, et cetera.)

Ah, between the toes, where the skin was thin. Perfect. Linda adjusted her grip on the strip of staples, and, taking aim, swiped between the big toe and the piggy who stayed home and *ooh ooh ooh* there it was: a bright, keening, nasal passage–clearing pain. She dropped the strip of staples onto the carpet and threw her head back, bringing the heel of her hand up to her mouth and biting down. *Good one.* Definitely more intense than she was expecting. She imagined herself turning suddenly into a gas, fully present in the moment for a good two or three seconds before the pain receded and she was called upon, once again, to forget herself.

A chiming sounded from her wrist as orange light swept back and forth. Time for the first session of the day. Linda looked down at her foot. The cut was beautiful, a thin red line with little red beads adorning both sides, tapering off just before meeting the top-most slash across her foot.

She placed her foot on the floor and took a breath. Did she have what she needed? A glass of water might be nice, but never mind. She again turned on the monitor and watched as Carl, hearing his own chime, stood and began puttering about, adjusting the curtains, straightening a lampshade, making his bed. Carl made a bed faster than anyone Linda knew. And he smiled all the time. After another moment of watching, Linda cleared her throat and said good morning.

MAY FY20___

USoFA WorldWide War-Related PTSD Individualized Therapy Program (Pilot), "SoldierWell" Therapy Session #49

May 1, FY20____

1105EST

LINDA HELD

Interviewing:

PRIVATE* CARL BOXER, US Army (Associate, Transportation Services, "Free2Fight," USoFA WorldWide)

(BEGIN)

LINDA HELD: Well, Carl, here we are.

PVT.* CARL BOXER: Can I ask you something, Linda? It's really you, right? Because sometimes I look up at this monitor and I just start talking, pretending you're there. Is that crazy?

LH: No, Carl. I always look forward to sitting down with you. You know that.

CB: Sure feels crazy.

LH: I know what you mean.

[*pause*]

But now it's on to something new.

CB: Yeah. The end of one thing, the beginning of another. I'm not a sentimental person, though. I'm not one for a lot of carrying on. [*laughs*]

LH: Well, some days I still wonder if you're up for the challenge. The challenge you've made for yourself.

CB: Oh, I can do it. I'm not worried. Linda, can I say something?

LH: Go ahead.

CB: I was thinking...you're a good therapist, Linda. Sorry if that sounds forward or something.

LH: Not at all. Thank you.

CB: You're welcome!

LH: What will you do when you leave here, Carl?

CB: I'm going to take the shuttle to the holding area. I will fill out my release forms and...

[*pause*]

LH: You will undergo a medical exam...

CB: Right, right, sorry. I will undergo a medical exam, then fill out my release forms, and request payment for my time with the SoldierWell program.

LH: How will you receive the payment?

CB: Half check, half cash payment.

LH: Good. And so, along with the traveling stipend, how much money will you have in cash?

CB: Enough to purchase a Beretta 92 and the Murphy accessory. And plenty of bullets.

LH: Caliber of bullets?

CB: The nine-millimeter NATO round.

LH: Good, and where will you make these purchases?

CB: Washington, DC.

LH: How do you plan on getting to Washington, DC?

CB: USoFA WorldWide allows all graduates of the SoldierWell program the option to fly anywhere one-way within the continental United States. My choice will be Washington, DC.

LH: And that is where you will purchase the gun and accessories.

CB: Our nation's capital has many options when it comes to purchasing a firearm. It will be the first thing I do after leaving the airport.

LH: That's right. Also, your traveling stipend will allow you to stay for one night at any mid-priced hotel in the District.

CB: Linda, sorry, but I had the idea last night… may I ask a question?

LH: Yes?

CB: Since I'm with the SoldierWell program, or, at least, since I'm an employee with the Company and everything, why can't I get a room at one of those Freedom America hotels the Company owns? I'm not trying to say I need a big room, but it seems like it might make more sense to let me stay there, maybe even...

LH: Yes?

CB: Maybe...I was just thinking...maybe you could make a reservation...

LH: Carl, I thought this was something you'd thought through. This is your mission.

CB: No, I know...

LH: Heroes take care of themselves. You said that.

CB: Right, you're right. No, I agree. I can find my own hotel room. [*laughs*] Forget I said anything.

LH: If you're not going to take this seriously, Carl, we might as well just go back to talking about your prison days ...

CB: No, Linda, please.

LH: All right. And the next day?

CB: The next day, I shower, shave, dress in my civilian clothes, and walk to the Washington National Mall.

LH: The mission has now begun in earnest...

CB: I'll walk to the Washington National Mall, which should take approximately ten minutes. I'll get as close as I can to the stage as quickly as I can. While still blending in.

LH: And if a police officer stops you?

CB: Hello, I'm here for pleasure, my tour of the Lincoln Memorial finished early, and I understand Chelsea Daye is going to be here. The wife and I are such big fans of her movies.

LH: Excellent.

CB: Thank you.

LH: I'd say you're ready.

CB: I am, Linda. I am ready.

LH: How are you feeling?

CB: About the mission?

LH: Yes, can you still see yourself accomplishing it, now that it's so close? Or do you find your resolve weakening in any way?

CB: No, no. This is a task that needs to be completed, and I'm capable of completing it. There's no sense inviting emotion into it because it's going to happen. I've made my decision. How I feel has nothing to do with it. Not anymore. But... I had a dream last night, about her. She was sitting on a swing, one of those old homemade kinds where it's just a rope knotted into a plank of wood, and you wrap your legs around…it's a warm day, she's swinging back and forth and wearing this very thin, very clean white dress. Spotless summer dress, it's so bright…and her hair's cut short…and I'm standing a few feet away, watching her and crying…only it's not that I'm crying, I mean, I don't feel the feeling or anything but I can feel the wet on my cheeks… Maybe I just finished crying… Anyway, I'm watching her, and these tears are running down my cheeks, and she's looking at me real cold, like I'm something that just disgusts her. There's more to it, I just can't remember…it was one of those real tiring dreams, running from place to place…this was the one quiet, still moment of the whole thing…[*laughs*] What were we talking about? Oh yeah, my resolve is not weakening. Thanks for asking.

LH: You're aware of her announcement, then? That the Washington stop is one of a whole string of public appearances?

CB: I heard that, yes.

LH: Does it interest you, the things she has to say?

CB: No. I don't care, honestly. Probably something else to damage our reputation in the world. That's what I think. Here she is, getting paid millions because of a little bit of talent and the generous support of USoFA WorldWide, which, you know, basically helped put her out there, in the world.

She's living off of us, off of America. And then, in this high and mighty position, she decides to denigrate the War? Denigrate our Armed Forces? That's just biting the hand that feeds.

LH: Like a dog.

CB: Right, a dog. A mad dog.

LH: I'm pleased to see you taking control of your future, Carl. This is what a hero does. A couple of weeks ago I wasn't so sure.

CB: Oh, well, I just had no clue then. [*laughs*] I didn't recognize the opportunities. It's a matter of imagination, because I'm young, in good health, pretty bright…do you think I'm bright, Linda?

LH: I think you're very bright.

CB: Thank you. I feel like I see things more clearly than a lot of people. Sometimes…I'd like to think I'm like you in that way, Linda. You see things real clearly. I mean, I know I'm not where you are, but one day…I think we're kindred souls. Like with Chelsea Daye and stuff, you expressed my wishes to me so clearly…

LH: No, Carl. That was you.

CB: No, Linda…the way you helped me see my situation in that light…I love our time together. Sometimes I remember this or that thing I said, you know, like I gave away too much, or like I said something I didn't want to say. But you don't judge. It's almost as if…as if the things I was saying, it was almost like you already knew them, like they'd happened to you. And I know it's not my place to ask, but sometimes it felt like, like by helping me you were also helping yourself. Maybe every doctor feels this way.

[*pause*]

Well… I don't really have anything more to say. I've got this peace now. There's this clarity I have, like this vibrating going on underneath everything, and it's building… Do you feel it, Linda?

LH: Yes, I feel it. But it's coming from you, Carl. You're vibrating.

CB: Yeah! I see it now!

LH: There are many, many people, Carl, who would envy you in your position. Here you are, heading out into the world, fully aware of your destiny. When you step out of that building and onto the shuttle, you'll know exactly what needs to be done.

CB: That's true.

LH: Most people go their whole lives without that sense of purpose. So many of us are just making it up as we go along. But not you.

CB: Not me.

LH: Would you like to go over the where and when? One more time?

CB: I don't think so. I've got it figured out.

LH: Do you have everything you need for now?

CB: Yes, and I can't wait. I can't wait…I look forward to feeling the gun in my hand almost more than anything… I'd like to find a place close to the stage, take a deep breath…it's all so clear in my head. It's going to be glorious, but also calm. I'll be thinking of you the whole time.

LH: I'm glad, Carl. I believe you're ready.

CB: Oh, I am. Thank you, Linda. I just…I can't remember the last time I was this happy.

END TRANSCRIPT

Carl had been on this street before. He remembered the long black bench and the overturned potted plant outside the glass doors of that apartment building and the chained-up iron tables of the closed café. He kept walking.

"John-Boy, hey. You got someplace to go? Nah, you don't. Hey, I'm talking to you."

The cop stayed about five paces behind Carl at all times, but Carl never turned around, not once. And he knew that if he so much as glanced backward, the cop would stop-and-frisk him. That couldn't happen.

"What's the plan, John-Boy? You sleeping out-of-doors tonight? I see you looking at that bench, don't do it! *Don't do it!*"

Carl removed his hand from the bench and continued walking. He was so tired, all he wanted to do was lie down. It had been a long day and now he was aching all over, even after downing three-quarters of the bottle of whiskey he'd bought a couple of hours before. His feet were aching and his arms were aching and his eyeballs were aching. His right ankle also ached, in an itchy, pinched way.

That morning, Carl had walked out of Reagan National Airport and used one of his three allotted passes to jump on a shuttle bound for Washington, DC. The plan he'd come up with, with Linda's help, was to ride into Union Station, and from there walk the five or so blocks to the Washington National Mall and get the lay of the land before checking into a nearby hotel. When that was done, he would head back out and make his purchases.

But while on the shuttle, Carl had seen a billboard showing a huge Jericho 941 with BEST PRICES ALL YEAR!!! in big red letters across it, and underneath ALL WEEKEND LONG AT THE LINCOLN MEMORIAL. Carl looked over the shuttle route and saw that, hey, if he got off just a little bit earlier, he would be right where this thing was going on, and then could just cross the street and be at the Mall. Best prices of the year…

He hadn't shopped around, though, which was stupid. One of the first booths that he passed had a Beretta on a retractable cord, with a handwritten price tag on a little white string hanging from the trigger guard. The second Carl saw it, some guy came up and started talking about what a great piece it was—polymer frame, adjustable sights, all this stuff, and Carl had no idea what he was talking about. Springing the gun from its retractable cord, the guy invited Carl to check it out for himself, pointing him to a mirror next to the cash register.

Carl had expected the Beretta to be heavy, but it wasn't. It just felt like all of a piece, like a block of nice wood that had been carved to fit his hand perfectly, with these cool finger grooves along the handle. It felt like an extension of himself, which, yeah, was the kind of dumbass thing a first-timer at a gun show might say, but still, it was true. Carl stood before the mirror and the guy said go ahead, show me your stance, and that's when everything felt real, twice as real as before. He was going to buy this gun. The guy laughed and said all right, brother, it looks like you know what you're doing, and Carl replied that he was just gripping it like his uncle taught him. Then the guy came over and looked at him in the mirror and said, *Damn if it ain't one razorblade motherfucker I'm looking at* and right there Carl knew this guy had done time, no doubt, so then Carl said you know what, I could use a Murphy to go with it and the guy took him over to the cash register and reached underneath and came up with one, out of its package.

Then Carl asked what about a holster and the guy made a face and started showing him waistband holsters and Carl had to say actually I'm looking for an ankle holster and the guy laughed and said what for, this a gift for your wife? But Carl kept his cool and said have you got one or not and the guy clucked his tongue and said he didn't bring his full stock but there was one made from carbon fiber that he'd be willing to throw in with the weapon and the accessory for two hundred. Carl pulled out his bills and said let's do it, and three minutes later he was back on the Washington National Mall with a loaded Beretta 92 strapped to his ankle.

With nowhere to go, Carl burned an hour or so in the lobby of a Freedom America Hotel, watching kids in dripping bathing suits snapping their towels at one another. Just as it started to get dark, a security guy came up and asked him if he was meeting somebody or what, so Carl had no choice but to leave. The next couple of hours Carl spent hanging around outside the museums along the Mall, feeling lonely, a little on edge, but free. After the sun went all the way down, he bought a hot dog and ate it and then purchased a flat pint bottle of whiskey, taking pulls while walking up and down streets as the traffic thinned and homeless people started coming out of the churches and libraries to make their beds on the grates of Metro ventilation shafts. All that seemed like a year ago now, with the whiskey almost gone and a cop following him, waiting for the opening to take him in.

"Which way now, John-Boy? Right or left? All right… left it is."

Carl turned the corner and started walking faster. He didn't know where he was, but it didn't matter because there, not a hundred feet away, stood a ShuttleShell.

Lit from within, its walls curving outward, the ShuttleShell glowed peach in the darkness. Carl checked his jeans pockets and, yes, there it was, his shuttle pass. He stopped, listening for the cop's footfalls to stop. Harsh laughter followed.

"What are we stopping here for, John-Boy? You think you're getting in there?" The cop came closer, close, by his side.

"Come on, son. This is USoFA WorldWide property. Here, let me take you in. We'll get you a cot or something, you can sleep this off. Seriously, man, I'm tired of walking."

Carl approached the ShuttleShell door. The cop let out a long sigh that halted when Carl pulled out his shuttle pass. He held it up to the sensor. It turned green and Carl walked inside. The light and warmth enveloped him, as if he had stepped into a gorgeous new dimension.

In one corner stood a water cooler, three-quarters full, *We Take Care of Our Own!* in friendly cursive stenciled across the jug. Before him sat a cushioned bench, about six feet wide, perfect for lying down. Carl turned to see the cop walking away, shaking his head, and so in celebration he brought out his bottle of whiskey and raised it to the light before taking one last pull.

Carl drank a cup of water before sitting down, allowing himself to feel every last inch of his relief. He reached down to loosen the straps on his ankle holster.

"Hi there!"

Carl flinched, looking around. A beautiful girl seemed to be looking directly at him from a panel on the wall to his right.

"How are you?"

Carl measured his words carefully. "I'm OK."

The beautiful girl put on a caring, sympathetic face. "Look," she said, "I get it. You're tired. Aren't we all? Studies show that the average American manages fewer than six hours of sleep every night. That's not enough, is it?"

"I guess?"

"Don't you wish there was something to make you feel like you've gotten a full night's sleep?"

Carl slumped. "Off," he said. "Off, please. Off."

But the beautiful girl kept talking, pitching Gatorade AM. When she finished, Carl closed his eyes and allowed his head to fall back...

"Hi there!"

Pause.

"How are you?"

The ad played through, all over again. Carl closed his eyes again, and the world started fading away, spinning away from him, growing distant...

"Hi there!"

⌒

Carl opened his eyes to two blue hills, very far off. They were quaking. He then remembered himself, where he was. He released his arms from around his knees and turned over onto his back.

Finally, it was morning.

Pushing his legs out and placing his feet on the ground, Carl stood up slowly. The street was quiet. Everything around him, from the sidewalk to the street signs to the red fire hydrant down the street, held a silvery, newborn tint, everything except for the puddle of barf on the curb. Carl swallowed. Whiskey had been a bad idea…

The ShuttleShell's peach-colored light was flickering. Carl looked to find a spiderweb of cracks in the center of the panel where the Gatorade girl had been. The water cooler lay on its side, its jug dented and empty. Water was everywhere. Carl walked away as quickly as he could.

At some point last night, after realizing that the girl in the Gatorade AM ad wasn't going to let him sleep, he'd started talking to her, telling her he loved her and wanted to run away with her. It was just drunk bullshit, but then the girl started responding to him, or at least he thought she did. She told him how he could get to meet her, how maybe he could contact the advertising company and find out her name, and from there he could do one of those paid searches on the CUP where you can find out where somebody lives, and then he could go and start hanging around the places she regularly goes—restaurants, coffee shops, yoga studios. She even told him how to approach her, how he ought to be friendly but not too friendly, then how to ask her out, how to be a good boyfriend, what meeting her folks would be like, getting engaged, marriage, kids. She said she wanted to buy a farm somewhere, away from any city, where they could raise llamas or something. Then Linda came into his head, asking questions about was he betraying her, talking to this girl. That's all he could remember.

Breakfast—that's what he needed. Union Station probably had a breakfast place somewhere inside. He had a little money left. He could go back there and get a bite, settle this funny electric feeling that was making his hands shake. Maybe eggs and bacon, or pancakes and syrup and a side of fresh fruit. SoldierWell had spoiled him; he couldn't go one morning without needing to stuff his face.

He stopped and bent forward and unsnapped the holster around his ankle, allowing it to fall away from his calf, and scratched the itch underneath. The skin there was damp, hair pasted against skin. After getting a little air on it, he refastened the holster straps.

Carl began walking again, not knowing exactly where he was but confident he'd make it to Union Station sooner or later. He took the morning air deep into his lungs, smiling. Things were going to happen today.

The ice in Linda's drink rattled as she took the den's last available seat. Everyone was looking at her expectantly, as if she owed them either her thanks or an apology. Vera and Deva were sitting together on the couch, Vera perched on its edge with her hands clasped together, the hematite magnetic therapy bracelet on her left wrist knocking against the gold watch on her right, emitting a chalky, billiard balls kissing sound. Both were gifts from Deva, who lounged cross-legged next to her, sporting too-short khaki shorts and oxblood penny loafers without socks. Robert (who, unless Linda was mistaken, should have been at school with

Danny right now) stood behind them, mannequin-like in fresh nursing scrubs.

Fear glowed in the center of Linda's chest. "Is it Danny? Is he all right?"

"Danny is fine," Vera said. "But we wanted to talk with you." She leaned forward and smiled. Her eyes were red.

Linda brought up her drink and gulped, trying to wash down a trio of melting Sertanin. She had swallowed them dry just a minute before, coming down the hallway as Vera called for her to please join everyone in the den, and they had gotten lodged in her throat, the active ingredients going to waste...

"Linda, we are worried," Vera said. "About you."

Linda looked at each of her accusers' faces. Vera remained smiling, with a desperate, pathetic hope in her eyes. Deva's face was impossible to read, though the set of his jaw betrayed unease. And Robert was Robert: cheerful, alert, eager to help.

"Aha," Linda said, laughing. "So that's what this is. Wow, an intervention with three people. And one of them works for me."

Vera blinked at the floor. "I'm hoping we can figure something out," she said. "Some options."

"OK, so Mom's the leader." Linda tightened the sash of her bathrobe and crossed her legs. "All right, what is everybody worried about? Start there."

"Your... your behavior."

"What about my behavior, specifically? You have to have concrete examples to present to the addict, Mom. Is this an intervention or not?"

Vera glared at the floor, acting like she didn't know where to start. "You're not taking care of yourself, Linda."

"*Concrete* examples, Mom." Linda slapped her palm with her fist to emphasize the need for organized thought. "Dates. Times. Eyewitness accounts." Again, she looked everyone in the face. "You guys should have talked to someone before trying this," she said. "I'm pretty sure consultation with a professional interventionist is covered by my insurance. So far, this is just…"

"You want a concrete example, Linda? What about last night?"

Last night…last night had been fine. Miles had called that afternoon, treating Linda to one last round of compliments and thanks. She remembered him saying that, whatever happened, he would make it known to the powers that be that she was, hands down, the best therapist he had worked with, across all SoldierWell programs.

A perfectly lovely evening followed. she and Danny and Robert walked around East Quadrant Park, grabbing hot dogs and fries from the food trucks that gathered near the fountains on Friday evenings. Later, Deva and Vera joined them, and together they took in the sunset. And then back home, Vera had cornered her in the kitchen to ask how come she was in such a good mood, and Linda shrugged and said, oh, nothing, just good news at work. Soon after, she hustled back to her bedroom and shut all doors, the better to wonder what exactly she had murdered inside herself to be able to say such a thing. Then she remembered the fresh bottle of vodka in the pantry, the fresh lime in the fruit bowl…

"What *about* last night?" she asked now, daring Vera to find fault. "I might've gotten up to check if the stove was off, but then I went right back to bed."

"You were *singing*, Linda. Singing and crying. And you fell in the kitchen. Robert had to carry you to bed."

Linda looked at Robert, unbelieving. "How's your arm?" he asked.

"For the last time…" Linda said, "when you *work* odd hours, you tend to *relax* at odd hours. Why does no one get that? Has everyone forgotten what it's like to work?"

Vera put on one of her sad smiles. "That doesn't make sense, Linda. You were with us all afternoon."

"Right. I was with you all afternoon. *Not* drinking. I thought we had a nice time, but then I didn't know you guys had this little surprise planned. And by the way, this is like the opposite of an effective intervention, Mom. You've got no *plan*, no *script*..."

Linda stood, and for a moment everything lurched to the right. She would have fallen for sure if she hadn't had the presence of mind to hold onto the arm of her chair. Vera gasped, drama queen that she was, but this was a good thing—it meant the Sertanin was kicking in.

"I don't have time for this," Linda said. "Mom, this was not your best idea. Try talking to *me* next time you want to try this, and I'll walk you through it. Everybody, all three of you, thanks for your concern, but I can't do this right now. I can't."

Vera looked around. "Would anyone else like to say anything?"

"I'd like to say," Robert said, "I've been picking up on some hostility..."

Linda turned to Robert. "Robert, sweetie, I love what you do for my son, but if you don't shut your mouth right now I swear to Christ I will come over there and bite your nose clean off."

Linda fled the room, embarrassed for her mother. She entered the kitchen, went to the sink. "Here I am, pouring out my drink!" she yelled. "Not because of you but because I don't want it right now! See, everybody? That's the difference between Dad and me! Dad was not capable! I am *perfectly* capable!"

She paused for a response but could only hear Vera moaning, "Now do you see what I'm up against?"

"What *you're* up against?" Laughing, Linda walked back toward the den to ensure she could be heard. "What is it that you're up against, Mom? Your own wing of this house? This house full of food? The uninterrupted free time? Or maybe it's being able to live here in perfect security? Is that what you're up against?"

She waited for a response. Nothing. Dammit, now she had to leave. No way could she spar with Vera all morning.

Fortunately, she was OK to drive. She went to her bedroom to fetch her car keys, which were on top of the dresser, right where she'd left them the day they moved in. She ditched her bathrobe and threw on jeans and sneakers, then worked out the knots in her hair with a brush. She grabbed her wallet and her phone and her Sertanin and got going, the urgency of wanting to be gone doubling with every passing second.

Vera stood in front of the door to the garage, hugging her arms. Linda stopped.

"What are you doing, Linda?" Vera's voice was singsongy, strange.

"Getting out of here. Excuse me."

Vera stepped forward and reached for Linda's wrists. "Linda," she said, "listen, honey. You are not in a good way."

Linda shook off her mother's hands. "Mom, for God's sake…" She stepped around Vera and, after securing both hands on the doorknob, shoved her away with her hip. Vera fell back, allowing Linda just enough room to pass.

"Mom, please," Linda said, almost to her car now. "I'm just going to get out of here for an hour or so. We can talk later."

She had the key in the car door when Vera caught up to her, falling to her knees and wrapping her arms around Linda's ankles.

"Mom?" Linda laughed as she shimmied one leg and then the other from Vera's embrace. "You sure *you're* not drunk?"

Vera remained on the floor, her arms splayed out, her shoulders shaking. "This happened to your father, I won't let it happen to you!"

Linda looked up to see Robert and Deva, watching from the kitchen, their mouths wide open. "Nice job, guys. Way to be involved."

Deva snapped to attention and went to attend to Vera, wrapping his arms around her and helping her into a sitting position. She was going to be fine, Linda was certain of it.

"I'll be home soon," Linda said. "I just need to be somewhere else right now."

Her eyes shut tight, Vera wailed, "I'll call the police! I'll call Harvey!"

"Mom, please. You are making a scene." It was the most cutting thing she could think of in the moment, and it worked— Vera dropped the operatics and went catatonic, staring into space, breathing hard.

Linda turned away and grabbed her keys and got into her car. The garage door opener was in the passenger seat. She shut the door and fit the key into the ignition while pumping the gas. The Hyundai roared to life.

"That's my girl." Linda patted the dashboard as she pulled out.

Union Station was a busy place. It felt just like the airport from the day before, only the ceilings were higher and there was this sense that nobody wanted to be here. No way was some cop going to pull him out of the crowd and demand he state his business.

He had to wait forever to get breakfast, cordoned off at one end of the counter with five other people, everybody with their faces in their phones, looking up only to scowl at the lady who was running the whole operation by herself. After receiving his clamshell of scrambled eggs and toast and grabbing a Gatorade AM out of the display fridge, he grabbed the least dirty table in the food court and scarfed everything down. Everything was hot and solid and made him kick back and burp when it was all done, which caught the eye of an old man, ten feet away, who pushed off the pillar he'd been leaning against to approach his table. Carl got a bad feeling. The old man's gaze was steady, like he was suspicious of Carl or else looking for a fight. The backpack on his shoulder looked like it had been run over by a truck.

"Hi there," the man said when he got close. "Beautiful morning, no?"

"Sure." As the old man sat down, Carl took his empty clamshell in his hands. He was just about to get up and walk away when he felt his ankle holster shift. One of the straps had come undone, now the Beretta had swung around to the front of his leg, pulling at the cuff of his jeans.

The old man looked away as a grin overtook one side of his mouth. "Hell with it, I'm just an old soldier, what do I know?"

"You were in the War?"

The old man folded his cracked, bruised hands on the table and nodded. "Operation Iraqi Freedom."

Carl noticed a security guard, muscle-bound and feather-haired, standing roughly twenty feet away. He had eyes on the old man. Carl sat up carefully. "Where'd you serve?"

"Army. Baghdad."

"I had an uncle in Samarra," Carl said.

"Is that right?"

"Raymond Denny? First Battalion, 46th Air Defense. He was awarded the Silver Star. But he's dead now."

The man nodded before saying, "Didn't know him. I was Baghdad." Slowly, he held out his hand. "Gordo Turnbull. 3rd Squadron, 71st Cavalry Regiment, 1st Brigade Combat Team, 10th Mountain Division."

"Carl Boxer. I was there, too. For a few weeks."

"Where at?"

"Mosul, mostly."

The security guard had spread his feet apart and hitched his thumbs behind his belt as he continued to watch them.

"Doing what?"

"Just driving trucks. Freight."

"And you stayed out of trouble."

"I was only there two months. Not much trouble to be had."

"Two months?" Gordo shut one eye. "How'd you pull that?"

"I was there…just as part of this program. I'd come from jail, they had me drive freight to knock down my time."

Gordo looked away again. He didn't seem to have any idea they were being watched. "Well, you served your country, right?"

"That's what they tell me."

"And you made it back in one piece."

"Yup."

"Drive on."

Gordo started recounting his years of fighting with the God-damn Department of Veterans Goddamn Affairs, before USoFA WorldWide took over and modernized everything. Things were OK for the first six months, he said, but then his status as a veteran got redefined, recategorized, something, and eventually Gordo lost coverage for his medication, which made him lose his job, which made him lose his apartment. Carl had trouble paying attention to these grievances; the security guard had come closer without taking a noticeable step.

The sound of Gordo snapping his fingers made Carl flinch.

"Here, let me show you something." Gordo unzipped his back-pack and began rifling through it. The security guard turned toward them, mouth hanging slack.

"It's OK," Carl said, "I should go."

"No, come on," Gordo said. "It's of me, from back in the day. Dammit, why can't I…" He set his backpack on his lap. "I just had it…"

Carl watched it all: the security guard running at them, laying out across the empty table and grabbing Gordo's head like it was a football. Gordo and his backpack hit the ground, hard, as the backpack slid sideways, dashing its contents across the floor. Carl saw a wadded towel, some newspapers, a wooden box with a small brass handle protruding from its side, and a photograph, probably the one Gordo had been searching for.

"Do! Not! Move!" the security guard yelled, his lips pulled back in a snarl. Gordo, his face against the floor, did not move.

Carl reached down at his ankle and re-strapped the holster before shouting, "Is he OK?"

The security guard righted himself, placing a knee in the small of Gordo's back. "Don't you fucking move," he muttered, reaching into his shirt pocket and whipping out a plastic zip tie. Exhaling hard through his nose, he pawed at Gordo's empty hands, trying to join them together.

Carl knelt next to Gordo, peering into his face. Gordo's eyes were closed. His forehead was dark red from hitting the floor. "You OK?" Carl asked. "Can you say something?"

Gordo slowly opened his eyes. His pupils didn't match.

Not knowing what else to do, Carl looked around and picked up the photograph. It showed a much younger Gordo—lean, bird-shouldered, short curls matted against his forehead, leaning against a tank.

"You, put that down!" The security guard snatched the photo and tossed it aside. "That's evidence."

Carl watched the security guard, who didn't seem to know how zip ties worked. "It's his *stuff*," he said.

"You want to join him?"

Carl stood and fought his way to the breakfast counter, where the lady was filming everything on her phone. "Excuse me," he said, ducking out of her shot. "We need an ambulance."

The woman looked up. "Was that homeless man bothering you?"

"No...but this guard might've just killed him. Can you call for a doctor, please?"

"I don't know the situation, and I can't make any kind of medical authorization when I don't know the situation."

"I'm telling you the situation," Carl said. His voice was shaking. "That rent-a-cop just tackled that old man. You saw it, right?"

"I don't know the situation."

"You said that already."

Placing the phone to one side, the woman looked Carl up and down. "Where are *you* coming from?"

Carl turned away just in time to see the security guard dragging Gordo by his still-untied wrists, the empty backpack pressed under his bicep.

Carl caught up to them. "Where are you taking him?"

The guard stopped and held a beefy hand in front of Carl's face. "Sir, I need you to go ahead and let me do my job, please."

"Where are you taking him?"

"Sir..."

Carl stepped back and looked into Gordo's face. "Gordo? Hey, can you hear me? You don't have to go with him. You didn't do anything. I'll vouch for you."

Gordo blinked slowly. "It's all right, young man. These things happen."

The guard dragged Gordo across the dining area to an elevator near the restrooms. A second later, the elevator doors parted and Gordo was heaved inside.

Carl went back and began righting overturned tables and chairs, shooing people away so that they wouldn't step on the old man's things. He picked up the photograph, the wooden box, a torn map of Cleveland, half a dozen newspapers, and a laminated badge that read THE CITIZEN—LICENSED VENDOR. He stuffed the badge into his pocket and dumped everything else except for a single copy of *The Citizen*.

After taking an escalator up to the main floor, Carl passed through the center arch of Union Station's front entrance and crossed Mass Avenue, weaving through the driverless vehicles and tourist buses stuck in traffic. He sat down in front of a big statue of Christopher Columbus on a pedestal, with a winged girl nearer to the ground, a look chiseled into her face that might have been ecstasy. Carl crossed his legs at the ankle so that he could feel the Beretta on the underside of his calf before snapping open *The Citizen*.

What he saw made him laugh out loud. His hands shook as he studied the small picture of his target.

Damn, she was pretty.

He wasn't going to do this. The whole idea seemed not so much stupid or crazy as just plain *bad*, a desperate move he didn't need to make. Linda wanted him to feel like he *had* to do it, but he had choices. He could stand up and run into traffic right now. He could do that.

And this thing, it was killing Linda, too. Carl could tell just by her voice, which had gotten lower and more monotone since they'd first met. And that's not even starting on what she looked like anymore, with the lines under her eyes and her hair—she used to have real thick black hair but recently it had gotten lighter and brittle and thin, like it was getting ready to fall out of her head. Still beautiful, though.

He got it. She was telling him to do this to save Danny. She was a loving mom, what else could she do? Carl felt lucky to see that love firsthand. He got to see the sacrifice she was making because *he was the sacrifice*. And that felt like something good enough to die for.

Carl stood, leaving *The Citizen* behind. The Beretta was hot against his ankle. He spun himself southwest, toward the Washington National Mall.

Linda figured traffic would be bad, but also that she had a whole two hours to make the eight-mile trip to the Mall. Her heart sang a little once she had made up her mind, but then traffic started getting bad in Rosslyn, everything at a standstill. After nosing into a quicker lane, she finally breached the intersection of Lee Highway and North Lynn Street, where two unmanned shuttles sat facing each other, their front fenders just inches apart. Police officers were waving passing cars this way and that.

Linda got close to one of the cops and rolled down her window. "What is this?"

"Those two shuttles are stopped."

"No reason?"

The cop shrugged. "Some wreck in Georgetown and *we* get jammed up. Hey, let's go, sweetie, you're blocking the box."

Traffic loosened up on the other side of the intersection, and tunnel traffic moved swiftly. Things didn't jam up again until the entrance onto Key Bridge, with two lines of cars snaking back a few hundred yards. Some cars had shut off their engines, drivers standing around, stretching, getting up on fenders to see if there was any movement ahead. Linda uncurled her fingers from around the wheel and rolled down all her windows, inhaling the exhaust fumes all around her. The sun was too strong. She should've eaten something. She turned on the radio—nothing but skin cream infomercials and historical conspiracy theories: Nazis and aliens, the Mafia and JFK.

Traffic leaving the District looked OK. She could turn around right now and go home. She could hear Vera out, promise to get help, maybe even get Deva to drive her to some luxury rehab center where she could spend the next ninety days in her bathrobe, catch up on her REM sleep, play Spades between group therapy sessions. She could do that. It probably wouldn't even affect Danny's transplant chances.

Seriously, what kind of mother was she? Why was she *here*, in this car, trying to stop the one thing certain to ensure and prolong the life of her child? For four months she had done nothing but contribute to the Company's goals, Miles's goals. Why go against that now? Why didn't she tell Miles that she couldn't go through with this yesterday, two weeks ago, two months ago? Why hadn't she jumped out of his car the moment he told her? Well, Danny was in the backseat, but still...

Was she in love with Carl, or what?

Linda paid the toll to get onto Key Bridge. Things were moving again. She got into the right lane and turned onto Whitehurst Freeway, which was wide open for a mile or so. She would make it to Carl, with time to spare...

So she *was* in love with Carl. Wait, no she wasn't. Did she have to be, to want to stop him from doing this? Was that the world now?

Twenty-Seventh Street was the most pothole-riddled road Linda had ever driven, and her car sounded like it might fall apart any second. Then a left on Virginia Avenue. Traffic not too bad. Linda felt faint again. She watched her hands slip off the steering wheel and for a second wondered why that mattered.

Still plenty of time. More than an hour. She was going to intercept Carl, take him somewhere quiet, a booth in a fast-food restaurant. They would order large sodas and talk. She would say she had been wrong about Chelsea Daye, that he ought to just forget it. She would ask him to come live with them. They could get a house somewhere and she could wean herself off the Sertanin and finish up her studies and get her degree and start a practice for veterans. And Carl could continue to heal.

And Danny could go back to constantly coughing, spitting up sputum, waking up choking in the middle of the night. Dying young.

A firefighter stood in the road ahead, his oversized glove raised to stop oncoming traffic. Behind him was a firetruck, its ladder extended toward a building belching dark smoke from its fifth floor. Just one lane lay open. Linda banged the heels of her hands softly on the steering wheel before checking the time. Less than one hour now.

To her left stood a dark statue of Benito Juarez, president of Mexico at some point in the 1800s, his face grimly defying all the pigeon shit on his shoulders. The Watergate was somewhere around here. Off in the distance stood the Washington Monument. That was where she needed to be. Traffic wasn't moving.

She did love Carl, though. He wasn't ever really a patient, not to her. He was a friend. He needed protection.

Linda put the Hyundai in gear and swerved around the firetruck, into oncoming traffic. The firefighter who had been directing traffic made a show of jumping to one side as Linda flew down Virginia Avenue, the Washington Monument bisecting her windshield.

It fell out of view when she turned onto Nineteenth Street, with its wide white sidewalks and the leafy trees of Constitution Gardens dead ahead. People were everywhere—tourists and diplomat types and cyclists and Haters with signs. Traffic not too bad. Then a left on Constitution Avenue, its four lanes congested but moving. Art museums on her left, the park on her right. It was a beautiful May day, the sky a deep blue, clouds like flour dashed against stained glass. Sunshine highlighted the water spots on her windshield.

Bad traffic now. All four lanes. Linda stopped at a light. Hater types passed in front of her, holding signs under their arms, smiling, glad for the weather as they traipsed across the bright landscape of trees and grass and black metal fence posts. Some were young and walked with a raggedness. Others were old, die-hard hippies, their walking more purposeful, like they knew the way.

Carl is exactly the kind of man that Danny needs. Someone sensitive and kind, who knows what the War is really like. Linda wiped her eyes with her sleeve. It felt like a fantasy, her saving him today, but it also felt within her reach. So long as she could make it to him in time.

The light turned green but nothing moved. Haters surrounded her car, their voices close as if they were addressing her directly.

She could park somewhere around here if she wanted. Walk the rest of the way. Where to park, though? The light turned red. A spry older man in shorts shouted *Cold drinks!* while hustling between cars.

Linda checked the time on her phone and cried out. Chelsea Daye was scheduled to speak in twenty minutes. Carl must be there already, waiting, with a gun. She unbuckled her seat belt. In her rearview mirror, she watched a young man with a greasy brown pompadour exit his car and look over the traffic, his hands on his hips. She got out and went to him.

By the time she reached him, the young man had pulled out his phone and was speaking Spanish into it, but, noticing Linda's approach, he covered the receiver with his hand and smiled.

"Do you think we'll ever get moving?" Linda laughed at her own helplessness.

The man shook his head. "Haters," he said. "Holding everything up. We don't go anywhere until they come through."

Linda looked past the man to see another wave of people coming toward them, many with their signs up: ABIDE NO LONGER! The President with an X over his face. Edna H eating the world in wide, watermelon-shaped slices.

Linda turned back to the young man. "Hey, I have to use the bathroom," she said. "I'll just run into one of these museums, I'll be right back."

"Take your time."

Linda went back to her car and killed the engine, checking to make sure she hadn't left anything she might need. She then crossed the lanes and stepped onto the sidewalk, falling in with a group of Haters on their way to the Mall.

At Seventeenth Street, a cop stepped in front of traffic to let them cross. "I hope you all get struck by lightning out there today," he said while waving them along. "I'm praying for that."

"All the best to you, officer!" shouted one of their group.

This gang wasn't going fast enough. At the African American History Museum, Linda broke off and fell into a jog. Her ankle hurt but she could handle it. At Fourteenth Street, she turned right, her panic increasing as she continued, making her way through the throng.

Finally, the Mall. Gravel underfoot. All cars were stopped as pedestrian traffic dominated the scene. Carl was somewhere nearby. She checked her phone; Chelsea Daye was scheduled to go on in eight minutes. Her ankle was starting to hurt badly—it felt like a sharpened bamboo chute was being pushed between her tibia and her talus. She had traversed along the first square of Mall grass and saw nothing, nothing but people. Finally, a setup of some kind rose into the middle distance, a wood stage that stood maybe five feet off the ground. Yellow police tape cordoned off the area. A long trailer and two police cars abutted the back of the stage. Even though there seemed to be thousands of people on this side, Linda felt suddenly focused, capable of complex navigation. She pressed her way around the stage, shouldering past people to get to where she thought Carl might be.

He was close. She could feel him. Maybe it *was* love...

The crowd was beyond dense now. Linda wondered if she could lift her feet and just be carried along. A beach ball bounced off of her head, and a tall black woman in an Army jacket jumped over her to swipe at it. Someone had had their hand on her ass for the last five seconds; Linda turned but saw no one worthy of her suspicion. Everyone seemed to be getting pushed away from the stage now, back toward the gravel walkways. Not good—Linda needed to get to the front of the seating area. She tried lowering her shoulder and pushing against the current of bodies. She tried jumping to see if maybe she could by chance catch a glimpse of Carl, maybe shout something to him.

This was stupid. She was going to have to do something drastic to get to Carl. She searched her pockets, thinking maybe she could use her car keys to gouge her way through the crowd—such was her desperation—but what she found was much better: an orange security clearance tag.

"Excuse me," she shouted at a police officer a few feet away. The cop stepped toward her, bending down to hear her request.

"I need to get to the front row," Linda said, holding her security clearance tag up to the cop's face. "It's an emergency."

"What's the emergency?"

"There's a man in the front row. He's not well. He may have a gun."

The cop stood on tiptoes, surveying the area. "Where is he?"

"Up front."

The police officer sighed before taking Linda by the wrist and winding her back into the crowd. "Let's go, people!" he hollered, waving his free hand into the air. "Coming through! Police business!"

They had gotten about ten feet closer to the seating area when a female voice boomed, "Can everybody hear me?"

Everyone whooped and hollered. Linda looked up to find a young woman standing behind a microphone. She had blonde hair and thick glasses and wore a cardigan that looked way too warm in this weather.

"OK, I'm just going to get moving," the young woman said. "Uh…OK, I'll do announcements later." She looked off to one side of the stage. "Ladies and gentlemen, Chelsea Daye."

The entire Washington National Mall cheered as Linda's police escort continued to gently push bodies out of their way.

After a few more steps, Linda saw Carl. He was standing with all the others, his head and shoulders no taller or shorter than anyone else. There was a strange look of open, eyebrows-raised resignation on his face. She called out to him but he couldn't hear her. The crowd was still on its feet, cheering. She called out to him again.

The cop turned to her. He was resting his hand on the snap-closed holster on his hip. "You see him?"

"Not yet," she said. "His name is Carl."

The cop nodded and turned back, searching. She slinked around in front of him—getting that much closer—and called for Carl again.

People in the crowd began seating themselves. She called for him again. Carl began surveying the crowd, left to right. His head was slowly turning, eyes bright with intent. Linda waved her arms.

Carl stopped surveying and blinked as recognition took hold. He then broke into a wide smile, his entire face beaming. Linda laughed at his glee upon seeing her. She went to him, stepping lightly around the corners of blankets and legs, not taking her eyes off him. Carl was staying put, which was fine. Linda didn't want him going anywhere.

"Oh my God, you guys, thank you so much for coming out today."

More whooping and hollering. Linda glanced back at the stage. There was Chelsea Daye, standing behind the microphone. She was smaller than Linda had imagined. Someone had set up a teleprompter just to her left.

Carl remained standing, the look on his face wild with delight. Maybe he loved her too. Just a few more seconds, fifteen feet more to go, ten, and she would be at Carl's side. How come he was still standing?

As if hearing her question, Carl bent down, reaching for something at his feet, and *oh God the gun he's got a gun he's here he's going to do it...*

Linda swiped at the empty air behind her. The cop had fallen behind. Linda shouted for him, waving her hands and yelling *there he is, he's got a gun*. The cop fell into a defensive crouch and unsnapped his holster. Linda watched his eyes go wide as he opened his mouth.

"Gun!"

Linda turned back to Carl, twisting her ankle again in the process. A shock of pain seized her and she collapsed. She reached out for a nearby shoulder to help break the fall but the shoulder vanished under her hand.

Bodies were everywhere, a wave of bodies and clothes. A squall of feedback sailed out over the rushing crowd. Linda heard nearby a wicker picnic basket getting crushed underfoot, then again, then again, followed by a mass keening sound. No one needed to hear *gun* twice.

From the ground, Linda kept her eyes on Carl. His face was suddenly serious. She watched the gun as it traversed the span of Carl's torso. Linda cried out for Carl to put down the gun when somebody stepped on her back.

Carl had the gun pointed at himself. He had the gun to his head. The look on his face remained serious, almost thoughtful.

Then he fired, falling as if shoved, his shoulders striking an overturned chair before settling on the gravel. Linda began crawling toward him, thinking he was probably very hurt, that he should definitely get medical attention for that gunshot to his head. Someone needed to get to him to stanch the blood...

The crushed wicker picnic basket exploded, sending up a hail of splinters. The cop shouted "Hold fire!" over and over.

Linda looked left and right. The crowd had dissipated, though further down the Mall, more people could be seen stampeding, the screams rolling and splitting like waves.

She reached Carl. Oh, yes, he was very hurt. His jacket was steeped in red, redder than Linda had ever seen before, the red fabric pressing against his red chest with a fast-growing pool of red gravel underneath. The grass was red, the gun was red, Linda's hands were red as she began pressing her sweater to his head, finally locating the wound—a clean little pocket, really not much more than a slit, just above one eyebrow. The underside of the wound flapped a little, a child's mouth coughing up red. She took off her sweater and moved it around, trying to make it cover more, soak up more. She pressed against the wound with her elbows and hands. God, so much red...

Sirens. The cop came up behind her, his walkie-talkie squawking furiously. He kicked the gun away. It flipped end over end about five or six feet, coming to a rest against a protest sign.

"Dead?"

Linda pressed the jacket harder against the wound, but the puddle underneath Carl's head was growing fast.

The cop re-holstered his gun and raised one hand high in the air. He brought his walkie-talkie to his lips as another cop came running up to him. The second cop looked down at Linda and Carl. "Is he dead? Ma'am? Can you tell me what happened?"

"Nah, don't," the first cop said. "She's in shock." Then he pressed his finger to the side of the walkie-talkie and described the scene in what, to Linda's ears, sounded like poetry: *West side of Mall/I got a body/Likely suicide/Area secure but we're gonna have to do something/It's chaos down here.*

Then a pop, a hiss, and the walkie-talkie finished the verse: *All right all right/sit tight for me/Medics on the way.*

FULL TRANSCRIPT

Meeting of Principals: USoFA WorldWide War-Related PTSD Individualized Therapy Program (Pilot), "SoldierWell"

May 3, FY20__

0946EST

TIM NESTOR, Executive Vice President of Media Relations, Region 1, USoFA WorldWide

and

GEN. (ORDNANCE CORPS) TYLER BURROWS, Commander, US Northern Command Region 1 and US-Canadian North American Aerospace Defense Command (NORAD)

and

DR. MILES YOUNG, Director, USoFA WorldWide War-Related PTSD Individualized Therapy Program (Pilot) "SoldierWell"

(BEGIN)

TIM NESTOR: OK, calling to order this meeting regarding the SoldierWell East program and SoldierWell overall. General? I've got Miles here with me. General, can you hear me OK?

GEN. (ORDNANCE CORPS) TYLER BURROWS: ████████ ████████

TN: Yes, sir. Loud and clear. OK, so I just got off the phone with Edna H, and we've discussed things as they stand… OK, I'd like to go over the events of May 1[1], try and see things from all perspectives. Let's start with you, Miles, and… General, feel free to jump in here at any time… and then I'd like to give you all a rundown of things as they stand with the media and where to go from this point. Miles?

DR. MILES YOUNG: Yeah?

TN: Do you have anything to say at this time?

MY: About?

TN: About SoldierWell East? About your program? About the events of May 1?

[*pause*]

Miles? Are you feeling OK?

---

[1] Patriot Media, a division of USoFA WorldWide Media Relations and USoFA WorldWide Compliance Unit Publishing, "The CUP"

May 1, FY20___ Saturday 1113 EST

BREAKING: DISTRICT POLICE REPORT SHOOTING ON NATIONAL MALL

Washington, D.C.—District police reported a shooting at approximately 1100 this morning during a protest on the National Mall. They are advising citizens to take refuge indoors and stay away from windows.

No further details are available.

ALSO ON THE CUP:
Three Dead in Brooklyn Public Swimming Pool Mass Shooting
Five Pleasant Surprises About Famous Dictators
15 Hottest Syrian Refugees

MY: Look, what is there to say? It didn't work. I thought it was going to work, it didn't.

TN: And you have no opinion, no idea what might have gone differently to achieve the desired outcome.

MY: No, Tim. I don't. I guess you could say my work speaks for itself.

TB: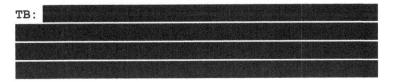

MY: You're asking me, General?

TB: ███

MY: It was called the INSIST Technique, General. It's been pretty much my entire working life for the last decade or so. The INSIST Technique. Maybe write it down.

TN: Miles, hey…

TB: ████████

MY: Yes, that's right, sir. The Subjugation phase, that's the second S of the INSIST Technique. That's where we were supposed to quell the patient's suicidal ideation. And it was my professional opinion that Miss Held did a pretty good job of getting our boy past that, getting him to take those thoughts and tendencies and push them outward, toward our Darling, specifically. But, as you know, General, I was on a tight schedule and certain corners were cut.

[*pause*]

I'm...I'm sorry, General, Tim... It's just so damn disappointing.

TN: About Miss Held... Do you have any idea what she was doing there? At the scene?[2]

---

[2] Patriot Media, a division of USoFA WorldWide Media Relations and USoFA WorldWide Compliance Unit Publishing, "The CUP"

May 1, FY20__ Saturday 1221 EST

BREAKING: AT LEAST 1 KILLED IN D.C. SHOOTING, SUSPECT ARRESTED

Washington, D.C.—A suspect has been arrested and taken in for questioning regarding the shooting incident that took place during the so-called "Rally for Peace" on the Washington National Mall this morning.

Gunfire erupted at approximately 1100 Saturday, killing one and causing untold property damage as bystanders, many of them Hater-related, attempted to flee the scene.

District police told citizens to stay indoors and away from windows as they sweep the area and work to establish whether the gunman acted alone. Government officials with knowledge of the incident told Patriot Media that more casualties were a possibility.

All roads leading to and from the National Mall have been blockaded, and all scheduled events have been canceled through the rest of the week. A hospital spokesperson said three people were treated for injuries.

"There's just a lot of commotion right now," said Brian Kitt, Supervisory Exhibits Specialist with the Smithsonian/USoFA WorldWide National Museum of American History, which faces the Mall.

MY: No idea. None. I spoke with her the day before. She sounded glad to be finished with the therapy, optimistic about the outcome. I can't imagine what she thought she was doing.

TN: I had to personally pull some strings to spring her from police custody, you know.

MY: That figures, yes.

TB: ██

TN: Yes, General. She's back with her family. As a matter of fact, I believe her son underwent major surgery just last night.

MY: Oh yeah?

TN: Yeah. A lung replacement, I believe?

MY: Yeah. It must've been.

TN: I believe her doctors found a donor so... I guess there's no waiting around on something like that. It's probably been a heavy couple of days for her. You haven't heard from her at all, Miles?

MY: No, not at all. I hope she's OK.

This marks the seventh time in less than a year that the Mall has been closed due to a shooting incident.

ALSO ON THE CUP:
Fourteen Dead, Two Wounded in Shooting at Miami Retirement Home
Four Things No One Tells You About Sharing Your Dessert
Blocks of Cheese That Will Make You Look Twice

TB: ████████████████████████

TN: [*laughs*] That's exactly right, General. We take care of our own. But Miles, let me ask you something. I think it was during one of the interviews with Miss Held, the one you had me sit in on…I remember her talking about…I think it was called transference, patient transference. Like when a patient has erotic…ideas, I guess, about his therapist. Do I have that right?

MY: Right. She'd written a paper about its practical advantages.

TN: Right. Can that ever go in the other direction? Maybe because of the intensity of her work with Private Boxer, all those sessions…is that ever a two-way street, do you think?

[*pause*]

MY: I don't think that's what was going on.

TN: OK. Why not?

MY: It's just…the INSIST Technique…well, theoretically, anyway, though I guess it's all in the shitter now, but it's a very intimate process. The therapist has to dehumanize the patient before applying the technique. You can't have actual affection for a patient, then coerce them into doing this, not without some serious cognitive dissonance. And that would be extremely uncomfortable, mentally, emotionally…

TN: Which might explain her being on the Mall on Sunday.

MY: Maybe. But it doesn't jibe with what I know about her.

TB: ███████████████████████████████████

MY: She's a very practical person, General. When I first presented this work to her, this project, she was able to handle it in such a way that it made… a kind of algebraic sense to her. She accepted pretty much on the spot. There was some wavering as we continued, but she was always able to compartmentalize.

TN: So there *was* some wavering. To the Company, to you, what?

MY: Not any more than I'd seen with my other therapists.

TN: Who also couldn't pull this off.

MY: Right, Tim. Who also couldn't pull this off.

TN: Couldn't? Or wouldn't?

MY: Look, it's my fault, all right? I don't see the point of entertaining ideas about what my therapists could have or should have done. I'm the one who failed the Company. I designed the technique, I selected the patients, I researched the drugs, I hired the therapists…it's on me. This failure is on me. And I'm prepared to accept whatever's coming. I'm not afraid.

[*pause*]

TN: [*laughs*]

TB: ▮▮▮▮▮▮▮▮

MY: That's…nice, guys. A man stands before you, prepared to accept what he has coming, and you laugh at him.

TN: [*laughs*] No one's out to get you, Miles. Like I said, I just got off the phone with Edna H, so what I'm about to say is in light of all that, but… [*laughs*] I'm not afraid! [*laughs*] Classic!

TB: ▮▮▮▮▮▮▮

MY: What are you talking about?

TN: OK, Miles… So while SoldierWell East didn't turn out the way you wanted, the fact is we are sitting here, as of today, operating under pretty much the same circumstances as if it had. And it's actually turned out *better* for us, in some ways. That's what I wanted to go over with you this morning.

MY: I don't understand.

TN: [*laughs*] Chelsea Daye is giving up. She's retiring from activism. The speaking tour is canceled, she's written her last *Citizen* column, all of it. She's done.

MY: When?

TN: Just this morning, a couple of hours ago[3]. She's going back to Hollywood. [*laughs*] Can you believe it?

---

[3] Patriot Media, a division of USoFA WorldWide Media Relations and USoFA WorldWide Compliance Unit Publishing, "The CUP"

May 3, FY20__ Tuesday 0821 MST

Chelsea Daye Announces Return to Acting

Billings, Mont.—In an announcement that has sent shockwaves across Washington, D.C., Hollywood, and all points in between, Academy Award nominee Chelsea Daye announced her return to acting, effective immediately.

The decision stunned the 100 or so attendees of the press conference, held on the grounds of Heavenslice, the Billings, Mont., ranch home of USoFA WorldWide CEO and chair Edna H. Appearing fatigued and wearing dark sunglasses despite the cloudy sky overhead, Daye read from a written statement that was later passed out to attendees:

> For the past forty-eight hours, I have been in mourning for Carl Boxer, the young man who took his own life during the Rally for Peace in Washington, D.C. I was looking right into his face during his last moments, and I would like to say now to his family: I am deeply sorry for your loss. My parents and I are only too familiar with the death of a loved one in the prime of life.
>
> While the tragic events of this past Saturday have done nothing to alter my personal politics, I now feel it would be counterproductive, both to the anti-War cause and to the nation as a whole, to continue pursuing activist journalism. While I have nothing but well wishes for my colleagues at *The Citizen*, it is with sound mind that I announce a return to my first love: acting. I am hereby seeking new representation and new film roles.
>
> I would also like to thank my parents for their continued support, as well as Edna H for being there for us during this difficult time. There will be no questions. Thank you.

ALSO ON THE CUP:
Gatorade Looks to Disrupt Baby Formula Market
Tucson Gunman Attacks Ice Cream Parlor, Killing Four
This Man Wasn't Allowed to Eat Waffles on a Roller Coaster. That May Change.

MY: Why?

TN: Oh, something about…

TB: ██████████████████████████████████████

TN: That's right, she did. Said she was looking right into his eyes when he pulled the trigger.

MY: Are you messing with me?

TN: Not at all. She said she talked it over with her folks, and this is the decision. They're probably talking about it on the CUP right now. Everyone's going crazy, it's like her big return to acting. Even the skeptics, the ones you'd expect to be saying she's selling out her principles, they're all saying they can't blame her.

MY: Well…that is good news.

TN: You kidding? It's great news! Edna H is pleased, Miles. You might not have worked everything out all scientifically, but the effect is the same. [*laughs*] Relax, man! You're safe!

TB: ██████████████████████████████████████

MY: And we can trust it?

TN: No reason not to. Which segues into some of the other stuff I wanted to go over with you guys. General, how much time did you say you have?

TB: ██████████████████████████████████████

TN: OK, in that case, I'll just give you the quick and dirty…

[*pause*]

Now, because this was such a surprise, my department is still trying to game this thing out. But it's hard not to look at this and see good news, mostly.

MY: I'm stunned.

TN: I'm going to take these points one at a time, so just, you know, refrain from your questions until I'm finished. Things are moving very fast now… First thing I want to say, no one got seriously hurt. That was one of the things about this project, SoldierWell East in particular, that gave me pause, personally speaking. The idea that some innocent so-and-so might get hurt in the crossfire or whatever, that just…I might not have said anything, but it was there, that fear. And with the crowds on the Mall… Anyway, there were some minor arrests, and I know the CUP reported some woman getting trampled or something, but no actual deaths. Aside from Boxer, I mean. OK, second point, and I really love this…there's no decent footage of the incident, as far as we know. Which is amazing, considering all the people who were there to film Chelsea Daye on their phones… plus the fact that there were six separate camera crews down by the stage, but those big cameras, they all got knocked down in the stampede. They got nothing. All anyone's got is Chelsea Daye coming out onto the stage, she says two words and then all hell breaks loose. There are some audio clips making the rounds but…audio doesn't make for good TV, as the old saying goes. Then yesterday, the FBI did us a biggie and confiscated all surrounding security camera footage, museums, places like that, and there was one thing taken off a very old security camera at the elevator of the Smithsonian Metro stop, but it's shot at a real distance. I watched it this morning.

TB: ███████████████████████

TN: Yeah, it's quite bizarre. It shows our girl, Miss Held, running toward Boxer, and she's got a cop with her, and then she just stops and watches as he puts the gun to his head. She just…stops. Then after he's pulled the trigger, she goes to him, trying to do something…it reminded me a little of that old photograph of that girl in Berkeley…you know the one, she's screaming over that dead kid's body…

TB: ████████████████████████████

TN: Kent State, right. Whatever. OK, so with no civilian deaths and no usable footage, the story pivots somewhat, because there just aren't very many journalists left who have the resources or the will to dig into the motivation behind the guy whose suicide is responsible for Chelsea Daye's return to acting. And he fits a pattern, which, Miles, is why you selected him in the first place, I believe. Troubled kid, a lone wolf type, kept mostly to himself… Carl Boxer just isn't that interesting of a story. Here's a guy who gets out of prison, an arsonist who gets out of prison, he does some menial work in Iraq, and then, as soon as he makes it home, he goes crazy and kills himself. Happens every day. As American as apple pie.

[*pause*]

One more thing, I don't foresee a lot of kicking from his family. All he had was his mother, and with her appearance, I mean… Let's just say she's not ready for prime time.

TB: ████████████████████████████████
████████████████████████████████

TN: No, because according to the paperwork, Carl Boxer was in Iraq for the past four months. He was still getting paid by the Company, so he's been with the Free2Fight program this entire time, as far as anyone can tell. There's no mention of SoldierWell anywhere on his official record. Everything related to his being with the SoldierWell program is now classified. I'm talking burn after reading type stuff. Just like this conversation. This isn't happening. As far as the public knows or ever will know, General, you and I have never met. You and Miles have never met. Miles and I have never met.

[*pause*]

OK, where was I…point four…OK, as this thing evolves, Chelsea Daye's announcement this morning becomes the story. We now are in the transition from a hard news story[4] to an entertainment news

---

[4] Patriot Media, a division of USoFA WorldWide Media Relations and USoFA WorldWide Compliance Unit Publishing, "The CUP"

May 2, FY20__ Sunday 1411 EST

President finds support for tougher gun laws in the wake of Mall shooting

Washington, D.C.—President Halliday held a press conference on the patio of his macadamia nut farm in Kalawao, Hawaii, late this morning announcing the creation of a bipartisan committee to address the need for more vigorous gun laws. This comes in light of Saturday's shooting on the Washington National Mall.

"The events yesterday at the National Mall highlight the need for greater gun control in this country," the president said. "That is why I have invited my friends in the House and Senate to join me in creating a group to research the effects of broader, more vigorous background checks for first-time purchasers of the Murphy, as well as new registration requirements for automatic and semiautomatic weapons."

The Multipartisan Subcommittee to Reinvigorate U.S. Gun Laws is made up of legislators across the political spectrum, as well as two private citizens and one high-ranking member of the U.S. Armed Forces:

Sen. Tasha Orr (Americans for Prosperity-Tex.), co-chair
Rep. Fred Wingo (Libertad!-Maine), co-chair
Sen. Katherine Boertman (Democrat-Tenn.)
Sen. Noah Roundtree III (Crunk-Ga.)
Sen. Jocelyn Unger (Green-Fla.)
Rep. Keith Dierkoski (Republican-N.Y.)
Rep. Douglass H. Craig (KISS Army-Mich.)
Sen. Marcia Grace (Workers World-Ore.)
Sen. Mac Devlin (Friends of Our Reptilian Overlords-Neb.)
Rep. Kevin Howard (Politique Concrete-Calif.)

Sheila Cargill, Executive Vice President, Moms Demand Action, Rhode Island Chapter
Walton T. Kreske, Executive Vice President, Public Affairs, National Rifle Association
General Tyler Burrows, Commander, U.S. Northern Command Region 1 and U.S.-Canadian North American Aerospace Defense Command (NORAD)

ALSO ON THE CUP:
Fifteen Dead, Six Wounded in Mass Shooting at Houston Gas Station
Nine Famous Fictional Cities You Won't Believe Are Real
Does This Time Machine Really Work?

story.[5] Let's see, what else…

TB: ████████████████████████████████
████████████████

TN: Hard to say, General, and of course we're going to have to keep our eye on Chelsea Daye for the rest of her life, but honestly, I think this

---

[5] Patriot Media, a division of USoFA WorldWide Media Relations and USoFA WorldWide Compliance Unit Publishing, "The CUP"

May 3, FY20__ Monday 1110 EST

Will Daye Don the Catsuit?

Los Angeles—With former Hollywood sweetheart Chelsea Daye's recent declaration that she would be returning to acting, director Trey Bongo speculated this could mean she would be his next Catwoman.

"Who's to say?" Bongo said from his Malibu beachfront penthouse. "I haven't had a chance to talk to Chelsea about it, obviously, but if she feels like coming back, yeah, I'm ready to talk."

If you ask us, Daye would be purr-fect for the part.

Batman fans are lapping up the news like so much milk left on the back porch. Phlogger Jason Amgen of BATMAN SUCKS! fame speculated that the onetime Academy Award nominee's Catwoman could bring "a certain youthful vigor" to the latest Caped Crusader installment.

"I'm cautiously optimistic," Amgen said. "Until Hollywood manages to create a believable facsimile of Eartha Kitt's groundbreaking turn as the Pilfering Pussy, [Chelsea Daye] seems like a good choice. If she can stay sober. We'll see."

Bongo's fourth Batman installment (working title: *The Dark Knight Dies*) has been in production hell for a year, beset by script rewrites, costuming disagreements, and behind-the-scenes bickering. Filming was scheduled to begin in Abu Dhabi last October, but investors pulled funding after an altercation with the camera crew.

ALSO ON THE CUP:
Breaking: National Mall Gunman Killed, Identified
Seriously Comfortable Sweatpants No One Will Mistake for Pajamas (NSFW)
Here's What's Coming to (and Leaving) Your Health Insurance Plan in June

time next week it will all be over. And the reason I say that is this…a poll came out, the day before yesterday, and it found that fifty-nine percent of Americans still think Chelsea Daye left acting for drug-related reasons. That's *fifty-nine percent* who have no idea she was ever an anti-War activist. And that's on top of thirteen percent who didn't even know she left. So none of what's happening is on the radar for most Americans, God bless 'em.

[*pause*]

Honestly, Miles, I know you're disappointed with your technique or whatever, but I cannot get over how clean an operation this turned out to be. Back in February, I was skeptical, maybe not as much as others, of course, who shall remain nameless…but from where I'm sitting, this is a big win for the Company. A big win.

TB: ████████████████████████████████████
████████████████████████

TN: Yeah, well, that's why I wear the big boy pants around here. [*laughs*] All right, gentlemen, I know you're all busy, so I'm ready to call it. Miles, do I need to say anything before I stop this?

MY: Nah, just turn it off.

TN: Terrific. So, listen, now might be a good time to get out of town for a few days. I've got plans to take Marcia and the kids around Hong Kong this weekend... Something about a Taoist festival, a bunch of floats, fireworks...dammit, where is the off button on this thing?

MY: Maybe I should.

TN: Sure, take a few days off. Take a week off. And Edna H might have something for you when you get back... Jesus, where is the off button on this thing?

MY: I did go to Portland last month. Maybe I'll go back.

TN: Oh yeah? Maine or Oregon?

MY: Oregon. I kind of met someone there.

TN: There you go. Jesus, am I staring right at it and I'm just too dumb to realize?

MY: No, it's on the side, you've got to...

END TRANSCRIPT

JUNE FY20___

USoFA WorldWide Internal Services: Orange-Level
Employee Psychological Consultation

Session # 6

June 5, FY20__

1012EST

**DR. AMANDA KANT, Internal Services, Department of
Military Information Support Operations (MISO),
Region 1, USoFA WorldWide**

and

**DR. LINDA HELD, Independent Consultant, Depart-
ment of Military Information Support Operations
(MISO), Region 1, USoFA WorldWide**

(BEGIN)

DR. AMANDA KANT: Settling in?

DR. LINDA HELD: Yes. Settling in. The Company
has a good program in place. I feel very welcome.
The common kitchen area smells like pee, dog or
cat pee. I've cleaned it three times, scrubbed
the floor, wiped down the cabinets, refrigerator… it's not completely gone but it's better. I
like having other people around. I like hearing
footsteps in the hall, running into people, and
just talking. Of course, what I'd really love to
hear is people inside my place. That's what I'm

most looking forward to when I get out...when I'm invited to leave, I mean.

AK: I understand you've taken to the horses.

LH: Oh, yes. Orpheus and Pearl. They're very... therapeutic.

AK: There's just something about them, isn't there? That natural ability to read a person, without judgment.

LH: Right. Uncanny.

AK: Every few weeks, when I have to be up there for a meeting, I make a point of arriving early so I can walk the grounds a little, just be with them. Anyway, tell me about your therapy. How is it going?

LH: Good. One day at a time, as Patrick says.

AK: And you're still attending daily group sessions?

LH: Yes. Sometimes twice a day. Once in the morning and once before lights out. They're a big part of my life right now.

AK: Good. You mentioned, last time, some trouble getting to sleep. Has that gotten better?

LH: Yes, actually. Quite a bit better. I've been doing some Jungian dreamwork with Patrick. It's been helpful. He's good at offering alternative interpretations of my dreams. [*laughs*]

AK: That's good. And what about...the things?

LH: The things...I don't think about them as often. You get exhausted after a while, thinking the same things over and over. I came across this line in a book I've been reading. It said something...how the mind eventually discards the thoughts that haunt her. That may be where I am now, I think. Close to it.

AK: You've discarded your troubling thoughts because of exhaustion?

LH: I was just saying, that was something I read in an old book, and I got to thinking about how it applied to my situation. The way one does.

AK: Right.

LH: No, I think I've come much more to terms with my situation. Thanks to my therapists. And to you. I appreciate these little check-ins. I owe a lot to everyone. It's humbling.

AK: In what way?

LH: Well, like we were saying last time, I just think, I mean you've helped me to see that I don't always need to take responsibility for what happened to Private Boxer. It was a Company decision, one made long before I was hired. There were other applicants for my position. If it hadn't been me, it would have been someone else, and Danny's health would have stayed just the same. The part that I had in applying the INSIST

Technique was significant, but not the whole. In the big picture, I don't need to take any more responsibility for what happened than the guy on the production line who made the trigger that Private Boxer pulled on himself.

AK: Do you still think about him?

LH: Not as much.

AK: Any more outbursts? Emotional outbursts?

LH: Not really. That's another thing they've helped me with. Seeing that he made the choice. There were any number of things he could have done when he was released from the SoldierWell program. It comes down to his making that choice. I think about how you described it last time we spoke. A narcissistic, borderline psychopath with pyromaniac tendencies harboring possibly dangerous delusions and suffering acute war-related PTSD. It was foolish, or at least naïve, for me to think I could've saved him.

AK: And while we all want to help as much as we can…

LH: And while we all want to help as much as we can, there's only so much we can do, as medical professionals. Some people don't want to be saved, and that's a tragedy.

[*pause*]

Oh, I've been meaning to tell you. I graduated. I'm officially Doctor Linda Held now.

AK: Wonderful, Linda. Congratulations.

LH: Got my degree yesterday. It was there on the front desk… I guess it had been kicked around a couple of different places before finding me. The envelope looked like a chew toy.

AK: Was the diploma damaged?

LH: It was, actually. But it's fine…

AK: You worked hard for that, Linda. I'm sure you could return it for a new one.

LH: It doesn't matter.

[*pause*]

AK: When do you see Danny next?

LH: Tomorrow morning.

AK: And how's it been?

LH: Well, he's getting more comfortable with me. And he looks so good! He's gained most of his weight back, and his appetite is really good, they say. The nurse let me see his scar last time, it's huge… They're supposed to remove the rest of the dressing soon. Whatever else happens, you know, I'm thankful for the CF Clinic, Dr. Bolaño. I couldn't change a thing.

AK: Excellent. And how are you getting on without Danny, day to day? You mentioned once before some feelings of alienation. Pining, you said.

LH: Yeah... I just try and look forward to next time. It's not that long between visits, so when the nurse comes in and says time's up, I'm able to reset the clock, somewhat. It's never more than seventy-one hours away. Unless they reschedule, which they haven't done since that one time... I think I'm ready, Dr. Kant, for him to come visit. At the facility.

AK: Just give it some time, Linda. It's only been six weeks.

LH: Seven.

AK: Seven weeks.

LH: I'll do anything I can, anything I have to.

AK: I know. But surely you understand, there's a process. You have to get healthy. And with Danny, in his condition...

LH: Yes. I know.

[*pause*]

AK: I'd like to talk about Vera, your mother, your feelings of betrayal...

LH: Oh...I don't blame her anymore.

AK: That's good.

LH: I mean, she was worried for me. And I was acting nuts toward the end there, the end of the program.

AK: But how she went about it, getting you into treatment. Agree or disagree?

LH: Do I have to? [*laughs*] I mean, I was a mess. That's why I'm here. But all her stuff about the negative coping, you know, the pills and the drinking…try and make that clear to Dependent Protective Services, they don't want to hear it. And now I've got this reputation for being aggressive, anger issues. It's just…my mother exaggerates sometimes, so when she told them that I'd been hiding from them, I mean…I wasn't hiding…

AK: It's all right if you were, Linda. Sometimes when we're under pressure, we want to hide.

LH: I know that, but it's not true. Seriously. It's just…not knowing what Mom and Deva tell him, how I'm talked about when I'm not there…I'm sure Deva's fine…he gets it, I think.

AK: He's a high-level Company employee.

LH: Right. But Mom, like I said, she exaggerates sometimes.

AK: I doubt she's talking about you behind your back, Linda. But even if she is, your relationship with Danny is strong enough, certainly, to withstand it.

LH: I hope you're right.

AK: I must say, I'm impressed with how you're handling all this. There's been a lot of upheaval lately, a lot of potential stressors. I'm seeing real improvement.

LH: Thank you, Doctor. I think this, you and me, it's helpful.

AK: I'm glad to hear you say that.

[*pause*]

I was hoping today we could talk a little bit about your future.

LH: My future?

AK: Your future with the Company. Would you like to hear about an opportunity? I think it could be really good for you. It's pretty exciting.

LH: OK.

AK: So, as you are probably aware, the Soldier-Well program has been deemed a success, overall, and so the Company is looking to build on that success. Now, it's very much in the pilot phase, but we're looking to expand SoldierWell to the civilian market. The thinking is we try and build out from war-related PTSD to see if the INSIST Technique can be applied to other common behavioral disorders. Anxiety, depression, bipolar... Of course, just as with SoldierWell, we'd be looking for a certain *type* of applicant, but eventually, we'd want to treat more common issues. I have the drafted press release if you'd like to take a look… I'll need it back when you're finished.

LH: Project Heal? That's the name?

AK: For now. We floated CitizenWell, but it didn't go over.

[*pause*]

LH: For victims of child abuse, rape, natural disasters, neglect…

AK: That's the thinking right now, yes. The PTSD piece is essential, as you know, and Edna H is looking to cast a wide net on this. Double the budget of SoldierWell. There are plans to garner the necessary public support, but I won't bother you with that right now.[1] Would you like to know your part in all this?

LH: Sure.

---

[1] Patriot Media, a division of USoFA WorldWide Media Relations and USoFA WorldWide Compliance Unit Publishing, "The CUP"

June 2, FY20__ Wednesday 0816 EST

Candidacy Announcement Video Garners Public Interest, Beltway Criticism in Ex-Marine

In the announcement video for his candidacy for Congress, Marine Sergeant Todd Sparrow blames extremists and party bosses for dysfunction in Washington. While this is nothing new, it's the manner in which he does it that has tongues wagging inside and outside the Beltway.

AK: Well, as I said, we're looking to expand on

"It's time to clean up Washington like we cleaned up the Middle East," he says, before loading and charging an AR-15 semi-automatic rifle. "And I'm just the man to do it."

The video, which has 9 million views since its release two days ago, has been denounced by Union leaders, elected officials, and gun control advocates for its aggressive rhetoric. However, Sparrow stands by it, saying it showcases nothing more than his willingness to defend freedom at all costs.

"I abhor violence," he said. "But this nation suffers from a kind of infestation, if you will. We need big, bold solutions. I wanted the video to reflect that."

Sparrow is the first candidate competing for the Republican nomination to challenge Rep. Karen Barbieri (D-Md) in FY20__. He seeks to win the seat of Maryland's 8th Congressional District, which spans from the northern Washington, D.C. suburbs north toward the Pennsylvania border.

Sparrow grew up in Chevy Chase, Md., graduating from Michael Flynn High School and joining the Marines immediately after graduation. Since his first deployment in FY20__, he has fought for freedom in Iraq, Iran, and Tasmania.

Still considered a long shot in most polls, Sparrow recently won the support of the Association of Republican Congressional Committees. While the ARCC does not endorse during primary season, the candidate said he has been making calls and sending texts since last week from association headquarters in Washington, adding that the group has been "extremely helpful" with media training, wardrobe, and other preparations.

We caught up with Sparrow at his mother's home yesterday afternoon to ask his thoughts on various topics.

On why he is running for office

"I've noticed over the last few years a lack of leadership in Congress, and government in general. Leadership is about never being deterred from the mission and always looking out for the interests of others over my own. I'm running to bring that attitude of service-before-self to Congress."

On the current political climate

"Look, we've got to get the government opened up and working again, and that process begins only when we stop the partisan bickering and violent rhetoric. But our initial success, but at the same time we're looking to operate under similar guidelines. The geography, keeping patients separate, therapists separate... We'll probably still go with one program in the east, one in the west, north, south, but we were thinking you might be the one to lead the east program. You'd be a board member. You'd have a say in the program's overall direction. What do you think?

LH: I don't know what to say.

AK: Say yes!

LH: Oh...OK.

AK: Does that mean...

LH: Could I have some time to think about it?

AK: Are you serious?

LH: I *can't* think about it?

---

my future colleagues in Congress should know, there's nothing I love more than a fight. And I'm coming locked and loaded."

On veterans' health

"Speaking as a veteran, the issue of PTSD is close to my heart. That is why I think the groundbreaking therapies designed by USoFA WorldWide ought to be shared with the civilian population. PTSD isn't just a veteran disorder. It affects people from all walks of life. I'll work hard to expand such lines of care to all citizens."

ALSO ON THE CUP:
Mass Shooting in Lansing High School Leaves Six Dead, Sixteen Injured
Why This Measuring Tape Has Single Moms So Obsessed
The 20 Most Dangerous Criminal Minds of All Time

AK: Linda… [*laughs*] This is a wonderful opportunity. Fresh out of medical school and you're being asked to head up a multimillion-dollar program. For USoFA WorldWide. Do you realize how many people, how many of your contemporaries, would kill to be a part of this?

LH: I realize.

AK: And I'm sure you realize it would be a strong signal to the Company, including those in Dependent Protective Services, if you were working full-time again. Keep the position for a few months, without incident, and I bet we could start negotiating down your separation period. It would depend on the work, of course, but again, you'd be in more of a management position this time around. Less intense, much less hands-on… You can continue working on your recovery. And I'll be here for you, we can keep doing this. There's no need to be afraid.

[*pause*]

Linda, your work for USoFA WorldWide is highly valued by the powers that be. Let's come together. We can take this thing to the next level.

LH: I can't win.

AK: Excuse me?

LH: No matter what, I can't win.

AK: Linda…

LH: No matter what I or anybody does, the Company always wins.

AK: Linda, we've gone over this. When the Company wins, we all win. Freedom wins.

LH: [*laughs*] There's no way you believe that.

AK: Excuse me, Linda, but I'm your only way out. You may want to be more careful.

LH: And I bet I'm your only way out. This is what you've been doing this whole time, isn't it? Softening me up? Establishing Nexus, so I'll take this job?

AK: My dear girl. I could never hope to apply any aspect of the INSIST Technique as well as you. You can't blame the Company for wanting to bring in its ace again.

LH: And together we'll murder the last few honest voices out there, all so USoFA WorldWide can keep making war. Killing people, telling lies. Eating up the world.

AK: OK…would you like to know who the donor was that saved your son's life?

LH: You don't have that information.

AK: [*laughs*] Of course I do.

[*pause*]

LH: Yes…no, wait…

AK: Private Carl Boxer was the donor. Your Carl. He filled out an application before his release. He insisted on it. Isn't that wonderful? The gesture?

LH: You sad bitch. God, I hate you.

AK: [*laughs*] You do see how that worked out, right? How it all comes together in the end? You gave us your all and the Company, we took care of you. We're still taking care of you.

[*pause*]

Look. You *will* say yes to this. I think you know that already. You'll say yes, you'll do an excellent job mentoring some new therapists, you'll guide them through this process, and in a few months, you'll move back in with your son. Then a year from now, maybe two, you'll look back and laugh at how foolish you were for not jumping on this. But OK, take some time to think about it. Just know that the Company is eager to get going on this, and I'd rather not disappoint.

END EXCERPT

The shuttle slowed to a halt, sounding its familiar hiss of brakes before the entrance of Pathway Acres. Linda had been the shuttle's only passenger, which made it ideal for a good cry. She cried every day over Carl. Sometimes it happened first thing in the morning, while she was still in bed, but more often it happened later in the day, in the bathroom, closed off from the world by a stall door, though she had to be quick about it or else someone was liable to come in and ask what was taking her so long.

Linda exited the shuttle, checking herself in its rearview mirror. She looked presentable, somewhat. The whiteness of her eyeballs these days was striking, even after a long crying jag. One thing you could say about sober living—she was looking the healthiest she had in years. The early nights and early mornings had sharpened her.

A young man, new to Linda, stepped out from a booth at the side of Pathway's entrance. He held a clipboard in one pudgy hand, its sign-in sheet curling upward as he hustled toward her.

Linda affixed a look of perfect innocence to her face as the shuttle drove away. "Good morning," she said. "Linda Held, I'm coming back from a pre-scheduled meeting."

"Sign here."

Linda signed, handing the clipboard back.

The young man looked over her signature and nodded. "Dr. Held...you have an appointment with Patrick Johnson in twenty minutes."

"Good, that gives me some time to visit Orpheus and Pearl." Linda began walking toward the Pathway entrance.

"Dr. Held! Excuse me?" From an inner pocket of his jacket the young man produced a clear plastic cup. "You have to fill this."

Linda took a deep breath. "Fine," she said, taking the cup.

"Just one second," the young man said. "I need to get someone up here to supervise."

Linda slumped. There was almost nothing she could say to keep this young man from traipsing back to his booth and calling for a monitor, and she didn't have much time. "I'd like to say good morning to them *now*," she said, following the young man as he made his way back to the booth. "It helps keep me centered, you know?"

"It shouldn't be too long, Dr. Held."

"I *really* have to go," Linda said, making her voice soft. "And it always takes like fifteen minutes before somebody gets up here."

"I understand, but it's how we do things."

Linda halted, which caused the young man to halt as well. It was at this moment that Linda knew she could work something out. "I haven't seen you before. What's your name?"

"Kyle."

"You know what, Kyle," she said, "why don't you and I just knock it out? Then you'll have what you need and I'll be on my way."

The quick rise-and-fall of the zipper on his jacket gave him away. "Yeah, OK," he said. "We could do that."

Linda approached the ash-colored split rail fence and placed her hands on the top rail. The sun felt hot on her neck. Ten feet away, Orpheus and Pearl stood side by side, their tails whipping at flies. Pearl, white with dark brown spots across her back, was the first to see Linda. She bucked her head once before turning away to nose at a patch of scrub grass. A second later, Orpheus turned to catch sight of Linda. He broke into a trot that went all the way to the other side of the pen, as far away from Linda as physically possible. Pearl soon joined him.

"Good morning to you, too," Linda muttered, turning away. Through the sunlight, she saw Jocelyn walking toward her, wearing gray sweatpants and a dark blue hooded sweatshirt, hugging herself against the morning cool.

"Good morning," Jocelyn said, joining Linda at the fence. She leaned over the top rail and spit into a mud puddle. Linda smiled. Jocelyn was vulgar in just about every way Linda appreciated. A good ten years her junior, Jocelyn had a user's knowledge of every hard drug in existence and enjoyed bragging on how many people—men, women, trans—she had been with. She was a born Hater. Jocelyn was not her real name.

"How is it in there?" Linda asked.

Jocelyn lowered her head to her forearms. "Patrick's got his guitar out."

"Oh, God."

"How are Pearl and Orpheus today?"

"The usual."

Jocelyn snickered, catching the attention of Orpheus and Pearl, who immediately began cantering toward her. "They really do hate you," she said. "It's weird."

Linda watched as the horses nudged one another to get under Jocelyn's waiting hand. Jocelyn could pet them like cats, not just on the nose or mane but all over. The first time Linda had been led to the horse pen—weak and appalled at the universe's cruelty after three days' detox, her voice shot from screaming—she spooked Pearl so badly that the horse reared back onto her hind legs and came down on the fence, splitting the top rail in two. Patrick and a team of orderlies had to run out and help free her as she stiffly pumped her front legs, stuck halfway out of the pen. Things had gotten better, slightly, since then, but the prospect of Linda ever petting either animal was out of the question.

"So…" Jocelyn said, taking Pearl's nose in both hands. She never looked at Linda when they talked business. "What's our friend up to now?"

"Apparently my son is breathing with Carl Boxer's lungs."

Jocelyn smirked. "Who told you that?"

"She did."

"She's full of shit."

Linda crossed her arms. "The timing makes sense, though. I remember, they released me from custody, and they're giving me back my phone, and at that exact moment, Dr. Bolaño calls, and she's saying it's time, get Danny here right now…"

"Did Carl ever fill out a donor card, do you know?"

"He said he did, yeah."

Jocelyn paused, then shook her head. "No. Carl was a full-grown man and Danny is, what, twelve? It wouldn't fit."

Linda shrugged, supposing that made sense.

"Trust me," Jocelyn said. "Carl might be somebody's hero, but he's not your son's."

Linda swooned, the world lurching. Tears filled her eyes. She steadied herself on the fence as Orpheus nodded roughly in response.

"What else?" Jocelyn asked. "Or did you get me out here just for that?"

"Oh. Well. They want to expand SoldierWell. Bring it into the mainstream."

Jocelyn nodded. She had predicted this. "Who's it for?"

"Anyone with trauma. Child abuse, rape, natural disaster…"

"Jesus Christ." Jocelyn softly swatted Pearl away, turning her attention to Orpheus. "What's the budget?"

"Double SoldierWell."

"Fuck. Who's heading it? Did she say?"

"They're asking me. When I get out."

Jocelyn froze. Linda could feel her fighting the urge to jump up and down. "You're kidding me."

Linda shook her head. "In the east, anyway. I'd be on the Board."

"Holy…" Jocelyn looked back at Building A. "My guys are going to *love* this."

"I told her I'd think about it."

"What? Why?"

Linda kicked at a patch of grass. When she looked up, Pearl was standing before her, her eyes kind between effortful blinks. Linda stepped back.

"Linda?"

Linda took a second, measuring her words. "I don't know. I didn't want to say yes right away. It's hard for me. They need to know that."

"But you're going to say yes," Jocelyn said. "This is huge, Linda."

"I know. I just couldn't. Not right away."

"OK, well, let me know when you do. My guys need to make plans." Jocelyn bent forward and placed her hands on her knees. "*Linda*. This is *huge*."

Linda unfolded her arms. Pearl stood still in front of her, blinking.

"I have to go," Linda said, taking a half-step forward.

"This can't slip away, Linda."

"I know. It won't." Linda reached out, and Pearl, for the first time, did not retreat. Her muzzle was smooth and strong and warm, nostrils puffing, everything alive in Linda's hand.

ACKNOWLEDGMENTS

I am deeply grateful to the following people:

John Rak for his superb editing and sincere encouragement. Charlie Franco and everyone at Montag Press.

David McMillan, Ph.D., for his expertise, feedback, and support. Eric Barth, Ph.D., for his expertise and imagination. Charles Hearn, LCSW, for his support and sympathy.

Marine combat veteran Roman J. Fontana, Esq., for his invaluable assistance with military terminology. Daniel Edwards of the Nashville Vet Center for his generosity of time and resources.

The Pediatric Cystic Fibrosis Diagnosis and Treatment Center at Monroe Carell Jr. Children's Hospital at Vanderbilt for their time and resources.

Katie McDougall, Susannah Felts, and Lisa Bubert of The Porch Writers' Collective in Nashville. Rosie Forrest and OZ Arts Nashville. The kind folks at Aethon Books and Unsolicited Press.

Anne Fentress for her feedback, instruction, and encouragement in the early going. Jim McAteer for his feedback, encouragement, and support. Haven Clancy for her help and feedback. Jennifer Doll. John Minichillo. Kermit Moyer. Nathan Elias. Jennie Fields. Mary Sanford. Christine LePorte. Doug Craig. JJ Hornblass.

My brothers, Pat and Mike, for inspiration and encouragement. Martha Orr. Dan McMillen. John and Melissa Orr.

My parents, Pat and Mary Anne Clancy, for their unwavering support in all things.

Most of all I'd like to thank my beautiful wife, Paige, for her years (and years) of patience, feedback, and encouragement.

ABOUT THE AUTHOR

Christopher Clancy holds an MFA in Creative Writing from American University. He lives in Nashville with his wife and two daughters. *We Take Care of Our Own* is his first novel.

Made in the USA
Coppell, TX
14 February 2022

73591320R00246